1. A TOCSIN TOLL

August 1929

It was market day in the village of Nansk, Novgorod province, Northern Russia, fifteen miles south of Leningrad, where a warm wind weaved its way over narrow, cobbled streets lined with stalls selling food, simple clothing such as the course linen Rubakha — a tunic like shirt down to knee length with a narrow sash at the waist worn by all the peasants — and the traditional trousers, again made of course linen worn and tucked into felt boots. Such a market was a traditional meeting place where peasants exchanged news and relaxed after the harvest. But those days were gone. Now the faces displayed suspicion, eyes cast down, body language that of a down trodden people.

Their unease increased as the wind began to carry a sound, a sound that villagers knew meant an emergency, one that fed on the low mood of the peasants and built fear; this was the plaintive sound of the Tocsin, a church bell announcing danger — its steady toll interspersed by the crack of gunfire.

At the centre of the village, amongst a group of teenagers gathered around the village well, two youths sat playing chess. One of the youths alarmed by the sound leapt up knocking over the chess board and listened intently to the wind. The other youth frustrated by his friend's carelessness shouted, 'Yuri. So you are losing, no need...'

But Yuri — six feet two and powerfully built — was already starting to run in the direction of the gunfire, his muscular legs carrying him effortlessly over the cobbled street towards the recently harvested land on the outskirts of the town. His progress slowed as most of his momentum was absorbed by the soft ground; his felt boots sinking in the dark rich soil. He pushed himself to the limit chasing wild speculation as to why the bell was ringing. He powered on, deep breaths filling his lungs as his boots crushed the sharp stubble of the recently harvested wheat, driving it into the rich dark earth.

As he headed toward the bell he heard a different sound; the explosive boom of a shotgun. His legs pumped harder as, full of fire and energy, he headed toward the sound that had alarmed him. He didn't notice the wind as it blew against his fuzzy beard and into his green eyes; his focus was upon the sporadic sound of gunfire coming from the town of Pulkova.

In the distance, at the edge of an adjoining strip of land another figure was also running in the same direction and waved as he saw Yuri, shouting inaudibly as he gesticulated toward the village in the distance. The two figures converged at a gate in the corner of the land.

'Vladimir!' Yuri shouted, as they both stopped and leant against the gate.

Vladimir gasped for breath. 'I heard the bell and just ran. Do you know what's happening?'

'No.'

Vladimir wiped sweat from his forehead onto the sleeve of his course linen rubakha. 'Come on!' He climbed over the gate and ran on through the next piece of land toward another gate in the distance. Yuri followed closely behind gradually catching him up as they came to the gate which his friend scrambled over onto a rutted track. Yuri climbed it effortlessly and caught up his friend. Yuri ran alongside him glancing anxiously at his friend as another boom of the shot gun rattled the trees lining the road. Beneath the crack of the gun fire he could hear raised voices — male and female — but he was unable to hear what they were saying.

The two friends reached the edge of the town and headed toward the raised voices echoing off a cobbled street facing them. They ran on between rough stone buildings and rounded a corner straight into the rear of an angry crowd making its way toward the town offices brandishing spikes, pitchforks and some with long pieces of wood sharpened to a point. In front of them were women wearing brightly coloured kerchiefs with their hands on the shoulders of children walking before them.

Yuri ran up to one of the men. 'What's happening? Who's shooting?'

'They're scared and boarded themselves in. Cowards!'

Yuri's friend caught up with him. 'Well?'

Yuri wiped sweat from his face. 'The officials have boarded themselves in the offices. It must have been them firing.' He bent over with his hands on his knees fighting for breath. As he looked up he saw Vladimir pushing through the men toward the front. He wearily began to follow but with relief found the men had stopped. Now that the pounding in his ears had lessened he could hear the women's voices jeering and shouting abuse, the men less vocal but with grim expressions fiercely protective of their women, angrily waving their weapons.

Yuri asked one of the men, 'What's happening?'

The man sneered, 'They think if they hide we will go away like last time, but we won't. We're going inside and they'll listen.'

'What's it about?'

The man spat on the road. 'Taking our farms and threatening our village.'

The shouting grew louder as more shots came from the building. The firing stopped and a voice from the crowd shouted, 'They've run out of ammunition!' At this the crowd surged forward — the women taking the children to one side — as with anything to hand the men battered the doors open and flooded in. Yuri stood like a boulder in a torrential wave of anger as the crowd flooded past. He saw Vladimir near to the doors hesitating unsure whether to enter. Yuri shouted to him but he didn't hear and was carried in on the turbulent sea of bodies.

Yuri was not used to such violence although his father had been warning for some time that it would come. Now, Yuri stood in the middle of the street; a lone, silent witness to what would become a black stain on the town and mark the beginning of his hatred of the *State Machine*.

The warm wind that had carried the sound of the Tocsin would soon change as the summer drew to a close allowing autumn to bring the first of its chilling winds. These would sweep down from the Arctic sea prompting the inhabitants of the Novgorod province to prepare for the onset of winter when temperatures could plummet to minus ten degrees; sometimes as much as minus forty five. Rivers starved of water during the brief summer heat now ready to swell with the coming winter wound their way through a landscape of pine forest and gently undulating rich agricultural land. This fertile land was divided into meagre strips; a legacy from the land being taken from the wealthy and parcelled out to the peasants after the revolution in 1917 as part of Lenin's Great Revolution.

But another wind also blew, stirred by this great uprising; one of change and uncertainty that swept this vast country, touching cities, towns and villages seeking out the weak and greedy alike. Unlike the artic wind there was no shelter from this wind as it penetrated deep into every nook and cranny of the country; affecting the peasants who formed eighty two percent of the population most of all.

These peasants were a hardy down to earth people whose very existence was dependent upon their ability to read the weather, but whose survival was not only threatened by the Russian seasons but also the stormy political backdrop of change. This change that had torn the country apart with the promise of equality required a violent revolution costing the lives of many; especially the young men from the villages. The current generation was the first to be spared.

Each village had a number of such teenagers who were no trouble in the summer — being occupied in the fields — but as the winter took hold their interests could turn to mischief. One such was Yuri Kazakof, powerfully built from most of his eighteen years spent toiling with his father on the land. Yuri had a wide smile that lit up his deep mischievous green eyes; eyes that seemed to look deep into the soul of another. His father, Ivan, knowing full well that his son was hot headed and likely to get in trouble if given half a chance, made sure his son was kept busy in the winter repairing equipment and maintaining their small strip of land.

In his day Ivan had been a fighter — scrapping in barns and back streets of the town — and he supposed this gene had been passed to his son Yuri who on many occasions would come home bloody from a fight. Ivan decided he needed to channel Yuri's natural aggression and put him to training his body for organised fights. Ivan had had a fearsome reputation for winning fights through sheer determination and doggedness. Yuri had proven, having the advantage of his father's experience, to be a natural; understanding fear and how to control it, reading his opponent — looking for signs of weakness usually displayed in the eyes — and knowing when to strike. He had taught him how to instil fear in a man; a necessary requirement to make him stay down marking the end of the fight.

Ivan Kazakof, put his tools away for the day and, absently rubbing his back — stiff from his efforts on their tiny allotment alongside the strip of land he farmed — walked slowly toward the backdoor across the tiny piece of dusty ground that fronted their modest wooden house. He stopped and looked to the shed that housed the horses thinking he needed to feed them; well later he would. He heaved a sigh of relief as he looked past the barn where he stored his tools and equipment to his strip of land waiting to be plowed; the meagre harvest safely in.

Everytime he entered the house he thought of his father; how he had dreamt of owning more than just a hut, but a grand wooden house on the land he had toiled as a serf during the Tsar's rule. Ivan had been determined to see his father's dream come true and had built onto the old hut by adding another bedroom. He even built a small loft where he and Yena could have some privacy from their three children.It saddened him that his father had not been able to see his dream comwe true having been killed during the uprising in 1917.

He paused with a hand on the door knob as he became aware of the Tocsin tolling. He listened for a moment then decided he ached too much to go and see what was happening. He entered the kitchen smiling to himself as the smells of cooking wafted over him and after hanging up his coat went over to his wife, Yena, who stood at a stove preparing the evening meal.

She said without looking up as she stirred the soup in an old blackened pot, 'Your back hurts again?'

He ambled up behind her, sighed and caressed her shoulders, 'It is the usual, nothing to worry about.' He turned and with a soft grunt sat heavily at an old wooden table and began picking at grains of buckwheat he found in the cracks of the old wood, savouring the cooking smells as he silently watched her work. He felt warm and comfortable in their small farm house as he looked around at the children's toys scattered about beneath the table and children's drawings on the walls. But most of all it was that wonderful smell of cooking that seemed to instill a sense of safety and stabilty.

Their youngest two children, Georgi, seven, and Yelena, nine, were running in and out of the kitchen making a nuisance of themselves, half expecting a look from their Papa — one of which would be more than sufficient to stop them in their tracks. Ivan had an aura of authority that emanated from from his sharp brown eyes, the wildness of his thick grey beard, tangle of long brown curly hair and a deep resonant voice.

The peasant population had not been encouraged to be literate when they were serfs of the aristocracy before the revolution in 1917 but now many had — through free access to schools — learnt the basic skills. Ivan had excelled at school but in retrospect felt angry that the only books available were those that taught Stalin's propaganda. He was angry that the outside world was not available to him (censorship being a dominant factor in preventing this). However, it didn't prevent him from having spirited discussions with close friends about what could be going on or questioning the rare foreign visitor he could corner in a sheltered spot away from prying eyes.

Ivan was proud of his heritage as a peasant farmer and enjoyed being close to the earth. Money held little attraction to him as it had to others who had turned their farms to making as much profit as they could selling their produce wherever possible. Such men became wealthy and considered by Stalin to be enemies of the people and labelled them "Kulaks" as were the previous landowners who had held onto the largest and best pieces of land; a term which would later threaten their very existence.

Ivan was not a kulak; he only owned one strip of land, two cows, a few chickens and two horses. The small area of land was barely sufficient to sustain them but he was good with his hands and hired out his practical skills to people in the town. Ivan was a thinker and his life as a farmer battling the vagaries of the Russian weather had taught him to watch and look beyond the current blue sky to what might be on the horizon. This same sensing he also applied to the political horizon, looking beyond the promises of blue skies to what really lay ahead. He felt bitterness and anger toward the socialist system that had promised a new start for his country, but was now destroying it through incompetent men hurriedly promoted beyond their capacities to deliver a programme of collectivisation; something that was despised and fiercely resisted by the peasant population.

Ivan and Yena had married when they were sixteen and after twenty four years Yena knew when something was troubling her husband. She sensed it now from the brooding figure behind her as she stood at the cooking range stirring the boiling pot. 'You're going to the meeting next week?'

Ivan grunted. 'Of course. Not that it will make any difference.'

She sighed. 'They talk at us about how we would be better off; Education, electricity, communal nurseries, communal kitchens, clubs, equality but they do not listen to what we think.'

He smiled tiredly. 'What men can be so foolish as to ignore the voice of so many women?'

She looked over her shoulder to check he was not mocking her, satisfied she continued, 'I fear they won't listen to you men either and then...'

Ivan studied her backside beneath her skirt. 'I'm sure our wonderful comrade Stalin will...'

She shushed him, looking anxiously out of the window.

He continued, 'What? Is the bucket going to give me up?'

She turned and gave him one of her looks. 'You know quite well there are secret police everywhere. You may joke...but one day it will slip out at the wrong time.'

He grunted. 'Konstantin was a fool speaking out the way he did.' He picked at the table and chewed a grain of buckwheat he managed to prise from a crack. 'He was a good man. Ten years Gulag for saying what we all thought.'

The door burst open and he stood as the children rushed in, Georgie crying, red in the face with tears streaming. He looked sternly at him as Yelena entered, contrite.

Georgi railed, 'She splashed me all over and—'

'Enough!'He roared. 'Stop snivelling, telling stories on your sister.'

To Yelena he said, 'Stop upsetting your brother or I'll take the belt to you.'

Both children looked at each other and said in unison, 'Sorry Papa.'

'Hmm. Now go outside and play nicely or I'll set your big brother on you.' He thought for a moment. 'Wait! Why are you not studying?'

Yena said, 'They did when they got home from school.'

He gave a deep scowl as he said, 'Hmm. Lucky for you both, this time.'

They ran out giggling and he sat down again.

Yena muttered, 'Take the belt to you! You would sooner cut your arm off than raise a hand to them.'

He smiled. I can dream...'

'So what does it mean for us Ivan? Should we be worried?'

'It would do us no good to worry my sweet.'

Yena stopped and looked out of the window again. 'Why can't we just live in peace?'

Ivan stood and put his arms around her whispering in her ear, 'Quite right...' He kissed her neck. 'The children are out now...'

She slapped his hand playfully, enjoying the earthy smell of his shirt and nodded at a figure running across the yard. 'There see!' 'Your son would have caught us then what would you say eh!'

He squeezed her tighter as Yuri burst in, Ivan swung her round to face him and said, 'Ah and here he is!' Ivan let her down to the ground and looked Yuri over, secretly enjoying how he was developing, not so sure about his fuzzy beard and long hair but... 'See mother he gets bigger every day, eighteen years old, eats us out of house and home. Another I should have shown the belt.' His eyes twinkled as he teased his son. Yena put her hand to her mouth with a silent gasp as she saw the tear stains beneath the sweat on her son's face.

Yuri bent forward hands on hips to get his breath then said, 'Pulkova. I heard gun shots...I ran there...Papa! They hung two officials, there in the town square and beat to death three others!'

Ivan went to his son and held him. 'And you witnessed this?' Yuri nodded into his father's shoulder. Ivan muttered, 'A boy should not see such a thing. Are you ok? Are you hurt?'

Yuri pulled away and sat down at the table. 'It was horrible! People went crazy. Dimitrii and his wife were there and...'

'Dimitrii and his wife?'

'The crowd smashed all the windows and furniture.' He put his head in his hands, 'Why Papa?'

Ivan sat next to him. 'Because bad things are happening and there are more to come. Collectivisation is going ahead. That's why they rioted, they're frustrated and angry. This will make matters much worse. The State will seek out people to punish; innocent or otherwise.'

'Collectivisation is not fair! Why should we have to give them everything? We should fight them!'

'I shan't if I can hold out. My father worked this land and I intend to do the same. It might not be much but it's ours.' He looked hard into his son's eyes seeing the black cloud of anger growing, 'Now listen to me. You have to keep away from there. It is going to turn nasty. Do you promise?' Yuri looked at the floor, his fists clenched. Ivan shook him, 'Promise! I know you're hot headed diving in without thinking, but this is serious. Understand?'

Yuri looked up and into his father's powerful eyes. 'Yes Papa...but — '

Ivan frowned, 'But?' Yuri looked down. Ivan turned to his wife. 'Mother, let's clean him up and feed him. He looks exhausted.'

As she tended to him Ivan sat in thought then said, 'Yuri. I think it is important that you fully understand what is happening to our country. Tomorrow evening there is a meeting to explain some of the changes we are experiencing. Would you like to come with me?'

Yuri smiled, 'Yes! Very much.'

'Ok then, tomorrow we go by train to Leningrad.'

2. A MEETING OF MINDS

In the city of Leningrad, life moved at a more frantic pace as city dwellers watched in alarm thousands of peasants — desperate to avoid collectivisation — enter the city seeking accommodation they assumed under the Soviet social policy would be provided for them. Within a short time the municipal housing authority creaked beneath the overwhelming numbers as it desperately tried to find accommodation. This led to peasants having to move in with working class families to share their space — often a very tiny space or even a bed in a corridor — which added to the misery of both parties.

This pressure touched the Reinhardt family. Gustav and his wife Maya and their daughter Nadya, all shared a two bedroom apartment beautifully decorated — Maya was fastidious and had carefully selected items that suggested opulence — in the centre of Leningrad. Gustav lectured in politics at the Leningrad University and was acutely aware that his position as an academic did not fit with Stalin's vision of a proletariat society.

Nadya, a beautiful young woman of eighteen with long black hair and intense brown eyes attended the Leningrad Academy of Art studying the violin. Nadya was a vibrant and passionate girl full of life with an infectious laugh. Up to now her life had been organised and respectable as her father's position as a college lecturer enabled them many luxuries and protected her from the excesses of communist dogma. The violin provided an outlet for her emotional energy much to the relief of her parents who loved her dearly but at times found themselves exhausted. Nadya had always been a handful, being an only child her parents had lavished attention on her determined to give her the opportunities they had been denied. Now eighteen, she held strong views — her friends would say opinionated — about everything and not frightened to express them loudly.

The crisis built as thousands of refugees arrived every week. Gustav became seriously concerned, so much so, that he felt he had to raise the matter with his family. One evening his wife Maya had created a beautiful beef stew and they were quietly enjoying it with a bottle of white wine, always a civilised affair his wife insisted on. He casually said after clearing his throat, 'The situation with homeless peasants is becoming acute. I hear there are quite a few entering the city with nowhere to live.'

Maya stopped midway with a fork full of food to her mouth. 'Surely they can't stay?'

Nadya snorted. 'I don't want smelly peasants near where we live thank you very much! Papa. You must stop them.'

He smiled. 'Sadly my influence would have no effect, in fact it could endanger us all. Don't forget I have German ancestry, something our friend Stalin doesn't like.'

Nadya snorted again. 'He's a horrible man! Someone should shoot him.'

Gustav picked up his wine glass and looked into it as he said, 'Nadya, such statements if overheard by someone out for mischief would put us all in the Gulag. Please consider your words more carefully. I know it is safe here, but you are developing the habit of carelessness, and in this climate that could prove fatal.'

'Sorry Papa...but he *is* evil!'

Gustav sighed and looked to his wife. 'Please try and talk some sense into your daughter Maya.'

Maya waved her fork at Nadya. 'Listen to your father Nadya.' Nadya took a mouthful of food and rolled her eyes.

Maya put down her knife and fork. 'How serious is it Gustav? Should we move do you think?' She thought for a moment, 'No. We have too many friends here.'

Gustav sipped his wine. 'I think you'll find the situation similar wherever you go in this torn country.' He sat back savouring his wine. 'There is a meeting tomorrow night at the Municipal building to explain the Five Year Plan, not that I don't understand it of course but I would like to hear how our *Friend* intends to put it into effect. It appears that he and the Central Committee have made a complete mess of it so far.'

Nadya sat forward. 'Can I go with you Papa?'

He considered for a moment and looked to Maya who shrugged. 'Very well. You can come with me. But behave!'

The next evening Ivan and Yuri set off on their long walk to the railway station where they caught the 5.15 train to Leningrad. Yuri took in the musty smell of the carriage and smoke from the engine as it leaked around the old windows and wooden slatted sides. Yuri was also excited at the journey having only been to the city once before with his father — again to a political meeting — and although remembered little of the visit did recall the excitement of so many people talking at once, of raised voices and the smell of tobacco and alcohol.

He remembered his father had held his hand as they walked up a
wide street — wider than any road he had ever seen with large
grand buildings and brown stoned ornate facades looking down
on horses and carts and the bustle of people — and taken him
into a large building full of men who seemed to tower over him
with loud voices. He remembered the smell of tobacco, how
their voices bounced off the walls, some of them looking angry
with red faces. He felt dwarfed by them and had no idea what
they were focused on so he looked up at the ornate ceiling
with its chandeliers, the oak wooden panelling on the walls,
all adding to the mystery of the big room. He remembered a man
he stood next to who seemed like a giant to the little boy and
who stamped his foot with rage, shouting, spittle flying as he
roared his disapproval, vigorously shaking his head..Yuri had
clutched his father's leg for reassurance as his father smiled
down to him reassuringly.

Yuri recalled the safety he had experienced in that moment
as his father put his arm around the little boy's shoulders
whispering, 'Empty vessels make the most noise.' He didn't
understand what he meant but felt the diffusion of his fear by
his father's joking tone. He remembered as they filed out of
the hall his father explaining what the meeting was about but
what he remembered most of all was the feeling of safety and
strength that emanated from him.

Now, as they made their way from the station up Nevsky
Prospekt toward the Municipal building he had wisps of memory
as he noted a vague familiarity some of the large imposing
buildings evoked. Not enough to know his way but sufficient to
stir his excitement. They turned a corner into a large square
where groups of men and women were gathering and heading
toward the Municipal building. It was clear the majority of
the gathering was peasants; as here and there the more formal
attire of expensive weaved material was in stark contrast to
the more rough linen of the peasants. They joined the throng
and patiently filed forward toward the ornate entrance.

Yuri said, 'It's a pity Mama can't be here.'

Ivan smiled. 'Believe me she knows what is happening. The
women know if it were left to the men at village meetings it
wpould most likely end in violence. But if *they* strike an
official it is put down to ignorance; the authorities consider
women, especially peasant women, to be childish and stupid,
preferring to push them away. But this meeting is more a
public announcement with the men delivering it well
protected.'

Yuri nodded. 'It was the women making the noise at
Pulkova.'

Ivan said, 'Exactly.' He laughed to himself, 'They have strategies we would never think of in a million years! For instance, the women might all talk loudly at once and drown out the speaker every time he asks a question, then they walk out. Or get so drunk they cause a riot.' He became serious. 'But the women are becoming angrier now and I suspect their violence could be far worse than a man losing his temper.' He looked thoughtful as they walked for a few minutes. 'You're Mama and I hate violence. The peasant way has always been to resist through silence and non cooperation. If all else fails we move away to some place different.'

Behind them Gustav and Nadya also slowly moved with the crowd. Nadya loved to watch people, to wonder who they were, where they came from, what they did, and so she looked around with interest noting how different every individual was. Her eyes settled on the broad shoulders of a tall young man a few yards in front of them talking passionately to an older man beside him. She looked away but then found herself drawn back to him. As she studied the pair she came to the conclusion that there were enough similarities — even though she could only see the backs of their heads and a brief profile — to assume them to be father and son. As the crowd slowly moved forward, she managed to manoeuvre her and Gustav to immediately behind them.

Nadya leant forward to catch their conversation not yet able to get a good look at the young man's face. She studied their clothing deciding they were roughly dressed by comparison to city folk and therefore peasants. Her interest began to wane. But then she heard the young man quote Lenin! Surely a peasant can't read? She turned to her father and oblivious of how loudly she talked when excited said, 'Papa? If peasants are illiterate how could they read political literature?'

Gustav felt uncomfortably aware that they were surrounded by peasants as he leant in to her and said through gritted teeth, 'Nadya, there is a time and a place for such comments; this is not one of them! Please remember our conversation last night at dinner.'

She huffed and swept her hair back — a gesture she used to signal annoyance — and focused once again on the pair in front of them.

Yuri glanced at his father as they both heard Nadya's question. He said loudly to his father directing his voice over his shoulder, 'I thought working class people would have better manners, being so clever.'

Nadya snorted. 'Pah. What would a grave digger know of manners?'

Yuri said even louder to his father, 'Wasn't it last year when a group of engineers from the Shakhty region of the Donbass tried to wreck machinery?'

Ivan said trying to suppress a smile, 'I believe it was.'

'You would think an engineer being working class and therefore far more intelligent than a mere peasant would have seen the futility of such an action?'

Ivan coughed to cover a laugh and sneaked a quick peek over his shoulder at the source of the provocative remarks that had riled his son.

A male voice from behind Nadya said, 'People should be careful what they say. Especially girls.' The voice was guttural and carried an undertone of threat.

Nadya swung round to see a large thick set peasant of about twenty watching her and leering.

She said, 'I'll say what I like.'

Gustav groaned, deeply regretting bringing her and began looking for a gap they could escape through. 'Nadya, there is gap over there we can —'

'I'm fine here Papa, thank you, although,' she said over her shoulder, 'I don't care much for the company behind us.'

The man behind her growled, 'I think you should shut up you working class whore.'

It was Ivan's turn to groan knowing Yuri would not let it go. The man shoved Nadya hard in the back pushing her onto Yuri knocking him forward almost off his feet. He stumbled for a second before regaining his balance and turned slowly to see who this female was and why she had pushed him.

Nadya flashed a tight smile at him and said without conviction and an underlying tone of mischief, 'Sorry. That oaf behind us pushed me.'

For an instant he was stunned by the sheer beauty of the woman who had been angering him taken aback by her deep brown eyes. He smiled at her and said, 'Excuse me.' He gently moved her to one side and stepped toward the man who was laughing and sharing a joke with a friend. Yuri took another step forward and stood close to the man. People nearby moved on as quickly as they could.

Calm and relaxed he looked deep into the man's eyes and said, 'I think you owe the lady an apology.'

The man looked to his friend and laughed. He shook his arms loose as if preparing for a fight. 'And I suppose you are going to make me?'

Yuri nodded with just the faint hint of a smile.

The man growled, 'Get out of my way.'

People close by pulled away in fear. Ivan turned to Gustav and said quietly, 'Not good.'

Gustav studied Ivan. 'You are his father?'

Ivan nodded with a smile. 'Children can be such a problem can't they?'

Gustav replied, 'I should have known better than bring her. I apologise for her comments. She can be outspoken...'

Ivan said looking at Yuri, 'And mine looks for fights.'

Yuri remained staring into the man's face, the smile lingering but beneath it now a hint of menace.

The man raised his fist to strike and Yuri stepped back and as the man's fist moved toward him, sidestepped grabbed his arm, twisted it and put him on the ground. He held the man's wrist under tension for a moment until he could see he was in deep pain then released him.

He turned to Nadya and said, 'He will apologise, but he's hurting at the moment.' The man struggled to his feet and reaching for his belt took out a vicious knife which he then lunged at him. Yuri stepped back and with a fluid motion grabbed the knife hand and bent the arm back against the joint at the same time lowering it over his knee. He applied more pressure and the man shrieked in agony. The knife clattered tot the ground. Yuri said softly, 'Now apologise to the lady. Tell her you are very sorry and in future you will be more respectful.'

The man feebly tried to struggle free but it only added to the pressure on his wrist and elbow. He nodded agreement. A crowd had now gathered.

Yuri released him and the man fell to one knee breathing deeply. Yuri bent down to him and hissed, 'Apologise to the lady.'

The man nodded again and stood up. Yuri took a step back watching the man closely. The man seemed to turn toward her but then swung a furious blow at Yuri's face catching him on the cheek. The force of the blow put the man off balance and he steadied himself to find Yuri waiting for him. The man aimed another blow at Yuri who gave him a solid punch to the face knocking the man on his back. Yuri bent over him and said, 'Stay down.' The man spat a tooth out and blood trickled down his chin. His expression suggested — apart from extreme pain — that he was considering trying to get up. Yuri raised an eyebrow questioningly. The man looked at Yuri's knuckles and realised what he was up against. He laid his head back to the ground.

Yuri pulled him up by his collar and heaved him round to Nadya. 'Apologise to the lady.'

The man hung his head and whispered, 'I'm sorry.'

Nadya looked at him with horror then to Yuri. She turned and pushed her way through the crowd. Yuri dropped him to the ground and hurried after her as she merged with the crowd.

Gustav said to Ivan, 'I see what you mean.'

Ivan offered his hand. 'Ivan Kasakof.'

'Gustav Reinhardt. It seems we both owe your son our thanks.'

Ivan replied looking around at the people close to them. 'In these troubled times, feelings run high.' He looked around for Yuri. 'You have a beautiful daughter Gustav.'

Gustav nodded graciously. 'And you have a powerful son!'

Ivan took off his cap and scratched his head. 'True. I've taught him how to look after himself. Yuri hates bullies but I get the feeling he and your daughter were attracted to each other despite the sharp words.'

Gustav laughed. 'Yes! You could be right. Although,' he leant in close to Ivan, 'he will need to be careful, she too has a temper!'

Yuri caught up with Nadya and walked alongside her the crowd slowing as they neared the entrance. She gave him a haughty look and then looked away. He continued to walk beside her. She continued to ignore him. Inwardly, her heart was racing, her palms sweating.

Yuri said, 'I was only trying to defend you. I'm sorry if...'

She rounded on him and said, 'Defending me? So you think I can't defend myself against...' she looked him up and down with contempt, 'peasants and bullies.' She relented a little as she saw the look of hurt on his face. 'Ok an educated one. And I didn't mean you are a bully.'

He smiled with relief. 'I can't stand bullies, it makes me angry.'

'I can see that!' She noticed his calloused knuckles.

He said, 'Perhaps you should think a little more before making judgements on people.'

She looked at him noticing for the first time his deep green eyes. Her pulse was still racing and she felt herself blushing, her usual composure slipping away.

Yuri's mouth was dry as he took in her stunning beauty, more intense the closer he got to her. He said gently, 'I'm sorry if I acted wrongly.'

She looked at him as she fought the feelings that were overtaking her. 'You didn't. I was rude, I apologise too.'

Ivan caught up with them. 'Yuri, we must get inside.'

Yuri tore his eyes away from her. 'Yes Papa.' He turned back to her as he moved away. 'My name's Yuri.'

She smiled. 'Nadya.'

As he followed his father he smiled and said, 'I'm going to marry *her*!'

They moved ahead as Gustav walked alongside his daughter. He looked at her expecting a scowl but found instead a gentle smile. He looked for Yuri and saw him disappearing ahead. He smiled to himself.

3. A ROUGH PATH

After a long and torrid meeting with officials spouting party language about "class enemies, backwardness (anything that related to old Russia) peasant's intelligentsia as opposed to bourgeois intelligentsia" and the wonders of Stalin's Five Year Plan, people left exhausted and frightened. Some were fired up with excitement of the Cultural Revolution of course and exalted others to join them, but many — especially the peasants — felt disillusioned and angry. Ivan was one of them as he walked silently out with the crowd into the late evening city looking straight ahead with his head held high, containing his frustration.

Yuri had spent most of the meeting scanning the sea of heads looking for Nadya without success. He too found the party rhetoric exhausting and too good to be true, but his focus was elsewhere as he continued to scan the mass of people. And then, as they walked down the steps there she was! She was about fifty yards ahead with her father as they made their way through the crowd.

Yuri looked to his father as he said, 'I'm going over there Papa, I've seen her!'

Ivan smiled. 'Ah! The girl you will marry?'

Nadya was hoping she might see Yuri again but with so many people about...and then a tap on her shoulder, 'Hello again Nadya.'

She turned in surprise and laughed as she saw him standing there. She said to her father, 'Papa this is...'

He said with a smile, 'Yuri isn't it?'

Yuri said politely, 'Yes sir.'

Gustav added, 'And here is your father!' Ivan joined them and shook hands with Gustav.

Ivan had considered that Gustav was certainly not a peasant — that was clear from his dress — and was aware of his own personal assumptions about the working class. But this man appeared open and accepting, certainly not giving the impression of any class distinction. Both men watched with amusement as their respective children — albeit both eighteen — looked at each other their eyes seemingly locked as they both tried to find something to say.

Gustav said to Ivan, 'It's not often my daughter is lost for words.'

Nadya bridled. 'Perhaps Papa I was musing about the meeting?'

He understood he had stepped over the line. 'Yes of course.' To Yuri he said, 'And you Yuri? What did you think?'

Yuri looked to his father then spoke. 'I think Sir, that the Five Year Plan is flawed. We are being pressured — although clothed in clever language — to force us either into collective farms where we lose our identity or off the land into industry. Either way we lose.'

Ivan said, 'And you Gustav?'

Gustav looked at the people milling around talking in small groups, here and there raised voices. 'I think you are right Yuri. Sadly the working class is being favoured, but only if you are a factory worker; intelligentsia, people like myself who are teachers or writers are definitely a target for the militants of the Cultural Revolution. Anything to suggest we hold any views counter to the party are sufficient for deportation.' He stopped abruptly, 'Pardon me. I have said too much. Come Nadya we must go.'

She had been watching Yuri as her father spoke and was drawn back suddenly by his quick change of mood. 'Then you go on Papa and I will make my own way.'

'I'm sorry my dear, confident as you may feel, I am not prepared for you to walk through the city alone at night, especially when emotions are high.'

Yuri jumped in quickly looking at Nadya as he said. 'With your permission sir I would gladly escort your daughter home.'

Nadya was about to object on the grounds of not being in need of protection— again — but instead simply looked at her father and smiled sweetly.

Gustav said, Very well.' He turned to Ivan. 'What do you think Ivan?'

Ivan looked to Yuri and could see the desperation in his eyes pleading for his permission. He felt a swell of pride that his son — certainly big enough to go his own way — had respect for him which he displayed before his pride in front of these people. 'Of course. I shall make my way to the station. Yuri, remember the last train leaves at eleven.'

Gustav and Ivan watched the pair move away. They shook hands and Gustav said, 'It's been an interesting evening. Pleasant to meet you Ivan.'

Ivan said as he watched his son, 'Yes it has, although I sense my son's attention was not on the speakers!'

Gustav smiled. 'Goodnight.'

Yuri and Nadya walked through the Tavrichesky gardens toward the river Neva discussing the meeting. Secretly she was impressed by his comments to her father but she wasn't going to let him know that. She said after a few moments silence as they entered the gardens, 'So you consider yourself a political expert then?'

Yuri was unsure how to be with this woman — previous conversations with females had been simple affairs, mostly about friends or the village — not a challenge like this. He felt defensive. 'Why do you say that? Because I take an interest you mock me?'

'Do I? I just asked if you considered you have extensive knowledge of what president Stalin intends, that's all.'

'Of course not. So tell me what you think then.'

'Me? Oh I'm just a woman.'

He was wrong footed and blushed retreating into silence as he kicked a stone — with some force.

She smile inwardly and stroked a shrub as she passed it. 'Aren't the gardens lovely?'

He struggled to understand why he suddenly felt so uncomfortable.

She continued, 'My Papa teaches at the University.'

Yuri felt the pressure lessen and asked, 'What does he teach?'

'Politics.'

He realised he was a fly caught in a trap, hopelessly out of his depth. She laughed heartily. He looked to see if she was mocking him but she linked her arm in his and speeded them up. 'Let's go and look at the river. I love the lights at night.'

Yuri began to experience feelings totally new to him; his heart was racing, he felt sweaty despite the evening chill, and excitement coursed through his body as he caught a sense of her smell; sweet and clean, as her hair brushed his face. They reached the river and sat on the wall watching the current swirl around the bridge. She kept her arm linked into his and leaned a little closer.

She said, 'I thought what you said to my father was right. He talks to me about his views.'

Yuri felt peaceful as he watched the water, feeling her warmth through his sleeve. He asked gently, 'Your Papa seemed worried just before we left them.'

She sighed. 'He is frightened. His father was German and he believes he is under threat. If they decide to get rid of anyone not purely Russian, he fears he will be deported. Especially being a teacher.'

'I can see that. My Papa is worried we will lose our farm.' She didn't know what to say to that. She continued to look at the lights. He continued, 'It's not big but it's ours, we own it and can just about make a living; although Papa thinks we will be taxed so heavily if we refuse to be part of the collective and have to leave.'

'Where would you go?'

'I don't know. I think a lot of us are going into the cities for work and a roof of any sort.'

Before she could stop herself she said in horror, 'Not Leningrad?' She regretted it immediately. 'I mean it would be horrible after the countryside and where would you live?'

'Hopefully we won't have to. The farm has been in our family since 1917.'

There was a difficult silence as she waited for him to say something else. He didn't. But then after a while he asked,

'Where do you live?'

She said tentatively, 'We have a little apartment, here in the city. Mama loves to buy expensive things to make it look grand.' She'd done it again!

This time she sensed him withdraw a little. Then he said softly, 'That must be nice.'

She cringed. How could she be so insensitive? The preconceptions she had held only a few hours ago now lay shattered on the damp pavement at her feet. Now she felt ashamed.

After a few minutes he said softly, 'Isn't the water quiet?'

She replied gently, 'Hmm.' Here with this man she realised her whole world was becoming disoriented as he blasted away her misconceptions about the peasant class. She felt shame at the disparaging language she had used when talking about them with her working class friends. She had considered peasants inferior beings who worked on the land, illiterate and unable to think beyond the next potato whilst living in squalor. She had not imagined in a million years she would be sitting with one watching the river and feeling so warm and safe. Another realisation struck her; she wanted to remain here with him forever, just like this. She sighed.

He said softly, 'Ok?'

She replied dreamily, 'Uhuh.'

He shifted a little to get comfortable on the hard stone wall but made sure he kept her arm linked to his. He was confused. First she was haughty, then apologetic then clever with her remarks then — he realised they were from such different backgrounds, how could this possibly work? Would you like to visit our hovel Nadya, but don't bring your best lace; it gets very muddy in the winter...His spirits suddenly sank as he thought she was just having some fun. She would be able to tell her friends that she had spent an evening with a peasant. How different that would be. Anger began to rise. He said curtly, 'We'd better go. Is it far to your grand apartment?'

Nadya realised she had blown it; her arrogance had driven a wedge between them already. She stood and straightened her coat, 'It's not far, about five minutes. But you don't have to bother. I will be fine.'

'I said I would escort you home and I will.'

They walked in silence. She felt wretched, desperately trying to think of something she could say to put it right. She said, 'It's not a very big apartment, not like some of the really grand ones.'

He looked straight ahead as he said, 'You don't have to say that. I'm sure it's lovely.'

They walked in silence again for a few minutes then she stopped. 'Here it is.'

He stopped and turned to her. 'We come from different classes Nadya. It's best we leave it as this.' He began to leave then turned and said, 'Sorry. I don't think I'm good enough for you. Goodnight.' He quickly disappeared amongst the many people coming back from the meeting.

Nadya watched him hurry away. A tear began to trickle down her cheek which she swiped away as she swished her hair back in frustration. Angrily she went inside.

Yuri walked quickly kicking at anything on the pavement he came across. How could he have been so stupid in thinking they could have made anything from such different backgrounds? And she was stuck up. Who did she think she was, talking about his class the way she did? Ok she tricked him with her beauty and soft voice and deep brown eyes and she was intelligent and

feisty — but...no it wouldn't work. And to think he wanted to
marry her!

4. REGRETS

The next evening, Nadya sat in her bedroom staring out of the window in a reverie about last night. She was confused. She had assumed peasants to be dirty and ignorant. Yuri was certainly a peasant but not as she had expected; he wasn't dirty, in fact smelled clean. And quoting Lenin? And so strong and confident! She felt a shiver and smiled. Ok he was violent but he had been provoked and was doing it for the right reasons. And those eyes...This is silly she thought. She went to her bookcase and began rearranging books (although being so preoccupied she was in fact simply moving them around).

He's just a peasant who happened to be there, she thought, and then he turned out to be so cold. The way he walked off like that. Huh. Yuri's face drifted in her memory and she huffed moving some of the books she had just repositioned. What is it with boys and fighting? His scarred knuckles drifted into her mind. Pride, that's what it is. Well he can go and be as proud as he likes! I don't care. She put a book back to where she had just moved it and put it somewhere else. She took out another which she idly shoved in between two unrelated books. This was ridiculous. She flounced into the lounge and plonked herself down beside her mother who was reading. She put down her book aware that when Nadya entered like that, she was angry about something.

She took off her reading glasses and said, 'Yes dear?' Nadya picked up a newspaper and flipped over the pages — obviously not reading anything. 'Is there something bothering you my sweet?'

Nadya threw down the paper onto a coffee table. 'Why are boys so stupid?'

'Bit of a sweeping statement perhaps...'

Nadya picked up the paper again and opened it with a snap then slapped it down on the coffee table shaking the cup and saucer.

'Nadya!'

'Sorry Mama. Aargh! Boys!'

Her mother asked, 'Is it the boy you met last night?' Nadya nodded. Her mother continued, 'What has he done to make you so angry?'

'He was horrible!'

Maya looked concerned. 'Your Papa thought he was wonderful...'

'Well, Papa didn't have to be told he was too grand.'

'Is that what,' she thought for a moment, 'Yuri said?'

'Just about, yes. He thinks our class difference is a problem.'

Maya said, 'Class difference?'

'He's a peasant.'

'Oh.' Maya felt a shudder. 'Well I think he's right dear, we can't expect them to be like us, after all they live in...' she shuddered again, 'sheds or even mud huts I believe. No dear, I think you are better off finding someone of our class.'

Nadya said angrily, 'He's intelligent and clever and really strong but gentle. And funny.' She jumped up and hurried back into her bedroom slamming the door.

Gustav appeared from his study and asked, 'Nadya?' She nodded picking up her book. 'Why is she so angry?'

'Oh just something about a boy she met last night, the one you told me about although,' she looked cross as she opened her book, 'you left out the bit about him being a peasant.' She reached for her glasses and put them on.

Gustav sighed and went to Nadya's room. He knocked on her door and entered. Nadya was face down on the bed crying. 'Hey what's all this about?'

She turned over and sat up, tears streaming down her face.

'He's different to any other boys I've met. Mama doesn't understand.'

Gustav sat on the bed and looked at her with a kindly smile. 'Your Mama has her faults like all of us. Unfortunately, despite her being a wonderful woman, she can be a snob.' Nadya stopped crying shocked at his words. 'I'm sorry if I shocked you but it's true as it is of many of our friends. I thought he was delightfully open and honest, as was his father, a man I would like to spend more time with. Tell me what happened.'

'We walked to the river and sat and watched the water. He asked where I lived and I told him.' He gave an enquiring look. 'I said Mama liked to buy expensive things to make it look grand.'

He rolled his eyes. 'Nadya...'

'He said we were from different classes and it wouldn't work, then he said goodnight and walked away. Just like that!'

'Did he escort you home as he said he would?' She nodded.

'So despite being insulted by you he still honoured his agreement?'

'I'm a horrible person Papa.' She began crying again.

He touched her shoulder. 'No you're not but perhaps now you will think more before you speak? All I can say from my observations is that he is very struck by you and if he has anything about him he will come back.'

'But he said coming from different classes won't work. He said he was not good enough for me.' She flung herself back onto the bed and buried her face in the blanket as she wailed.

'He was hurt by your remarks Nadya. He did the grown up thing and walked away before his anger got the better of him. I like him.'

She wailed even louder, 'So do I!'

The next week the bombshell Gustav feared, exploded in the form of a starkly worded letter informing him that a family of four would be sharing his fourth floor apartment in three days time — it also contained thinly veiled threats that non - compliance would lead to eviction. Of course he argued as much as he dared but was acutely aware of the political climate in which anybody regardless of rank or position could be labelled as an "enemy of the people" and deported to a far flung area of Siberia or sent to prison. In either case the family would be destroyed.

Gustav sat at the dining table and stroked the softness of the lace tablecloth beneath his shaking hands as he looked around the apartment that had been their home for twenty years; the familiar family ornaments and furniture, paintings and flowers in vases, all representing elements of his family's life. He looked up to the ornate chandelier that hung over the table as if for inspiration as he watched his wife Maya cry into her lace handkerchief. He looked around in desperation for his daughter.

Nadya was sitting on her bed holding her violin, listlessly staring at a piece of sheet music; as she had done every evening since last week. She hadn't told her friends about the night she met Yuri — she felt too ashamed and angry with herself. The subject was not discussed at home but her moody presence made it clear she was unhappy. Gustav had considered broaching it with her but decided it was best left to heal of its own accord with time. And anyway since the letter had arrived his attention was solely on that.

She came back to earth as she heard her father calling out for her. Nadya jumped up and went through to the kitchen where her parents sat at the table. Her mother's crying became louder as Nadya sat down beside her father who sighed with relief.

Her mother was unable to take in the enormity of the impending invasion of their home and lives by peasants. She had no conception of what it would entail as she cried looking past Gustav to their comfortable and well furnished lounge.

Between sobs she cried plaintively, 'But where..? I mean we have only two bedrooms. I can't bear the thought of...' she shuddered, '...peasants in...' She broke down into floods of tears as Gustav glanced anxiously to his daughter for help.

Nadya reached over and took her mother's hand as she looked at her father, shocked by the sadness in his eyes, his expression suggesting he had aged ten years overnight. 'Mama we just have to take each day at a time; perhaps it will only be for a few days until something more permanent is found for them.'

He quickly agreed. 'Yes! Do you see Maya? It may not be as bad as...'

Maya leapt up crying hysterically and rushed into her bedroom slamming the door. Nadya moved closer to her father and put her arm around his shoulders. 'It's not likely though is it Papa?'

He rubbed his face with his hands, 'No darling, I don't think it is. Families are sleeping anywhere they can. Our lives are about to change. Hopefully your mother will accept it and we can deal with it as best we can.'

Nadya's eyes flashed anger. 'It's not fair! Why do we have to take them in?' But then she thought of Yuri describing exactly that situation. Shame burnt her cheeks.

He took her hand. 'It's not just us. I have two colleagues in the same situation.'

Nadya sighed. 'Sorry Papa.'

He looked into her brown eyes. 'I think you know now that your assumptions are not always right.' She nodded, her head down. 'His father commented on how beautiful you are.'

She looked aghast. 'You talked to his father? Not about me I hope.'

He smiled. 'Hmm. A little.'

'Papa!'

He laughed. 'You can "Papa" me all you like. I knew when I saw the way you avoided him. A sure sign you liked him.'

She reddened and swished her hair back, 'Well it's too late now.'

He turned serious again. 'But I fear we have more pressing matters to deal with.'

'How will we do it Papa?'

He looked perplexed. 'Well, there is only your room, and the lounge. The kitchen of course and my study.'

Nadya was outraged, 'Not your study Papa! You can't...'

He took her hand. 'Darling this is beyond anything we could have imagined. My study is where I escape to. Now I will have to find another way. And you...' he squeezed her hand playfully, '...will have to move in with your mother and me.' She nodded understanding the enormity of what was coming. He continued, 'As for your beloved violin...'

She smiled. 'Inber will let me practice at her's.'

'And her parents?'

She said vaguely, 'They died remember?' She became lost in thoughts for awhile as she tried to ignore her mother's hysterical crying in the bedroom. 'Perhaps I should see if I can move in with her?'

'Gustav sighed, 'I would prefer it if you could stay here, for your mother's sake... and mine.'

'Ok Papa we'll see how it goes, but if it would help the situation then I will.'

'Thank you Nadya. You know, when you were a little girl we thought you would be such a handful; all that energy! You tired us out. How could we have known you would grow into such a lovely...' he looked to the ceiling and smiled, 'usually calm, person.' He smiled, 'Although...'

She laughed. 'I was a handful wasn't I?' But you and Mama have been so good to me. It seems so unfair that everything has to change.' She thought for a moment. 'What do you think they will be like? Since meeting Yuri and his father I've come to change my mind. I don't believe the terrible stories about peasants, how they live in filth and steal from people. Do you think the tales are true Papa?' But she knew the answer.

Gustav sighed, 'There's always a grain of truth in such things before they get blown out of proportion, but we must hope and pray our visitors are not like that. You know, I have discovered over the years that everybody is basically kind; it's when power and greed take over, or fear of course, that can change people.'

Nadya stood and stretched. 'I'll go and see Inber now so at least we will know I could if it was necessary.' She gathered her coat and left shouting goodnight to her mother as she closed the door.

Maya sobbed quietly. Gustav sat in the silence, looking around the apartment as if for the last time, taking in the carefully draped curtains, soft carpet and furnishing creating a soft feel. He knew it was going to be hard both for them and their impending addition to the apartment. How would they all fit in? And the kitchen, how would that work?

Maya came back in and sat down at the table again, her face puffed from crying, her eyes red and sore. 'I'm sorry Gustav, I know we need to be strong. It's just...' She blew her nose into her crumpled lace handkerchief, 'so unfair. What have we done to deserve this?'

'Nothing my dear. It's because of the hair brained and poorly thought out state plan driving them from their farms.' he added ironically, 'I wonder how many party officials will be in the same boat as us?'

'Isn't there anyone you can talk to? Surely in your position at the university...'

'No my dear, I've tried as much as I dare. There are high political tensions within the party which may result in Stalin reacting by hitting out at anyone not of pure Russian descent.' He laughed. 'Interesting then that he chooses to target eighty two percent of the population as a means of raising revenue to benefit the working class minority! But still. We are entering dangerous uncharted territory Maya. We need to take each day as it comes and stick together.'

She reached over and took his hand. 'I know, and we will.'

'Then let's start right now and work out how we are going to deal with our new guests.'

5. RELUCTANT GUESTS?

Vadim Aminev leaned into the arms of his wooden cart and heaved it forward along the Nevsky Prospekt toward Rumyantsev Square, his sons Leonid and Maxim pushing from behind. His wife Lidiya sat on the cart trying to stop their belongings falling off. Despite the cold wind Vadim was sweating as he heaved and puffed along the wide street with his heavy load. At last he was nearing the end of the long journey having dragged all their belongings fifty miles into the city, fleeing their farm to avoid being shot by soldiers brought in to take the land and hand it over to the collective farms. Vadim had refused to join the Collectivisation believing it was evil as many rumours spread throughout the countryside that such farms were run by cruel tyrants or idiots. Vadim despised the working class and the city but now with no roof over his head he decided he had to swallow his pride and seek work and accommodation there.

When he arrived at the perimeter of the city and saw to his horror many other carts heading in the same direction, he knew it was going to be bad, but he had not expected to be told to sleep in the corridor of an apartment block until something could be found. If he had not made such a fuss he and his family would probably still be in that smelly, drafty corridor. After a few days he was given an address and told to take his family there, it being made clear to him that it was his and others like him that had caused the crisis. His argumentative nature could have lost him even that if his wife had not intervened and dragged him away.

Now, he stopped pulling as he noted the name of the building and dropped the handles of the cart unceremoniously as he looked up to the fourth floor. He walked stiffly to the entrance and pressed the bell for number twenty three. He noted the name Rheinhardt thinking it didn't sound very Russian. He stabbed the button with a grubby finger as he shouted to his wife. 'Stay with Maxim and the cart until I know it is safe.'

Upstairs, Gustav had been watching from their lounge window to the street below and felt his stomach drop as he saw the cart being pulled by a man and a boy slowly toward the direction of the apartment. He knew it had to be them; if not by the presence of a peasant cart then certainly from the way they were dressed in typical peasant trousers with their felt boots, woollen tops and flat hats. He could just make out a female figure wrapped in a shawl buried in a pile of blankets and what looked like rags. How was he expected to accommodate them and all their belongings? He moved away from the window and sat beside his wife on their large flower patterned sofa. 'They are here.'

Maya sighed. Already?'

'Yes. We must be kind dear, they look like they have little in their lives.'

'Poor things. I will try Gustav, I promise.'

He smiled. 'I know dear. We both will.'

'What about Nadya?'

'Nadya? She's strong willed and sulky but I think growing up very fast. Do you remember when she was little and refused to have the light on at night? She said it was us who was frightened not her. How old was she?'

Maya laughed. 'Four!'

He laughed with her. The door bell rang, stopping their momentary respite. He stood and went to the door, speaking into an intercom. 'Come up please, fourth floor.'

Downstairs, Vadim waved to his wife as he and his oldest son Leonid entered the building and climbed the stairs to the fourth floor.

'I hope they are nice people Papa.' His son said between breaths as they climbed the stairs.

Vadim snarled, 'Don't hold your breath they're townies and I'm sure they aren't too pleased we are moving in with them.' They reached the fourth floor and number twenty three. Vadim knocked on the door. Gustav opened it and there was a long moment of silence.

Vadim snatched off his hat. 'We were told to come here.' He looked awkward.

Gustav felt sad for this man who must feel awful as circumstances ate away his confidence and pride. How would he feel in this position? He smiled. 'Come in, please.' He looked past the man down the corridor. 'Your wife?'

'She's with our cart in case anyone tries to steal anything. She has our youngest with her as well.'

Gustav replied as he ushered the man inside. 'There is a yard at the back. You can leave the cart there.'

Vadim nodded and turned to his son. 'Go and pull it where the man says then bring your mother and brother back up here.'

The boy hurried off down the stairs as Vadim entered and Gustav closed the door. Vadim felt overwhelmed by the apartment and its "softness", the silence, flowered patterns on the walls, fancy lights hanging down from high ceilings, but perhaps most of all, the smell of polished wood and scent. His eyes drifted to the large sofa then over to the kitchen with its worktops, cupboards, cooking implements stored on walls, saucepans hanging from large stainless steel hooks. He thought of their farm which was nothing in comparison.

It was obvious to Gustav the man was overwhelmed as he took him into the kitchen. 'You must be thirsty. Would you like something to drink? Water, coffee or tea?'

Vadim replied quietly, 'Tea. Please.'

Gustav put the kettle onto to boil and said, 'How far have you come?'

Vadim shrugged tiredly. 'Who knows. Perhaps fifty miles?'

Gustav gasped. 'Pulling that cart? Have you not got a horse?'

'They shot it.'

Gustav realised he had no idea what this man had been through.

As the kettle began to boil Maya came through and with a tight smile said, 'We must help you bring up your belongings.'

Gustav poured the hot water into the teapot, 'I suggested they put their cart in the yard out of the way of prying eyes.'

Maya took some china cups out of the cupboard. 'Of course.'

A pregnant silence settled then Gustav said, 'We have emptied a bedroom and my study. It's not much I'm afraid. Hopefully you will have enough room.'

Vadim looked around struggling to cope. He had expected a hostile reception and been prepared for a confrontation, even violence, but now he was lost, deeply out of his comfort zone.

Maya handed a cup of tea to him and pointed to the sugar bowl. He nodded and she spooned in one small spoonful. She handed him the spoon and he stirred it, desperately thinking what he should do.

Gustav smiled at him. 'I think this is difficult for all of us. We must take our time and work things out.'

Vadim nodded and drank his tea quickly. 'I'd better go and help bring things upstairs.'

Gustav said, 'I'd be glad to help but I have a bad leg from the war, but I can organise things up here as you bring them up.'

Maya said, 'Our daughter Nadya will be here in a moment, she is young and strong. I can carry some light things?'

Vadim put on his cap and went to the door. He turned and said humbly, 'Thank you both.' He hurried out.

Maya looked at Gustav and her gaunt face said everything.

Gustav looked grim. 'We have no idea what they have been through.' He began making a space in the lounge.

As Vadim got back downstairs Nadya arrived on her bicycle and leant it against the wall. She could see this man must be the one they were expecting and said slightly out of breath, 'Hello.'

Maya appeared and said, 'Nadya this is...' she said awkwardly, 'sorry I don't...'

'Vadim. Vadim Aminev.'

Nadya smiled, 'I'm Nadya. Can I help with your things?'

He nodded and headed for the alleyway to the yard. Nadya looked to her mother and smiled then wheeled her bicycle into the alleyway. Maya followed her. In the yard Vadim's wife was untying ropes and freeing up parcels and bags as they all arrived.

Nadya took control. 'Hello I'm Nadya have you met my mother Maya?' Maya felt a swell of pride in her daughter and a little ashamed at her own reticence.

Vadim began pulling boxes off the cart and handing them to his sons, 'This is my wife Lidiya and these are my boys Leonid and Maxim.' Maxim, the youngest, seemed shy and just looked down at the ground. Leonid being fourteen and grown up — in the eyes of his brother who was three years younger — said, 'Hello.'

Nadya moved forward and took a couple of boxes from Leonid. She turned and carried them away. Vadim offered some bedding for Maya to carry and she bundled the blankets in her arms and turned trying to see over the pile. She soon became aware of their earthy smell and bits of straw fell onto her face as she struggled up the stairs. She felt as if it was all a dream and she would wake up any minute soon, but her reverie was broken by Nadya as she hurried past her and smiled. Maya eventually dropped the blankets in the lounge and turned to go down again.

Gustav hugged her. 'It will be ok Maya.'

She smiled stoically and went back downstairs meeting Leonid carrying some boxes. She stood aside for him and he smiled awkwardly as he struggled past. When she got back down to the cart Lidiya had emptied everything and piled it as best she could on the cobbled stones of the yard. As Maya approached she felt a wave of sadness engulf her; to imagine her own life distilled into an old wooden cart? Her eyes drifted over the assorted bits and pieces; bowls, pots, boxes of food, candles (Maya realised they probably hadn't had electricity) and more bedding.

Lidiya sat on a box holding a crucifix which she was whispering to. Maya touched her shoulder and pointed to the blankets. Lidiya looked up, her eyes wet and nodded yes. Maya gathered up the bedding and made her way back up stairs. Leonid stood aside to let her pass and they avoided eye contact as Maxim appeared with Vadim and they both made way for her.

In the apartment she looked in horror as all the bits and pieces which when in the cart had appeared small but now dominated the lounge incongruously beside the patterned sofa and the elaborately woven carpet which was now virtually covered, spilling into the kitchen and the empty bedroom that was Nadya's.

Gustav looked helplessly at his daughter and shrugged. She began trying to move things around to make a space for the rest, huffing at the untidy way Gustav had attempted to organise it. He realised he had not done a very good job and decided to organise his many books in some semblance of order on hastily put up shelves in their bedroom.

Vadim entered with his family and all four stood in the hallway unsure what to do next.

Gustav appeared and said, 'I've moved your bedding into the bedroom, and some of the boxes. Perhaps you want to see where to put things?' Vadim nodded. Gustav gestured to what used to be his study. 'Here is the other room. I'll let you decide how you want to organise it. As for the kitchen...' He looked bemused. 'We must sit down and think how we can make that work.'

Maya came through and said to Lidiya, 'You must be thirsty.' Then to the two boys, 'And you as well. Come into the kitchen and we'll make some drinks.'

Vadim cleared his throat. 'It must be a great shock. I'll do everything I can to find accommodation and work. You have been very kind.'

Lidiya held his arm. 'I too am very sorry. It was not easy leaving our farm.' She looked around at the apartment. 'It was nothing grand like this but it was our home.'

Vadim put his hand on hers.

Maya held out her hand and *almost* touched her arm. 'Tea?'

6. A STORM BREWS

September 1929

A week later, in the old town hall of Nansk, a gust of wind rattled the doors and blew dust across the floor toward a long wooden table behind which sat a committee of five men. In the centre Vladmir Molotov, District Secretary and Plenipotentiary — his demeanour and imperious manner replacing the absence of any insignia denoting his position as a civil servant (the cultural revolution forbade it) — impatiently tapped his foot as he glanced toward the doors and up to a clock above it as its hands seemed to take forever to reach seven o'clock. He sat upright, hands clasped on the bare table top in front of him, tense with nervous energy, which eventually expressed itself by a single loud cough.

The men continued to sit in silence until a clap of thunder rattled the windows and wind howled through any gap it could find. Outside, the evening sky was filled with black clouds laden with rain, harbingers of an impending storm. The wind brought the first few drops of rain splattering on the town and a group of peasants striding purposefully through its streets towards the town hall. Their mood was as black as the sky above them — their grim expressions highlighted by a flash of lightening as they approached the steps.

They burst open the doors and flooded in — many voices raised in angry discussion — and crowded before the committee, their faces reflecting a single purpose; defiance. The District Secretary Molotov stood and put his hand up for silence. Some of them looked back toward the doors as four armed soldiers appeared but most stood shoulder to shoulder resolute as they watched Molotov with venomous anger, their eyes shouting for an explanation.

Molotov surveyed the angry faces, his eyes drifting to the reassuring presence of the armed guards at the rear. He waited for the angry voices to subside. 'I know you are angry. I was advised to call off this meeting because of the violence last week in Stetzin but I believe it right that we should share with you the great vision of our leader Stalin.' He put his hands behind his back to conceal them shaking and took a deep breath to remove the tremor from his voice. 'None of us like change.' He avoided the eyes of the men immediately in front of him, instead addressing the guns at the back. 'In order for our motherland to be the greatest country in the world we must build our industries to provide the money we need to look after our citizens, educate our children!' He attempted a smile but it faded before it could take hold on his sweating face. 'You. You are the means toward this great and wonderful plan. Your grain is essential to the rebirth of our motherland, to the dawning of a new age making the Soviet Union the greatest country in the world! In order to ensure your produce is used in the most efficient way, the Central Committee has decreed that as part of the Five Year Plan, private ownership will be illegal and from now on your farms will be taken over by the state.'

The crowd erupted. He put up his hand again. 'Comrades! You will be paid by the state for your produce! Surely you can see it is wrong to make a profit at the expense of the people of the motherland?'

A powerful voice came from the middle of the crowd bringing an immediate silence. 'So Lenin freed us from being serfs to the rich and now we are to be serfs to the state!'

'That sort of talk is what undermines our...'

'And yours is all lies.' The crowd roared approval.

Molotov shouted, 'Such talk is illegal. It is against the law to...'

'Speak freely, as Lenin wanted? So now I am to be arrested? Like the priest? As an enemy of the people. For anti — party thoughts!'

The crowd erupted, jeering and jostling to throw insults at the official who turned and whispered to the man beside him. 'Who is this man?'

The man replied speaking behind his hand, 'Ivan Kazakof.'

Molotov held up his hand again. 'It has been thought through carefully and you have all been assessed on your yearly output and will be paid accordingly.'

Another voice came from the crowd. 'How much will we be paid?'

'Everything is in hand as part of the Five Year Plan our great leader President Stalin has designed for us. Industrial growth is vital for our country; we cannot afford the Imperialist backwardness that was removed by the Great Revolution. Now we must work together! Go back to your homes and rejoice in our great party leadership!'

'What choice do we have?' came from a voice from within the crowd.

Molotov pressed on, 'All over the country people are sacrificing for the good of the state. Now it is your responsibility to do your part.'

Ivan Kazakof bellowed again, 'And what sacrifices have you made comrade Molotov, apart from a better apartment and rich food?' A man standing beside him cheered and shook Ivan's hand.

Molotov reddened and began to bluster, 'I...I have...'

Ivan turned and spoke to the angry crowd, 'We are being lied to and used. Let's go, there's nothing for us here!'

The soldiers quickly stood aside as the crowd angrily left the hall.

Later, a small gathering of peasants crowded beneath a barn roof as the rain and wind drove against the rough wooden sides. Ivan sat on a bale of hay in the middle. 'We know how little they intend to pay us. It will not be enough to live on. Already, I've heard rumours many of us are deserting our farms and moving into the towns to be housed by the state; if we're lucky there will be a space in a corridor. It is not what I want for my family.'

'So what do you suggest we do Ivan?' asked his friend Boris Frenkel,

'I don't know.'

'Well I do!' retorted Boris, 'I'm going to the town Committee Office and demand to be heard.' There was a murmur of agreement from the other men.

Ivan stood and said, 'Like Stetzin last week, how many of our friends have been arrested whether they were there or not?' He sighed. 'It will do you no good Boris. You'll be arrested and then what happens to your family huh?'

Boris shouted angrily, 'What happens to my family when they starve anyway?' He turned to the others; 'Are you with me?'

The murmurs grew into a swell of anger as they all stood and followed Boris as he stormed off into the rain toward the Committee Office. One of them stopped and turned to Ivan. 'Will you not come with us Ivan? We need your strength.'

'This will achieve nothing. We must try through argument first.'

The man pulled his hat tight to his head as left. 'We have.'

Ivan put on his hat and went out into the rain — hesitating for a second watching his friends marching purposefully toward the centre of the town — then sadly turned in the opposite direction and began the walk home.

After thirty minutes of trudging down a dark muddy track, a figure loomed out of the darkness and came towards him. The hearty voice of Sergo, the local policeman penetrated the wind and rain. 'Ivan, where are you off to on such a night?' Ivan waved as they past, 'My bed! Goodnight.'

The policeman stopped and called out, 'Ivan, a moment of your time?'

Ivan stopped and turned slowly — recent events had made him cautious — to face the policeman.

Sergo drew closer and, because of the wind and rain, whispered close to Ivan, 'Would you have a little grain left over? My wife thinks yours is the best and with prices...'

With a feeling of relief Ivan said, 'Of course. Call round tomorrow and we'll see what we can do.'

Sergo patted Ivan's shoulder. 'Wonderful. Now she won't nag me!'

Ivan turned back into the wind to continue his journey. The policemen shouted after him, 'I'm glad you're not with the others.'

Ivan hesitated then returned, a questioning look on his face.

The policeman leant in close looking around furtively. 'I received a call from Mikhail who is on duty in the town tonight that feelings were running high. Molotov has been seriously hurt Ivan.'

Ivan blinked into the rain. 'Tensions are increasing now. I fear we are in for trouble. Yena said the women's group has been ignored and after last week...'

The policeman nodded. 'I have noticed some of the younger ones — not Yuri thank God — meeting in the forest. I've heard that in some regions they are forming groups of bandits. I don't want to see that here Ivan. Please make sure you keep your young man at home.' He drew closer. 'I hear in Nivorsk they are moving Bolsheviks into the town to stir up trouble with the poor. Already in some areas there have been threats against officials, like last week and now tonight. Even arson Ivan! Violence, burning crops and killing livestock.'

Ivan shielded his eyes from the rain, 'Hmm. Things could get a lot worse when they take the grain.'

The policemen sighed into the wind and slapped Ivan's back. 'Take care my friend. Goodnight.'

Ivan walked on into the rain oblivious of it getting under his collar and trickling down his neck. His mind was racing as he thought about what the policeman had said about bandits and rioting. Is that happening here already? He knew it was rife in the Black Country but then trouble usually sprang from there, but here in Nansk? And Yuri, was it only a matter of time before his anger spilt over into physical action? No. He needed to occupy his son in hard physical work which would help them when matters got worse, and Ivan knew they would.

Yena greeted him anxiously as he entered their warm comfortable kitchen immediately calming his anger as she took off his jacket and hung it up to dry. She handed him a towel.

'So?'

Ivan sat at the table and rubbed his head with the towel then over his face as if to clear his thoughts. 'It's true, they have tried to coerce and scare us into it and now it is to be the law.' He stood and went to a cupboard taking out a bottle of vodka and two glasses. He sat back down at the table holding the bottle in one hand and the glasses in the other. 'I knew it would come.' He placed the glasses on the table and slid one over the rough wooden surface to her. 'The farm becomes owned by the state and' he sneered, 'we are to be paid accordingly.'

Yena sat beside him and watched as he poured the drinks, 'We've worked so hard.'

'If I believed it was going to help us and our motherland then I could cope with it but I know it won't. It will put profit into the pockets of corrupt officials and starve us.'

'What happened after the meeting?'

He picked at his fingers, 'They stormed off toward the Committee Offices.'

'Oh.'

'Hmm. I tried to tell them it would do no good.' He poured their drinks and she watched with surprise to see his hands shaking.

'That's all you could do Ivan.'

He took a swig of the vodka. 'I know but...'

Yuri came out from a bedroom, 'I think we should smash their windows.'

'I'm sure you do, fortunately we are not all eighteen.'

Yuri sat down. 'But it's not right!'

'You will learn that a lot of things are not right, that's just how it is.'

'But you've always said we must try and do the right thing.'

Ivan sighed, 'Yes I have. But we must be careful. These are difficult times; people are being encouraged to tell tales on others for their own gain. At the meeting there was a man I have not seen before who was very keen to be friendly. It is best nowadays not to trust anyone unless you know them well. Even then...'

'Who was he Papa?'

'I don't know. I suspect he was planted by the authorities to spy on us and report back.'

'Will we stay here Papa?'

'If it is possible, yes Yuri, we will, this is our home.' He studied his son for a few seconds. 'I bumped into Sergo the policeman, you remember him don't you?'

Yuri blushed. He didn't need reminding about the one and only time he was cheeky to the policeman after being caught stealing cakes from the town shop. He expected his father to explode with rage but he didn't. Instead he told him he had done something similar himself but was deeply ashamed of it. He hoped Yuri would learn from it. Yuri was then required by his father to provide two hours of his time every Saturday for a month in reparation sweeping up and moving boxes for the shop owner.

Ivan smiled, his eyes twinkling with mischief. 'So your friends would like to smash windows too?'

Yuri looked into his father's eyes checking for signs of accusation but found none. 'They are angry. Some of them talk about forming a gang.'

'And would that include you?'

'No Papa I wouldn't...ever.'

Ivan smiled. 'I hope not. If they pressure you come to me.' He looked appraisingly at his son. 'Although it's more likely you would end up being the leader.'

Yena huffed, 'If you want to talk about fighting I shall go.'

Ivan chuckled. 'You should be proud Yena that the men in your family can look after themselves...and you.'

'Huh. I can look after myself thank you very much.' She stood and went outside.

Ivan laughed. 'Yuri! Now see what you've done!' He became serious again. 'Would you help me with something?'

'Of course Papa.'

'I need those muscles of yours.'

7. A WARNING SHOT

The next day as Ivan was feeding the horses a black car pulled up outside and two policemen got out looking around furtively before heading towards Ivan. He put down the pail and turned to them as they reached him.

One of them asked in a cold impersonal voice, 'You are Ivan Kazanof?'

Ivan nodded maintaining eye contact with the man.

'You are to come with us.'

Ivan shrugged. 'Let me speak to my wife.'

The second man grabbed his arm and said as the two of them turned him toward their car, 'No.'

Ivan was bundled into the car and taken to the The People's Commissariat for Internal Affairs building (NKVD) infamous for the methods of interrogation that were used there by the Secret Police. He felt a sense of dread as the car pulled in behind the building and he was roughly pushed inside. He was thrown into a dark, empty cell and by the time he was dragged out he was shivering with cold.

He was taken to an interview room. It had blank bare walls, a single electric light bulb dangling on dusty cobwebbed flex and a wobbly wooden table with two chairs. A third chair was against a wall. Sitting in one of the chairs at the table was the Chief of Security Ivor Tamnsky, overweight, balding and smoking a cigar. His nondescript uniform was crumpled, struggling to restrain the fat belly trying to force its way past the strained buttons of his tunic. His round, tight face was shiny red. He looked up as Ivan was brought in and seated in the chair opposite him. Ivan sat upright and studied the man about to interrogate him, noting with a suppressed smile the words his mother would have used in such a situation. 'His eyes are too close together, don't trust a man whose eyes are too close together.'

Tamnsky shuffled a few papers in front of him and said, 'You are Ivan Kazakof. Forty two years old born in the village of Nansk.' He looked up. 'You are a farmer?'

Ivan looked down to his work toughened hands and back to the man opposite him. He couldn't resist a wry smile.

'Where were you last night?'

'I was in my bed asleep.'

Tamnsky sighed, 'Last *evening*.'

'I attended the meeting at the Town Hall.'

'Did you speak at the meeting?'

Ivan considered for a moment, 'Yes.'

'Who to?'

'You want me to list everyone I spoke to?'

Tamnsky glared at him, 'On the Committee.'

Ivan thought for a moment knowing quite well that there would have been "eyes" at the meeting. 'I reminded the chairman about a few facts.'

'A few facts?'

Ivan sighed. 'I pointed out that Lenin freed us from being serfs to the rich and now we are to be serfs to the State.'

'Such talk is dangerous. It undermines the good work of the party and encourages those with weak minds to complain. What else did you point out?'

'I asked if I was to be arrested.'

'So you knew you were speaking out of turn?'

Ivan checked himself as a sarcastic retort rose to the surface. 'There seem to be a lot of pointless arrests recently. I simply asked if I might be another.'

Tamnsky asked, 'What were you doing last night after the meeting with the District Secretary?'

'I went home.'

Tamnsky consulted his papers. He spoke without looking up, 'You met with some others in a barn belonging to Vasili Kalinin. What did you discuss?'

Ivan shrugged. 'Given we attended a meeting concerning the state taking over our farms I would have thought it obvious.'

'Plotting subversive activity is a criminal offence and can lead to twenty years in a work camp — to be rehabilitated.' He glanced up. 'So you didn't go into the town to the Committee Offices?'

'No.'

'And you went straight home?'

'Yes. I've already told you.'

'What did you discuss in the barn?'

'I've told you that as well.'

'Tell me again.'

'We discussed the Five Year Plan.'

'That is enough to get you the Gulag.'

'I didn't say I said anything against it.'

'But you agreed with the sentiment?'

'What sentiment?'

Tamnsky stubbed out his cigar. 'It is not wise to play games with me.' To a guard he barked, 'Put him back in his cell.'

Ivan sat in the dark cell thinking through what was happening, aware that he had to be careful. These people were only interested in trapping and removing anyone vaguely suspected of anti—party activity to satisfy Stalin's paranoia. Ivan could tell that the man interrogating him was not bright; his manner demonstrated that, but he was dangerous having the power, the ability to falsify evidence.

After what seemed hours Ivan was taken to the interview room again and sat at the table. Tamnsky entered and sat opposite Ivan wobbling the table as he settled his bulk down.

'What did you discuss in the barn?'

'I've told you.'

'Tell me again.'

'We discussed the Five Year Plan.'

Tamnsky sat back and studied Ivan. 'And what do you think of it?'

'It's not my place to make judgements about it.'

'Why else would you be in the barn?'

Ivan looked at him trying not to make a sarcastic comment.

'And you plotted the murder of the District Secretary?'

Ivan's blood ran cold. He sat forward. 'We discussed the Plan that's all.'

'And the smashing of the office windows?'

'I know nothing about that.'

Tamnsky sat forward and said quietly, 'Attempted murder is an offence punishable by death.'

Ivan rubbed his hands over his face. 'I am not a violent man.'

Tamnsky flipped over a sheet in his file and read for a moment. 'If you are not a violent man why were you renowned in the villages for fighting?'

'That was many years ago. Boxing is not violent in the sense you are referring to.'

Tamnsky laughed dryly, 'Bare knuckle fighting is not violent?'

'No.'

'And you don't hurt each other?'

'Of course we do. But both fighters are there from choice.'

Tamnsky changed tack. 'Tell me about your views.'

Ivan replied, 'What views?'

'What you think of the Party for instance?'

'I'm not interested in causing trouble but I believe we must speak out if we think something is wrong.'

Tamnsky sat forward eagerly. 'And what is wrong?'

'Violence is wrong.'

Tamnsky sat back. 'You say you believe violence is wrong and yet you plot to murder the District Secretary?'

Ivan shook his head in disbelief.

'Windows were smashed. The District Secretary Molotov was badly injured. He is very ill in hospital and I find it hard to believe it wasn't plotted in that barn, and that you weren't part of it.' He lit a cigar blowing a cloud of blue smoke at Ivan. 'You are a trouble maker.' He studied his cigar and said, 'Tell me about Boris Frenkel.'

'What is there to tell? He is an honest man. He works hard on his farm.'

'He was there, in the barn. Don't deny it we have a witness.'

'If you know then why ask me?'

'You're insolence is not helping your case.' He scratched his fat belly. 'We know he was there and you were the ring leader, plotting the murder.'

'Then your witness is either a liar or stupid.'

'What did you do after the meeting in the barn?'

'I went straight home.'

'Did you have a knife?'

Ivan smiled. 'We're peasant farmers, of course. We all do, they're our tools.'

'And Boris had a knife?'

'Probably.'

Tamnsky shuffled through his papers on the desk. 'We have been watching you for some time. You like to stir up trouble don't you? Spread unease amongst people with anti party talk.' He drew on the cigar. 'What are your views?'

Ivan smiled again. 'I only want what is best for my country.'

'Are you suggesting the Five Year Plan and President Stalin's dedicated work is wrong?'

'Look. I didn't attack the District Secretary. You cannot prove something that I didn't do, unless of course you falsify evidence.'

Tamnsky's face went even redder as he blustered angrily, 'How dare you accuse an officer of the police with such outrageous nonsense!'

Ivan said quietly, 'It's no more preposterous than you accusing me of a murder I could not have committed because I went straight home.' He thought for a moment, 'Ask one of your policemen, Sergo.'

Tamnsky sat back and puffed his cigar studying him. 'You tread a dangerous path my friend. We will get you eventually.' To the guard he said, 'Take him back to his cell.'

Ivan again sat in the dark reflecting on the conversation trying to ignore the cold floor and filth of the cell. He deeply regretted not being able to stop his friends from their actions but at the same time he could understand their frustration. If he got out from here — and he was beginning to think it might not happen — he would have to be very careful.

Hours later he was once again taken to the interrogation room and sat before Tamnsky who was reading a file. He looked up disinterested. 'Comrade Sergo Yeltzin corroborates your story.' He studied Ivan carefully. 'We know you are a trouble maker Kazakof and eventually we will have evidence with which we can charge you as an enemy of the people. As for the matter here,' he glanced at his papers, 'You can go.'

8. A KULAK

One of the members of the Committee at the Town Hall on that fateful evening was Alexander Pavlov a peasant who had taken it upon himself to build a small empire of trading food and goods to the city, which he obtained from the peasant farmers. It was a congenial arrangement which suited everyone; especially Alexander. Over the years Alexander had become involved in village and then town politics fighting to get his friends a fair deal. Because of this he was regarded as a trusted and vital member of the village. Labelled a "Kulak" he was protected by the peasants from the Kulak witch hunt but now that all the local farms were to be properties of the state, Alexander — like all successful entrepreneurs — began to worry for his safety.

He was an astute man and suspected the real idea behind the collective was to fund an industrial base, by paying the peasants a pittance and utilising their produce. Knowing how communist double talk and fake promises operated he could see that the farmers were not going to be paid enough which offered a golden opportunity for him to act on their behalf and move some of their produce into the city of Leningrad. He was tempted knowing the officials responsible for organising and controlling the farmer's produce to central depots, were mainly simple folk moved in to do a job they were not equipped for and therefore open to the age old and well established use of bribery. However, Alexander was also aware that the protection the villagers gave him could not last. It was only a mtter of time before he was arrested.

A few hours after Ivan had been released Alexander visited him at his farm. Ivan opened the door surprised — but perhaps not totally so given their business arrangement — and waved the man in. Alexander took off his coat and stood before the wood fire that burned steadily in the hearth. Ivan poured vodka for them both.

'Bad times Ivan. I knew the meeting would be stormy, but....' He sat down, 'You've heard of course about the District Secretary?'

Ivan picked up a poker as he stared into the fire. 'After a day at the NKVD offices it became clear yes, and in case you ask, I went straight home.'

Alexander touched his shoulder, 'I would not consider you a brutal man Ivan. Strong fighter yes. Ah that match with

Dmitrii, ha! How long did it take you to put him down, and to stay down? But a thug, no.' He stroked his beard in thought. 'They won't give up until they have the culprit, although I suspect they would have to arrest most of the local farmers.'

Ivan prodded the fire causing embers to scurry up the chimney. 'They were pretty stirred up when they left the barn. Anything could have happened.'

Ivan sat down opposite him and offered him another glass as he held up the bottle. Alexander smiled glancing at his time piece, 'It's four in the afternoon, why not?'

Ivan poured them a glass each.

'Listen Ivan, you know I am wealthy because I chose to sell my farm and go into retailing and made a good profit from it. But people like me are feared by Stalin. He fears we will stir up trouble to keep our power.'

Ivan smiled grimly. 'I don't intend to let the State have my land and livestock. I have no choice in handing over my grain but I know they will pay me a pittance and tax me heavily. Even so, I refuse to join a collective farm. However, I have a plan which you might find interesting and which would be of mutual benefit to us both.'

Alexander sighed, 'Once I would have jumped at the idea, but...I'm frightened Ivan. Many such as myself have been deported to God knows where in Siberia. The Kulak witchhunt is gaining momentum. I have no choice but to hide.'

The next day Ivan took Yuri to the rear of their barn with a shovel. He marked out a square on the ground and said, 'Dig a pit here. If I whistle, pull that old tarpaulin over it and look innocent digging over the vegetable plot.' He patted Yuri on the shoulder and went about his business repairing some tools inside the barn.

An hour later as Yuri was well into his task he heard a whistle. Quickly, his heart pounding both with exertion and anxiety, he pulled the tarpaulin over his project and began furiously digging the vegetable plot. Sergo the policeman got off his bicycle and meandered into the yard where he leant his bike against the wooden wall of the barn. He peeked inside to see Ivan filing something at a vice on a large wooden bench. He went past the door and being inquisitive looked around the yard where he stumbled across Yuri furiously digging the vegetable patch.

Yuri looked up in surprise as the tall figure of the policeman loomed into sight.

'Yuri, you look busy. I see your father has you working?'

Yuri leant on his shovel and wiped sweat from his brow. 'Yes digging this vegetable patch.'

Sergo looked puzzled by the stressed tone of the young man but put it down to his intimidating presence as a policeman.

'Well don't let me stop you! I'm here for a chat with your father.' He disappeared back round the corner. Yuri sighed and collapsed on the shovel.

Sergo entered the barn and called out, 'Ivan!'

Ivan stopped what he was doing and wiping his hands, turned. 'Sergo. Ah I remember, our chat the other night.'

Sergo picked up a hatchet and ran his finger gingerly along its keen edge. 'If it is ok of course?'

Ivan smiled. 'Of course. Come inside and I will show you what I have for you.' Sergo put down the hatchet and glanced over the other tools on the bench. They left the barn heading toward the house, weak sunshine breaking through the clouds.

Sergo said, 'I see you have your son hard at work!'

Ivan glanced anxiously behind him to see Yuri digging the vegetable patch. 'I took your advice Sergo, keep him busy and out of trouble.'

Sergo stood aside as Ivan opened the door. 'You are a wise man Ivan.'

Ivan smiled to himself as he entered and called out, 'Yena, we have a visitor!'

Yena appeared and for a second looked alarmed as she noted the looming presence of the policeman who seemed to fill the space of the kitchen. 'Sergo...'

Ivan quickly gestured toward a chair, 'Sergo take the weight off your tired feet. Yena, Sergo has asked if we could supply him a little grain, for his wife.'

Yena tried to hide her relief. 'Oh, yes of course. I'll get a sack.' She hurried out.

Ivan sighed, 'Since these disturbances she has been a little anxious.'

Sergo gave him an understanding look, 'Women...?'

Ivan smiled in response and winked conspirationally. Sergo whispered, 'I'm very grateful to you for this favour Ivan. It's good to know who your friends are in such times.' He looked around and said quietly, 'I've heard they are replacing Molotov with a new man who, I believe, has built a reputation for himself.'

Ivan asked, 'Reputation?'

Sergo looked over his shoulder then said, 'It's rumoured he is the devil. Of course that is nonsense but it would be wise to avoid him.'

Yena reappeared carrying a small which she put on the table in front of the policeman. 'That should be enough?'

Sergo kissed her hand. 'Yes, plenty. Thank you both so much. So how much do I owe you?'

Ivan glanced at Yena and said, 'You are a friend Sergo. How about a little donation toward repairing the barn door?'

Sergo stood and reached into his trouser pocket. 'Here.' He handed over a few rubles.

Ivan took them without looking. 'Thank you Sergo. Anytime...' He thought for a moment. 'As long as we have any left after the state has taken its share of course.'

Sergo sighed heavily as he turned toward the door. 'These are bad times for sure. Good day to you both.' He opened the door and went out.

Ivan watched him as he mounted his bike and peddled away. 'Big oaf, I hope he falls off.' He opened the door and returned to kiss his wife on the cheek. 'I don't trust him.'

Yena hugged him. 'Good.'

'I'd better go and see how our son is getting on.'

Ivan stood and watched his son digging furiously suddenly stopping as Ivan's shadow fell before him.

Yuri said between breaths, 'How deep do you want it Papa?'

Ivan paced around the hole Yuri had dug and checked the depth. 'Another three feet will be perfect. I've got to go out so keep a look out for visitors. The existence of this is between you, me and your mother. Certainly don't let your brother and sister see it or the whole village will know. At the moment they are at your aunt's house but look out for them coming back.'

'I still don't understand'

Ivan put his hand up. 'You'll find out soon enough. You're doing a great job.'

9. THE BIG GUNS ARRIVE

The Regional Party Secretary, Anatoly Boykov, looked with distaste at the flat forested countryside around the town of Pulkova as his chauffeured car bumped over the uneven roads churned up by cart wheels. Boykov was heavily built with a bullish neck and jutting chin, his eyes hard and penetrating.

He struggled to light a cigar as the car bounced around but eventually managed it. He puffed on it as he began reading a report lying on his lap. Beside him sat Assistant Secretary Valentin Grankin a slender man with darting, weasel like eyes and thin hair combed over in a vain attempt to cover his baldness.

Boykov stopped reading and groaned, 'These peasants are not going to give in easily Valentin. This recent event in Pulkova cannot be allowed to enter into their folklore system of rumour. It will spread like wild fire. It's the women who are the problem; the men will fall in line if we can control the women.'

Valentin took out a cigarette and lit it unsteadily as they hit a large rut. 'Public executions had some effect in the black country. Perhaps...'

Boykov looked out of the window. 'Hmm, I fear that would enrage the women more unless of course we include them in the process. Were any women found to be guilty?'

'I'm not sure.'

'Arrange for a military presence in the surrounding villages. Chase out any peasants suspected of being "difficult" and flog them. What about this Kulak Alexander Pavlov?'

'You signed the papers for him to be resettled in Siberia Regional Secretary. Unfortunately he has disappeared.'

'We must find him. He's probably hiding in these damn forests somewhere waiting for us to go away. Send some men in to have a look. Shoot him if necessary.'

The car entered the edge of the town and made its way to the NKVD office; a large imposing block of a building. The driver pulled up outside, switched off the engine and after checking the path was clear, got out and opened the door for his passengers.

Boykov got out, straightened his coat and said curtly to the driver, 'Wait here. We might be some time.' He strutted purposefully into the building noting with distaste the ornate interior considering it excessive; certainly his own offices were shabby in comparison. It was obvious to him that Stalin granted special privileges to the NKVD because he needed them to do his dirty work for him.

Boykov entered the office of Anatol Petroff who was standing in as District Secretary and a man totally out of his depth. Boykov tersly introduced himself and began pacing, pinning Petroff with a steely glare. 'So you have not found this Kulak or the ring leader of the riot? What have you done so far? Have you ransacked their huts? Taken suspects in for questioning?'

Petroff was terrified, frozen to the spot his mouth dry but his hands sweating. 'Sir, I...this job is new to me. I am used to accounting. Please. Give me guidance; tell me what I must do.'

Boykov took out a cigar and sat down in an armchair facing the window overlooking the streets of the town below. 'Listen, these peasants are cunning. They work together covering for each other. The women are the key players. Get your men to seek out the vocal ones, any faces that were recognised at the scene. Create fear Petroff! Fear is what motivates them to give each other up. And greed of course. Offer rewards for information. If none of that works get a gun and shoot yourself or I will have you sent to the Gulag for twenty years.' He lit his cigar. 'Is that clear?'

Petroff muttered, 'Yes Sir.'

Boykov looked out of the window. It was clear this idiot was so frightened he couldn't concentrate. He tried a different tack. 'Listen Petroff, our country is undergoing vast change. The working class are vital to our industrialisation programme but we need to finance this expensive process to allow them to succeed.' He blew a large plume of smoke. 'Come here Petroff.' Petroff hurried over to him and Boykov gestured to him to sit in a chair next to him. He nodded to the street below. 'What do you see?'

'People sir.'

'Yes, working class people. Men and women with brains; factory workers, typists, with skills we need for the Great Plan.'

Petroff watched the people below. 'Yes sir, I see.'

'Now the peasant is different, he is of the earth. He is a simple creature that needs to be told what to do. Not like the Kulak, he is clever. He has made money, exerts his influence over them. The Kulak must be eliminated, removed from the motherland permanently, if we are to continue with our great revolution. The peasants must be controlled and encouraged to work for the state and not just themselves. I have to deliver the Five Year Plan. These...' he spat out the word, 'peasants cannot be allowed to stand in my way. So, you will work closely with your officers; use the police to instil fear. Arrest anyone who has any history of troublemaking. If you think they look suspicious then send them to the Gulag. I will back up any paperwork required. They need to see us being strong, exerting control. Now, is that clearer for you?'

'Yes Sir.'

'Very well, get your Chief of Security to bring me what he has and we will go over it. Before I leave today we will have some names for you to follow up.'

The shadowy figure of Valantin Grankin came to life from a chair at the back of the room. 'Sir' He walked over to Boykov. 'Perhaps I can be of assistance here?' Boykov waved him to go on. Grankin opened a file. 'Recently Chief of Security Tamnsky interviewed a peasant called Kasakof. Get him in again; let's see if we can get him to give up some names.'

With District Secretary Molotov, in hospital and unlikely to return, it was incumbent upon Party Secretary Chupin to swiftly find a replacement now that Boykov had made it clear the "stand in" Petroff was not up to the job. He had little choice in the matter when he was informed that the position would be filled by Nikita Sidorov, the son of General Sidorov who had great influence with Stalin himself. Chupin mused on why Sidorov had escaped the increasing purges Stalin ordered on anyone vaguely suspected of posing a threat to the State; a fear he himself shared along with his fellow members of the Party.

Chupin inwardly fumed. Molotov, although a little soft, had been efficient and fair, which meant Chupin did not have to concern himself too much with the affairs of that District. He had hoped to find another with the same credentials and thereby allow himself to concentrate on his own job and not have to baby sit some half wit. Chupin sat back in the leather chair behind the large mahogany desk and drew on his cigarette. He looked around his large office with its wooden panelled walls that reminded him how lonely his job was. Sometimes he felt even the walls were watching him, ready to turn him in. He frowned as the stress of his job washed over him.

There was a knock at the door. He sat forward and called, 'Come'.

The door opened and a young man entered, closed the door and waited to be invited in. Chupin waved him to a chair at his desk. The young man walked briskly over to it and sat down, sitting back with his legs crossed.

Chupin inwardly sighed as he made an instant appraisal of the young man sitting opposite him; Nikita Sidorov. Chupin drew on his cigarette which he held between his forefinger and thumb, the palm of his hand pointing upward which cupped his chin as if in deep thought as he drew on the cigarette. His eyes travelling over the tightly slicked down hair, round face sporting a Stalin moustache — as was the fashion — and fat stomach stretching the young man's uniform. His eyes drifted down to pudgy little hands with chewed nails, constantly fidgeting. Chupin's gaze went back up and settled on the man's eyes which, behind round wire glasses, were piggish, greedy and dishonest. Chupin stubbed out his cigarette into an ornate china ashtray wishing he could do the same to the object sitting opposite him. Chupin was a fair man and tried to avoid stereotyping people — but he couldn't avoid it; this man was a typical example of a wealthy upbringing, protected from the ramifications of his actions by his father, the General. Chupin had seen such young men before, keen to attain positions of power which they believed was their entitlement and then use that position to gain pleasure from bullying.

Sidorov felt uncomfortable as the penetrating gaze of Chupin swept over him as Chupin sat back and lit another cigarette. Sidorov was fascinated by the way the older man held it thinking it made him look intellectual.

Chupin asked, 'How old are you?'

'Thirty one Party Secretary Chupin.'

'And you are ready to take up the position of District Secretary?'

The young man took out a silver cigarette case and tilted his head as if to say 'May I?' Chupin nodded. Sidorov replied as he took out a cigarette, 'Of course Party Secretary Chupin.'

Chupin blew a smoke ring above the head of Sidorov. 'These are difficult times.' He knocked the ash off his cigarette watching Sidorov, 'It is vital we deliver the Five Year Plan.' He took a deep drag on the cigarette holding it in his inimitable fashion. 'Listen Sidorov, the peasants are making it clear they want nothing to do with collectivisation. We have to make it clear to them that they have no choice.' He sat forward. 'I want you to work closely with the local police; use their information. Get together a plan that will quash this rebellion before it takes hold. Do you understand what I am expecting from you?'

Sidorov lit his cigarette and appeared to be avidly listening; in fact he was wondering whether he should hold his cigarette in the same way. It seemed to give an impression of authority. 'Of course Party Secretary Chupin. Rest assured I will stamp out such illegal activity.'

Chupin said, 'I understand when you were an assistant to the Commissar in the East district your methods were....'

'Thorough, Party Secretary Chupin. I use whatever means required to obtain the information.'

Chupin felt a chill wash over him. 'I don't need to know the details; I just need evidence to give Comrade Stalin.' He knocked the ash of his cigarette and inhaled deeply.

A smile crept over Sidorov's face although it did not reach his eyes. 'My methods are effective in getting arrests. You can rely on me.'

Chupin stubbed out his cigarette and stood. 'Yes, I'm sure they are. Very well off you go and do your job. I would prefer if you don't bother me unless necessary.' He waved a hand over a pile of files and numerous letters on the side of his desk. 'As you can see...'

Sidorov stood and leaned over to stub out his cigarette taking note of the large china ashtray.

Chupin felt a wave of distaste for this creature that had been foisted upon him. 'Of course, I leave that sort of detail to your discretion.'

'Thank you Sir.' Sidorov turned and swiftly exited.

Chupin slumped down in his chair hoping he could ignore what would be happening in his District and turned to yet another letter from a peasant complaining about unfair treatment which he read with a sigh. A sigh perhaps for the laborious task he had set himself to read every single letter but also because he understood their frustrations and secretly admired their courage. He picked up a letter and began concentrating on the matters before him trying to ignore the voice of warning in the back of his mind. There was something very wrong about Sidorov that ran a chill down his back.

Nikita Sidorov looked out of his car window at the flat heavily forested land flashing by and gave a deep sigh, pleased with the task given him and relishing the challenge, but why did it have to be in this miserable outback? The less time he had to spend here the better. He looked around with distaste — it was just as depressing as he had imagined — as they entered the town and made their way to the district offices.

Inside the grand entrance of the NKVD, Sidorov waited impatiently whilst a security officer, sitting at a desk completed a form and looked up. 'Can I help you?'

Sidorov, feeling powerful in his long grey coat banged on the man's desk with a leather gloved hand and said through gritted teeth, 'I am District Secretary Sidorov. Petroff is expecting me?'

The security man leapt off his seat and hurried away down a corridor as Sidorov looked around at the ornate furniture and decor. The man hurried back with Petroff close behind him and as they approached Sidorov, Petroff ran past the security man and said whilst giving the security man a black look, 'District Secretary Sidorov! Please, come this way.' He led him back down the corridor to a door halfway along and opened it ushering Sidorov in. He waved toward a large desk and chair. 'Your desk Sir!'

Sidorov ambled in and slowly sat at the desk feeling its size and looking around the room.

Petroff sat opposite him. 'Welcome Sir. I'm glad to be handing this job over to you I don't mind saying. Don't think I've slept a wink. I'm an accountant you see. Not used to this sort of work. Mind you we have made some headway.' He leant forward and pushed a file toward Sidorov. 'Those names are high on the list of suspects. Chief of Security Tamnsky has interviewed some of them.'

Sidorov opened his silver box and took out a cigarette which he tapped on it before snapping the box shut and putting it back in his pocket. He lit the cigarette and held it in the fashion of Chupin — something he had been practising — as he eyed Petroff as if watching an animal in a cage. 'Some of them?'

Petroff stiffened, his stomach suddenly churning with fear. 'Yes, well there are quite a lot of them, and they're not always easy to track down. They seem to know we are coming.'

Sidorov leaned back and blew a smoke ring. 'Quite a lot of them?'

Petroff feared he was about to lose control of his bladder as panic enveloped him. He nodded.

Sidorov stood and paced around causing Petroff to keep squirming in his chair to see him. 'So let me get this straight. As acting District Secretary, in charge of people like this Tamnsky, you have allowed the trail of these swine to go cold?'

Petroff tried to interrupt. 'I err...'

'Shut up! I will not tolerate weak excuses. Our great leader Comrade Stalin has a job for us all to do in making our motherland the greatest in the world. Do you think we can achieve this if people like you are in charge?'

Petroff felt sick. Fear enveloped him as a warm trickle of liquid run down his leg. 'I...'

Sidorov stopped him with a raised eyebrow and raised hand. 'Enough, you are incompetent. Such incompetence is considered anti party and as an enemy of the people you must be dealt with accordingly. There is no place here for a weakling like you.' He paced again, hands behind his back, deep in thought as Petroff felt the warmth trickle into his right shoe. 'I sentence you to fifteen years in the Gulag. Guard!'

Petroff slumped to his knees whimpering. 'Sir! I have done my best. I did not ask for this post! Please I beg of you. I have a wife and three children. Sir...'

The guard rushed in and stood in shock staring at Petroff kneeling in supplication, crying and with a dark stain spreading down his right leg. Sidorov pointed at Petroff.

'Take this idiot to the cells until I can arrange transport. And send Tamnsky here.'

Sidorov returned to his seat and stubbed out his cigarette in a small metal ash tray which he eyed with distate. He imagined a large china ash tray like Chupin's sitting there. He smiled to himself. He opened and closed draws taking in the grandeur of the room with its fine oak panelled walls and plush red carpet. A pile of files sat on the edge of the desk from which he picked up the top one and opened it.

He sat back and was reading the file as Chief of Security Tamnsky entered, and after shutting the door behind him waited to be invited in to sit down. Sidorov felt a little annoyed that the man had not knocked, and waited a few seconds, continuing to read before issuing a terse, 'Yes?'

'Chief of Security Tamnsky, District Secretary.'

Sidorov looked him up and down deciding from the tired uniform he was a peasant oaf promoted beyond his means.

Sidorov said testily, 'Sit down.' Tamnsky did so.

Sidorov took out his silver case and removed a cigarette which he held between his lips as he put the case back into his inside jacket pocket. He took out his gold lighter and lit the cigarette carefully holding it the "Chupin way". 'Tell me about the suspects.'

Tamnsky decided this man was someone to be wary of. 'Quite a long list but some key names. Known agitators are the ones I am focusing on.'

'Can you tie them to the assault?'

'Not yet, but two women are in custody and I have others to interview. Regional Secretary Boykov wanted me to re—interview a man called Kazakof but his alibi for the night is sound. However, I'm not convinced he was not involved in the planning. But without proof...'

Sidorov smiled but it didn't include his eyes. 'Proof hmm. We can't always afford the luxury. As long as *we* are sure he is guilty, that's all we need to send him on his way to the Gulag.'

Tamnsky made a note to himself not to cross this man. 'Of course, I'll get him back in.'

Sidorov blew a smoke ring and asked, 'How many men do you have?

'Five Sir. If we need reinforcements we call them in from neighbouring towns.'

'I see. And you know these villagers well?'

Tamnsky nodded. 'I used to live a few villages away and was lucky enough to join the force.'

Sidorov smiled inwardly. So he is a peasant! He asked, 'And you are not troubled by arresting,' he almost said "fellow peasants" but managed to stop himself, 'fellow villagers?'

Tamnsky scratched his balding head. 'No sir. If someone has broken the law they should be brought to account.'

Sidorov stubbed out his cigarette. 'Like this Kasakof.' He thought for a moment. 'How do they communicate between villages so quickly?'

'The Tocsin sir.'

'That's the town bell? Well the first thing we must do is remove them all. See to it.' He stood indicating the conversation was ended. 'When you have this fellow in custody I will conduct the interrogation myself, is that clear?'

Tamnsky stood. 'Yes District Secretary Sidorov.'

'You may go.'

10. A BULLY

Sidorov picked up a file from his desk and headed for the door but caught sight of himself in a full length mirror he had had put up. He stopped and stroked his moustache admiring himself — tugging at the bottom of his jacket in the vain hope he could cover his bulging belly — then saluted himself and stood to attention, clicking his heels together as his father had taught him. He turned and gripping the file strolled down the corridor to the interrogation room.

He entered and sat down at the table where he laid the file and placed a pen beside it. He set a china ashtray on the desk (it was the best he could find to match that of Chupin) and moved it a little until he was satisfied. He opened the file and began reading.

Tamnsky entered and hesitated, thrown for a second by Sidorov in his chair. As he stood there unsure what to do, a tall, frightened man with thinning hair revealing a large bald patch and eyes wide with terror was brought in and sat at the other side of the table facing Sidorov. The man's hands were secured behind his back. Sidorov ignored him and gestured to Tamnsky to sit on a chair behind the prisoner. Sidorov picked up his pen and began to write slowly and meticulously in the file on a fresh sheet of paper. After a few minutes he placed the cap on his pen and laid it beside the file, sat back and took out his silver cigarette case and removed a cigarette.

He studied the man as he held the cigarette in the "Chupin" manner and lit it. He said coldly, 'You are Vladimir Fastenco, a peasant farmer from the village of Nansk. You are fifty five years old. You have been arrested for...' he turned the sheet of paper over and read, 'acting suspiciously in the town of Kivorsk on the twenty eighth of August.'

Vladimir stuttered, 'There must be some mistake. I...'

Sidorov put his hand up impatiently, 'We don't make mistakes. We have witnesses that you were seen putting a poster up inciting other peasants to revolt against collective farms.'

Vladimir squirmed on the chair his face reddening with fear, his eyes darting around the room as if looking for a way to escape.

Sidorov dragged on his cigarette as he watched his victim, secretly enjoying the power he could wield over another human being. 'You will be going to the Gulag for...' he considered for a moment, 'fifteen years.' He leant forward and read the file. 'I see you have a son and a daughter, both teenagers.

They are such a handful at that age aren't they? How will your poor wife Anna, cope? You understand that the wife of a convict is not allowed to remain in the property — she will be evicted, along with any other relatives?'

Vladimir burst into tears pulling in vain at his secured hands against the back of the chair. 'I have done nothing wrong! I know nothing about a poster. How can there be wit—'

Sidorov sat back and drew on his cigarette as he once again silenced him with a raised hand. 'Also your mother lives with you, a frail old lady I understand.' He glanced over to Tamnsky. 'Is that correct Chief of Security Tamnsky?'

Tamnsky nodded and said, 'Yes that's correct District Party Secretary.'

Vladimir was now sobbing and wriggling around in misery and fear.

Sidorov stubbed out his cigarette in the china ash tray as he watched Vladimir closely. 'There is perhaps a way out of your dilemma.'

Vladimir looked up with tears running down his face, mucus hanging from his nose.

'I need to ensure there is no further trouble in the villages. To do this I need to remove a known trouble maker by the name of Ivan Kazakof. I'm sure you know him?'

Vladimir nodded as the look of terror changed to confusion. 'Ivan is my friend; I have known him all my life.'

'Then you will know he is...outspoken?'

Vladimir's mouth tried to produce a sound but nothing came out as he looked around bewildered, a knowing dread building.

'Here is my solution to your problem. If you want to save the life of your elderly mother, to stop Anna from starving to death and your children taken from her, all you have to do is sign a letter.'

Vladimir was struggling to comprehend. 'A letter?'

Sidorov lit another cigarette and with studied movements held it as before as he said, 'Yes a letter. A letter stating that you witnessed Ivan Kazakof inciting other peasants in a barn after the committee meeting and in particular encouraging Boris Frenkel to take a group of men and kill District Secretary Molotov. For this courageous act of patriotism all charges against you will be dropped.'

Vladimir had been listening intently to make sure he was hearing what he thought he was hearing. 'Dropped?'

'Yes.' Sidorov looked questioningly at him, waiting. Vladimir nodded imperceptivity. Sidorov motioned to the guard to release his hands. As Vladimir rubbed his wrists and wiped his face with the back of his hand Sidorov slid a typed letter toward him, picked up his pen and took off the top. He drew on his cigarette as Vladimir leant forward and with a shaking hand took the pen and signed the letter.

Sidorov took his pen back and with obvious disgust wiped it with a cloth before putting it back in his pocket. 'You may go.'

Bewildered, Fastenco stood and walked shakily toward the door, hesitating before leaving to check he could leave. Sidorov stood, closed the file and said to Tamnsky as he turned toward the door, 'I shall be conducting all the important interrogations from now on.' He turned on his heels to leave but returned to the desk and picked up the china ashtray which he emptied in a bin and carried out.

Tamnsky remained sitting staring at the table as he thought over what he had just seen. He was not averse to applying a little pressure occasionally, but this...

11. THE SHADOW STRIKES

Ivan stood with Yuri and examined the deep rectangular hole behind the barn. He walked back and forth deep in thought then said, 'Ok very good. Now then, we must line it with tarpaulin and strong wooden boards, then construct a strong trap door over it and cover it with turf.'

Yuri looked puzzled as he asked, 'But what is it Papa?'

Ivan laughed and patted the boy's shoulder. 'A secret grain store. One only you, me and your mother know exist. They are going to do everything they can to force me into joining the collective. I won't. They will then let me take my grain to the depot but will tax me so heavily I will have virtually nothing to show for it. So, we will put enough away to keep us alive until matters change. I will have to do more odd jobs and so will you but...' he nodded to the hole, 'hopefully this will keep us alive.'

Yuri laughed. 'Can I make the hatch?'

'Of course my boy, you dug the hole! Just be careful to keep it hidden. I will line it and then we keep it covered until the hatch is made.'

The screech of tyres and slamming car doors interrupted him. Quickly Ivan and his son covered the pit just in time as two security police appeared looking around the yard. They spotted Ivan and with no explanation dragged him to their car.

Yuri followed, bewildered, shouting for them to stop but they took no notice and after bundling Ivan into the back of their car, slammed the doors and drove off in a cloud of dust. Yuri watched it grow smaller within the dust cloud before the vague image disappeared round a bend. He ran toward the kitchen where his mother stood in the doorway crying.

She wiped her eyes and said, 'We knew it was going to happen sometime. This is what they do, how they try to scare us. Your Papa is a strong man; he won't be intimidated by them. I know it is hard for you, but you must be patient.'

Georgie and Yelena, home from school, ran into the yard excited by the speeding car as it hurtled past them. 'Did you see that car Yuri?!' Exclaimed Georgie.

Yelena could see her mother had been crying and Yuri standing beside her looking angry. 'What's happened Mama?'

Yena pulled them both to her and said softly, 'Your father has been arrested.'

'Will he go to prison Mama?' Georgie asked matter of factly.

Yuri said, 'No it is all a mistake.'

Yelena hugged her mother tightly and whined into her skirt, 'But what if they send him away?'

Yena sighed as she stroked daughter's hair. 'How can they? He didn't do anything wrong.'

Sidorov sat and studied the man sitting before him in the interrogation room thinking how different he was to the previous prisoner. He laid his pen down and took out his silver cigarette case taking one out, lighting it and holding it in what he now considered was his own stylish manner. Ivan returned his stare trying to weigh the man up deciding he looked too smug, like so many officials.

Sidorov opened a file and read, 'You are Ivan Kazakof. Forty two years old, wife and three children. You are a farmer.' He looked up enquiringly. Ivan watched him.

Sidorov continued. 'You are a trouble maker. That makes you an enemy of the people.' Ivan returned his gaze not giving anything away.Sidorov continued. 'Unless you help me bring peace to the villages you will find yourself in serious trouble my friend. So, tell me the names of your friends who also like to cause trouble. Let's start with the violence in Stetzin.'

Ivan shrugged. 'I was not there when it happened.'

'No. But you know who was involved.'

Ivan shrugged again. 'I don't.'

Sidorov drew on his cigarette thoughtfully. 'Ok then. Who else in your village was involved in the violence at the town hall?'

Ivan watched him steadily and said, 'I've already told him,' he waved his head at Tamnsky sitting behind him, 'him that I was not there.'

'I'm not sure you grasp the situation you are in Kasakof. With a stroke of my pen I can send you to the Gulag under special powers granted by the Central Committee. Unless you tell me your co-conspirators, life will get very grim for you.'

Ivan smiled. 'Give up my friends to you? People I have known all my life?'

'Very well, I'll take that as a no. I have had you arrested because evidence has been obtained from a witness to prove you have been lying.' Ivan listened in silence. 'This witness has signed a letter stating they saw you deliberately incite a group of men to attack District Secretary Molotov with the intention of murdering him.' Ivan remained still, desperately trying to hold himself together. 'For this heinous crime I could sentence you to death, but I don't want to provide your peasant friends with a martyr. Instead I sentence you to twenty five years in the Gulag. That will give you plenty of time to consider your actions. Is there anything you want to say?'

Ivan sat forward. 'Would it make any difference?'

Sidorov sneered, 'No. I just like to conduct matters correctly. Unless you want to reconsider and give me the information I require.'

Ivan leaned forward and said with quiet authority, 'I am loyal to my beloved country. I despair at the way Stalin and his cohorts are destroying our culture, murdering thousands of innocent people for a flawed ideology distorted to serve his ego. As long as I remain free I will fight such tyranny as will my friends.'

Sidorov smiled and clapped slowly, mocking the man before him. 'You are an enemy of the people spreading dissention, inciting people to rebel.' He nodded to the guard to take him away. 'And good riddance to you. Oh, and of course your family will be evicted.' He stood and closed the file, picked up his ashtray and left.

Yena watched from her kitchen window as Yuri tidied up the barn and finished off the work his father had been doing at the vice. She had a feeling of dread about Ivan's arrest despite the reassurances she had given her son. She fetched her coat and pulled on her boots, then went outside and called to Yuri that she was going out for awhile but would be back for the children after school. He waved to her without looking up, concentrating on his work repairing a saw handle.

She walked quickly down the road to the centre of the village and a row of wooden peasant huts where she stopped at the second one along and banged on the door.

It was opened by a woman who, on seeing the expression on Yena's face exclaimed, 'Yena?'

'Can I come in?'

Her friend stood aside and ushered her in closing the door behind them. Once inside Yena burst into tears. 'They've arrested him again Anna.'

Anna put her hand to her mouth in shock. 'Yena...'

'I hear there is a new one at the NKVD; a man who will stop at nothing to get what he wants.'

'Yes. This I have heard as well.'

Yena sat down. 'Ivan is a proud man. He won't allow some small minded official to get the better of him and he hasn't done anything wrong! So why do I worry so?'

'We all worry about our men folk. I was scared stiff when they arrested Vladimir, but thankfully they let him go. He had a terrible time of it in there. He's taken to his bed, it's really scared him.' She sat down beside her and said, 'How long has he been in there?'

'Ten hours.'

Anna sighed and put her arm around her friend. 'I'm sure he'll be home soon.'

Yuri cleaned his hands and went into the house. It was eerily quiet. He sat at the table and idly ran his fingers along the cracks in the table as his father often did when he was working out something — now it was Yuri's time to do so. He looked around at the familiar surroundings and down to the table top with its rough but reassuring surface as an understanding began to emerge; his father was not coming back. He stood as the realisation swept over him. He grabbed his coat and hurried out.

He knew where his mother had gone and ran down the road to find her. He knocked at the door and asked anxiously, 'Is my mother here?'

Anna beckoned him in. Yena came out to see what was going on. 'Yuri?'

'Mama, I'm worried about Papa. I'm going to find out what's going on.'

She pulled him into the kitchen and sat him down. 'Now you listen. It is dangerous to go there. We have to be patient.'

Anna sat with them. 'Your mother is right Yuri. Vladimir had a terrible time in there.'

Yuri exclaimed, 'Your husband was arrested?'

'It was a shock I can tell you. Vladimir is a very quiet man, not interested in politics.'

Yena asked. 'What was he arrested for Anna?'

Anna looked uncomfortable. 'He didn't tell me what happened; he just said it was frightening. He had bruises on his body too. Now he just lies in his bed.'

Yuri leapt up. 'I'm going to find out what's happened to my father.' He quickly left despite his mother calling out to him.

As he made his way to the town he tried to keep focused on what he would say when he got there as many things his father had told him about soviet rule were becoming real to him. At times he had thought his father too suspicious and distrustful of people but he was beginning to understand nothing was safe anymore — perhaps had never been as the State tried to force its policies on the population — especially the peasants.

His mind was in turmoil as he approached the hateful NKVD building; his nerves on edge. He hurried in and saw a security guard sitting at a desk in the foyer. The security man looked up as Yuri reached the desk. Yuri took a deep breath and said, 'My father was arrested hours ago and brought here. I need to find out what is happening please?'

The security man yawned. 'If he was arrested he must have broken the law. He will be kept here until the matter is resolved.'

Yuri tried to keep calm. 'His name is Ivan Kazakof.'

The security man looked bored and went back to reading his newspaper. 'I can't tell you anything.' Yuri stood watching him with disbelief. The man looked up and growled, 'Go away or you will get arrested as well.'

Yuri shouted angrily, 'Then arrest me!' He looked around the foyer and saw a rubbish bin which he ran to and kicked over, then picked it up and threw it at a window. It bounced off the wall and across the floor spilling its contents everywhere. Yuri was fired up now, angry at the impersonal system and how his family was being mistreated. The security guard hurried round his desk toward Yuri who took up an aggressive fighting stance which stopped the guard in his tracks. The guard took out a whistle and blew a loud shrill at the same time taking out his revolver. Two other guards appeared and overpowered Yuri taking him down on the floor and handcuffing him then dragged him up and took him downstairs to a cell.

He was thrown onto the floor of a windowless cell, his arms trapped beneath him. He waited for his eyes to adjust to the dark and gradually began to make out the size of the cell from light seeping in from the corridor around the ill fitting door. The cell was not much longer than him and the same in width. Yuri tried to manoeuvre his arms so that his weight was not on his hands, which also helped to disperse the adrenalin that was coursing through him. After a few minutes he felt calmer and eventually his eyes began to close as he thought about his father and where he might be in this terrible place.

Later, he was woken by a heavy key ring clattering against the door and the sudden influx of bright light. He was heaved to his feet and dragged out into the corridor toward a door further along and pushed into the interrogation room where he was roughly sat down opposite the table his hands tied behind him and round the chair.

Security Chief Tamnsky entered, sat at the table and yawned. 'I don't like idiots trying to damage our building. What were you trying to prove? How big you are?' Yuri gave him a venomous glare.

Tamnsky continued. 'What is your name?'

'Yuri Kasakof. I want—'

Tamnsky barked, 'Be quiet.' He turned to the guard and said, 'Go and get the District Secretary.'

The guard knocked on the door of the District Secretary and waited — he knew better than to knock and enter from the last time. Sidorov was looking at some photographs that were giving him considerable pleasure; the aperitif to later when he would have the main course. He looked up at the knock on the door and hurriedly put the photographs in his drawer and locked it. He said irritably, 'Come.' The guard entered.

Yuri said to Tamnsky, 'I want to know what's happened to my father.'

Tamnsky stood and considered him for moment. 'You idiot. Do you think you can just turn up here like this?' He took a step back from the chair as Sidorov entered. He moved to sit behind Yuri.

Sidorov said irritably to Tamnsky, 'Well?'

'He came into the foyer and was arrested for causing a disturbance and threatening a guard.'

Sidorov was not in the mood to play games; he had more interesting personal business on his mind. 'So?'

'His name is Kazakof. I thought you should know Sir.'

'I see.' He sat down and took out a cigarette which he lit. 'So, what was so important that you got yourself arrested?'

Yuri said, 'I want to know what is happening to my father.'

Sidorov blew a smoke ring and said tauntingly, 'That's easy. He is on his way to the Gulag for twenty five years.'

Despite being handcuffed, Yuri leap to his feet dragging the chair with him intent on getting at the smarmy little man on the other side of the desk. Tamnsky jumped forward and slammed a choke hold from behind, wrestling him back down onto the chair. Yuri coughed for air until the hold was released. Sidorov had retreated to the door where he watched as Tamnsky dealt with the angry figure.

When he was satisfied it was safe to return to his seat, Sidorov sat down again. 'You're not doing yourself any favours acting like that. However, I shall overlook it because it must have come as a shock to you. But don't try my patience further or you will join him.' He glanced over at Tamnsky. 'I think perhaps we will let him go; he can take a message back to his village for us.' He looked at Yuri with sheer malice as he said quietly, 'Take him downstairs, teach him a lesson he won't forget, then dump him back in the hovel he calls his home.' He stood and left.

Yena heard the sound of the car engine outside and hurried into the yard as Yuri was pushed roughly out of the rear of the car and left in the dust as the car drove off. She ran to him, crying out at his swollen and bruised face as she fell to her knees beside him. The two younger children ran out to see what was happening and she shushed them back inside as she got him to his feet.

In the kitchen she helped him to a chair and got a bowl of water and towel which she put on the table and dipped the towel in the water as she examined his battered face.

Goergi was spellbound looking at his hero covered in blood. He asked in an awed tone, 'Did you win Yuri? Was he bigger?'

Yena tutted disapproval as she gently wiped at the dried blood on Yuri's face.

Yuri said through split and swollen lips, 'Sort of.' He tried to smile but could only groan.

Yelena was sitting with her chin resting on her hands watching in fascination. 'Bet it hurts.'

Yena squeezed out the towel in the water as she said, 'Both of you go away and let me tend to your brother. You can ask him questions when he's better.'

Georgi whined, 'But I want to watch.'

Yelena joined in, 'So do I.'

Yena returned to Yuri's face as she said sternly, 'Now!'

They vanished knowing that tone meant business. She said softly, 'I did warn you not to go. What on earth happened?'

He tried to force the less swollen eye open but gave up with a grimace of pain. 'Papa has been sent to the Gulag.'

She wavered a little as her hands began to shake and asked quietly, 'How long?'

'Twenty five years.' A tear forced its way out of his eye and mingled with the blood on his cheek.'

Yena stopped and said in hushed tone, 'God help us.'

Yuri forced his eye open and focused on his mother. Painfully he muttered, 'I won't stop until I get him released Mama. I promise.'

She looked at him and realised that he was no longer a boy. She stroked his battered face.

Ivan was taken from his cell and pushed and shoved outside with other prisoners toward a rail car previously used to transport coal and had not been cleaned out for its current purpose of transporting prisoners. He was forced to scramble into the wagon encouraged by rifle butts that slammed into his back and legs. As he stood up and the door slammed shut behind him he could just make out — once his eyes adjusted to the darkness — the many eyes of perhaps twenty five people watching him with disinterest; staring vacantly as if in a dream state. He pushed his way forward to get away from the door and decided to try and get to the rear of the carriage and perhaps find a space to sit down. As he pushed his way through the manikin like figures, his shuffling feet caught on a metal edge and the next step went into a hole in the floor causing him to reach out as he stumbled. He grabbed at the figures around him but nobody helped. He felt around with his foot and guessed it was a hole in the floor; presumably a toilet.

Eventually he reached the far side of the carriage and squeezed and pushed until he found some space and sunk to the floor where he hoped to be left alone — he was in no mood for talking although nobody appeared to notice him anyway — it was as if he was invisible as they stood in a paralysed state, their eyes focused way beyond the confines of the truck. The carriage lurched as they began to move forward, the clack of the wheels running over the roughly built track adding to the somnambulistic effect on those inside.

His eyes were now adjusting to the dim light and he looked around to find a bizarre sight of men and women in various attire obviously still wearing the clothes they wore when arrested. He wondered how long they had been in here but by their lethargic body language he suspected some time. The train picked up speed and the steady motion gradually sent him to sleep.

Yena watched her son tidy up items in the yard but she knew he was in the process of coming to terms with losing his father. She felt heartbroken, devastated by what had happened — she was not ready to face up to the harsh reality of it yet, secretly hoping that he would return — but life had to go on and she had to explain it to the youngest two without breaking down herself. She needed to lean on Yuri but it was hard enough for him already, she also knew his impetuous nature could get the upper hand and then...

Yuri finished sweeping and went into the barn closing the big wooden door behind him. She wiped away a tear and began washing up. Yuri sat on a workbench in the barn his head spinning with thoughts about his father and what happens next. He knew he had to be strong for his mother and help her with his brother and sister, but how? How could he be strong when he felt so wretched? He looked around the barn at his father's belongings — the tools he had taught Yuri how to use — and his heart sank as he remembered the times they had worked alongside each other, his father gently teasing him. A tear trickled down his cheek as he picked up a hammer his father often used and hefted it in his hand feeling the familiar weight, the smoothness of the handle from years of work. Anger was not far away now as he remembered the interrogation he had experienced, the coldness of them, their abuse of power — what right had they...who do they think they are...? Anger was closer now, his tears drying up, adrenalin beginning to course through his body as he looked around seeing their smug faces in every tool, every corner of the barn. He had to silence them. The rage burst out as he hurled the hammer with all his force at the side of the barn where it bounced off the wooden side and crashed into other tools knocking some onto the floor. Now he looked for anything he could smash to stop their faces leering at him, he picked up a chair and threw it at the bench where it broke in half. Now he was out of control as he careered around the barn flinging things in every direction shouting and swearing at the nameless faces jeering at him.

Yena stopped what she was doing as she heard the first crash come from the barn. She watched to see if he would come out but the following crash and then a series of crashes and noise made her think it best he was left alone. She waited anxiously as the crashes and shouting reached a crescendo and then it became quiet. She bit her nails anxiously watching.

He appeared sweating and covered in dust but calm, a determined look on his face as he approached the house. She felt a wave of relief; he had survived his anger.

He came into the kitchen and hugged her whispering, 'I will look after us Mama. I've been talking to some men in the village who say this man Sidorov is sweeping through the villages for kulaks and people who he thinks are causing trouble. They are saying now if you have two horses and two cows you are a Kulak and will be deported. I know he will come after us so I think we should take our things and go to our relatives in Pskov.' He looked anxiously at her desperate for her to agree.

Yena chewed at a broken nail on her left hand. 'I understand. That has always been the way of a peasant in time of trouble; to move and hide. Your father is gone and we have to think of the little ones.'

Yuri's face darkened. 'I will get my father free.'

She stroked his hand. 'I know you will try Yuri. But these are bad times now and will get worse. I will write to Anotolly and ask him if—'

'We don't have time Mama. They're coming for us, I know it. We have to go today.'

She ran a hand through her hair, 'You're right Yuri. There are soldiers everywhere now and secret police. You sort out the cart and I will see what we need.' Yuri jumped up and went outside. Yena watched her son proud that he was becoming a man. She thought of Ivan and her chest tightened. She busied herself getting prepared for their journey.

Over the next two days Yuri and his mother sorted through their belongings throwing out everything not necessary for survival; some of which were hotly disputed by his younger brother and sister insisting all their toys had to go with them. By the evening of the second day the cart was loaded to capacity, the two horses in harness and the children wrapped in blankets on top of the loaded cart. Yena sat at the front of the cart and Yuri walked alongside the horses with the two cows tethered behind.

It took sixteen hours of heavy trudging over partly paved roads to reach the village of Pskov. As the cart pulled into the tiny farm owned by Yena's sister the door opened spilling out warm light onto the darkness of the dusty ground outside.

A short plump woman hurried out closely followed by a tall
thin man. Yena jumped down and hurried to her sister in a
flood of tears, unable to keep them in any more. Her sister
hugged her close and said in alarm, 'What's happened?'

'Nika! They've taken him!'

Her husband, Leonid asked, 'Who have they taken?'

'Nika gave him a dark look as she hugged her sister. Ivan of
course, who else?'

Yena sobbed into her. 'Twenty five years in the Gulag for
something he didn't do.'

'There, there. Don't fret now. Let's get you all inside.'

Leonid looked at the loaded cart and sighed.

After a long evening explaining what had happened and the
children settled in bed with Nika's two children, the adults
sat down to discuss what to do next.

Leonid was a grey placid man who made little impact on the
world around him and seldom spoke. However, he was the first
to speak as they sat around a large wooden dining table. 'We
have one cow and one horse and one strip of land. That means
we are seen as peasants and not Kulaks. If you intend to stay
you will have to get rid of your animals.'

Yuri thought for a moment. 'Won't we be classed as one
family?'

Leonid said tiredly, 'No. I am the land owner. They will
assess it on me and say the extra animals are mine. Then we
will all have to leave!'

Nika said, 'We have a friend in the village who has not got
a cow or a horse. We could ask him to look after them for you
until you can find somewhere else to go.'

Yuri looked anxiously to Leonid, the head of the family and
who would make the final decision.

Leonid closed his eyes deep in thought. 'I suppose so.'

Yuri said quickly, 'We can't risk selling them. We will
need them when we move on.'

Yena touched her sister's arm and said, 'We thank you for
letting us stay Nika. I know it makes it hard for you. We will
try and do something else.' She looked at Yuri who smiled at
her.

Yuri said, 'Tomorrow I'll see if we can go into the city and
find work there. Then we could get a little apartment.'

Leonid watched him realising he was not a troublesome teenager any more. 'I feel badly about Ivan. It puts a big responsibility on you Yuri.'

Yuri flushed and said quietly, 'My father will come home — soon. I swear it.'

12. SECRET PLEASURES

Sidorov was satisfied his staff at the NKVD building knew their place and he had made it clear that any important interrogations were to be done by him. However, this evening, his main focus was on his personal entertainment which he looked forward to one evening a week which necessitated a trip to Leningrad. A small inconvenience for his indulgence he thought as he looked out of the train window to the flat countryside blurring past. His dislike for the area grew deeper every day; especially the peasants.

On his lap sat his briefcase which he held tightly to his body as if it contained top secret documents — and given his needs it probably could be seen in that light as the contents had been difficult to obtain requiring considerable bribery. He revelled in his mounting excitement at times finding it difficult to conceal.

The train pulled into Vitebsk station and he hurried down the platform and into the darkness of Leningrad city. After a few minutes he arrived at the Summer Gardens, near to the Peter and Paul Fortress, where he waited in the shadows of a row of trees. He lit a cigarette noting his hands were shaking with excitement as he looked out for his friend. This area had begun to have associations with pleasure as it was now his tenth visit since moving to this district. He sometimes thought this part of it — the planning by hushed telephone calls, the secrecy — the most exciting part, but of course the eventual event was the prize.

He finished the cigarette and was about to light another when a figure appeared in the distance, which he instantly recognised by the stoop of a tall man trying to hide his six feet three frame also carrying a brief case. As he drew nearer and Sidorov was confident it was Vasili he stepped out of the shadows. Vasili looked up, his long gaunt face brightly lit by a street lamp which picked out his thin hair swept over his bald scalp and deep set eyes that constantly looked for danger in every nook and cranny.

'Nikita! You frightened me.' He drew near and leaned close to him, 'it's on!' The excitement was clear on his deeply wrinkled face as he tapped his briefcase.

Sidorov took his arm and led him into the shadows. He looked around them furtively. 'In these times one can't be too careful.'

Vasili nodded and then said excitedly, 'I understand there will be four there tonight.'

Sidorov smiled. 'Then we should hurry. Do you know their ages?'

They moved away quickly toward the dock area as Vasili thought for a moment. 'I know one is eight. I think two are ten. Not sure about the fourth.'

Sidorov squeezed his friend's arm excitedly and said in a lascivious tone, 'Ten eh?'

Vasili whispered, 'I hope the fourth is perhaps seven? That would be perfect.'

The two figures hurried out of the gardens toward the Mariinsky opera house where their interests — certainly not operatic ones — would be fully indulged late into the night in a seedy bar far from prying eyes behind the grand building and its grand occupants.

The next morning Sidorov sat at his desk replaying the events of last night idly moving the china ashtray to and fro until he settled it on its right resting place on the desk. The events of last night — although he was now fully sated sexually at least for a couple of days — left in him a restlessness which he needed to quell by activity. Today, this would take the form of interrogating a few peasants; more aggressively than usual as necessitated by his inflated libido.

He stood and put on his long coat and flat police cap as he walked down the corridor calling out for his driver. Tamnsky appeared from an office. Sidorov waved for him to follow. 'It's about time we shook this rabble up — show them we mean business and make sure rebellion is far from their minds; then I can get out of this dump. Tamnsky fervently wished for the latter.'Sidorov continued, 'So we know Kazakof's wife is active in this rebellion?'

Tamnskey hesitated making sure he was covering himself. 'Getting witnesses is tricky Sir, they stick together.'

Sidorov stopped for a moment and turned to him. 'But we strongly suspect she is?'

'Yes Sir.'

'Good enough for me. We'll go there now and arrest them then deport the lot to Siberia.'

Sidorov's black car entered the village followed by a lorry carrying armed police. Villagers gathered at a distance waiting to see who they were after this time. The women gathered in a group, fierce looks upon their faces with their husbands close by. Sidorov strutted to the Kazakof's farm and banged on the door. He was aware of laughter coming from the women as he turned to his guards shouting, 'Break it down!' As soon as the door was smashed open he rushed in behind two guards.

From the crowd came, 'Your too late, they've gone!'

Sidorov collected three guards and strutted over to the crowd. 'What do you mean? Where?'

A woman boldly stepped forward and said, 'Where you won't find them. They hadn't done anything wrong. You're pigs, all of you.' She spat on the ground narrowly missing Sidorov's boot.

He took a step back and shouted, 'I could have you all arrested. In fact, I'll start with you! Guard! Put her in the truck.'

As they went to grab her arm they were surrounded by the crowd and shoved away from her as she quickly slipped away. A large powerfully built man stepped closer to Sidorov and clamped a vice like hand on his wrist as he tried to get out his pistol. He held on and pulled Sidorov close to him. 'Now listen. We won't be beaten down by the likes of you and your bullies with their guns. We have guns as well and we'll use them if we have to.'

Sidorov felt trapped as the man steadily looked into his eyes before releasing him. Sidorov massaged his wrist as the man withdrew into the crowd. 'You dare to threaten officers of the state? Go to your homes and think carefully about what you are doing. You might find the army arriving...' He pushed his way through the crowd and back to his car. He got in and slammed the door closed trying to ignore the jeers and taunts of the crowd. He felt shaken by the man and would make sure he had guards closer to him in the future.

13. LEARNING THE GAME

Ivan was woken by the clank of couplings as the carriage slowed down after what seemed an eternity of monotonous travel. The large door slid open and handfuls of dried herring and bread were thrown in. He managed to grab a few scraps in the ensuing fight for food when everyone seemed to suddenly become animated. Ivan wondered if it could get much worse? Perhaps when they reached the prison it would improve.

After long intervals of monotonous travel interspersed by sudden stops and searches, the guards bellowed for them to get out. Ivan tried to stand but realised his legs were cramped from sitting for so long. The guard jumped in and dragged him out of the carriage. Ivan fell to the ground unable to stand grimacing as the circulation returned to his legs. He looked around peering past the guards dirty boots through a low lying mist that hugged the ground obscuring anything other than a few hundred metres. Crying out as his circulation flooded back into his legs he was pulled up and pushed forward; the point of a bayonet prodding him in his back.

All he could see in the dark were railway sidings and a station a few hundred metres away. They were pushed into single file and prodded with bayonets to move along toward a line of lorries some way in the gloomy distance, their headlights piercing the mist with long tubes of diffused light. After much shouting and prodding they were loaded into the lorries which trundled away into the mist. Ivan tried to think where they could be; he had been travelling for around fourteen hours and by guess work thought they might be a few hundred miles away which — although he had no idea what direction they had been travelling —could be nearing Siberia. (The majority of prison camps were clustered there)

He felt the lorry slow down bouncing over bumps in the road before it ground to a halt, the rumble of large metal gates being opened accompanied by more shouting. The lorry ground forward again and powerful searchlights mounted high on towers pierced through the gaps in the sides of the truck highlighting fearful eyes trying to see what was happening. After a few more minutes the back of the truck opened to reveal the lorry was parked, along with the others, in a large rectangular concreted area with search lights at each corner. Guards were running back and forth issuing orders to men and women scrambling out of the lorries to get into single file and march toward a number of buildings looming out of the mist.

Inside they were ordered to strip and were searched, then shoved toward rows of baths full of filthy water from previous prisoners. After this they were thrown striped prison uniforms and lined up again to have heads shaved (to reduce the lice population) with what Ivan could see was a dirty razor, before shuffling back outside into the misty night to stand in line for a roll call. As the roll call went on — as if forever as the three or four hundred prisoners stood in the cold air — Ivan began to get angry, looking around impatiently, becoming agitated.

The man next to him said quietly, 'Don't. They'll just shoot you.'

Ivan was startled to hear a voice after so many hours of silence. He glanced sideways at the man deciding his demeanour suggested he knew what he was talking about. His face was pale as if he had been out of the sun for a long time, his skin patchy with eczema, spots and sores on his shaved scalp, but when Ivan looked to the man's eyes he could see a lifetime of hardship and yet there was a light there, almost an amused twinkle!

The man smiled to reveal blackened teeth as he said, 'You are you from freedom. Have you any news?' Ivan didn't understand. 'What's your name friend?'

'Ivan Kazakof.'

'Erik Pushkin.'

Ivan said grimly, 'This place is...'

Erik said casually, 'There are much worse...You get used to it eventually. You might find it safer to not admit it's your first time.'

'How long have you been here?'

Erik smiled, but it was not a joyful one, more ironic. 'Here? As long as you.' Ivan looked puzzled as Erik continued, 'This is a transit prison. You might see twenty or more of these before you reach your final destination. But even then...'

'Are the proper prisons better?'

'This is not bad compared to some. Now Vologda for instance. An ancient building. The toilets are on top of each other and so bad they leak through the floor to the one below. Mind you at least they had toilets...' He said thoughtfully, 'I could go on, but you will learn for yourself. So how long have you got?'

'Twenty five years.'

Erik laughed. 'You'll soon learn how to be a Zek. Then you can deal with it.'

Ivan asked, 'Zek?'

'That's what we are called.'

'How long have you served?'

'Ten. I got twenty five.'

Ivan felt his knees growing weak, whether through lack of food or the thought of what lay before him he wasn't sure.

Erik said, 'You look a reasonable fellow but one not versed in the ways of the Gulag that's clear.' He looked Ivan up and down focusing on his knuckles. 'I can see you can look after yourself.' He looked around at the lines of prisoners, 'You will find a mix of men here; political prisoners, thieves, murderers and to survive you must learn the rules, they're not written anywhere but they apply which ever prison you go to. Stick with me, I'll give you some tips. The first one is; don't trust anyone. They send in snitches to catch us out. If a Zek is too friendly, keep out of his way. Second, watch out for the trustees, they are the ones with privelages. Many of them are criminals and enjoy inflicting pain.'

Yuri worked alongside Leonid repairing farm equipment thinking how different it was to being with his father who was always teasing him but at the same time, teaching him so much about life without Yuri being aware of it. Leonid was a kind man but plagued with depressive thoughts that drove him into his own private world that Yuri couldn't penetrate. And so they worked in silence. Yuri's mind was full of how he could get his father freed but all his schemes were fanciful without any basis in reality. He decided he needed to understand the system in order to find how he could make a complaint to someone in authority who could reverse Sidorov's decision. Perhaps he should go to the city and seek advice — this brought a flush of excitement as he remembered Nadya.

Thoughts of her flooded his mind as he relived those few minutes with her. He realised, again, that there was no future in it, and felt guilty thinking what his father must be going through. Leonid stopped what he was doing without saying anything and went inside the house. Yuri stopped working and looked around at the strangeness of the barn; how different it was to theirs, the same smells and yet alien. He longed for his old farm house with its leaking roof when it rained heavily, despite his father's determination to fix it. He put down the chisel he had been sharpening, grabbed his coat and left the barn.

He entered the kitchen and put his arm around his mother who was helping her sister mend clothes. 'I'm going into Leningrad Mama, I have to try and find Papa. I have enough rubles for the train.'

Yena stopped sewing, 'Be careful Yuri, please?'

'Of course Mama.'

After a bumpy journey of two hours, Yuri arrived at Vitebsky station in Leningrad and stood between the wide marble columns trying to decide where to go for advice. He wandered around for awhile before noticing a large government building. He entered the large grand vestibule and headed for a polished mahogany counter behind which he saw a man in a smart uniform (although no rank was evident) who looked up at him and smiled. Yuri asked, 'I need to get some advice please.'

The man asked, 'What sort of advice?'

'I need to get my father out of prison?' The man looked slightly amused. Yuri wanted to grab him by his smart uniform and drag him over the counter. Yuri drew a deep breath and said, 'He was wrongly accused and I want to write to someone.'

The man sat back. 'I see.'

Yuri watched him with a steady gaze as he seemed to think over the request before he said, 'You need to have someone petition on your behalf. Do you know anyone here?' Yuri shook his head. 'There's nobody here you can see in that case.'

'How do I get someone to do that then?'

The man smiled, 'You need to make a friend.' He winked but then he saw darkness enter the young man's eyes, 'Or, you write a letter yourself to your local Party Secretary who, if he agrees, will write on your behalf to the Regional Party Secretary and get it delivered for you.'

'Would he be at the Town Hall?'

'Yes.'

Yuri thanked him and left going back out to the busy streets bustling with people returning from work. He looked up at the grand buildings on Nevsky Prospekt and thought about

Nadya again wondering where she worked and lived. Perhaps if he were to stroll around he might bump in to her? He laughed at himself realising how slim the chances of that were. He tried to imagine what she did. Was she an officer worker, a student or worked in a factory? As he walked around looking out for her he noticed how many people were dressed like him shuffling about; many begging on street corners.

Ivan sat squeezed up beside Erik in a filthy and damp cell with twenty other men. Ivan was acutely aware of the smell they generated in this confined space which he found difficult to ignore. There was a dim lightbulb in the ceiling and no windows which increased his sense of feeling trapped. Ivan had been given a dented metal mug but had not received anything to drink.

Erik pointed to it. 'Hang onto that or someone will try and steal it. It's good to have as few possessions as possible; they can't be stolen then. I've seen a couple of men eying your coat as well.'

Ivan asked, 'So we just sit here?'

'You will learn the art of patience Ivan. These places are overcrowded and the guards don't have a good time of it so they take it out on us. You have to learn to look down and not draw attention to yourself. When it comes to eating time watch what I do. We will probably have to line up for it and whatever it is will be ladled out.'

'But we have no bowls or forks.'

'Like I say, watch what I do. If you don't get given a bowl — and it's not likely in a transit camp — use your cap. Hold it open and get the soup or whatever. You must eat, and believe me, you won't want to when you see what it is!'

'What is it usually?'

'Fish bones in a thin watery soup, and if you're lucky, crushed grits.'

'What about taking a piss? I'm getting desperate.'

'Sometimes it's only once a day. The guards have so many prisoners. If you get really bad then do this.' He took off his long felt boot and turned it upside down, then turned the soft top inside out to form a container around the boot.

A guard entered and pointed to Ivan to get up. As he stood the guard dragged him out and took him to an interrogation room where two officers stood waiting for him. One was tall and thin with a bushy beard; the other shorter, but stocky and well muscled, with cropped hair. Ivan looked around the room and noted a large clock at the back of the room; he had to find something to keep track knowing how long these interrogations can last.

The one with the beard sat at a desk and gestured for Ivan to sit opposite him. The other man handed him a file which he opened and read, 'You are Ivan Kazakof. I see here you have been convicted as an enemy of the people under Articles 58—10, Part2 and 58—11 of the Criminal Code of the Russian Republic on the testimony of a brave comrade. What is missing is a signature admitting your guilt.'

Ivan sat watching the man in disbelief. 'What's the point? You have your false "testimony".'

The man leant forward. 'It is necessary that for you to be rehabilitated into society you must accept the error of your ways!'

Ivan said, 'Go to hell.'

He felt a crashing blow on the back of his head from the man behind him with a truncheon who screamed, 'You will admit your guilt! The system requires it.'

Ivan was dazed by the blow and swayed on the chair.

The bearded man leaned forward shouting — spittle spraying from his fat lips — 'Sit up!' The second man grabbed him by his collar and dragged him up on the seat.

The bearded man pushed a sheet of paper across the desk and snarled, 'Sign at the bottom.'

Ivan shook his head. There came another blow to his head causing him to fall forward and then to be dragged back to the sitting position.

The bearded man tapped the piece of paper angrily. 'Sign the damn paper!'

Ivan looked up at him and down to the floor again. The man behind him swung the truncheon and Ivan slumped forward unconscious.

Later, he was dragged back into the room noting the clock; it had been four hours. He couldn't tell if it was day or night. His head throbbed viciously. Again the bearded man pushed the piece of paper toward him. 'It is important that you admit you acted as an enemy of the Soviet republic and betrayed the communist principle.'

Ivan moved his head which immediately roared in pain from the previous beatings. He said groggily, 'Go to hell.'

The bearded man signalled to his associate who grabbed Ivan by his shoulders pulling him off balance onto the floor where he then proceeded to viciously kick him in the back, stomach and head until Ivan lay still. The bearded man crouched beside him and offered a glass of water smiling as he said gently, 'Come now Ivan enough of this barbarity. I apologise for my friend's over zealousness. Here take a sip.' Ivan shakily accepted the glass and took a few sips. The bearded man took the glass from him and helped him back in the chair. He carried on in a reasonable and gentle tone, 'Look here Ivan, let's be done with all this nasty business. You are going to be locked up for twenty five years what difference does it make if you sign a piece of paper? Sign it and we can all get some sleep.'

Ivan looked up out of pain bleared eyes and spat on the floor. 'I will not sign something and condemn my friends to your system.'

The bearded man sighed sadly. 'Then we must encourage you a little more.' To his associate he said, 'Put him in the punishment cell for twelve hours.'

Ivan was dragged between two guards down a corridor and pushed into what could only be described as a cupboard; a cell no wider than a body and as deep. He was cramped up between the walls as the door slammed shut putting him in total darkness. He tried to sit down but it was impossible. He had no option but to remain in a slumped standing position. His mind raced as he tried to make sense of it all. Why was it so important to them to get a signed confession? He knew they weren't going to let him go; more likely they were going to kill him anyway. He thought of his family and tears ran down his face as he pictured Maya cooking and him teasing her, Yuri, his fearless, brave son. And the two little ones.

He felt the beginnings of panic as he realised he was over breathing. He tried to take some deep breaths to calm himself but his body was so confined he could only take quick shallow breaths. His legs were already beginning to shake, sweat was starting on his forehead but the cold damp walls and floor soon made him cold. He began to shiver.

Ivan was beginning to see that his life was over. He began reflecting on recent events — some of which he thought bitterly he should have seen coming — and how much he hated Stalin, the architect of his misery. Anger grew in him but had nowhere to vent itself. He tried to force the walls further apart in a struggle to feel free then suddenly stopped as he heard screaming. Frantically, he looked around in the solid blackness with wide flitting eyes the pupils dilated to maximum. It was his screams. He began to sob softly.

Twelve hours later the door suddenly opened and without its support he fell forward unable to support his weight on numb legs. The guards didn't bother helping him up, they simply dragged him along the rough concrete floor back to the interrogation room. The two familiar men met him with blank gazes as he was dumped in the chair.

The bearded man, again sitting at the table, pushed the piece of paper over to him. 'Sign it.' He proffered a pen.

Ivan was barely conscious, his mind a blank after semi standing in the box for twelve hours. He shook his head. The bearded man nodded to his associate who dragged Ivan to his feet. Ivan promptly collapsed because his legs were still numb and then the two of them dragged him into the corner of the room and pinned him against the wall. The bearded man hissed in his face, his bad breath and spittle assailing Ivan's senses, 'Now you stand there until we are ready for you. If you try and sit or sleep we will beat the shit out of you.' He and the other man left and a guard entered and sat at the desk.

Ivan felt weaker than he had ever felt before. He remembered when he had had pneumonia which had left him weak for sometime but even that was not as bad as this. His legs screamed as the circulation returned causing him to lose his balance and lean against the wall. The guard seemed to sense it and stopped reading his newspaper looking up at him with a fierce expression. Ivan balanced forward and knew it wouldn't be long before his legs gave way. He tried to breath slowly and concentrate on keeping his mind busy. He looked around the room trying to remember every detail of it, then shutting his eyes and recalling it. He began with the ceiling which was a dirty grey with cobwebs in the corners and one light bulb in the centre hanging on a dirty wire flex. The walls were similar in colour and in the corner there were spats of dried blood. There were larger dried spots on the asphalt floor. He watched the guard, trying to guess where he came from, did he have a family? Did he enjoy his work? He would be a peasant glad of the work probably. He shut his eyes to think and everything began to drift from lack of sleep, he wobbled back against the wall again. The guard shouted at him making him snap awake. And so it went on for five hours.

The two familiar interrogators entered and as usual the bearded one sat at the desk. Ivan was in a trance like state and had to be pushed and shoved to sit down at the desk. His legs were immediately on fire, his whole body aching and his mind desperate for sleep.

The bearded man pushed the piece of paper toward him across the desk and said pleasantly, 'Here is the confession. Sign it now and you can rest. If you don't you can stand again for a few hours. Perhaps then you will reconsider. Think about it Ivan. Is it really so difficult to sign a piece of paper? We will get your friends anyway so what's the point in putting yourself through this?' Ivan stared defiantly at him through bloodshot eyes.

The man sighed, 'Very well. Guard!' A new guard appeared and roughly pulled Ivan from the chair pushing him to stand against the wall again. Ivan knew he would not be able to stand for very long. The two men left and the guard sat at the desk where he began reading the newspaper. He looked relaxed and glanced at Ivan a couple of times with a faint but not friendly smile.

After an hour Ivan's legs gave way and he slumped to the floor. The guard leapt up and shouted for him to stand up. Ivan was drifting into sleep. The guard kicked him hard several times then pounded his body and head with the butt of his rifle. As Ivan drifted into unconsciousness he thought at least he could now sleep. He was dragged into awareness as a bucket of cold water was sloshed over him. The shouting and beating carried on until the process had been repeated several times before he was dragged to his feet and stood against the wall again. His mind was drifting in and out; memories of his family becoming a distant thing as his body began to close down.

After another two hours during which time he wobbled on numb feet — feeling the bruises from the beatings becoming a deeper ache — the two men entered and took up their usual positions.

They waited whilst Ivan was dragged to the chair and seated by the guard who then left and the bearded man said, 'Ivan, I must inform you that we have arrested your son and his mother — she was not like you, she gave us all the names — and taken the two younger ones into better care under the authorities. There they can learn the right way of thinking and not be contaminated by your dissenting ways. So, you see? What need do you have to resist signing a piece of paper?'

Ivan tried to drag his mind into thinking clearly but he couldn't. He had a vague idea about his family being mentioned but perhaps he was dreaming.

A hard slap in the face cleared his mind for an instant as the bearded man sat back and said, 'Let me repeat what I said. We have arrested your son and his mother — she was not like you, she gave us all the names — and we have taken the two younger ones into better care under the authorities. So, sign now, you are not saving anyone by your stubbornness, and,' he leaned further forward, 'we can reduce your sentence and make life a little easier in here.' He pushed the piece of paper toward Ivan again and held the pen for him to take.

Ivan was slipping in and out of consciousness, his thoughts far away — his son laughing as he teased, his youngsters giggling as he threatened them with their older brother — to a piece of paper? Was it floating in front of him? He felt something in his hand but wasn't concerned what it was as he felt his hand moved by some unknown force the cold table top under it now, a voice somewhere saying, 'That's right, just there'.

14. THE PAST CATCHES UP

Vladimir Fastenco came down from the bedroom and told his wife he was going into the barn. She noticed he was still withdrawn but pleased he had got up; this being the first time since his arrest a few weeks ago. Hopefully whatever had frightened him at the police station was leaving him now. She hurried upstairs relieved she could change the sheets at last. She busied herself in the bedroom as she watched him from the window slowly make his way to the barn and go inside. She heard the old wooden door rattle shut and a bolt thrown.

Inside the barn Vladimir Fastenco looked around for a length of rope which he gathered into a coil and laid on a bench. Slowly as if everything was an effort he manoeuvred a stool to below a high beam. He took hold of the rope and slung it over the beam hanging onto it testing it would hold his weight. He tied one end into a noose and climbed up onto the stool putting the noose over his head. As if in a dream, without any further thought he kicked the stool away.

Anna was finishing the bed when she became suspicious. Perhaps it was second sight — her sister always told her she could sense things about to happen — or at a deep unconscious level her mind had noted the incongruous sound of the door being bolted; something Vldimir never did. She sat on the bed and the feeling grew worse. Something was wrong, but what? Her thoughts immediately went to Vladimir. There was something about the way he looked as he went out to the barn. Why would he suddenly — she leapt up and raced downstairs and out to the barn pulling at the door although she knew it was bolted. She shouted to him in panic but he didn't answer. Desperately she looked around for anything she could find to break the door in. She called his name again but still no answer. She remembered a side window which was always unlocked and she raced around the side of the barn. She spotted a barrel and pulled it below the window. Frantically she clambered onto it and climbed up to see her husband standing on the stool.

To her horror he kicked the stool away. She pounded the old wooden window frame with her fists watching aghast as her husband swung from the rope; his feet dancing as he kicked the air. The glass shattered and she reached in to release the catch then scrambled through cutting herself on the remains of the glass as she wriggled through and tumbled onto a workbench. She scrambled off the bench and sobbing with fear grabbed his flailing legs to take the weight from his neck. He was turning purple and twitching as she tried to pull the

stool back into position with her foot. Anna was a strong
woman used to physical work and her muscles saved his life as
she held him up until she could lower his feet onto the stool.
As the pressure was released from his neck he gasped and
gurgled. She let go for a second and snatched a knife from the
bench. She grabbed another stool and reaching up managed to
cut him free of the rope holding him as steady as she could
balancing on the stool.

She sobbed as she laid him on the ground. 'Why? What made
you do that?'

He croaked, 'I can't live with what I did.'

'I don't understand Vladimir. What did you do?' She thought
for a moment, 'You've been like this since you came back from
the police station. Was it something they made you do?'

He began crying and wailed, 'You should have left me up
there Anna. I sent him to his death.'

She pulled him into a sitting position. 'Now you listen. We
will talk about this. You have to promise me you won't do this
again. It hurts me as well. How would I cope if you weren't
here? Now let's get you inside.' She helped him up and back
into the house.

As soon as Yuri woke up each day he instantly focused on the
two things that occupied his mind; to free his father and
speak to Nadya again. His emotions were scrambled as the pain
of his father's imprisonment mingled with the deep regrets he
felt about what he had said to Nadya. He wasn't sleeping
properly or eating as he usually did and thought how he could
meet her again and what he could say to heal it. But then was
there any real chance for them coming from different classes?

Beneath his ruminations about Nadya lay the aching chasm of
his father's absence, the constant fear for him and the rest
of the family. He decided to write to the local Party
Secretary and asked his mother for help. Together they wrote a
letter asking to get his father freed. They tried to make it
short and explained what had led to his father's arrest.

Maya said when it was finished, 'Now you must be patient.
These things cannot be rushed and the more you pester him the
longer it will take.'

Yuri realised he was clenching his fists. 'I know Mama. I
just hate the thought of what is happening to Papa in prison.'

Maya put her hand on his and gently prised his fingers out of his palms. 'Your Papa is a strong man. He knows we will do what we can. He will be proud of you.'

Yuri took the letter and placed it carefully in an envelope then put on his coat. 'I'll take it there now. I think I will go to Leningrad this afternoon, there's not much for me to do here at the moment.'

'Be careful Yuri, please?'

'Of course Mama.'

When he was in the town of Pulkova and had delivered the letter he bumped into his friend Andrei who exclaimed, 'Yuri!'

'Hey Andrei.'

Andrei became solemn. 'The village is not the same anymore. When I go there, everyone seems scared. We used to have good fun. You heard about Vladimir Fastenco?'

'No?'

'He tried to hang himself.'

'Do you know why?'

Andrei shrugged. 'Anyway, how are you?'

Yuri was preoccupied with the news and after a few more exchanges about life in their villages Yuri made his way to the station where he got the train to Leningrad and headed toward the apartment where Nadya lived. He kept thinking about Vladimir and how his wife had been anxious about him. She had mentioned him being arrested and questioned. Alarm bells began to ring. What if he had given information about his father? And what would that be? But they were good friends, why would he do that? He decided he needed to find out for himself when he got back. Now he wanted to see Nadya to try and make it right.

He reached her apartment but was not brave enough to call there. Instead he waited down the road in a position where he could see her if she approached. He had no idea what he was going to say, he would have to make it up as he went along. A couple of hours passed and it became late afternoon busy with people returning home from work.

Nadya was heading for home when she saw Yuri. She dashed down an alley. Her heart was racing as she leant against the wall trying to slow her breathing. The last few days had been strained with the other family in her home. It had not been made any better by her constant thoughts about Yuri. She longed to hear his voice and see those lovely eyes. But how could she? Nothing had changed; they were still from different classes only now she had peasants living in their house! She peeked round the corner and he was still there. A deep longing overcame her and she knew she had to speak to him. She left the alley and headed toward home staring at the pavement rehearsing what she was going to say, but when she looked up he was not there. Her stomach churned as she quickened her pace to see if he was anywhere near but he wasn't. She stood looking up and down the street but he was gone.

Yuri despondently made his way back to the station telling himself what an idiot he had been to think she would appear. He had to let her go; there was no future in it. His thoughts were back with his father and Vladimir Fastenco. Tomorrow he would visit him and find out if there was a connection to his father's arrest.

When he arrived back to his Aunt's farm he sought out his mother who was returning from a walk. He met her at the gate.

'Mama. I'm taking one of the horses to our village; I need to talk to Fastenco.'

'Is that wise Yuri? The Secret Police are everywhere!'

'I know and I will be careful, I promise.'

The next day he made the long journey by horse to his old village and knocked on the door of Vladimir Fastenco. Anna opened it and greeted him warmly inviting him in looking over his shoulder to see if his mother was with him.

'Thank you Anna,' he said as she sat him before a fire and heated some water for a drink.

'How's your mother coping Yuri?'

'She's ok, my younger brother and sister keep her busy.'

'And how have they been with your father away?'

'They're sad but we try and keep them occupied.'

Upstairs Vladimir sat in their bedroom shaking as he heard Yuri's voice. He had to escape. Yuri's reputation as a fighter was well known. He looked out of the window but decided the drop was too much. He was trembling with fear and guilt as he crawled under the bed.

Downstairs Yuri looked into the fire and said, 'My father was innocent Anna. He would never have done anything wrong; that wasn't his way. Somebody must have made a false statement against him.'

Anna began to feel uncomfortable. 'Why would anyone do that?'

'I've been interrogated by this new man there, Sidorov. He's a bad man. He had me beaten up.'

Anna looked up to the ceiling as she said, 'And this man would force someone to sign a document telling lies?'

'Yes he would.'

'Wait here.' She got up and went up the stairs into the bedroom expecting to find him there. 'Vladimir?' She sat on the bed and realised with deep sadness and a little irritation where he was. 'Come out, Now!'

A voice from under the bed said, 'I can't Anna, he'll kill me.'

'If you don't I will kill you. Listen, he's hurting for his father and just wants to get him free. He's met this new man at the police station and he knows what he is capable of. Please, Vladimir, just come and talk with him. I'll go downstairs now and you come down, please. It might help you feel a little better if you talk to him.' She went back downstairs and busied herself making tea for Yuri. 'Vladimir's frightened of you Yuri. He thinks you want to hurt him.'

Yuri shook his head. 'I just want to get my father out of prison. If Vladimir had been forced to sign a false statement I can get him to write down what happened and send it to someone in Authority who can get my father released.'

She handed him his drink and looked up to the bedroom. 'He's too frightened to come down Yuri. Go up and talk to him. He's hiding under the bed.' She flushed a little with embarrassment. Yuri tried to understand how desperate the man must be. He put his drink down and went up the stairs into the tiny bedroom with its floral wall paper and female items on a small dressing table.

'Vladimir, it's Yuri. I don't want to hurt you; I just need to know what the man did to you. He had me beaten up so I know what he is capable of. I just want to talk, please.'

From under the bed Vladimir said weakly, 'I didn't mean to. He threatened my family.'

'Come out and talk. Please. If I was angry I would have pulled you out by now.'

A pair of hands appeared as Vladimir struggled out and sat on the floor leaning against the wall.

'His name is Sidorov. He showed me a piece of paper and said if I didn't sign it he would arrest my family. He said horrible things Yuri.' He began crying. 'I tried not to but he made me.'

Yuri said, 'I know. And I'm not angry. I know you tried to hang yourself Valdimir. That tells me how bad you feel. So help me get this monster removed so he can't hurt other people. Will you sit with me and we will write a letter that I can send to the Party Secretary and get my father released? If we get Sidorov out he can't hurt you.' Vladimir nodded and struggled to his feet.

15. MENDING FENCES

October 1929

Yuri felt he had done all he could by sending the second letter. He just hoped the Regional Party Secretary was an honourable man. Now feeling he could do no more his thoughts returned to Nadya. Once again he made the journey to Leningrad and as he walked toward her apartment tried to rehearse what to say if he managed to see her. He would rather take on a man twice his size than have to go through this. He reached her apartment and decided to wait by the entrance door to make sure he didn't miss her.

Nadya left the Academy as usual and made her way home carrying her precious violin. She was not in any hurry. The situation there was proving onerous for everyone; especially her mother who was becoming ill with the strain. Nadya did not blame their guests but all the same she wished they could find somewhere else because the tensions were unbearable; not that their guests were troublesome, they were doing their best to make it work but they couldn't find employment which only added to the pressure on Gustav to feed them.

Full of these concerns Nadya approached her apartment and saw a figure in the doorway. She felt a flood of confusion as she found she desperately wanted it to be Yuri but at the same time dreaded it would be. She drew nearer and Yuri stepped out to meet her. Her stomach did summersaults, her head swam. Her mind went blank.

Yuri stood before her and said, 'If you want me to go I will, but first just hear me out?' She nodded and he continued, 'can we walk for a little, perhaps go to the river again?'

She smiled trying to catch the words before they left her mouth. All she could allow was, 'Ok.'

Yuri could see she was finding it difficult. 'So you play the violin?' She nodded. He went on, 'I want to apologise for my behaviour last time. I was upset and didn't want to say something I would regret.' She fought desperately not to tell him how much she had missed him. 'Some bad things have happened to us since I saw you and they have been hard to sort out. But even then, I have thought about you all the time Nadya, all the time.'

They walked in silence for a few minutes as she thought what she wanted to say but gave up. 'I've missed you to. We have also had distressing things happen but like you I have thought about you all the time.'

Yuri looked concerned. 'What has happened?'

She didn't know how to explain it. 'It's complicated, I'll tell you later.'

'Are you angry with me for walking away?'

She smiled. 'I was. But you were right. I said some horrible things.'

Yuri relaxed a little. 'That evening was the best time I've ever had. When you put your arm through mine I felt I was floating on air. And the water was so beautiful. Like you,' he added bashfully. 'I've been thinking a lot and I know we are from different classes but so what?' She put her arm through his and smiled. 'What do you think Nadya?'

She clutched him tighter to her and said, 'I'd like to think we could.'

'But?'

'It's difficult. I don't know how to explain.'

'Is it to do with me? Are you still angry?'

'No. Ok I'll tell you. There have been thousands of,' she stopped the word in time, 'people being driven from their land into Leningrad. But when they get here there is no accommodation for them...' She didn't know how to put it.

He finished the sentence for her. 'And many of them are on the streets begging. Yes I know.'

'The authorities have moved many of them in with families who have apartments, with no discussion about it.'

Yuri stopped and looked at her, shocked. 'This has happened to you?'

'Yes. It's strange isn't it, I mean it's like a lesson I've been made to learn.'

'It must be awful. What about your parents?'

'It has hit my mother the worst. She has always suffered with her nerves. She has not been well for some months and this has proved too much for her.'

They reached the river and sat where they had before. She kept her arm linked to his and moved closer to him. 'They are good people. I've learnt a lot about many things since they have been with us. I don't think anyone would be comfortable with such a situation.'

Yuri exclaimed angrily, 'I wouldn't be! But then our farm,' he was about to say *is* but had to change it to, '*was* very small anyway. But I can understand how hard it is for your family and the family forced to live with you. We have been forced out of our home and have had to move in with my aunt and her family in a farm not much bigger than ours.'

She was shocked. 'Why, what happened?'

'Our local District Secretary died and a new man took his place. He is the sort that does whatever he likes to get want he wants, he enjoys having people beaten up or locked in a tiny dark damp cell for hours; I know this because he has done it to me.'

'Why? What had you done?'

'My father was arrested and put in the Gulag. I can't find out anything so I went to the police station to ask and...' He ran his hand down his face, 'I caused them a bit of trouble and they arrested me had me beaten up and dumped outside our farm.' He realised she was looking at his clenched fists and he relaxed them.

She looked at him and touched a bruise still visible on his face. 'So you know what's it like to live in somebody else's home and I know what it is like the other way.'

He said, 'Perhaps we both had lessons to learn. I'm trying to get my father released; we know a friend of my father was arrested and forced to sign a false document incriminating my father in something he did not do.'

'That's terrible.'

'I've spoken to his friend and we've sent a letter to the Party Secretary.'

'I hope he helps you.' They sat in silence watching the water flow by, the evening air becoming chill. 'It must be horrible.'

'Yes it is. I don't think anyone is safe.'

'I worry for my father. He is constantly frightened of being deported because his father was German.'

'That's sad. I like him even from the brief converstion we've had.'

She sighed as she relaxed against his powerful body. 'He likes you as well.' She felt safe. They could make it work. Yuri felt her relax against him and felt good for the first time in ages.

Yuri said quietly, 'let's sit here forever just like this.'

She laughed. 'Hmm, obviously you are not very practical!'

She became serious. 'How will we do it Yuri? We want our families to know about us but how?'

'I don't know. If you come to meet my mother she will feel awkward because we are not in our own house, and how can I come to yours, especially with your *guests* there?'

She rubbed his arm. 'I know. At the moment it is not practical. We have to wait.' She snuggled up to him. 'My father does think you are wonderful though.'

He said with a chuckle, 'Suppose I am really...' She poked him. He said, 'Let's take it a day at a time. We don't know what's going to happen. For now I will come and meet you and we can talk, ok?'

She snuggled up to him. He saw Sidorov's smarmy face and a flush of anger flowed through him. He knew the stirrings of hate building would not go away as he tried to remind himself how lucky he was to be here with this beautiful woman. He wanted to kill him.

Nadya felt him becoming tense and said, 'Are you ok?'

'I'm fine, just memories.'

Two months had passed since Yuri had sent his letter to the local Party Secretary who didn't want anything to do with it. He wasn't going to rock the boat, his position was comfortable and that was that. And so he passed it as quickly as he could on to someone higher than himself.

Party Secretary Chupin sat at his desk trying to deal with the mountain of complaints from peasants about unfair treatment. Chupin was not a fool; he understood the pressure districts were under to meet Stalin's targets fully aware the punishment for failing was imprisonment or deportation. Chupin himself was in no way immune from the wrath of Stalin if he failed but nevertheless he was determined to carry out his office with honour.

He lit a cigarette and looked at the pile of letters waiting for him. He blew a smoke ring and picked up the next letter. The majority were badly written but he had developed the knack of making sense of them. This letter though was set out properly with good spelling and sentences constructed correctly. He sat back and read puffing on his cigarette. As he read he became still and sat forward attentively as the import of the letter hit home. Sidorov! He knew he was trouble and now he had proved it. He should have refused to have him; well it was too late now.

A grave miscarriage had occurred and it was up to him to put it right. He did not shrink from sending men to the Gulag — he was a realist living in a cruel regime of which he had no choice — and he knew some of the evidence was poor at best, but he would set matters straight using his authority when he could. He read the letter again then laid it down and reached for his telephone.

15. NEAR AND YET SO FAR

It was November and the Russian weather was bitter cold and wet with sleet building up amongst the squalls of heavy rain. Nadya hurried home from the academy with her violin case beneath her coat for added protection from the driving rain. She climbed the stairs to her apartment thinking about seeing Yuri tonight. Her pulse still raced every time she thought of him especially how he had kissed her for the first time last night. She opened the door and went in to find her mother slumped on the sofa. She hurried over to her. 'Mama?'

Maya opened her eyes which were puffed and red. 'Oh Nadya. I must have fallen asleep.'

'Is Papa home yet?'

'No dear, he had to attend another of those awful meetings after work.'

'Are Vadim and his family out as well?'

Maya stiffened still unable to call their guest by his first name, 'Mr Aminov and his family are out looking for work I believe.' Nadya looked around the apartment as her mother spoke, thinking how different it was now full of alien belongings of another family. They had done their best to keep things in their two rooms but it was inevitable that space would be at a premium. It was good that she had Yuri to talk to about it knowing her parents were struggling to cope; especially her mother.

'Mama I need to tell you something.' Her mother sat a little straighter. 'I'm seeing someone. He's really nice.'

'Oh does he go to the academy? What does he play dear?'

'No he isn't from the academy. Why should that make any difference anyway?'

Maya sniffled into her lace handkerchief. 'Because boys who go to the Acadamy are educated Nadya.'

'Educated? Yuri is worth ten of them.'

'You're talking about the peasant boy from the meeting again? Nadya! How could you be so insensitive after all they've put us through!'

Nadya replied testily, 'It was the authorities not them that put us all in this predicament.'

'Why must you make everything so difficult? What's wrong with good working class boys?'

'I'm sorry Mama but I will continue seeing him. I'm going to Inber's and will probably stay over there. I'm sorry you feel this way because I really care for him. Goodnight Mama.'

She hurried out and down the stairs back into the street where heavy snow flakes were replacing the rain, some flakes beginning to settle on the tops of walls and window sills.

She went to her friend Inber's flat and left her violin there asking if she could stay the night. She hurried off to the station and looked anxiously for the train. At last the train pulled in —it's smoke and steam mingling with the snow — and people stepped down to the platform pulling up their collars as they scurried against the cold. She moved closer to the platform looking out for Yuri and then there he was. She ran to him and threw her arms around him snuffling into his neck to smell his earthy clean smell. They walked back off the platform hand in hand enjoying each other without speaking until well clear of the station.

She looked him up and down noting his fresh shirt beneath his linen coat. He had freshly ironed trousers and his felt boots had been scrubbed. She laughed and said, 'Come on!'

He yelled as she dragged him along, 'Where are we going?'

'You'll see!' He had no difficulty keeping up with her and in the end they were racing to the end of a street leaving mushy footprints in the light frosting of snow. He stopped and waited for her and laughed, 'Now where?'

She grabbed his hand. 'This way, come on!' They headed back toward Inber's flat.

As they ran up the concrete stairs to the flat he shouted, 'Who lives here?' She stopped, took out a key and went inside. He followed her. 'Who's is this?'

'It's my friend Inber's. It's very tiny but she likes it. She said we could have it this evening; just the two of us.'

Yuri took off his coat looking around at the strangeness of another person's home. 'And she doesn't mind?'

'She has a boyfriend and spends a lot of time at his place. So...'

She sat down on the sofa and patted the seat beside her flashing her eyes at him. He jumped over the back of the sofa beside her. She snuggled up to him. 'I tried to tell my mother about you but she wouldn't listen. She thinks I should meet a boy from the academy. Pah! Don't think so. There's nobody there like you anyway.' She squeezed his arm and snuggled closer.

Yuri said, 'I told my mother but she has so many worries about my younger brother and sister and how we are so cramped up in her sister's home, I don't think she really heard. She seems distant sometimes. I will try again, I promise.' He turned to face her and brought her close to him then kissed her deeply getting totally lost in the experience. He pulled away a little and smelt her neck then sighed. She brought his mouth back to hers and they kissed again slowly. She pulled his hat off and flung it across the room laughing within the kiss then ran her hand through his long hair to the back of his neck. She marvelled at how strong the muscles felt there and in his shoulders as she ran her hand into the front of his shirt and entwined her fingers in the hair of his chest. Their breathing became heavier as he responded running his hand through her hair and down her neck to her shoulder then further down and rested it on her left breast. She sighed and he unbuttoned her blouse then slipped his hand inside and felt her brassier where he slipped his hand beneath and touched her nipple. She gasped and kissed him passionately. Her hands explored his chest touching his nipples and enjoying the feel of the hair on his chest.

Their passion was growing fast as he pulled her bra up and felt the weight of her breast. It was his time to gasp and he pulled away from her a little and looked into her deep brown eyes. 'Nadya you are so beautiful.'

She sighed deeply. 'So are you. My God you do something to me!'

He drew back a little more. 'I don't want to do anything we might regret. I respect you too much for that. Also, I love you and nothing can change that. I don't care if we wait. Just being with you is enough.'

She laughed. 'Really? I think you are a liar Yuri Kazakof. I think you desperately want to make love to me!'

'He laughed with her. 'Ok so yes I do.'

She kissed him again. 'And we will make love and it will be perfect. But not yet. We must give it time ok?'

'Yes,' he said then pounced on her saying, 'But we could get pretty close don't you think?'

She screamed with delight as he nuzzled her breast.

Yuri got back to the farm full of his evening with Nadya. Even the constant background sadness about his father could not take away how exhilarated he felt. Nadya was something he had never experienced before; like a force of nature overwhelming him with her voice, her eyes, her laughter, her body... As he opened the door Nika stood from the kitchen table and took his arm, an anxious look on her face. 'Yuri. I'm so glad you're here.'

'Why what's happened?'

Nika looked concerned. 'It's your mother Yuri. She collapsed not long after you'd gone. I think it must be the stress of everything that's happened. Your brother and sister were arguing and fighting. She screamed at them. That's not how she is.'

'Where is she now?'

Nika stroked his arm. 'She's in bed. The children are fine; I put them to bed a little while ago. I think she just needs rest Yuri,' she looked deep into his eyes. 'I think you need to be here, I don't think she has the strength to carry on at the moment, what with your Father and the farm.'

'Yuri sighed. 'I understand. I'll go and talk to her.'

'Leave it till the morning. She needs to sleep.'

The next morning he took his mother a cup of tea and sat on the edge of the bed. 'How are you today Mama?'

She smiled wanly. 'I feel so weak. It's not like me Yuri, I don't understand it. Nika thinks it's the stress of everything.' Yuri nodded. She went on, 'and how are you?'

'He smiled. 'I have met the girl I told you about again.'

She looked confused. 'A girl? I don't remember dear, sorry.'

'You've had a lot to worry about Mama.'

'Tell me again.'

He said shyly. 'She is wonderful Mama. I want to marry her!'

She smiled and took his hand, 'So where does she live?'

'In Leningrad.'

'That's a long way away.'

'I can get there by train, if I have the money.' He looked at her and realised how exhausted she was. 'Get some rest Mama.'

'I can't I have the children to...'

'I'll look after them. You need to rest.'

He got his younger brother and sister up and washed, making sure they ate some porridge for their breakfast. The local school had accepted them and they were making new friends. When they were sent off he sat down and thought about the situation. How could he make the journey to Leningrad without any money and how could he leave his mother at the moment not being able to cope? He felt a mixture of emotions flood him as he realised without his father he now had to be the man of the house. He had no choice; he would have to write to Nadya and explain the situation to her.

With a heavy heart he sat down and wrote.

Nadya sat looking out of the window with Yuri's letter in her hand. She was devasted that just as they were getting close he was taken away from her. She had thought about him every moment of every day looking forward to seeing him, to be with him, to feel him close to her. As far as she was concerned he was the man for her and everything else would sort itself out; but then this! She didn't blame him; she just felt thwarted, as if they were being kept apart by some unknown force. All she could hope for was that his mother would get better and he could come back to her.

17. SIDOROV WRIGGLES FREE

Chupin slammed his telephone down into its cradle and swore under his breath as he took out a cigarette and lit it blowing a cloud of swirling smoke toward the ceiling. It did little to appease his anger. It seemed that Sidorov was out to make a name for himself and considered torture something to enjoy; as opposed to a necessity. (Chupin had been around long enough to know that torture was part of the system's tools to get "enemies of the people" to confess; innocent or otherwise.) Chupin would not be part of that but he knew to what lengths Stalin would go to maintain control. Now he has to move Sidorov somewhere else and find another replacement for the District Secretary. He knocked the ash off his cigarette aggressively. General Sidorov had made it clear his son had done nothing wrong; simply over enthusiasm, but did reluctantly accept Chupin's advice to move him from that post because tensions were running high and it was imperative to get the Five Year Plan rolling successfully.

He had heard the Commissar for the south district in Leningrad was very ill; perhaps he could put Sidorov there? At least he would not be able to stir up the peasants as he had done so far. Chupin would not express his views openly but he believed the collectivisation to be a folly that would not be achieved without bloodshed.

Sidorov entered the offices of Party Secretary Chupin and waited outside his door for the customary 'come'. He entered to find Chupin standing with his back to the room looking out of the window to the streets below, a cloud of smoke hanging over his head. Sidorov entered and waited to be invited to sit at the desk. Chupin said without turning round, 'Remain standing.'

Sidorov was puzzled. He tentatively said, 'Good morning Sir.'

Chupin whirled round, his cigarette carving a swirl of smoke in the air behind it. 'Is it?'

Sidorov was becoming uncomfortable. 'I...'

Chupin sat and stubbed out his cigarette. He looked up at Sidorov. 'Do you know why I have told you to report here?'

'No Sir.'

Chupin picked up the letter from Yuri and waved it at him with a questioning look.

Sidorov shrugged. 'I don't understand Sir.'

'Then let me explain. This is a letter of complaint from a peasant stating that his father was sent to the Gulag on false evidence signed by a peasant who had been beaten and threatened his family would be thrown out of their home if he didn't do so.' He threw the letter down on the table.

Sidorov blushed. 'I have interrogated many enemies of the people Sir, you instructed me to make sure the peasants didn't cause trouble.'

'But I didn't instruct you to act illegally. God knows I have enough to deal with without having to clear up your mess. So you are going to be transferred to Leningrad and take up the position of Chief of Security. I want you in post within the next five days. If it was up to me I would have you sent to the Gulag, but it isn't. Now go away.' He picked up another letter and began reading.

Sidorov saluted and left. Outside he smiled to himself. Leningrad! Excellent!

18. A HOMECOMING

May 1930

Nine months had passed since Yuri wrote to Chupin. During that
time he had received a letter from him stating that his father
would be released and they could have their home back. With a
mixture of relief about their farm but sadness not knowing
when, or if, his father would return he drove the horses and
cart away from the farm of his Aunt and Uncle back to their
own. As he drove he thought about how much he missed Nadya;
the only contact being by letter which he kept close to him
and read everyday. How he longed for her!

As they entered their village it became clear a lot had
happened; many houses had been burnt down and people no longer
stood around talking. There was an air of gloom about the
place and a general feeling of neglect; beneath that he felt
suspicion and fear on people's faces as they watched the cart
pass, one or two guardedly acknowledging them. He stopped the
horse outside their farm and jumped down eagerly saying to his
mother who sat beside him, 'Wait here till I know it's safe
Mama.' He went to the door and found it was not locked. He
went inside and felt a sense of relief and warmth to be back
in it despite the neglect it showed. He hurried out and waved
to his mother who clambered slowly down and brought the two
children with her.

She sighed as she entered the kitchen and blew dust off the
old wooden table. 'Needs a good clean.' She sat down. 'But its
home Yuri.' A shadow crossed the doorway and a head poked
round. A voice said, 'I saw the cart and thought I'd better
check. I've been keeping an eye on it you see. Didn't know if
you would come back but...'

Yena turned in shock. 'Vladimir! Thank you.' She glanced to
Yuri, 'Wasn't that kind?'

The children ran through the house excitedly bustling past
Yuri as he put out his hand, 'Thanks. The village looks
different.'

Vladimir sat at the table and ran his hands through his
hair. He looked awkward. 'After...you know, I thought the
least I could do was keep an eye on your farm. Yes. A lot has
happened, just like with your father going to the Gulag. That
swine Sidorov has set fire to houses to drive folk out and a
group of youths have set up camp in the forest thinking they
are bandits. Pah, no idea. Every now and then they set a fire

or throw bricks at the police. Quite a few have gone to the city but I don't know how they've got on.'

Yuri gritted his teeth. 'Sidorov. Is he still here?'

'No he's been transferred somewhere else. There is a new man now who seems more human.'

Yuri sat at the table. 'Looks like our letter to the Party Secretary had some effect then. Hope they sent him to the Gulag.'

'Have you heard from your father?'

Yuri picked at the table as his father used to do. 'No. All I know is he will be released.'

'Then we must hope. Is there anything I can help with?'

'Thank you Vladimir, you've done enough already. No we will be fine once everything is unloaded.'

'I feared you were going to kill me when you came to my house that day. I'll go home and tell Anna you are back.' He hesitated struggling with something, 'do you think he will forgive me Yuri?'

Yuri stood and offered his hand again. 'There's nothing to forgive. I've seen what a monster Sidorov is.'

Vladimir stood and took his hand. 'Thank you. I'll go and see if we can find something for you to eat after your journey.' He hurried out.

A few weeks after the family had moved back in, Yuri was making preparations for sowing a crop on their modest piece of land. He was walking across the yard as a stooped figure appeared at the gate and stood as if waiting for permission to enter. Yuri looked for a moment then realised it was his father. He sprinted to him and threw his arms around him. 'Papa!'

Ivan was carrying a bag which he gripped tightly not responding to Yuri's embrace although Yuri was so excited he hardly noticed. 'Come! Come and surprise Mama!' He pulled him by the arm and dragged him joyfully into the kitchen. 'Mama! Look who's here!'

Yena hurried down the stairs and stopped at the sight before her as she put her hand to her mouth in shock. 'Ivan?' She ran to him and put her arms round him but he didn't respond continuing to grip his bag. She let him go and looked to Yuri. 'Take your Papa's bag Yuriso he can sit down. She pulled out his favourite chair and rubbed his shoulders as she said, 'I can't believe you're home! I'll make us a drink.' She bustled at the sink as Yuri went to take the bag. Ivan grunted and clung onto it as he sat down with it clasped in his lap. Yuri sat beside his father. Something was wrong but he couldn't understand what. 'Papa, it's wonderful to have you home. Was it a long journey?'

Ivan sat motionless staring straight ahead. Yena looked back at them and noticed it as well. 'Yuri! Don't hassle your father, let him catch his breath.' Yuri sat back not knowing what to do or say.

Georgi and Yelena burst in Georgi shouting with glee, Mama we found...'He stopped in mid sentence as he noticed the figure at the table. The two children suddenly became awkward shifting their eyes from Yuri to Ivan waiting for him to show them what to do. Ivan did not respond to them.

Yuri laughed nervously. 'Hey don't you recognise your Papa?!' Both children sidled closer to Yuri sensing something was different. 'Your Papa's very tired from a long train journey, let him get his breath. Ok?' They both nodded and continued to stare.

Yelena asked quietly as she stared at her father, 'Can we go out and play now?' Yuri nodded and they walked out quietly. Yuri and his mother exchanged glances. Ivan did not move; it was as if he was waiting for instructions. Yuri looked closer at his father and noticed he was thin, very thin and his eyes — which usually sparkled with fun and mischief — were dull, unfocused. His hair was grey now and his face had new tight lines around his eyes. He had stubble and his skin was grey with the remains of sores.

He said gently, 'Papa? You're home now. You're safe.'

Ivan turned his head slowly as if noticing his son for the first time. When he spoke it was softly, almost like a whisper. 'Safe?' He looked around the kitchen and said, 'Safe. Like home?'

Yena put down their drinks down and sat at the table. 'Ivan? What's wrong?'

He slowly turned to the new voice. 'Safe?' A tear trickled down his cheek into the grey stubble.

She reached over and hugged him looking at Yuri over Ivan's shoulder. Her eyes were wet and fearful as she said gently, 'Yes you're safe now Ivan.' She closed her eyes and said softly, 'It was bad wasn't it?'

He nodded imperceptivity and silently began to sob. Yuri was shocked; he had never seen his father cry. He felt his own tears welling up feeling helpless as he looked at the broken man before him. He stood angrily and growled, 'Bastards!' He ran out and into the barn. Ivan gave a little shudder as he felt the violent outburst.

Yena held him tighter. 'Your son is angry at them for what they've done to you. You must rest and get your strength back.'

'He murmured, 'Rest. Sleep.'

She helped him to his feet and toward the stairs. 'Come on. Let's get you to bed.' He didn't resist as his eyes darted around him as if waiting for a threat. She realised he was filthy and probably lice ridden. 'Let's get you a nice warm bath.'

Outside, Yuri leant against a work bench deep in thought. He was shocked at the broken man his father had become. He recalled how strong he had always been — like a rock which the tribulations of life broke harmlessly against — always with an answer to a problem or a kind word of encouragement. Now he just sat and stared into the distance.

Later, he went back into the house and found his mother sitting at the table her hands clasped together, her face lined with worry, the two younger children sitting and watching her.

He sat besides her not knowing what to do or say. After a few minutes she said, 'Your father is very ill children.' To Yuri she said, 'He seems so distant and strange; almost like somebody else has come back in his place.'

Yuri laid his head on his arms at the table. 'Perhaps he's just very tired?'

'No. It's more than that. Something bad has happened to him. We've just got to give him time.'

Georgi put his head on his hands looking sideways up to his mother. 'Will Papa get better Mama?'

'Yes of course he will. He just needs some time. So that means you both have to behave and not worry him.'

Yelena said, 'Can I take him some soup Mama?'

'That would be very helpful Yelena.'

Yuri stood. 'I've got to get sowing while the weather is good. I'll make a start tomorrow. If Papa gets up I will take him to the field, perhaps that will help.'

'Yes it will. We just have to be patient. At least he is home now — thanks to you.'

He smiled. 'I couldn't just let him rot there. He'll be ok.' He hadn't said what he feared was wrong with his father but he was convinced he was right. Only time would tell.

The next day he gathered his equipment and a bag of seed then walked to the field looking up at glowering black clouds in the distance. He stopped and smelt the air confirming his fear that heavy rain was on its way. Now he had to decide whether to continue or wait. He sat down and watched the horizon as the clouds gathered.

Vladimir approached him and sat beside him. He chewed a piece of grass as he said, 'I've been watching them too. It feels cold for the time of year, too much rain already.'

Yuri nodded. 'The grounds still very wet.' They sat in silence for a few minutes watching the sky.

Yuri bit a finger nail. 'Papa is home.'

Vladimir picked a length of grass and chewed it. 'That's wonderful! How is he?'

'He's not right Vladimir. He's very quiet and doesn't talk. He's not my Papa.'

Vladimir spat out the grass and picked another piece which he began to chew. 'Despite what you say Yuri, I feel bad about what happened to your father, and it was because of me. I know I must speak to him but I'm scared he will hate me.'

Yuri turned to him. 'Sidorov is responsible for what happened to my father. Don't worry. I will make sure Papa understands before you see him.'

'When you were away things changed a lot in the village. That pig Sidorov sent many to the Gulag but there have been a few activists from the collective farm who believe what is happening is right and have burnt houses and attacked us. So now many farmers have hidden their grain and not handed it over but these people search our farms and if they find it they take it away. Now we don't have the proper seed to sow. Feelings are very high in the village. People are fearful of the collective farm peasants and resent them. I think it's only a matter of time before they openly start fighting. I've thought of going to the city but I've heard so many have died there.'

Yuri picked a piece of grass and said, 'What about the new District Secretary?'

'He seems a fair man but he has his orders. He knows if he doesn't push us to join he has to tax us. He told us we have to do our best, but what can I sow when they've taken it all?'

He noticed for the first time that Yuri had some seed. He asked, 'How have you got seed?'

'We hid some last year. I'm going to use that.'

'You know they will take everything from you — tax you so you have nothing left?'

Yuri spat. 'I don't care. This is our farm and I will sow, if the weather allows it.'

They both looked up at the clouds which were moving closer and growing darker.

Vladimir said, 'It was like this last year. Most of my crop died in the ground, water logged. We had to scratch around for food. I hope it doesn't happen again this year.' He stood. 'Take care Yuri, these are dangerous times.'

'I think you're right.' Yuri stood and gathered his equipment and took it back into the barn then went into the house. Large spatters of rain began to tap on the windows and a wind rustled across the yard.

He sat at the table and wrote a letter to Nadya telling her about his father and the bad weather delaying sowing. He longed to see her but he had to be there for his father. Although his mother was a little stronger, she was still weak and prone to losing her temper. He desperately wanted to hold Nadya but all he could do was pour his feeling out through his letter.

Over the summer the weather continued to thwart the farmers who doggedly continued with their crops. When Yuri should have been busily harvesting he was standing at the edge of their plot looking out at withered plants and heavy water soaked land. His father sat in a wheelchair beside him looking to the horizon, a blanket wrapped around his legs, his expression blank.

Yuri had grown used to it and accepted his fears were correct. He had seen it in a couple of fighters who hadn't known when to stop and suffered from too many blows to the head. Yuri knew his father had suffered brain damage from the beatings he must have received in the Gulag. He also knew it was Sidorov who had caused it and needed to pay for what he had done. Yuri sighed and said, 'It's bad again Papa.' He wheeled his father back to the house and inside to the kitchen. He went outside boiling with rage and punched the wooden barn door. That pig had ruined his father's life. Somehow, Yuri would make him pay dearly.

Gradually Ivan began to respond to their efforts to communicate with him but his speech was laboured and it seemed to take him a while to process answers to questions. The mischievous eyes were still dull; the joy gone. Any sudden noise would cause him to panic. He never spoke a word about the Gulag.

Yuri sighed at the ruined crop and wondered how they were to survive the winter with little grain and no money to buy food. He longed for Nadya and felt a recent letter in his pocket for comfort.

Only a little grain was harvested in August and villagers were becoming desperate for food as a famine took hold over large areas of the country. Yuri had secretly stored — in their pit near the barn — what little grain he had managed to grow. Yuri knew people were becoming desperate for food and hid it at night. He was sweeping the yard when a truck whined past heavily loaded with grain headed toward the city. He spat on the dusty ground and went inside. He knew they would be coming soon.

He walked into the village and saw a couple of friends near the well. They hardly noticed him as he went up to them. He sat on the well and picked at his hands.

One of the men said to him, 'So Yuri. You have much grain?'

Yuri had learnt that it was safest to keep to himself nowadays and say little. He replied, 'Not very much at all, the summer was shit wasn't it?'

They all nodded. Another said, 'I've hardly enough to get us through the winter. Did you see the lorry pass here a while ago loaded with grain?'

The first man nodded, 'It came past us. I've heard they're bringing secret police and soldiers to take it from us.'

Yuri grunted, 'Why? They like to tax us at the depot. Why come to our farms?'

'Because they don't intend to pay for it all. That bastard Stalin is exporting it.'

Yuri looked up. 'How do you know this?'

'My cousin works in administration in Moscow. He told me.'

Yuri stood up angrily. 'If they come for mine I'll shoot them.'

'They'll shoot you first.' Yuri looked at the faces of his friends and saw in their eyes desperation; and fear. He left and walked home.

He stopped in his yard and went to the covered secret store by the barn. He felt confident it wouldn't be found. He had been careful to leave enough out for them to see and hoped they would go away.

He went inside and Yena was making some soup. She turned as he entered. 'Your father seemed better this morning, he managed to dress himself.'

Yuri kissed her cheek tiredly. 'That's good. Where is he now?'

'He's gone for a walk down the road, not too far.'

'There's talk about soldiers coming for our grain.'

She stopped stirring and turned to him. 'Yuri. We don't know that's the case. Perhaps they will leave us alone.'

He sat and picked at the table. 'Like last year? We were starving then as well. They still took it and taxed us though. We've had another bad harvest, I don't know how we are going to get through the winter.'

'We did last year and we will this. I've been storing as many fruits from the summer that I could and made them into jams. We have a few vegetables from our garden as well.'

Yuri looked out of the window; he suddenly felt tired. Thoughts of Nadya came as always to haunt him. He shuddered.

'They won't steal any from the garden this year Mama. I'm going to sit up at night with the rifle.'

He opened the door and looked outside thinking he heard something. 'I can hear a lorry.' He went to grab his rifle but Yena had got to it first. She clasped it firmly to her body. He stormed outside and stood in the yard defiantly.

A lorry pulled in and four armed secret police got out. A tall thin man approached him and barked, 'You have grain?'

Yuri replied, 'Hardly enough to live off for the winter.'

'Where is it?'

Yuri said evenly, 'Why do you want to know?'

The man took out a pistol and drew nearer. 'Because we have been ordered to collect it. Don't make trouble now.'

Yuri pointed to the barn. 'What little we have is in there.'

The man looked inside and returned. 'That's all you've got?' Yuri nodded, his arms folded.

One of the others whispered to the thin man, 'He must have it hidden somewhere, like the others.'

The thin man studied Yuri for a moment. 'You look the sort to hide it.' He turned to the others, 'Search the farm.' He faced Yuri. 'I remember you from last year. You must be a rubbish farmer, you had little then as well.'

Yuri didn't rise to the bait. 'We've had poor weather. Did you notice the bodies lying around last winter in the streets?'

The thin man shrugged, 'Not my problem.'

'I bet if it was a relative you would see things differently?'

The thin man looked around at the farm. 'Why don't you join the collective like the others? At least they have enough to survive on. We don't have to take it from them because they're working for the state, whereas you comrade, are just looking after yourself.'

Yuri felt the bile rising as he clenched his fists hidden at his sides. 'And if you didn't have a gun I would knock the shit out of you.'

The thin man took a step back and brandished his pistol. 'You threaten me? A member of the NKVD? I could have you arrested for that.'

'Arrest me then. So what? At least I might get some food in a cell.'

The others returned empty handed. The thin man told them to take what there was in the barn. He held the pistol toward Yuri. 'Don't make any trouble now.'

Yuri smiled as he watched them load up the lorry with the few sacks from the barn.

The thin man said, 'We will find out if you have any hidden and we will come back and burn everything.'

'And I will be waiting for you.'

The man joined the others in the lorry and it reversed out.

Yuri went inside. 'They didn't find it.'

'How much do we have hidden Yuri?'

'If we are careful we might make it last but there won't be much. I don't think we will have enough to sow next year.'

Yena stroked his hair. 'You're a good boy Yuri. I know you do your best for us.'

'I'm going into the village Mama. Won't be long.' He kissed her and left.

In the village he looked around for his friend Boris who he spotted near to the store looking at the empty shelves. He tapped him on the shoulder.

Boris turned in surprise, 'Yuri! You want to be careful creeping up like that.'

Yuri laughed. 'Why?'

'Perhaps not you but someone smaller I would beat to the ground!'

'Of course...' Yuri kicked at a stone near his foot. 'I've had the goons round to take my grain.'

'They came to mine as well. Found my secret store the bastards. Somebody must have seen it and told them.'

Yuri spat on the ground. 'There are too many activists around here for my liking.'

Boris drew closer and whispered, 'I know one of them. Their farm is part of the collective. A couple of us are going to pay him a visit tonight.'

'Count me in. Bastards snitching on their own kind deserve what they get.'

Boris nodded. 'Meet us when it's dark. Let's see if we can talk some sense into him.'

That night Yuri met with his friends and they walked through the village to a farm a few hundred yards out. Boris knocked on the door and a young man opened it then immediately tried to shut it on them. All three bundled in. Yuri grabbed him by the collar and punched him in the belly. The man collapsed gasping for air on the floor.

Boris pulled him to his feet and said, 'We know it was you who told them where my secret store was, the same way you snitched on Erik. We are here to warn you if you pass anymore information to those pigs we will burn this place down. Do you understand?'

The young man nodded as he gasped for breath. 'I didn't want to tell them. They threatened me!'

Yuri hissed in his face, 'You're part of the collective and think you're better than us. Well think carefully. People are getting hungry. And we know you have stores of food.' He put his fist in the man's face. Do you want some of this?'

The man shook his head. Yuri released him and turned away in disgust.

19. DARKNESS FALLS

December 1932

In the city of Leningrad Nadya made her way home from the academy thinking about Yuri as she trudged through a thick layer of snow. His last letter was full of sadness and anger about his father's condition and the failed crop. She suspected matters were more serious than he was letting on from what she had heard about the failed crops last year and again this year. She was only too aware of the growing shortage of food in the shops; breadlines and queues growing daily. She had been following the desperate machinations of the Soviet to implement the Five Year Plan by listening to friends who had contacts telling her not to believe any of the propaganda pumped out by the authorities. Her views about peasants had undergone many changes since meeting Yuri and having a peasant family living in their home; her views of Party propaganda she now viewd more cynically.

She reached her apartment block and climbed the stairs. As she entered she found a letter on the floor which she snatched up and hurried into the bedroom. She sat on the bed and eagerly opened it. She read quickly, desperate to hear that he was coming to see her. Tears flooded as she read he has been refused permission to travel to the city because so many peasants were fleeing there. He said he was trying to get a passport which was now required for him to travel but it was illegal for peasants to have one. She could sense the anger in his writing and his frustration at not being able to see her. The front door opened and she hurriedly crammed the letter into her coat pocket.

She went into the lounge crowded with the other family's possessions as Vadim entered with his wife. He snatched his hat off and said apologetically, 'We are back too early? Should we...'

She went into the kitchen and put a pot onto boil as she said, 'No of course not. You must be thirsty?'

They both nodded. His wife said, 'We have walked a long way today for no work. I think we must try the factories again.'

Nadya smiled. 'It must be very hard for you both. How are the boys getting on? Any more luck?'

Vadim shrugged. 'There is just too many of us and too few jobs. We saw two people dead on the street this morning.'

Nadya gasped. 'That's awful.'

He sat down. 'Yes it is. We are doing everything we can to get out of here.'

Nadya poured the tea. 'I know you are. And please don't worry, it's not your fault.'

His wife said, 'I know your mother suffers so much. I don't know what to say to her.'

Nadya swept her hair back. 'My mother is not a very happy person. It's not you.'

Gustav bustled in. 'Nadya!' He nodded to Vadim and his wife. 'Oh what a dreadful, turgid meeting we've just had at work. Do you know every month we have to sit through an indoctrination meeting where we discuss any problems we have and listen to talks about how important it is for us all to look out for enemies of the people...'

'Papa, you didn't say anything?'

He fussed around with his bag. 'It's hard not to some times.'

'Well just be careful Papa. If as you say they are encouraging people to spy on each other...'

Vadim joined in, 'These are very bad times I think. And it will get worse I fear. If only we could find work...'

Gustav touched his shoulder. 'I know. We just have to keep calm. Now, where's that tea?'

That evening as Gustav sat in their bedroom with Maya and Nadya there was a loud bang on the door. Gustav hurriedly put on his slippers and in his dressing gown went to answer it but Vadim was already at the door. He opened it and three secret police stormed in. A tall thin man grabbed Vadim and said aggressively, 'You are Gustav Rheindhart?' Vadim shook his head. 'Show me your papers.' Vadim fumbled in his jacket pocket and handed them over. The policeman handed them back and turned to Gustav. 'You are Gustav Rheindhart?' Gustav nodded. The policeman barked, 'Come with us.' The other two grabbed him by his arms.

Gustav protested. 'But I've done nothing wrong!'

One of the other policemen said, 'Chief of security Sidorov has ordered your arrest. You were heard making comments that the party treats people unfairly. That makes you an enemy of the people.' To the others he said, 'Take him away.'

Maya cried out, 'Gustav! Your coat.' As the two men tussled him into the corridor the thin man turned to Maya. 'You are his wife?' She nodded weakly. Nadya joined her and took her arm. The man looked at Nadya. 'You are his daughter?' She nodded. 'Then you must both vacate the apartment immediately.'

Nadya gasped. 'But we have done nothing wrong!'

He said, 'You are relatives of a criminal. You are not entitled to be here. Pack your things and leave. Now.'

Vadim pleaded, 'Please don't do this. They are good, kind people.'

The policeman snapped, 'You are the tenant now. They have to leave.' To Maya he shouted, 'Get your belongings now and go.'

Nadya said angrily, 'And where are we supposed to go at this time of the night?'

He moved closer to her and sneered, 'Perhaps you would prefer a police cell?'

Nadya backed away from him and turned to her mother. 'We have to do as he says.' She took her mother into the bedroom and hurriedly packed two bags whilst her mother stood watching her in shock. Nadya had to quickly select essential items as the policeman shouted to them to hurry up. Vadim tried to intervene but was also threatened with arrest. Nadya put a coat and hat on her mother and put her own winter clothes on and with the two bags struggled into the lounge. Vadim and his wife stood with tears running down their faces helpless as they watched them hustled out of the door and into the snow covered street. Maya was in shock, unable to think or speak.

Nadya whispered, 'Come Mama. We'll go to Aunty Nina's in Vologda.' She took her mother by the hand and led her toward the station.

Yuri came in from the freezing weather stamping the snow from his boots. Ivan followed him in and stood waiting whilst Yuri took his father's hat and coat off him. 'Stamp your feet Papa.' Ivan stamped his feet vigorously. 'That's it. Sit down and I'll make us a drink.' Yuri took his own hat and coat off.

Ivan said slowly, 'I'm hungry.'

'Yuri said, 'I know, but we have little Papa. Your secret store of grain has served us well but we're running out.' Yena came into the kitchen and kissed Yuri on the cheek then Ivan.

She went to a pan and stirred. 'Those few potatoes are something anyway, even though it took me all day to find them.'

Georgi came in and smelt the boiling pot. 'What's for dinner Mama?'

'Potato soup.' He pulled a face and ran out of the room. She said as she stirred the pot, 'Yuri. We've got to find more food.'

Yuri went to her and put his arm round her. 'I know Mama. Leave it to me.' He went to his room and looked for his rifle. He took some bullets from a drawer and stuffed them in his pockets then put the rifle underneath his blanket. He went back downstairs. Yena was sitting with Ivan talking to him holding his hands as she did.

Yuri sat at the table and said quietly, 'Mama, I know you are tired but I need to go away for a day to get some food. Don't worry about me, just look after Papa.'

Yena looked exhausted both from losing weight and trying to deal with Ivan's problems. 'Just be careful Yuri. Please?'

'I will Mama.' He went to a cupboard and took a piece of bread which he wrapped in brown paper and put on the table while he put on his coat and stuffed the bread in his pocket. He ran upstairs and took his rifle and bullets which he stuffed in another pocket and returned downstairs with the gun concealed beneath his coat. He stopped and kissed his parents then went out into the snow and darkness. At the gate he stopped to collect his thoughts then headed down the road in the direction of the collective farms.

He trudged slowly through the snow conserving his energy thinking about Nadya. Would he ever see her again? He couldn't get into the city because as a peasant he was not allowed a passport despite pleading with the District Secretary. It seemed everything was against them being together and yet he could not give up hope. Every day he had to be a parent to his brother and sister because his mother would sometimes be too weak to get out of bed and he had to look after his father because he was unable to do so himself anymore. Anger boiled within him as he thought of the evil system that had destroyed the man he respected more than anyone. The system that arrived in the night and took away any grain the family had, that made it illegal to eat your own produce because it was considered "state property". Well, he had made a decision. He was not going to see his family starve to death like many in the village were doing.

He turned off the road onto a track and headed toward the collective farms where he knew there was a little food. If he was careful he hoped to get enough for a few days at least. He also hoped he didn't have to fight for it, because he knew he would.

As he drew nearer he kept close to the ground, his rifle ready if he needed it. He knew from a previous visit to check the area that there was an outhouse where vegetables were stored and with the weather as bad as it was he hoped the farmers there would not be too vigilant. He crept through the snow on his belly toward the store and reached it with no problems. He tested the door and found it was locked. He took out an iron bar and forced the lock as carefully as he could. It came free with a loud crack and he froze waiting to hear a door open and shouts; but nothing followed. He opened the door and filled a sack with as many vegetables as he could then crept out back to the track, where he stood and ran as fast as he could.

The next day he received a letter which he excitedly tore open. He sat at the old wooden table and read it then laid it down. His mother came into the kitchen and sat beside him. 'Bad news?'

He replied in a monotone, 'Nadya's father was arrested and taken away. Nadya and her mother were evicted and went to live with her mother's sister. Her mother died. The authorites were tipped off and Nadya was arrested and sent to the Gulag because they said she was a relative of a criminal. She got a friend of the family to write and post this letter.' He laid his head on his arms. 'She's gone Mama. I can't believe it after so much.'

His mother put her arm around him. There was nothing she could say.

After being arrested and interrogated Nadya was transferred to the police building to wait being shipped to a prison camp. The next morning she was transferred with other women and men to a railway carriage and bundled inside the cramped confines; the only light that which spilled through cracks in the wooden sides. It seemed an eternity as the train remained stationary until the large door slid open again and a handful of bread was thrown in.

In the darkness a scuffle immediately broke out as men and women fought for the meagre food on the filthy floor as the doors slammed shut. Nadya squeezed herself tighter to the carriage wall and clasped her knees trying to shut out the horror of the desperate grunts and shouts surrounding her.

From the light creeping through the cracks she watched helpless as a man punched an emaciated woman and grabbed a crust from her hand. She cried out and fell onto Nadya then rolled onto the floor. For a second their eyes met; the misery and fear she saw in them struck deep into Nadya's soul. The woman pushed herself away and vanished into the darkness whimpering. The scrapping died down and the strongest kept their prize pieces of crust closely guarded as they frantically chewed, their eyes darting about warily, like wild animals. Nadya listened in horror to the grunts and whimpers of her fellow prisoners wishing it was just a terrible dream from which she would awake.

As her eyes grew accustomed to the darkness — save from chinks of light coming through the gaps in the doors — Nadya watched the others in the train carriage. As she looked around she saw some were dressed in night clothes, others in coats or suits. She realised they were still in the clothes they had worn when arrested, creating a bizarre, surreal tableau. She thought back to the farce of her arrest and questioning, the foregone conclusion she was guilty — of what she still didn't know — and the inhumane way she was treated. Although not heavily beaten, it was enough to leave sore patches and deep bruises on her thighs and back.

Despite her aches and pains, the monotony of the train lulled her into a fitful sleep from which she was abruptly awoken by movement and the shuffling of feet near to her. Two men were dragging the lifeless body of the woman she had exchanged eye contact with earlier over to the door. Once, Nadya would have been shocked to her core, but now she simply drifted off to sleep again.

After a few more hours the clank of couplings indicated the train was slowing down and in the distance she could hear the chuffing of the steam engine as it ground to a halt. The door slid open and a guard looked in then stood back as the two men removed the coat from the dead woman and pushed the body out. As the door slid shut again, a wave of cold air rushed into the carriage. Nadya caught a glimpse of trees and fields in the distance covered in snow. She fought down a growing panic and the desire to throw herself out into the air and make a run for it. With despair she stared as the heavy door slammed shut, wondering how she was going to survive this hell, how much her life had changed in such a short time and how her whole world had become a hellish darkness haunting every waking minute. She shuddered as soldiers walked the length of the train banging to wooden sides to check for broken boards.

Eventually — after drifting in and out of a light sleep — she awoke with a start as the train jolted and began to slow down. She was desperately hungry and hoped it would be another food stop. She knew then she had to make an effort; everybody in that carriage was out for themselves. If she continued to remain passive she would die.

Another half hour passed before the door slid open again and a handful of bread was thrown in. This time Nadya leapt up and tried to grab whatever she could. Bodies crashed into her pushing in all directions as she fought to grab the meagre pieces of bread scattered on the floor. Joyfully she felt a piece of bread in her right hand and pushed her way back to her position at the rear of the carriage where she jealously guarded her prize and hungrily stuffed the stale crust into her mouth. As she chewed she thought ruefully that she was no better than the others now. In the space of a few hours she had been reduced to fighting like an animal for scraps of food.

She was too tired to examine the philosophical meaning of it all and anyway, what did it matter? She just knew she had to stay alive as long as she could, other than that she had no idea what her life meant anymore. She drifted off into a fitful sleep again listening to the monotonous sound of the wheels as they ran over the miles of track. Her mouth was dry; her lips cracked her whole body cramped by lack of food, all joining together with the aches from the beatings.

The sounds changed and she knew they were coming to a stop. Eventually the train ground to halt, the screeching wheels becoming silent. In the distance she could hear shouted commands getting louder until the door was slid back and three soldiers gruffly ordered them to get out gesturing aggressively with their guns. Nadya stood and tried to get some feeling back into her legs as they shuffled toward the open door. She struggled out and was pushed in the back by a soldier who told her to follow the others.

They shuffled in a line toward a lorry were they were instructed to climb in. She was squeezed in with a number of others and sat between two men on a narrow wooden bench. A canvas cover was pulled down over the back of the lorry plunging them into darkness. The lorry lurched forward, the wheels occasionally spinning to get a grip on the icy road. Nadya sat like an automaton waiting for whatever fate brought her. She was too tired to care.

The lorry bumped and jarred them for what seemed hours before it lurched to a stop. She could hear shouted commands outside as the canvass rear was lifted, the daylight temporarily blinding her before she saw heavy snow flakes falling and blowing into the lorry. Everybody was told to get out and she followed the two men she had been sitting beside as they were forced into a line and shuffled forward occasionally being prodded by the muzzle of a machine gun. She saw lines of prisoners joining them from the other carriages. She could just make out through the falling snow a row of wooden huts which they were being pushed toward. The vague outline of other buildings could just be made out in the distance.

She estimated there were at least sixty men and women with her as they shuffled through the snow along a rough path toward a row of huts adjacent to a larger wooden building set apart. As they approached the building she could make out two doors in the side of the building. The men were separated off toward the further door and the woman jostled inside the nearest. Once inside they entered a long narrow corridor lined with men in prison uniforms. These men were the privelaged ones; "trustees" who had snitched on their fellows to obtain more freedom.

Nadya looked for a way out but there was none; she had no option but to follow the other women as they fearfully ran the gauntlet of the men waiting to look them over. She saw a girl — no more than sixteen years old — pulled to one side by a man who then took her away through a door. The girl looked terrified and meekly followed him. This was repeated with two other women before Nadya was faced with a leering elderly man who grabbed her feeling her breasts and sniffing her. Nadya pulled away in disgust.

He sneered, 'You might regret that. I could get you privaleges.'

A guard shouted for her to keep moving and she was directed into a room. She and a few others were then told to strip by three guards who shut the door behind them. Nadya removed her clothes and they were snatched from her and thrown onto a heap with the others, then they were jostled into a wet area where they were told to get in large dirty and slippery baths full of cold scummy water. The guards watched them with amusement making lewd comments.

After a few minutes she was told to get out and line up for her hair to be cut — with what she could see were not only blunt but filthy clippers. She felt violated with no way of defending herself. She lined up with the others again and took the drab prison clothes thrust at her by a guard. They were marched down a damp dingy corridor and herded into cells with wet floors, mould on the walls, and nowhere to sit other than the floor. Nadya recoiled at the intimacy of the situation hating the close body contact. She sat and shivered for what felt like an eternity, not realising she had dropped off a number of times. There were no windows in the cell and it was stuffy despite the damp.

The door opened and they were told to line up in the corridor. She could hardly move her legs which were numb and her arms ached as she marched down the corridor with the others into a large eating area. It was silent apart from the shuffling of feet and clanking of metal ladles on metal boilers. She followed the line as it snaked toward a large boiler where steaming food was being ladled out to each person. Nadya began to panic; she had no bowl, knife or spoon. Should they have given her one? As she looked about her she realised they were all empty handed.

She looked ahead along the line and saw women holding out their caps, or a piece of cloth or the flap of their jacket; into or onto which something was being ladled. She snatched off her hat and when it was her turn held it out to be filled with a foul smelling fish soup. She followed the others to rough wooden benches and sat with her hat in front of her watching what the others did. She knew she had to eat and made an effort, spilling most of it down her front. Trying not to appear obvious she looked around and noticed a woman sitting next to her. She was thin and dirty with a shaved head, bent over her bowl and eating with a metal spoon. She held the bowl protectively, occasionally loking around at the others but keeping to her self.

   Nadya turned to her and said,'Excuse me?'

   The woman looked up and Nadya instantly regretted interrupting her as she was met with a face etched with contempt as the woman spat, 'Leave me alone. And stop looking at my bowl or I'll break your skinny neck.' She went back to eating.

   Nadya felt totally out of her depth as she looked around at the assortment of men and woman at the long wooden bench. A woman the other side of Nadya nudged her arm. She too wore prison uniform. Nadya turned to face her and with relief was met with a grim smile. 'Don't worry about her, just keep out of her way and don't touch her bowl or she'll kill you.'

   Nadya grimaced wondering how somebody could be so attached to a bowl.

   The woman said, 'You'll find out soon enough. It's best not to have any belongings then they can't be stolen. If you're lucky enough to find a bowl then keep it hidden. Look out for somebody on their last legs and snatch it if you can.'

   'Is this the Gulag?'

The woman ate a spoonful of soup. 'The Gulag means all the prison system. This is a transit camp. You might hit half a dozen of these before you get to your destination.'

After a few minutes a guard bellowed for them to line up again and they marched outside into the freezing air and snow to trudge back to the cells. Nadya was beginning to see that all she could do was take one minute at a time. Perhaps eventually it would be one day at a time. She had survived this one. Tomorrow was another day. She felt her leg itch and discovered a tiny red bite. Nadya didn't think she would be able to go on for long like this. Her life seemed to be at an end.

20. THE HAMMER FALLS

December 1931

It was late December and the winter had taken hold. Many people in Yuri's village had died of starvation; some in their homes others in the fields or beside the road. People were getting angry and riots were becoming common place in the towns. Yuri did what he could to stir villagers against joining collective farms by holding secret meetings and attacking farmers who had joined the system.

As Chief of Security in Leningrad, Sidorov was called to supply assistance by the District Secretary who was trapped in his office by the crowd and terrified after hearing about a riot in Stetzin. Yuri was with two friends amongst the crowd outside the District Secretary's building when they heard the roar of engines. Sidorov arrived in an armoured vehicle with a brigade of soldiers and told them to drive through the crowd, narrowly missing a few peasants slow to get out of the way. Yuri turned to see what the fuss was as the vehicles pulled up outside the district offices and Sidorov, surrounded by armed Secret Police, ran up the steps of the building. The jeers and boos from the crowd didn't bother him; after all he had the army with him and the authority from Stalin to do whatever it took to continue with the collectivisation. He held up his hand for silence and eventually the crowd quietened.

He shouted, 'This must stop! We are heavily armed, your weapons are nothing compared to ours. I know who the ring leaders are and they are to be arrested. Anyone who offers resistance will be shot. Do I make myself clear?'

A sea of angry faces met his gaze. He pointed to Yuri and his friends as he yelled to the guards, 'Arrest them.' The soldiers surged through the crowd toward them as the three tried to escape. A shot rang out and one of Yuri's friends fell to the ground. Hands roughly grabbed Yuri and he was dragged away with the other man.

At the NKVD building Yuri was thrown into a cell where he sat in the dark for what he felt must have been a few hours — he had lost track of time. Far away in another part of the building he could hear screams. He shuddered, waiting for his turn. Eventually the door was opened and two guards dragged him out to the interrogation room which he recognised from before. At the table sat Sidorov; smug, reading a file which he closed as Yuri was put in the chair opposite. Tamnsky sat behind Yuri ready for any trouble.

Sidorov sat back and lit a cigarette with his gold lighter and studied his prisoner. 'You are trouble just like your father. And look where it got him? Why do you people do it? Collectivisation will go ahead whatever you do, why not accept it; at least you would have some food.' He smiled but is eyes were blank holes of evil. 'Now what am I going to do with you? Your friend thought he was brave but in the end he told us all we need to know about your pathetic resistance group. Mind you, he did take some persuading but a few broken fingers — minus their nails first of course — had him singing like a canary. So you see, he saved you from a lot of pain. You should be grateful to him. But anyway, here we are again and this time I just want you to sign this.' He pushed a sheet of paper across the desk, 'then we can get on with business.'

Yuri glared at him with ill concealed venum.

'Cat got your tongue?' He nudged the sheet of paper a little closer.

Yuri spat on the floor and shook his head. Sidorov nodded to Tamnsky who came to the side of Yuri and punched him hard on the side of his face knocking him off balance. Yuri growled, 'Let's see you do that without my hands tied.' Another blow knocked him off the chair. He struggled back up.

Sidorov soothed, 'Now you see we what we have to do? All I need is your signature admitting your guilt and willingness to take part in our rehabilitation programme.'

Yuri sneered. 'In the Gulag of course.'

'Why of course, where else? So you see it makes no difference to you now, you're going there for twenty five years; plenty of time to reflect on your subversive behaviour. As of course did your father before he was saved by that idiot Chupin. But of course you know all about that because you sent the letter didn't you? That wasn't a very nice thing to do. But anyway, we need your signature and will get it. So...?'

Yuri sighed and sat forward. 'I'm going to the Gulag so what's the point of a signature?'

Sidorov got up and walked round to stand behind Yuri. He put his leather clad gloves on Yuri's shoulders and whispered in his ear, 'Please continue to refuse. I quite look forward to making you beg to sign it. And,' he squeezed his shoulders, 'you will beg; loudly.'

Yuri half turned and said, 'Go to hell.'

Sidorov chuckled and returned to his chair.

Yuri thought quickly. What was the point of putting himself through hell for the sake of a piece of paper? 'What would I be signing?'

'A simple confession.'

'I want to read it first.'

Sidorov moved back to his seat and held the paper out for Yuri to read. Yuri read it carefully but could not find anything that would incriminate any of his friends. 'Ok.'

Tamnsky released his hands and Yuri took the pen and signed.

Sidorov smiled. 'Pity I was looking forward to persuading you.' He nodded to Tamnsky to tie him up again and said, 'Of course now I have your signature it will prove very useful... 'Take him back to his cell.'

Yuri sat in the dim cell bitterly regretting his mistake. How stupid! He should have known a man like Sidorov had no morals. He felt desperately lonely as he thought about his mother having to look after the family on her own. How would they survive? Anger began to rise and he paced — as much as he was able — within his tiny cell. He had no hope and no future.

PART TWO

24. TEN YEARS LATER

22nd April 1941

Stalin, wary of Hitler's real intentions, used the Zeks as labour to to build defences against an invasion. One of the many camps used was ...where Yuri was imprisioned. And so,on a misty cold morning, Yuri was taken from the Gulag and crowded onto a train with hundreds of other prisoners bound for Leningrad. Yuri was now a hardened Zek with all the worldly knowledge about survival that he needed. His fighting skills had saved his life on a number of occasions and earned him respect from his fellow prisoners. Yuri had had ten years to develop a hatred of Sidorov so deep as to be an obsession; every day his mind filled with ways to find and kill him. When he wasn't plotting he would think of the distant memories of Nadya and his family but these he only allowed in at certain times otherwise he would have broken. Yuri had become adept at sealing off parts of his memory and decided he had to take one day at a time.

But his anger still boiled at a deep level like a volcano waiting for an opportunity to erupt with explosive violence. Having prepared himself for the full term of twenty five years he was now wrong footed by the sudden movement of so many prisoners to awaiting trains. Of course nobody was told why they were being moved but it was part of Gulag life that a prisoner would see perhaps fifty prisons.

He had developed a manner of slow movements (mostly because he was often weak from lack of food) and what was the rush anyway? He would only be moving from one part of the prison to another. Yuri was now thirty but looked ten years older. His hair had thinned and his skin was pale and covered with sores. His teeth were black and his nails brittle but what had not changed was the fierceness in his eyes. Yuri had become a man to fear; he had nothing to lose.

Over the days as Yuri travelled, he gradually learnt from guards that there was probably going to be trouble at the Polish border with the Germans. He knew they had invaded Poland with the help of the Soviet Union and supposed there was a breakdown between Hitler and Stalin. Yuri was furiously thinking what his options might be. His only priority was to get home but he had to be careful, if he went missing it would be the first place they would search.

What he needed was a body he could swap identities with to convince them he was dead. He was confident it wouldn't be long before he found one; men were dying every day and sometimes left where they dropped. All he had to do was swap their details with that of the dead man. He looked around the carriage to see if there was a possible victim and soon spotted one; Aleksei Kotchina, roughly his age and height. Yuri watched him with hooded eyes as the train rumbled endlessly on, looking for the signs he knew meant death was drawing near. He studied the man's emaciated face and thin limbs; he was well into malnutrition with dull eyes and skin stretched tight over his face, his lips permanently pulled back from protruding teeth with sores on his nose. Yuri had long ago forgotten what empathy felt like, seeing the man purely as a subject he required for his own ends. He tried to remember something about him but could only recall vague details about being a watch maker in Moscow. He moved closer to be ready if he should fall to the floor.

The train rumbled on until — after stops to transfer prisoners to other trains — they reached Leningrad. The train ground to a halt and they were escorted off and into waiting lorries under the watchful eye of armed guards. Yuri had stayed close to Aleksei and as soon as the man died and fell to the floor Yuri swapped their papers, quickly sticking the man's photograph into Yuri's papers now on the dead body.

Hopefully, as far as the system was concerned Yuri Kazakof was dead.

The lorry bounced and ground over rough roads until it pulled up with a squeal of rusty brakes to the usual sound of guards shouting instructions. The tarpaulin was pulled back and they were ordered out into single file. Yuri yawned, being used to the endless role calls and frisking. Eventually they were marched into a forest toward wooden huts beneath the trees. All around were felled trees and sawing equipment. So, Yuri thought, they were at a logging camp. He went along with the usual process of finding a cot and blanket and getting in the warm as quickly as possible. As he lay on his cot he began plotting his escape. Fortune had for once shone on him.

Yuri had been at the camp for a few days and had worked out his escape. He was in no hurry; patience was a virtue he had learnt in depth from the Gulag. The time had to be right to give him the maximum chance of getting away which he calculated would be in three days time when there would be no moon. He didn't know exactly where he was but once he was on a road he would be able to work it out.

The time came and he slipped out of his hut and on his belly to a hastily erected wire fence which he easily wriggled under. The guards were busy playing cards confident no Zek would risk inevitable death in the forest as he disappeared amongst the trees into the darkness. Yuri's body was used to working with few calories and he made steady progress eventually finding a familiar road which he followed out of sight in the trees. After a few hours he reached the town of Kirsk and knew he was about two hours away from his village. It was becoming daylight and he built himself a shelter made of tree branches to hide under until night fall. When it was dark he moved on, his mind focused on his goal; to find and kill Sidorov.

Yuri stood outside his home hesitating to go into the yard watching snowflakes settle on his coat. He felt little emotion; that was a luxury he had learnt to bury deep. He opened the gate and headed for the backdoor. It was dark and he could hardly see the door but his hand automatically found the door knob. He knocked on the door and waited. He heard movement inside and the door was opened by a tall thin young woman who looked quizzically at him and said, 'Can I help you?'

He smiled and replied, 'Don't you recognise me?'

She peered closer and saw his eyes, 'Yuri!'

She moved to him and hugged him pulling him inside. He was suddenly overcome by the familiar smells and sights around him of home and safety at last able to remember he was once human.

Yena came through to see what was going on and stopped, her hand to her mouth, 'Yuri? Is it you?' She looked closer, 'it is! Oh my, oh!' She burst into tears. Georgi came through to see who it was causing all the fuss and stopped in shock as he tried to recognise this stranger.

Yuri said to him, 'Hello Georgi. Remember me? Your big brother?'

Georgi studied him for a few seconds then said, 'I'm as big as you now!'

Yena grabbed Yuri and held him close whispering, 'You're safe you've come back.' She froze and pulled away from him suddenly confused. 'How are you here? You were sent away for twenty five years! We'd given up seeing you again and now... have you escaped?'

Yuri sat down weariy, realising he had forgotten how to speak without looking over his shoulder. 'I was moved to a logging camp and escaped with another man's papers. I left mine with him so they will think I'm dead.'

Georgi asked, 'Won't the other man tell?'

Yuri ran his hands over his face. 'No.' He looked up fearfully, 'Where is Papa?'

They all exchanged glances. Yena said, 'He's asleep. He sleeps a lot. But he is much better. You will see him in the morning. You must be hungry?'

He picked at the table. 'We are always hungry.' He eyes filled with tears. 'How have you survived with the famine?'

She sighed and he realised how old and tired she looked. 'It's been hard. Vladimir has helped a lot. He and your father spend a lot of time together. He has a relative in the collective who smuggle out bits and pieces when they can. He has been very generous. Many people in the village have starved Yuri. And now we hear we have invaded Poland with Hitler.'

Yuri said, 'We didn't hear much about the outside unless we had a rabbit from freedom.' Yena looked blankly at him. 'Sorry Mama. A new prisoner. They would tell us some of what was happening outside.'

There came a thump of boots upstairs and Yena looked to the ceiling. 'I think your father has woken up.' Yuri felt anxious as he watched the stairs, listening to heavy footsteps on the wooden treads. The shuffling figure of Ivan appeared then stopped at the foot of the stairs looking around at everyone watching him. Yena went to him and took his arm as he unsteadily moved toward Yuri. Yuri stood and waited, unsure how to be.

Ivan remained slightly stooped as he tried to understand what was happening. He studied Yuri and slowly reached out his hand and touched Yuri's roughly bearded face. He whispered, 'Is it you?'

'Yes Papa. It is me. Yuri.'

Ivan straightened and shook Yena's hand away. He looked into Yuri's eyes and they both knew a truth they could never tell anyone. Tears appeared and trickled down Ivan's cheek into his thick grey beard. With trembling fingers he traced his son's face then moved to him and put his arms around him. Yena watched with tears of her own, her two other children awed by the presence of their lost older brother. She busied herself making some soup from potatoes Vladimir had given them.

Later when they had eaten a meagre serving of thin soup Yena looked at Yuri as he cleaned the last vestige of soup from his dish with a small piece of bread. Ivan sat silently, his hands clasped in his lap.

Yena said, 'Will they come for you?'

'I don't think so. They're too busy getting supplies to the front. If they do I'll hide. I'm not going back to the Gulag.' He looked up to his father who nodded imperceptibly. Yuri said, 'I'm exhausted. I need to sleep.'

Yena took him to the communal bath house aware he was crawling with lice. Later, when he was in Georgi's room alone, Yuri looked around at the comforts he had forgotten, having been used to lice ridden cots and damp cells. His thoughts followed their usual path as he drifted to sleep; how he would find and kill Sidorov.

Downstairs Yena sat with Ivan and said, 'Your son is back.' Ivan looked up at her and nodded. She continued, 'You know what he has been through but you won't speak to us. Could you speak to him?'

Ivan's face darkened. He nodded imperceptibly, stood and clumped up the stairs to bed. She blew out the candle and touched the wooden table stroking it gently then followed her husband upstairs.

20. THE BULLY STRIKES

September 15th 1941

Yuri stood in their yard listening to the roll of gun fire in the distance. It was clearly why the number of carts passing through their village had increased every day. He approached an elderly man leading a horse and cart and walked alongside him. 'What's happening?'

The man grunted with effort and stopped. 'You don't know?'

Yuri said, 'We don't get much news but we can hear the guns.'

The Germans have doublecrossed us. We invade Poland with them and then they turn on us. We're going to Leningrad, it might be safer there.'

'Have you seen German soldiers?'

'No and I don't want to. I've heard what they're like. Some villages thought they might free us from our wonderful leader's insanity but they soon found out how cruel and evil they are. If I were you I'd do as we are and get out while you can. Once they reach Lake Lagoda Leningrad will be cut off.'

After consulting his mother, Yuri had called a family meeting. Yuri had talked his plans through with his father who as far Yuri felt — despite Ivan's brain damage — was still the head of the family. Inside their small wooden farm house, set amongst a collection of sheds and farming equipment, Yuri waited for his father to join them. Ivan scratched his thick grey beard as he joined them at the old wooden table. A candle burnt in the centre casting deep shadows around the small room making the windows thick black from the night outside. A wind had picked up and was carrying spots of rain that began tapping gently at the glass. The muffled rumble of guns rolled around in the distance and bounced off the clouds so that even inside they could be heard, carrying with them a terror it was hard to ignore.

With a weathered and gnarled hand Ivan scratched his walnut brown bald head as he held a glass of vodka in the other. The glass was chipped and dulled from age. He had regained many of his faculties but still had blackouts, memory loss and his speech was slurred. Yuri and his mother had developed an alliance to ensure Ivan felt the head of the family and that his impairment was not important. He knocked the vodka back and concentrated hard to get his words out. 'Motha plea! We have little time.'

Yena shrugged as she busily prepared bread, her hands covered in flour. 'Then go ahead, I can hear perfectly well from here. We will need all the food we can carry and it won't make itself.'

Ivan put his hands together in front of him on the old wooden table as he always did at family conferences although now he left most of the talking to Yuri. He clasped his hands tightly to reduce the tremor he had developed. Ivan rubbed his hand over the rough surface of the wooden table again finding a grain of salt in a crack which he put in his mouth. 'At firs ligh we hitch up the cart an make our way into the city.'

Yelena said, 'I hate the city! Why can't we stay here?'

Georgi, now almost a man said importantly, 'We don't have a choice.'

Still working at the stove Yena said, 'This is for the best. Georgi is right Yelena. Your father knows what he is doing. Don't argue. I know this is hard for you to understand, but now we must be strong. Trust your father.'

Yuri said, 'Papa is right, we have no choice. I'll prepare the cart and sort out supplies for the horse.'

Georgi stood. 'I'll help Yuri.'

Yuri smiled. 'Hey look at my little brother all grown up.'

It was evening as Yuri stood outside the modest farmhouse that he had been born in — his father and Grandfather before him — looking out toward the fires, smoke and flashes of artillery in the distance. The roar of the shells as they hurtled overhead toward the city shook the old farmhouse. He looked down at the wooden fence he had helped make years ago and gripped it in anger not wanting to believe what was happening. Their horse nearby that should have been grazing was pulling at its tether — spooked by the noise — and he went over to it stroking its muzzle and talking gently to it. 'They're not shooting at you.' He soothed. 'Not yet anyway.' He gave it a carrot and tickled its ear as he looked back at the fires burning in the distance, clouds of black smoke choking the already darkening sky.

Later, after everyone had gone to bed, Yuri poured himself a glass of vodka and looked around the room at the rough walls and empty shelves, highlighted by dancing shadows formed by candles standing on the worn wooden floor. His eyes rested on the sacks holding their belongings by the door as he mentally made an inventory of the equipment and tools he had to leave behind. It seemed heartless to leave them to rust and not be used to make things of beauty or to build a shed or repair a fence. He sighed as he knocked back the vodka grimacing as it bit the back of his throat. He couldn't believe he was leaving the farm which had been in the family for three generations.

He loved the rough wooden slats that made up the walls and the worn wooden floors scrubbed to within an inch of their lives by his mother... He smiled at her determination to keep up her "standards" as she referred to them. He lifted the bottle and tipped the last of the vodka into his glass. He stood and toasted the house, swaying slightly. He closed his eyes and listened to the room; the stories it told of his childhood; children laughing and crying, of family tragedies, triumphs, discussions and arguments.

Like his father, Yuri loved his country; the vagaries of the seasons, centuries of history, a lot of which was bloody, but feared along with his friends that the path set out by Stalin, and Lenin before him, promised much hardship clothed in the language of stoic propaganda. Yuri smiled as he remembered when he was five years old how his father would take him aside and sit down in the barn with him explaining patiently, 'Your mother means well, but don't be fooled, she's trying to wrap you in cotton wool and that won't save you from the terrors of the world that await. One day you will be a man and have to stand on your own. It's my job to give you that strength.'

    The little boy would look at his father in puzzled awe. 'Will Mama always do that Papa?'

    Yuri laughed remembering his father's sly grin as he would reply, 'If she had her way but...' he tapped his nose and pulled a sly face, 'your father knows a trick or two.'

    Yuri would climb onto his father's knee and smell his shirt; something that made him feel warm and safe. Then he would whisper in his father's ear so that his mother would not hear, 'Can I be strong like you Papa?'

Ivan would mask the pride he felt bursting from his chest by lifting him up in the air and swinging him around until he heard squeals of delight when he would throw him into the stacked straw behind him. At other times he would teach him how to fall and roll and put on a choke hold.

On one occasion Yena came into the barn as Yuri was midair on his flight into the hay. 'What on earth are you doing to that poor child!' She hurried toward the hay but stopped when Yuri's head appeared his eyes sparkling with joy laughing at the top of his lungs.

Ivan said defensively but with a mischievous twinkle, 'See he's fine! When he's older I'll try it off the roof...'

Yena poked him and said in disgust, 'You'll be the ruin of him, mark my words.' She scurried out holding her skirt up to avoid dragging straw into the house. Outside she smiled to herself and muttered, 'You old rogue...'

Yuri opened his eyes and surveyed the room smiling at the crooked shelf his father had never got around to fixing despite Yena's insistence that it be 'done immediately or else.' His eyes became moist as he knew he would not be able to pass the farm onto his own son one day. The memory of Nadya burned strongly as he thought of her and how it could have been. Yuri was a realist and knew the impending storm would not blow out overnight, and once they had left he knew that would be the end of a chapter in his family's life.

By first light Ivan, Yuri and Georgi were up and carrying supplies and family possessions out to the cart. Yena was checking around for anything they might have left *which could prove useful.* Ivan noticed what she was up to as she casually moved various items around putting the odd plate or cup to one side. He knew how much they meant to her.

Yuri and his father came into the kitchen. As Yuri followed him Yuri had noticed his father had recently developed a limp in his left leg. Ivan laughed as he said, 'So. Tweny minutes huh?'

Yuri laughed. 'Then I put him down with a right hook. And he stayed down.'

Ivan gave him an admiring look. 'Tha oaf always thought he was the strongest. You proved him wrong though.'

Yena tutted as she wrapped food in a piece of muslin. 'Why do you still talk about fighting? Anyone would think it was a good thing to do.'

Ivan said slowly, 'We don't know what to expect in the city Motha. These are bad times and good people sometimes do bad things. Feel proud tha your son can defend himself and his family with honour an strength. You migh not like it but our son is not afraid of any man.'

Georgi came in at the end of the conversation and added, 'And me Papa.'

Yuri laughed and clapped him on the back as he busied himself with more sacks but glowed with pride at the rare praise he received from his father... 'Of course, and you!'

With the cart loaded, horse in its livery, two cows tethered to the rear and the two teenagers buried amongst the family's possessions beneath a tarpaulin, Yuri sat beside his mother on the cart as Ivan set off pulling at a rope tied to the horse's bridle. Yuri watched as Ivan leaned into the rope, focused on what was before them never looking back at the family farm. Yuri watched fascinated by rain drops as they began to form on the shoulders of his father's rough cloth coat, trickling down his back. Yena, wrapped in as many clothes as she could put on whispered to Yuri, 'Your Papa is a strong man and proud, but you must insist on helping him. We have a long way to go.'

Yuri smiled at her. 'Don't worry, I'll look after him.'

She touched his shoulder. 'You're a good boy Yuri, I know you will. If only I was....'

Yuri put his arm around her shoulders. 'You have to think about yourself sometimes Mama.'

She shrugged. 'Just look after your father, don't mind me.' She looked ahead and whispered, 'I fear for Georgi, Yuri. He hasn't your strength since he had pneumonia.'

The wind brought thick grey clouds threatening snow as the temperature dropped; a harbinger that winter was approaching. In the distance the rumble of gunfire rolled around the skies and on the horizon black smoke drifted toward them. Yuri looked over his shoulder but their farm was already becoming a memory as it grew smaller being absorbed by the surrounding countryside. He turned back and looked ahead over the horse as it struggled with its heavy load, Ivan lending his weight to help it over the ruts as they moved slowly along the track toward Leningrad.

Flakes of snow began to drift past them in the wind, some settling on the horse's back and Ivan's felt hat and hide coat. The cart slowly lifted over humps in the track before it slid down the other side then rolled smoothly for a little before bumping in and out of another rut.

After an hour, Yuri jumped down and walked beside his father who was leaning forward pulling the horse as it struggled with the continuing ruts and mud on the track. He looked over his shoulder into the flurries of snow then to his father.

'They must be about twenty miles behind us.'

Ivan grunted as he leaned into the rope, his breath forming small clouds that merged with that from the horse. 'We should get to the city by tonight. Then hopefully we will be safe.'

Yuri grabbed the rope and helped to pull. 'Where will we go when we get there?'

Ivan turned to him as he pulled. 'We mus trus our great leader has made provision for his workers.' Yuri caught the bitterness in his father's voice.

They trudged in silence for a few minutes then Yuri said, 'You were right about the Germans.'

His father looked straight ahead. 'Little good it's done us.'

Yuri looked back at his mother huddled down in her clothes and coughing as she nodded at Yuri urging him to take over.

Yuri leaned into his father and said, Let me take over for a while.' Ivan turned to him and considered for a moment then nodded and let go of the rope.

'Don pull him too har, let him make his own pace.' Ivan heaved himself up onto the seat next to his wife.

She leant against him. 'He's a good boy Ivan. He's just like his father, stubborn.'

Ivan chuckled. 'Not like you then motha!' He kissed her cheek. 'You think I don know about the china cups you hid away?'

She coughed and covered it with a laugh. 'You might be glad of them one day.'

He watched Yuri leaning into the rope. He felt a rush of pride that he was so lucky to have a son like him. He smiled thinking he was glad he didn't have to go up against a man as powerful as Yuri in a bare knuckle fight.

Yena nudged him. 'What's amusing you now?'

He put his arm around her. 'Nothing.'

She gave him a look. 'Hmm.'

He looked ahead at the city skyline and wondered what awaited them.

21. NEAR AND YET SO FAR

It was mid morning as Nikita Sidorov sat back from his desk in Leningrad and scratched his fat belly which strained against the leather belt of his police uniform. He smoothed his moustache, and took off his small round wire glasses, then lit a cigarette as he perused the finished reports on five dissidents arrested for spreading alarm which would send them to the Gulag. Sidorov was a stickler for detail and keeping to the rules although of course, he knew how to bend the rules to his own advantage. Being the Commissar of this district gave him immense power; something he wielded with relish in response to Stalin's aggressive purges to eliminate any opposition he considered a threat.

Sidorov was only too aware that if he did not carry out his duties of tracking down and punishing those considered a threat to the motherland — or more precisely to Stalin's paranoia — he would himself join the seventy thousand officers already executed. But then he questioned his assumption; after all, his father always bailed him out...

He blew a cloud of smoke toward the ceiling as he thought about his task for the day. Hopefully he would be back by early evening, and if the shelling was not too heavy, indulge himself at the old bar behind the Opera house. He glanced down with a secret smile at the drawer which contained the photographs then stubbed out the cigarette, stood and took his jacket from the back of his chair shouting loudly, 'I need transport NOW!' He pulled on his jacket then took a heavy grey coat from a hook by the door which he struggled to get on. 'Sergie! Come here you oaf and help me with this damn coat.'

A heavily built man of middle age with a ruddy complexion from too much alcohol — once muscled but now fat — hurried in. Sergie hated Sidorov but feared him even more. He would have preferred to remain in his old district but he wasn't going to make Sidorov angry. He knew which side his bread was buttered on and his job as gaoler and *Interrogating Assistant* suited him fine. Stalin's paranoia fuelled the need for men like Sergie who could use their fists to make men cower. Coming from a peasant background he was illiterate but intelligent enough to know it was better to be on the inside than outside.

He pulled the coat over Sidorov's shoulders and handed him his cap.

Sidorov checked himself in his full length mirror and snapped, 'Get the lorry.' Sergie hurried out. Sidorov locked his office and went out to the rear of the building where the cold struck him like a knife. 'Hurry up you idiot', he hollered at Sergie who was trying to get the lorry to start. It irritated Sidorov that a man in his position should have to ride in a lorry, but since a shell had reduced his personal car to a mangled wreck — luckily with two of his men inside and not him — he had to put up with it. It was drafty, rattled and stunk of fuel which would do nothing to improve his mood. A clattering roar as the engine coughed into life together with a cloud of black smoke emitted from the exhaust pipe signalled he could at last get going. He struggled up into the passenger seat and impatiently made a "go ahead" gesture. The lorry trundled out of the compound bouncing over poorly repaired holes in the road.

After a bumpy journey during which Sidorov blamed his discomfort on Sergie's driving they approached a barbed wire enclosure surrounding a makeshift camp on the outskirts of the city. A guard swung open the gates and the lorry trundled in toward a wooden hut, bounced over a deep rut, then stopped. Sidorov clambered down from the lorry and growled with frustration as he felt his boots sinking in the mud.

He banged open a door to the hut and stomped in. Two men huddle around a stove leapt up. 'Commissar!'

Sidorov looked around the untidy area which served as their administration office and with a look of distaste asked, 'So is it ready?'

The man who had leapt up said, 'Yes Commissar. The fences are up and we have supplies ordered.'

Sidorov studied the man closely. 'What is your name?'

'Konstantin Merkov, Commissar.'

'Sidorov strutted back and forth and said imperiously, 'When we know the numbers I will be informed.'

'Yes Commissar.'

'These peasants will try anything to get more than their share. You must watch them carefully. Also, look out for trouble makers. I will decide on the rations. I have no control over the source of the supplies and no doubt too much will be sent here. We can't waste food on these people when it is needed in the city. I therefore intend that the majority of the food be kept back from them and transported into my jurisdiction. How you do it is up to you. I suggest keeping their ration cards and entering what you think fit.' He stopped and looked directly into the man's eyes. 'Can I rely on you to carry out my orders?'

Konstantin looked back at him in terror. 'Yes of course Commissar.'

'Good. Do as I say and you will be rewarded. Store the food where they can't see it and I will arrange for it to be collected each week.' He gave another cursory glance around and said with disgust, 'And clean this pigsty up. I expect impeccable records to be kept of all activities on this camp. In regards to the food, I assume you can be creative in your recording?'

Konstantin looked bewildered. His colleague, a man of twenty five with broody eyes and a hungry look jumped in, 'I understand Commissar.'

Sidorov turned to him, 'What's your name?'

'Viktor Volochik, Sir.'

'Very well. You will be in charge.'

'Yes, I understand Commissar.'

'Good. I shall return in a few days.' He turned and left. When he was gone the two men exchanged glances. Konstantin said, 'Phew.'

Viktor replied as he set to work clearing things up. 'If we don't do as he says we will be on our way to the Gulag, or a firing squad. I think he's the devil, Konstantin.'

It was evening by the time Ivan and his family reached the perimeter of the city where hundreds of families with carts from the outlying villages were gathered in lines waiting to enter the encampment.

Ivan jumped down and said to Yuri, 'We mus go and see wha's happening.'

Yuri nodded glad to rest. 'Why do you think we've stopped?'

Ivan shrugged. 'We'll find out.' He shouted over his shoulder, 'Look after your motha Georgi. We won't be long.' He and Yuri trudged through ground churned up by hundreds of wheels and boots along the rows of carts passing neighbours who stood on their cart seats, straining to see what was happening.

An elderly man jumped down and joined them. 'Any idea what's going on?'

Ivan patted him on the shoulder affectionately. 'Volkova, you old rogue! No idea but,' he leaned in close, 'if it can be done wron it will be.'

Volkova laughed. 'You old cynic!'

Ivan smiled thinly. 'I wonder why.'

After a few minutes they reached the head of the row of carts, passing horses steaming in the cold air partially melting the snow on their backs before it built up again — their owners stamping their feet to get warm — to a line of soldiers directing people toward a row of makeshift tables beside a wire fence with a gate just wide enough for a cart. They moved further along and saw that officials were taking people's details then directing them through the gate with their cart. Ivan and Volkava looked at each other quizzically. Ivan moved toward the table but a soldier blocked his way.

Ivan asked him, 'Wha is happening here?'

The soldier replied. 'You can't go any further. Orders from the Commissar.

Ivan looked at him. 'So we stay out here?' The soldier nodded.

Ivan asked softly, 'For how lon?'

The soldier shrugged believing this man was an idiot, his attention drawn to a man in uniform strutting toward him from inside the enclosure. The soldier looked around anxiously, trying to ignore the approaching figure then straightened and said aggressively, 'Move on or you will be arrested.'

Yuri realised who the figure approaching was and made a quick exit. Ivan turned to Volkava. 'It looks like we have no choice.'

Volkava sneered as he looked through the gate at the precession of carts being lined up in rows. 'It does.'

The officious man in uniform reached them and said to the soldier, 'What is the problem here?'

The soldier stood to attention. 'Nothing Commissar.'

The Commissar considered Ivan. 'Don't I know you?'

Ivan instantly recognised Sidorov.

Sidorov moved closer to him. 'I sent you to the Gulag. And your loud mouthed son. Did you escape?'

'I wa released.'

Sidorov scowled. He prodded Ivan in the chest and sneered, 'You have no food and yet you drink?'

Ivan said nothing. 'Volkava answered for him. 'His brain was hurt by beatings. He means no disrespect.'

Sidorov turned to Volkava. 'When a peasant addresses a Commissar he uses the term *Commissar* Do I make myself clear?'

Volkava stood his ground, a twinkle in his deep blue eyes. 'Very clear, Commissar...?'

Sidorov felt the power shift a little. 'Commissar Sidorov. I suggest you remember in future.'

Volkava smiled, 'Oh I will, Commissar Sidorov.'

Sidorov looked at Ivan. 'What about you?'

Ivan returned his stare. Sidorov started to turn to leave then faced them again. 'I will not tolerate any trouble making.'

Ivan asked innocently, 'Wha do you mean by trouble making Commissar Sidorov?'

Sidorov put his face close to Ivan's. Push me and find out, peasant.' He turned and left.

Ivan nudged his friend. 'I think we know?'

Volkava replied, 'Yes.'

Ivan returned to their cart and spoke to Yuri and Yena.

'They're not letting anyone into the city. It looks like they've made a camp where we will have to stay.'

Yuri looked worried. 'That was Sidorov, if he recognises me I will be sent back.'

Yena said, 'You are a lot older and have a thick beard, perhaps he won't.' She asked Ivan, 'What if the Germans reach here?'

Ivan rubbed his hands over his face, suddenly tired. 'Who knows. Is out of our hans.'

'But they will let us into the city won't they? Yena asked anxiously.'

Ivan brushed snow from the edge of the cart and leant against it looking at his wife huddled down under her coats looking worried. 'Of course.' He motioned for Yuri to follow him as he said, 'Yuri, come, hel me check the wheel.'

Yuri jumped down and joined him looking at the left wheel expecting a crack, or worse. Ivan beckoned him over a few feet to the side of the cart as another two carts pulled up behind them.

Yuri said, 'The wheel looks—'

Ivan nodded in the direction of Yena. He said with effort, 'Your motha is not well, I fear this cold will make her worse. We have no choice but to stay here and the sooner we get her inside the better. The only way we can achieve tha is to do as they order.' He saw Yuri bristle, 'This is not the time to crack heads. This is what I have been preparing you for. Not the German invasion but the system we are about to crash into.'

Yuri looked puzzled. 'Why are we being kept in a camp Papa?'

Because everything is being run by men who are only out for themselves. Remember? I told you about greed and power? Yuri nodded. 'Well here is your first taste of it. Don trust them. Do as they say. Don give them an excuse to bea you down.'

Yuri said, 'Yes. I remember. So what do we do now?'

'We wait.'

A man from the cart that had drawn up behind them shouted, 'Why are we stuck here?'

Ivan turned to him. 'We're being processed.'

'Processed? What do you mean?'

Yuri joined in. 'It's a camp of some sort. We have to wait.'

The man jumped down and began marching aggressively past them uttering, 'We'll see about that!'

Ivan whispered to Yuri, 'He won last long.'

After a couple of very long hours the cart in front began to move slowly forward and Ivan went to take hold of the rope.

Yuri gently took it from him. 'Let me do it, we'll need you when we get there. Anyway, I'm less likely to hit anyone if I'm holding the horse and I can keep my head down...'

Ivan nodded tiredly and got up onto the seat of the wagon. He put his arm around his wife. 'We'll be ok don worry.'

She leant against him staring ahead into the unknown.

The next day the snow turned to sleet as it pattered on the makeshift tarpaulin cover that Ivan, Yuri and Georgi had hastily hung over the cart when they finally stopped at their allotted area in the camp. Yena and her daughter huddled inside trying to keep warm beneath blankets. Ivan had gone with Yuri to find out about food, sanitation and water.

Ivan returned with Yuri and scrambled in out of the rain fighting to contain his anger. 'We are to be issued with ration cards an will ge a fair portion of foo twice a day.' He exchanged looks with Yuri. 'So everything will be fine.'

Yena looked questioningly to Ivan. 'Do you believe them?'

He snarled. 'Believe a bunch of corrupt incompetent idiots! No. I've heard from those here before us that the ration cards mean little. The "officials" it seems use them to their own ends an we get the scraps, if we're lucky. Already some families have sold their cattle for food.'

Yuri asked, 'Should we do that?'

Ivan scratched his beard. 'I'd prefer to eat them than sell them for a pittance. An another thing, we must be very careful an look out for thieves. Sadly such times bring out the worst in folk.'

Yena did her best to eke out the meagre food they had brought with them. When Ivan was talking quietly with a group of their neighbours nearby, she called Yelena to her. She whispered in her ear as she shoved a sausage wrapped in brown paper in her hand. 'Take this to Eva Nikolsky. Her husband looks ill. I know they had a bad harvest last year. And don't let your father see.'

As Yelena ran through the mud Ivan watched out of the corner of his eye as he listened to a point being made by one of the men and smiled secretly to himself. The group of men came to an agreement and went their separate ways.

Ivan nipped under the tarpaulin and grabbed Yena around the waist from behind as she peeled a potato. He murmured into her neck. 'You have a big heart. Just be careful.'

She smiled and said over her shoulder, 'I don't know what you are talking about...'

He squeezed her whispering in her ear, 'Charity begins at home.'

'And you be careful who you talk to.'

He looked out down the rows of carts with horses and cattle tethered nearby, myriad footprints in the mud between the carts forming a churned path.

He sighed. 'We can't stay here for long before we starve Yena. I've called a meeting for tonigh to make a plan of action.'

Yena stopped scraping. 'Ivan...'

He turned to her trying to conceal his anger. 'I won sit by an watch my family starve.' He sighed. 'Two families tha arrived here a week ago have lost their eldest. They said they have not seen their ration cards an get threatened if they question it.'

'Perhaps it just needs time for them to get it all sorted out.'

'Yena, you are an optimist. Me, I'm a realist, and I'm telling you now this place is corrupt.'

'How do you know? There must be a Commissar. Let's ask him.'

'I have met the Commissar, Yena. He is the worst type possible. The man who put me in the Gulag, and our son. A bully in a uniform. No. We need to get enough of us together an ask for help.'

'Ask who for help?'

He sneered. 'Our wonderful leader, President Stalin.'

22. THE FINAL STRAW

Yena could not remain in their tent for long without the need of female company. She hurried outside hoping to see a friendly female face. A guard appeared from between two tents and passed her. She said in surprise, 'Dmitri?'

He stopped and looked at her puzzled for a moment before recognising her. 'Yena Kasakof!'

She smiled. 'How is your family?'

His face darkened. 'I haven't heard from them. Everyday I look out to see if they are here.'

She looked into his face that was etched with pain, 'You left and went to the city a year ago. So you joined the army?'

He nodded. 'I thought I should fight for my motherland but,' he pointed to his foot, 'they said I was not good enough and put me here.'

Yena sighed. 'I knew your mother well. I am sorry Dmitri.' He smiled. She continued, 'What will become of us here? We are starving.'

He flushed, 'It's out of our hands Yena. The Commissar is,' he looked furtively around, 'an evil man. We are all scared of him. I had better go.'

She touched his arm, 'Don't let him make you like him Dmitri.'

He nodded and carried on trudging through the snow on his rounds.

Friendships were beginning to form between families camped next to each other as the community way of life became re-established. Despite Ivan's warning, Yena continued to share their meagre food with the Nikolsky family and was spending time with Eva Nikolsky and two other women nearby; Irena and Anna both with children and angry frustrated husbands used to being active on the land, finding captivity abhorrent.

As the four women sat in Anna's tent they discussed the plans of their men folk with concern. 'Eva touched Yena's arm as she said, 'Don't take offence Yena, but these men of ours are going to stir up trouble, and Ivan will lead them.'

Yena smiled and touched her hand, 'I know my husband Eva. He could no more sit back and watch us starve than the sun not shine...there is nothing I can say to him to change his mind once set.'

Anna sighed, 'All men are the same Yena, and it's not just yours. I know they mean well but this meeting they're having tonight...'

Yena's face clouded, 'But we are being starved by staying here. Something is not right. Where is the protection from —'

Eva looked around alarmed, 'Yena!' She signed for her to be quiet. Such was the paranoia felt by everyone.

That evening Ivan led a meeting of his neighbours gathered beneath a large tarpaulin. The noise of the pounding rain forced them to talk loudly and Ivan struggled to be heard and understood.

Ivan shouted above the roar of the rain. 'If we continue like this we will all starve. The ration cards are an insult. We know they are using them to get food for themselves an giving us virtually nothing. I have heard of two families now that have lost someone through lack of nourishment.'

A gruff voice from behind said, 'So what do you suggest? We take over?'

Another voice answered. 'And get shot. Good idea.'

Ivan put his hands up for silence. 'I suggest we deal with this by writing to our President explaining our plight an asking for help.'

A bitter voice said from the shadows, 'Stalin help us? He's too busy looking after Moscow.'

Ivan said pleadingly, 'We have to try. Ok if it fails then we must turn to other means but at least let's try?'

A worried voice from the shadows asked, 'And who will write this letter. I can't, I'm just a simple farmer.'

Ivan said, 'If you are all in agreement I will write it and read it to you before it is sent.' A murmur of agreement ended the meeting.

A week passed and conditions continued to worsen as families saw with horror their supplies vanishing. Ivan had completed the letter and shared it with the committee he had formed. They were in agreement that it was fair and reasonable.

Commissar Sidorov was extremely angry that his evening had been interrupted by a soldier from the camp banging on the door of his police station. When he opened the door he was handed a note from the man who quickly disappeared having done his duty. Sidorov went through to his office and opened the note.

A sour look of contempt crossed his face as he hollered, 'Sergie! Get my transport out the front NOW!' He gathered his coat and hat and aggressively stuffed the note in his coat pocket. He stomped out into the heavy falling snow and impatiently strutted back and forth in the snow waiting for Sergie.

As the worn out lorry roared away from the police station carrying Sidorov in a foul mood, Ivan's family settled down within their makeshift home now extended by tarpaulin on poles. Ivan felt the camp seemed especially quiet becoming aware that the usual sounds of the families around them seemed subdued as if a blanket of tension had descended and laid itself over them.

He said to Yena, 'If this snow continues we will have to make more supports for the tarpaulin.'

Yuri was whittling a piece of wood. He said without looking up, 'I can do it.'

Ivan smiled at Yena. 'See he is not brain dead like me...'

She was sewing and stopped, raising her eyes to his. 'Don't say that Ivan. But you and you're fighting!' She couldn't help a smile escaping, 'My father was right...'

He laughed. 'That you should have married that oaf from the next village? The one with crossed eyes?'

She went back to her sewing. 'He didn't have crossed eyes. He did have a big nose though!'

Yuri looked up at them smiling. He loved listening to their banter.

An hour later, Sidorov's lorry bounced and bumped to a halt outside the camp. He laboured through the mud and snow to the office where he burst in waving the note at the two men inside. 'What's the meaning of this?'

Viktor, the man he had earlier put in charge, stood to attention. 'I thought you should know as soon as possible Commissar.'

Sidorov read the note again then snarled. 'And you have proof of this?'

'Yes Commissar. I heard them myself.'

'Take me to the tent immediately.'

Viktor hurriedly put on his coat and led Sidorov with two soldiers down rows of tents and carts with tarpaulin draped over them forming makeshift protection from the elements. They stopped outside Ivan's encampment and Sidorov directed the soldiers to open the flap.

Inside, all hell broke loose as the tent flaps were torn open and torches shone into their small shelter. Ivan jumped up and stood defensively in front of Yena who was trying to stand up. Yuri slipped out under the tarpaulin and hid in the shadows. Georgi appeared and stood defiantly by his father.

Ivan asked, 'Whas going on?'

Two soldiers with guns entered followed by Sidorov who strutted back and forth looking with contempt at the family's life packed in around them. He pointed at Ivan. 'You again! Did I not warn you about making trouble? To the soldiers he barked, 'Arrest this man!'

Ivan tried to stand tall despite his weak leg. 'I have done nothing wrong.'

Sidorov smiled. 'You are a troublemaker.' He drew his pistol and pointed it at Ivan.

Georgi jumped in front of his father shouting, 'Leave my father alone!' Sidorov pistol whipped the boy who fell to the floor holding his bleeding cheek. For an instant Ivan froze then all the pent up anger from the years of cruel treatment burst from him in a violent eruption as he grabbed Sidorov and lifted him off the floor; his hands around his throat. Sidorov was still holding the pistol which was now between their bodies and pulled the trigger. The sound of the pistol rattled their ears as Ivan was thrown back onto the ground by the impact of the bullet at point blank range. Yena dropped by her husband's lifeless body, numb with shock. Yelena was screaming. Georgi leapt up and dived for Sidorov who shot him in the chest.

Sidorov turned and strutted out of the tent saying to the soldiers, 'You all saw, it was self defence.'

Outside, Yuri heard it all but knew he had to keep away until Sidorov and his men had gone; his anger trying to burst from him. When it was clear he ran into the tent and stood in shock at the sight of his father's lifeless body and his brother's, his mother kneeling beside Ivan shaking and his sister in shock. Yuri knelt beside his weeping mother and hissed, 'It was Sidorov wasn't it?'

She nodded stroking his father's face. 'I vow I will avenge them Mama. However long it takes.'

Later, unable to be contain his anger and grief he slipped quietly out of their enclosure but was stopped by two men slightly older than him.

They barred his way as one of them said, 'You're Yuri Kazakof. Your father stirred up trouble and now our fathers have disappeared.'

Yuri stood his ground. 'He tried to get a fair deal for everyone. I've lost my father too.'

The second man pushed Yuri hard in the chest causing him to take a step back to keep his balance. The man failed to see the anger flash in Yuri's deep green eyes. The first man threw a punch which Yuri dodged. The second man tried to grab Yuri by the arm but Yuri elbowed him in the face stunning him then turned to the second man and kicked his shin. The man howled in pain and let go. Yuri chopped him hard to the throat and he fell to the ground gasping for air. Yuri returned to the other man and punched him hard in the stomach and as he bent forward brought his knee up into his face. The man fell on his back groaning.

Yuri leant over him. 'Stay down. I didn't come looking to hurt you. I feel bad like you do. Do something to help your families instead of seeking revenge.' He walked away heading for the fence again.

The next day Yuri tried talking to his neighbours about reforming the committee but after hearing of the shooting their apathy was his only answer. He felt powerless knowing he could not do it alone.

Yuri's rage boiled at the injustice perpetrated against men who just wanted to be heard. His anger was like a solid block of ice within him stifling any positive emotions, but as long as he kept busy he didn't have to face the pain. Yuri spent his time tirelessly trying to find any source of food he could within the camp. At night he prowled, struggling with his anger which was like a heavy black blanket shrouding him. It was if a bright light in his life had been suddenly extinguished.

He knew he should be with his mother but he couldn't bear to see her putting on a brave face for her daughter and although he was surrounded by hundreds of people, he felt alone as he walked aimlessly around. Then one night he noticed the wire fence around the perimeter of the camp and wandered over to inspect it. It was not very strong and he was sure he could bend it sufficiently to wriggle underneath. He looked through the dark and heavy snow flakes to the vague presence of fields the other side. He checked he was not seen and pulled at the wire fence until the hole was enough for his large frame. He scrambled under and went into a nearby field looking for vegetables. After digging around with a piece of wood he found nearby, he dug up a few potatoes. He returned under the fence and took his booty home.

His mother was sitting sewing as she heard him undoing the tent flap. She wondered every day how she could carry on; the pain in her lungs was as nothing compared to the pain in her heart. She carried on sewing trying to get lost in the stitches ready to put on a brave front for her son.

He burst in. 'Look!' He held out his reddened and muddy hands holding the potatoes.

She looked up and his heart broke as he saw the grief for their previous lives in her eyes. It was as if she had aged ten years over night. She asked softly, 'How did you get those?'

'From a field! I got under the fence. Tomorrow night I'll get much more, you wait and see.'

She knew he needed to be busy and for once did not want to slow him down. She went back to her sewing. 'You will have to sleep soon Yuri or you will become ill.'

He put the potatoes down, kissed her cheek and went out again. He did not want to sleep. He didn't think he would ever be able to again. He kept the hole a secret to himself. The next night when his sister was asleep he sat with his mother as she sewed.

Yena reached out and grabbed his sleeve. 'Your father is proud of you Yuri.'

He turned to her. 'And he would have done just the same wouldn't he?'

She shook his arm gently. 'Yes he would.' A shadow of anger flashed across her face. 'Just be careful.'

Over the next few weeks he did his best to look after his
mother and sister. He began to realise his mother had been
concealing how ill she was and now without Ivan to hide behind
he could see it clearly.

That night, he crept out intent on finding out why a curfew
had been imposed. His anger boiled at the camp officials who
seemed to maintain their rotund figures as he and the other
families grew weaker, slowly starving. He made his way
carefully in the dark between carts toward the office. He
crouched down as armed guards passed by. He watched the office
and saw beyond it a large shed which he had not considered
before. He waited in the shadows and saw a lorry pull up by
the shed and men loading boxes and bags of food into it. He
had seen enough. His rage roared like a furnace. Rage at the
corrupt system for taking Nadya from him, for murdering his
father and brother, Sidorov for representing the worst of it
all and now he was stealing food from starving families for
his own ends. Yuri knew he had to do something but what?

Over the next few weeks time seemed to pass slowly within the
camp. Shells whistling overhead toward the city became part of
the everyday sounds; the crump as they landed in the city a
reminder that the Germans were intent on destroying them all.
Almost by stealth, starvation crept into their tent, as Yuri
realised in horror that his sister, usually a cheeky ball of
energy, had become lethargic not bothering to argue with him
or her mother, becoming quiet and withdrawn.

Yena had no strength left to line up every day, waiting
patiently for their food which meant Yelena had to do it, much
against her will. The camp shop, a hastily erected wooden shed
but with a substantial lock and guarded twenty four hours a
day, remained closed ignoring the hundreds of hungry eyes
watching expectantly. The time for it to open had long since
past and people were becoming restless, the tone of
conversation becoming that of anger. One of the guards headed
off to the camp office for instructions. He returned a few
minutes later with more guards, all heavily armed with machine
guns.

He stood on a wooden box and shouted, 'There are no
supplies today by order of the Commissar.'

A roar of angry voices began to rise quickly silenced by the
chatter of machine gun fire over their heads. A heavy silence
followed.

He continued, 'Go back to your homes and come back tomorrow.'

A voice from within the crowd shouted, 'You said that yesterday!''

Another voice. 'And the day before!'

He turned to his fellow guards for guidance. They looked away. He made his way back to the office and knocked.

A voice from inside said, 'What is it now?'

He entered. 'They're getting angry Commissar Sidorov. We've quietened them down but—'

Sidorov was sitting back drinking a coffee, picking from a bowl of fruit. He put down his mug. 'Then we will have to shoot a few as a warning.'

The guard looked perplexed. 'Shoot them?'

Sidorov studied him with a sinister smile. 'You have a problem following orders?'

'No Commissar.'

'So...?'

The guard nodded subserviently, 'I understand Commissar.'

'Good. Because if you disobey my orders I will send *you* to the Gulag.'

'Yes Commissar.'

'Would you like me to send you to the Gulag?'

'No Commissar.'

Sidorov picked up a piece of orange. 'Tomorrow, let them have some bread. Not a lot though. You know the amounts. If we are not careful they will eat the lot. Our President knows what is right and I am going to ensure we carry out our duties. Do you understand?'

'Yes Commissar.'

'Good. You may go. Oh, and send Viktor in here.' After the door closed Sidorov opened a drawer and took out a file. He ran his finger down a column of figures.

The door opened and Viktor entered looking wary 'Commissar?'

Sidorov nodded for him to sit down. 'I see from these figures we have enough produce to return to the city. I will arrange for the lorries to collect it tonight. To be on the safe side order another curfew for nine pm.'

As the crowd dispersed, Yelena idled back to the tent. Yuri
met her outside. 'No food again?' She shrugged listlessly. He
walked away trying to control his frustration and anger.
Surely people would band together now? No food had been issued
for three days! And then it had only been a small amount of
bread. People were starving becoming lethargic, not bothering
to discuss the signs that were posted at each row of carts
with the times of the curfew. Yuri fumed. He had long since
sold the cattle and the horse for whatever food he could get,
and now had little to barter with or bribe officials. His
mother had become bed ridden, her strength sapped by illness
and grief. His sister grew thinner and more sullen every day.

The next day he again tried to rally his neighbours telling
them what he had seen but they were too frightened. He idly
walked back to his tent trying to think what his father would
have done. He looked up at the thick grey sky heavy with
impending rain and entered the tent.

He sat with his mother, who was hidden under her blanket. He
began telling her what he had seen last night then sensed
something had changed, a stillness had settled around him. He
knew she had passed away. The past few months had left him
devoid of feeling and he hardly felt anything other than
numbness as he covered her face. He turned to his sister
huddled beneath her blankets sleeping, her skin a greyish
yellow, her eyes although shut, sunk into their sockets. He
had come to recognise the signs of starvation and was aware
that he was scarcely any better. How could he look after them
when he didn't have the strength to look after himself? He
began to cry softly; he missed his father's strength.

There was nobody to help him. He knew he could sit there
forever and nothing would change; he had to force his weak and
tired body into action. He placed his mother's body on a sled
and took her to a burial point where he was coldly instructed
to leave her. He did not have the strength to argue and turned
sullenly into the cold dark night to trudge back to their
shelter.

As he approached it he became alarmed that the flap in the
tarpaulin that formed the door was open. He couldn't be sure
he hadn't left it open but he felt something was different. As
he drew near he discovered with horror that somebody had
ripped open the tarpaulin; presumably to gain a quick entrance
without having to undo all the ties. He left the sled and ran
the last few yards staggering inside to find his worse fears
were true. Someone had ransacked it for anything worth
selling. He slumped on the floor as the last ounce of his
energy left him. How could he go on? It wasn't fair. Did life
have to be this hard?

He became aware of how quiet their new home had become — flashes of their familiar cosy farm house now a distant memory — and looked at his sister. She was lying very still. He sighed remembering how his mother used to tell them to be quiet and stop arguing. He heard his father growling with frustration as Georgi knocked over something as he tore about chasing his sister. He got up and felt her forehead noticing the palour of her skin. He knew she was dead. It was if she had just quietly slipped away leaving the husk of her body behind. This was too much for anyone to bear. He just wanted to curl up and sleep. He lay down beside her and holding her hand, wept.

He dreamt, through a troubled sleep, of sunny fields and his brother and sister chasing each other as his father reaped. Then it turned to blackness and they exploded into pieces as evil birds like vultures swept over them. He awoke from the nightmare gasping for breath, disoriented. He realised with horror, as he felt the cold body of his sister beside him, that this was the real nightmare. Despite having slept for a few hours he felt exhausted, hunger immediately overwhelming him. He just wanted to lie there and for it all to be like it was before the war. Is all of this misery down to the Germans? He knew his father would say 'Tosh Yuri! Stalin is the main culprit; just don't say it out loud.' The thought of his father — although a memory saturated with grief — gave him a little resolve and he carefully stood up beside his sister as she lay in silent accusation. But how could he have done more? The image of lorries being loaded with sacks of food filled his mind with hatred and anger toward, the nasty little strutting man; Sidorov.

He knew it would be light in a few hours as he gathered the body of the last of his family and placed her on the sled feeling the oppression of guilt that he had not provided his mother with a proper burial. His emotions were drained as was his physical strength as he sat in the dark listening to the wind outside as it brought more snow, quickly settling and forming a deeper white blanket over everything. His isolation felt like a darkness smothering him, threatening to take him. Sleep beckoned, but he knew this would be a sleep he would not awake from.

He looked tiredly around the pathetic space that had become their home; smelling the shadows left by those he had loved as his eyes settled on the bottom edge of the tarpaulin flapping in the wind; the old chipped and dulled vodka glass rolling back and forth as the tarpaulin nudged it. He leaned forward and picked it up, sniffing it. He put it in his trouser pocket. The memory of standing next to his father at the meeting in the city when he was a little boy swept over him flowing into his very being. It awakened something deep inside; an unwavering determination to bury the last remaining body of his family.

Beyond rational thought, operating from an instinctive need to do something for his family he pulled on his coat and then his father's over that, wrapped a scarf around his head, tying it carelessly under his chin and for a moment stopped, looking around. He rummaged through his parents belongings and found his father's woollen hat which he jammed down over his head. He found a shovel hidden under the edge of the tarpaulin which he placed on the sled beside the pitiful body of his sister, grabbed the rope at the front and dragged it into the grey early morning. He began dragging it toward the fence leaning forward into the rope focused on the hole in the fence. It wasn't long before he was spotted by a guard with a machine gun and dog which was pulling eagerly against its lead. Yuri took no notice; his focus on the hole in the fence.

The guard shouted, 'Stop! What are you doing? You can't—'

Yuri trudged passed him grunting as he pulled the rope. The guard blew a whistle and tried to stand in front of Yuri as he said, 'You've got to stop or we will have to shoot you!'

Another three guards appeared with dogs that were all barking and growling unaware of why, as the guards struggled to hold them back. The first guard shouted at Yuri, 'We'll let the dogs on you if you don't stop!'

Yuri became aware of the barking and stopped, looking up as is if from a dream. He looked around at the guards and snarling dogs. In a flat voice he mumbled quietly, 'I'm burying my family.' He leant into the rope again.

A few people came out to see what was happening making the guards uneasy as the first guard stood close to Yuri and allowed the dog within a foot of him. 'You can't. We have to stop you.'

It didn't appear that Yuri had heard as he mumbled, 'Have to bury them.' He stood straight and looked around with a thousand yard stare seeing nothing, 'amongst the trees, they would like that. Yelena loved trees.'

More people appeared forming a crowd, as more guards arrived trying to move people away but there were too many. The first guard shouted to one of the others, 'Go and get the Commissar!'

A voice from the crowd shouted, 'Let him be! Let him bury his family! We should be able to do the same. Why do you stop us?' An angry swell of voices agreed. The guard was becoming more nervous as he tried to swing his machine gun into the firing position whilst restraining the howling dog. More guards arrived and forced the crowd back a few yards but beyond that it was impossible.

Sidorov stirred in his sleep and became aware of banging on his apartment door. He sat up suddenly aware of a small, cold body beside him. For a second he recoiled before remembering last night. He jumped out of bed and hurried to the door which he snatched open.

'This had better be good!'

The guard stuttered, 'There's a riot at the camp Commissar!'

'Riot?! Wait there.' He slammed the door and hurried back into the bedroom to get dressed. He thought idly as he pulled on his uniform about the body. Normally he would dispose of it in the dark, down a side street. But an excess of alcohol had sent him into a deep sleep. Oh well, it's not going anywhere, he can do it later. He joined the driver and went down to the lorry parked outside. Snow was gradually covering it as he climbed inside, disgruntled that he had still not been given a replacement car.

As the lorry approached the camp Sidorov could see in the distance bright lights in a circle near the bottom fence. The lorry's headlights swung across the tents near the entrance picking out figures hurriedly pulling on coats and disappearing into the darkness toward the lights. He jumped out of the lorry almost slipping over in the snow as he unholstered his pistol and strode toward the lights, beckoning the driver to follow him. As he approached the illuminated circle of he saw through a few gaps in the crowd a tableau of five guards with snarling dogs surrounding a lone figure standing by a sled. It was almost surreal as snow covered the whole scene like a bizarre Christmas tableau.

He pushed his way through to the middle and joined the guards being careful to keep well clear of the dogs. He shouted above the noise of the crowd, 'What is the meaning of this?'

The first guard said, 'I stopped him from going through the fence Commissar.'

Sidorov looked at him pityingly, 'Why would he be going through the fence?' He looked down at the sled and pulled back the tarpaulin to reveal the body of Yelena then up to the figure standing beside it. He moved round out of the light and looked into the figure's face.

'Kazakof! I should have known it. I should have killed you at the beginning.' He turned to the guards. 'Get rid of these peasants. Shoot over their heads, if that doesn't move them then shoot the ones at the front.' A chatter of machine gun fire into the air shocked everyone into silence. Sidorov shouted, 'Go back to your tents. There's nothing to be seen here.'

A voice from the darkness shouted, 'Why can't we bury our dead?'

Another voice, 'Where's the food we were promised?'

Sidorov shouted, 'It's not my decision about burials, you will have to put a complaint into the commission. As for the food, we are doing our best, but if it isn't delivered what can I do? Now leave or I will have my guards open fire on you.' He nodded to the guards who fired more shots into the air. The crowd quickly dispersed.

Sidorov called a couple of guards over to him. 'Take him to where he wants to go, let him dig the grave, then shoot him.' He marched off to his office.

One of the guards said to Yuri, 'Ok come on then.' He nodded toward the hole and helped make it bigger then stood aside. To Yuri he said gently, 'Come on before he changes his mind.' He motioned to his fellow guards and one of them joined him. He whispered, 'Dmitri, this is not right. They should be allowed to bury their dead.'

Dmitri nodded, 'I know this man. His mother was kind to our family when we lived near to them. I even had play fights with him.'

The first guard replied as they slowly tracked behind Yuri with the sled, 'Sidorov will shoot us or send us to the Gulag if we don't follow orders.' To Yuri he called out, 'Where are you going to bury them?' There was no reply from the lone figure leaning into the rope ahead of them trudging stolidly through the deep snow. He said to Dmitri, 'The fellow's gone crazy. I've seen it before. You won't be able to reason with him. Perhaps it is kinder to shoot him.'

Eventually they reached a group of trees and Yuri stopped beneath them. Oblivious of the men around him and dogs eager to be off the lead, he went about digging a grave through the deep snow and frozen ground. He was not aware of the sweat pouring down his face as he laboured, not thinking to remove the two heavy coats, scarf and hat. Eventually it was deep enough and he gently removed his sister's body placing her gently in the ground. He fell to his knees looking at her.

Dmitri whispered, 'I can't do it. Leave him be.'

The first guard watched the lone figure kneeling at the edge of the hole.

'We could shoot into the ground then let him go.'

Dmitri nodded. He went over to Yuri and put a hand on his shoulder.

'Can you hear me Yuri? We're going to shoot into the ground and walk away but you must not come back to the camp or we'll all be sent to the Gulag. Do you understand?'

Yuri nodded imperceptibly as he stood and picked up the shovel. Dmitri looked to the other guards who all nodded back and a volley of shots dug into the snow and ground below. They turned and retraced their steps through the snow toward the camp.

Yuri filled in the grave and pulled a slat of wood from the sled which he stuck into the snow then stood and looked at it as he said, 'You will have lots of lovely summers here Yelena.'

He turned and trudged slowly through the snow toward the city of Leningrad.

23. WALK SOFTLY BUT CARRY A BIG STICK

There was still a slight moon but this was obscured by thick clouds allowing him to move without casting any shadows. He listened to the rolling sound of gunfire and constant flashes from the guns in the distance and headed in the opposite direction toward the city. He hardly had any thoughts, he just walked. The temperature was steadily dropping as he made his way causing him to pull his coats tighter around himself although at that moment he could have just sat down and gone to sleep for ever. His mind was frozen numb by the overwhelming pain which threatened to take him over. The only thing he could do was walk, walk and not think.

He counted his steps remembering rhymes from school as he watched his felt boots sink into the deep snow. He didn't look up, just followed the hedge which indicated the route of the track. At times Nadya came to him but he knew she was not real. He carried on like this for hours as the light grew slightly better, diluted by the heavy clouds and snow. Gradually his mind began to clear sufficiently to allow the pain to surface as anger, deep black hatred of everything, especially Sidorov. It was the depth of this anger which drove him on until eventually he began to pass rows of buildings and wide roads. He had reached Leningrad.

Now he had reached his target he felt overwhelmed with no idea of what to do next. He was past being hungry; his body was gradually shutting down, consuming itself. He walked on until he entered Aleksandrinskaya Square where he hesitated, trying to decide what to do next, aware of the damaged buildings, shell holes in the road and pavements. He was exhausted and would normally have been more careful about avoiding drawing attention to himself but his grief had left him careless.

A group of scruffy young men — gaunt from hunger— were hanging around and after watching for a few moments approached him. He was instantly wary and began to turn away.

The tallest of them came up to him and said, 'What have you got for us then?' Yuri said he had nothing of value. The man pointed at Yuri's coat. 'What's in there?'

Yuri gripped it tightly around him. 'It's just coats. I have no money or food.'

The leader poked him with a dirty finger, the nails bitten down, sores on the backs of his hands. 'Open it.'

Yuri began opening his father's coat. The leader pulled the coat open to reveal the second coat beneath it.

He sneered, 'This is all you've got? You come here expecting us to provide for you huh?' Yuri began doing up his coat. The leader pushed Yuri off balance and he fell in the dirty snow. 'We don't want your sort here.' He kicked him hard in the stomach and was preparing for another when one of the others shouted. 'Police!' They all ran off. Yuri grunted as he got to his knees as the two policemen came up to him.

They eyed him with suspicion and one said, 'What are you doing here?'

Yuri replied in a monotone, 'My family are all dead, I've got nowhere to go.'

'Show me your ration card.'

'It was stolen.'

The two policemen looked at each other sharing the same conclusion which the other voiced. 'Get out of the city, you won't survive here. We should arrest you but it's too much paper work. Now go.' They turned and walked away. Yuri hobbled quickly away into a side street. When he was out of their sight he stopped and bent over with his hands on his knees breathing deeply. He felt scared, helpless and overwhelmed, the adrenalin coursing through his body as exhaustion took over. His body relaxed and he slid down the wall and pulled his knees up to his chest as his body gave in. He fell into a deep sleep.

When he awoke an hour or so later he was immediately hit by another wave of intense hunger. Then his father's voice, clear as if he was next to him, 'Get on with it boy. You're intelligent, use it. Get food. Survive, do it for us.' He straightened up and looked around at the alley, formed by closed shops. This was a city. It had lots of people; they couldn't all be starving. Where would the survivors be? The wealthy part of the city! He got up aware that his muscles ached and his stomach was cramping. He continued down the side street and followed it until he entered what had until recently been an affluent shopping area. He walked around looking for houses of those with money. He soon found them.

He waited patiently in the shadows outside a house that looked as if it would be easy to get into unnoticed. He remained in the shadows as the shelling started, the shells whistling overhead. Flame erupted in a building a few hundred yards away but it didn't scare him. He concentrated on the house with hungry eyes. Eventually two figures came out and walked

quickly away ducking their heads as if it would protect them
from the tons of steel flying overhead.

He waited for a few minutes and crept around to the back. He
patiently checked for a poorly secured window which he
eventually found. He entered. Consumed by hunger he looked
around and found some ham, sausages and other bits and pieces
of food. He stuffed the ham in his mouth so eager that he
hardly chewed the first mouthful and choked. He put any food
he could he find in his pockets and looked around for knives,
spoons, matches and anything he could use. He empted cupboards
and found a small saucepan. He grabbed a bottle of wine and
rummaged through a drawer looking for a corkscrew and opened
the bottle being careful not to damage the cork. He emptied
the contents down the sink then filled the bottle with water.
In a cupboard he found a hessian bag which he filled with his
finds.

He walked away slowly, not to draw attention to himself and
looked for somewhere to cook his food. He soon found an empty
flat that had been left unlocked — he later learnt the
occupants had probably left in a hurry to join the evacuation
of women and children to a safer area — and quickly used bits
and pieces of wood he had collected to make a fire in the
lounge. He then put the saucepan on and filled it with water.
He hungrily stuffed more of the cooked ham into his mouth as
he waited for the water to boil. When it did he placed some
potatoes in the water and two of the sausages. He sat back and
remembered his mother cooking. His eyes welled with tears
thinking about the loss of his family. His mind refused to
focus, flitting from one memory to another. He felt empty.
Thoughts of Nadya became insistent now that he was in the city
and he remembered her parents flat and where it was. He had
nothing in the world except the memory of the woman he loved
and he was going to do his best to find her.

After he had eaten he felt his strength returning. Although
there was no heating or light in the apartment he knew it was
better than outside in the freezing cold and snow. He laid his
father's coat on the floor, took out his blanket and lay down.
His exhaustion ensured he quickly fell asleep.

The next day he awoke feeling stronger than he had felt for
some time. He checked out the flat and realised the previous
occupants had left little behind. He checked draws and
cupboards and found a small clock and a glass fruit bowl. He
stuffed them in his sack. He went outside and looked around at
the city. It was obvious that many people had fled before the
siege. That meant more empty properties and possibly things
left behind he could use.

But first he had to see if he could find Nadya; a long shot but he desperately needed a purpose to his life. He had to have some luck surely? So he made his way to the address he remembered, noting the odd landmarks he recognised giving him confidence. He came to the apartment and rang the bell but there was no answer. He stepped into the road and looked up at the windows which appeared dirty and with no curtains. He went back to the entrance and looked closely to check the names again; there was no Rheindhart listed. He kicked the door in frustration and walked away.

Yuri spent the next few days getting to know his way around the city; especially the previously affluent areas. He also knew where the gangs preyed on the weak. He recalled the times he had been bullied and his father teaching him how to fight. He smiled grimly to himself remembering that strength he had developed from the many fights that led to him becoming the champion of the village.

His father had said, 'Now that you are the strongest remember, "A measure of a man's power is in its restraint".' At the time he didn't understand what he meant but now he fully understood. He relished meeting the gang again, but on his terms. He looked down at his scarred knuckles and rubbed them.

He quickened his stride toward the poor quarter. Yuri now had a plan, a purpose, his father driving him forward. If he was to survive in this city — with the Germans trying to invade and probably to kill them all — then he had to ensure he would be in a position of strength. Even in their small village, factions within people of his age existed. There was always a group and always a leader. He knew from discussions with his father that some led by bullying and fear; others by tact and example. From what he saw of the yobs that had attacked him their leader was a bully. He had noted one of the four had hung back clearly uncomfortable with their actions. That meant there were tensions and where there were tensions cracks could be exploited.

He strode purposefully toward Aleksandrinskaya Square looking for the gang that had confronted him earlier. It wasn't long before he spotted them harassing another boy. He waited and watched listening to the guns and crump of shells in the distance. Snow was hanging in the air as a gentle wind began to stir, moving it into light flurries.

The leader punched the boy to the ground and began kicking him. Two of the others joined in, the same one standing back looking uncomfortable as before. Then the leader took out a knife and began threatening the boy on the ground with it. Yuri decided it was time to intervene.

The leader stood as Yuri reached them and said, 'Clear off. This is nothing to do with you.' He thought for a moment. 'Don't I recognise you?'

One of the others said, 'He was here before.'

The leader stepped closer to Yuri. 'Yeah that's right. Saved by the police.'

Yuri stood his ground surveying the men around him. There were four in the gang all around twenty years old, hungry and dirty. Yuri focused on the one who had threatened him keeping strong eye contact with him. He felt his father with him; as if advising him on what to do next. Yuri waited patiently, relaxed, confident.

The leader came close to him and said, 'We warned you before to go away. We don't want your sort in our city.'

Yuri smiled as he quickly raised his hand toward the leader's face making him flinch, Yuri continued the movement and scratched his nose. 'Hmm. Well it seems to me that your way of doing things doesn't seem to get you very far. You all stink.' The leader took a step back ready to throw a punch but Yuri head butted him to the ground.

Stunned, he quickly got to his knees, blood pouring from his nose and waved the knife snarling, 'You shouldn't have done that boy, I'm going to have to cut you.' He lunged forward only to find Yuri had moved and as he turned felt a boot drive into his belly. Winded he struggled to get up. Two of his friends moved toward Yuri but he was ready for them. Compared to some of the fights he had had in the village — and especially the prison — this was easy. He looked for the next strongest one who he quickly identified. As the man came towards him Yuri stabbed two fingers at his throat. He went down choking for breath. The other one hesitated, moving back to the one who had kept out of it. Yuri moved at them and they backed off. The leader was now on his feet and swung wildly at Yuri's head. Yuri stepped aside and smacked him hard in the face then got in close and punched him hard in the stomach. The leader staggered back winded but unable to lose face with his gang, made another wide stab at Yuri catching his left arm and drawing blood.

He smiled believing he had got the upper hand and made another swing. Yuri dodged sideways and grabbed the man's knife arm which he twisted and bent over his knee feeling it pop as it dislocated. The man screamed in agony and rolled to the floor grasping his arm sobbing. Yuri knelt down and picked up the knife which he stuck in his own belt.

He leant down to the man and said, 'Nobody draws a knife on me. Ever.' He became aware of the boy on the ground groaning. He looked back down at the leader and took out the knife again.

He turned to the others. 'Now listen, murdering people and stealing is wrong. It's over.' He turned back to the man on the ground. 'I'm going to let you live but you need to know that I, Yuri Kazakof could have killed you and I didn't. If you attack me again, I *will* kill you.' The leader rolled about in agony grasping his damaged shoulder. Yuri leant down to help him up and asked his name.

The man ignored his hand as he gasped, 'You will regret this.' He scrambled up and staggered away.

Yuri turned to the others. 'Anyone else?' He glared at each in turn. 'I'm not interested in taking anything from you, I just want to survive. We know the Germans are coming. They are ruthless and cruel. If we have any chance of surviving then we have to work together. It's us against them.'

They looked at each other and shifted around. One of them called Andre said, 'They want us to join the army but we hide.' He added quickly, 'We're not scared though.'

Yuri shivered. 'I am. But I want to fight as well.' He felt a wave of emotion flood him. He turned and walked away. He knew his name would be spread within their friends as someone to steer clear of.

After he had gone Andre said, 'Did you see how easily he put down Nicholie?'

Dmitri rubbed his throat. 'He sucker punched me. I'd have—'

Karl said, 'I saw his knuckles. He's a street fighter. He could kill you easy. That guy is tough.'

Andre asked, 'What about Nicholie? He won't let him get away with it.'

Karl said, 'I know he's my brother but he scares me. You're right. But we have to try and keep out of it. I nearly got caught by the police yesterday; I don't want to go to the front fighting with no weapons.'

Dmitri said hoarsely, 'What was that guy's name?'

Karl said, 'Yuri. Yuri Kasakof.'

Yuri looked around for more empty flats and eventually found one that suited him, for the moment at least. It was situated in the poor quarter where he was learning the street names and geography. As he broke into houses and stole food, he grew mentally and physically harder. Yuri had been brought up to be kind and honest, but now he was stealing to survive. He began a daily regime of fitness in the flat; if he had to fight he would be ready for it. He was living day to day, the pain of his loss still an ache he found hard to bear. He waited until dark before venturing out to explore the besieged city looking for Nadya, needing to avoid the police and security services that would either send him to prison or the army.

He wandered down a side street when three men appeared and blocked his way. Yuri could see Nicholie behind them brandishing a sword. He felt his heart beat faster, the adrenalin flowing to his muscles.

The man in the middle was Yuri's height but heavier and older, clearly a fighter like himself. He asked, 'You Yuri Kasakof?'

Yuri smiled.

From behind them Nicholie said, 'It's him alright.'

Yuri shouted past them, 'I warned you to leave me alone.'

He caught movement out of the corner of his left eye and a millisecond later the same from the right. Instinctively he knew which was the greater threat and turned quickly to the left as the dim street light reflected off a knife heading toward him. He rolled forward and kicked the one on the right sharply in the shins bringing him down. As he heard the clatter of the knife as it hit the wall he leapt onto the one he had brought down and elbowed him hard in the throat. He leapt up and faced the one who had thrown the knife and who had drawn another. Yuri waited for him to move aware of the big man nearby watching him, waiting. As the man with the knife thrust at him Yuri side stepped, got inside and elbowed him hard in the face. The man dropped the knife as Yuri viciously twisted his wrist pushing him to the ground. He jumped on him and punched him several times in the face. He quickly stood as he felt powerful arms grasp him from behind pinning his arms. He slammed his head back and felt the crunch of the man's nose. The steel like grip released and he wriggled free turned and squared up to the big man. They both locked eyes and circled slowly sizing each other up.

Yuri noted the many tattooes on the man and his heavily scarred knuckles; this man was no push over. After a minute of this the man struck out with a right which brushed Yuri's cheek as he moved to avoid it. He took the opening and slammed his fist into the man's solar plexus. The man grunted and backed off. Yuri followed straight in with a leading left to the face and then feigned delivering another slam in the same place. The man came back and landed a hard blow to the side of Yuri's head. They locked arms for a second and tussled, testing each other's strength. Yuri got another blow into the man's belly and then another but then felt the wind knocked out of him by a similar blow to his mid-riff. Both winded they moved apart again sizing each other up. Yuri studied the eyes of the man and saw only the desire to hurt, to inflict pain. Yuri hated men like him; to Yuri fighting was a noble sport and although without rules, carried with it a certain standard of behaviour. The other fighting was to survive. This man was a thug because he had taken advantage of Yuri fighting the other man.

They carried on circling making the odd punch land, both waiting for an opening. Then suddenly the man rushed forward hurling blows at him in a furious attack. Many of them landed on Yuri's face causing his eye to swell and blood to run freely from his nose. He brought his arms up in defence ready for the man to take advantage and go for his mid-riff. Yuri slammed his elbows down on the man's shoulders delivering an immense double blow that would temporarily weaken the man's arms. At the same time he brought his knee up and smashed it into the man's face repeating the process three times. The man staggered back looking groggy. Yuri moved in and delivered a left and right and left and right to the man's face until he fell backward unconscious. The two side men had run off leaving Yuri to face Nicholie swinging the sword slicing viciously at Yuri narrowly missing him as Yuri side stepped.

He shouted at Yuri, 'You didn't think I would let you get away with it did you?' Yuri sighed and kept direct eye contact waiting for the sign of an attack. Nicholie continued. 'You've driven my brother away; you've taken everything from me. Now you have to pay.' He made a wild swing with the sword which Yuri side stepped and got inside close to the man elbowing him hard in the ribs then grabbing his sword arm and twisting it hard. The man let out a cry of pain and the sword clattered to the ground. Yuri kicked it away and squared up to him. The man drew a knife and stabbed at Yuri. Yuri moved away and took out his own knife as they moved around in a circle looking for a way in. The man made a wild strike.

Yuri moved sideways shouting, 'Leave it! This is madness. Nobody has to die.'

The man was filled with rage as he sneered, 'You took my brother from me. I have nothing now.' He ran at Yuri wildly, determined to kill him. Yuri knew he would not stop and managed to get in close bringing his knife up hard into the man's stomach. He pushed it upward and held it there as the man's eyes grew wide in shock then closed as he slumped to the ground. Yuri knelt down and caught his breath. He pulled the body into an alley and quickly left.

Once he was further away he sat in a doorway out of sight and drew breath. The adrenalin would dissipate soon and he knew he would feel exhausted but he had to take time to think about what had happened. He glanced back to see that the big man had gone. He rubbed his knuckles and wiped the blood from his face. Is this how it's going to be from now on? Fighting for sport was one thing; fighting for survival another.

24. A THOUSAND MILE JOURNEY BEGINS WITH ONE STEP

LENINGRAD FEBRUARY 1942

Now, almost five months after Yuri had entered the city he trudged through a thick layer of snow in the Nevsky Prospekt, a boulevard of once elegant properties and shops now shut except for official food shops selling produce at extortionate prices. Beneath a thick grey coat he concealed a small bundle pressed tightly against a threadbare jacket and woollen sweater.

During those five months he had developed a reputation — from a number of tough fights — as someone not to be messed with. He had also become known as someone who knew where to go for virtually any item — if the price was right. He had made three friends; Andre Dmitir and Karl from the first gang despite having killed Kalr's brother. He had engendered loyalty and trust within his group and their underground community. He was learning about gangs and their rules and was tattooed both as a mark of respect to indicate his standing in the gang community and also to warn off strangers.

However, his driving aim was to survive, find Nadya and seek revenge on the man who had destroyed his family. Yuri knew Sidorov was selling the food — meant for those in the camp and sold at an extortionate price — to buyers in the city. Those who gained most were senior officials in the party and clearly not bothered by the city starving around them. Of course, the man who did best from the deal was Sidorov.

The usual barrage of shells rained down causing Yuri to keep to the shadows, instinctively ducking as he felt the ground tremble beneath his feet. A shell landed nearby creating billowing clouds of choking smoke and dust which hung in the air obscuring the dying embers of a rare blue evening sky above. The grey apartment blocks pock marked with shrapnel stood stoically against the regular barrage of shells, here and there bruised and battered where a shell had landed, roofs missing or sections of wall leaning at a skewed angle. With no mains electricity the buildings stood alone in the darkness occasionally lit by a fire raging inside. The majority of the two million inhabitants remained huddled in their unheated apartments or air raid shelters wrapped in layers of clothes trying their best to keep warm.

Yuri made his way around the city avoiding the dead bodies of those who had succumbed to the harsh winter — scattered around on the pavement like discarded refuse bags — the carpet of snow blurring their shapes into soft humps. Nobody had the energy to remove them and like the rest of the population, Yuri had become indifferent to them. It was as though they no longer represented people; more that of obstacles to avoid as was the rubble buried beneath the snow ready to turn an ankle. Even the most trivial injury could lead to death picking out the weakest to succumb to the simple matter of survival. Yuri averted his eyes from the faces of the recent who seemed to watch him, accusing him of treachery. He had been told that usually the first to die would be a grandfather, then an infant then Grandmother, father and finally Mother and eldest son.

Snow began to fall, at first a light dusting, settling on the consolidated snow packed down hard on the pavement. Then larger flakes floated down, blown by the currents created by the explosions forming flurries that obscured anything more than a few metres away. Yuri had wrapped a scarf beneath his chin, over his ears and the top of his head gathering it again below his chin and into his coat leaving a narrow slit through which he tried to see where he was going. Into this slit some of these large flakes found their way getting into his eyes causing them to sting.

Yuri stopped outside a hotel; its windows boarded over, and hastily made his way down some rubble strewn steps into a cellar. A boy arrived at the same time and followed close behind. They nodded to each other as they scrabbled down into a cellar so dark it was thick with blackness. They brushed the snow off their coats and heads as they stamped it off their boots. Yuri felt around for the candle they kept hidden in a corner and lit it.

He shivered as he turned to his friend. 'Yakov. It's so cold!'

'What's in the parcel?' Yakov asked shivering and hugging his dirty coat closer around him.

Yuri was evasive. 'Just a few bits I can sell.' He looked at Yakov as if to say *and don't touch*. Yakov shrugged. Yuri asked, 'Have you eaten today Yakov?'

His friend spoke to the floor. 'No.'

Yuri took a piece of bread from his coat and handed it to him. 'You have to try harder or you will starve. You can't rely on me to feed you. Why won't you work with us?'

Yakov took the bread with grubby fingers, the nails bitten down into his fingers, and carefully broke a piece off which he hungrily stuffed into his mouth. He gave Yuri a big grin exposing blackened teeth and red gums, an indicator of his advanced stage of malnutrition. He tore off another piece and smelled it then stuffed that in chewing with relish. He said through a mouthful, 'I hang around the food line but nobody gives me anything.'

Yuri took another piece of bread from his pocket which he stuffed into his mouth and chewed eagerly. He took out a package which he opened to reveal olives and a small jar of sunflower oil.

Yakov stared in silence then gasped, 'How...?'

Yuri tapped his nose. 'You have to know where to look. See, not everyone is starving. I know of three families connected to a factory manager who eat well.' He waved the parcel. 'Like this. So I followed them home and when they go to work I help myself. But, the secret is not to take too much. Just a little every other day. They have some ham which I will have a little of the day after tomorrow. But tomorrow I go to the other house and take some more bread and oil.'

Yakov looked at him admiringly. 'You make it sound so easy. I wish I could be like you.'

Yuri shrugged as he tore another piece of the loaf. 'You want to live you must take chances.' He took off his scarf and ran his fingers through his long dark hair then scratched at a stubbly chin.

Yakov crouched by the smoking candle. 'I don't think I can keep going like this Yuri. I hear the children's homes feed you at least.'

Yuri snorted. 'Orphanages and children's homes? Have you also heard they beat you and take most of your rations? They are stupid people only out for themselves. Last month they tried to evacuate a lot of kids and sent them toward the German lines. They were straffed by German stukas — at least here I'm in control of my own destiny. Anyway, we're too old. It's the army for us, but they've got to catch me first, I don't like the stories I've heard.'

Yakov rubbed his hands to get warm. 'You're stronger than me.'

Yuri nodded.'Yes, I am. I'm going to survive. I want to pay back those bastards for starving my family to death. But I'll do it my way.'

Yakov began sniffling, wiping tears away. 'Me too.'

Yuri playfully punched his arm. 'Then grow up! Join us.'

Yakov beat his arms against his sides to get warm. 'So why do you take things you can't eat?'

Yuri smiled as he huddled deeper into his coat. 'To sell. See, my father taught me that there are always greedy people in this world. I thought there must be some here. So I watched. I waited outside factories and food shops. I followed people who didn't look like they were starving and saw where they went. I discovered the black market.' Yakov looked puzzled. Yuri continued, 'My father used to get angry about the system and how we are all supposed to be equal but some are more equal than others...' Yakov looked confused. Yuri said, 'If you have power or influence you can have what you want. He said it's grown from the corruption that's wide spread amongst those in positions of authority, or in a position to be able to take more than their share. So I thought about what he told me and discovered that fashionable clothes are the best currency on the black market for those lucky enough to have a regular supply of food.'

He opened the parcel and held up a chiffon blouse and a yellow silk scarf. 'I can exchange these for bread and stuff to make cattle cake.'

'Cattle cake?'

Yuri smiled. 'See you are a city boy. Me, I grew up on a farm so I know these things. It's a mixture of linseed husks, cotton, hemp or sunflower seeds pressed into blocks. We fed it to cattle. Grated and fried in oil you can make pancakes. That is a luxury food compared to boiling off wallpaper paste.'

'A few months ago I was given a piece of cat to eat. Not very nice but...

Yuri grimaced. 'You hope it was cat... All their talk of how lovely they're sweet pet is — till they're starving. You have to be hard Karl. You must be number one.' He crouched by the candle warming his hands. 'I've learnt a lot about people these past few months. When my Mother died I took her body to one of the burial centres in the camp. While I was away a few kind people took the few bits we had and my ration card. No ration card, no identity to obtain the,' he said with a sneer, 'theoretical amount allowed of one hundred and twenty five grammes of bread. So I had a choice — either I stayed in the camp and starved or come to the city and survive. Then I discovered I either begged for scraps outside the food shops or I would have to steal. At first it didn't feel right — my father had taught me to be honest — but as my body continued to waste away I knew I had no choice; I had to learn how to steal to survive. I discovered I was good at it.

Anyway, I'm going to sell these items and get some food for tonight.' He wrapped his woollen scarf back around his head and scrabbled back out over the rubble shouting back to Karl, 'Get stealing!' He got to the top of the steps and stopped then went back down into the cellar. 'You must do it for yourself. 'Yakov nodded. Yuri continued. 'Come to the railway arches near Vitebsk station tonight at eight. Bring something we can sell and your in.' He turned and sprinted back up the stairs.

As he did everyday he searched in vain for any sign of Nadya — although he knew she had been sent to the Gulag — retracing his steps time and again around the area of her parent's apartment. The shelling became heavy as murderous pieces of metal packed with explosive shrieked overhead to land with an ear splitting roar nearby. Yuri knew it was too dangerous to be on the street and he huddled in the doorway to the apartment. A figure hurried from the street to enter the building. Yuri stood aside for them noting instantly that the man was a peasant by his dress.

The man unlocked the door to go in as Yuri asked, 'Do the Rheindharts still live here?'

The man hesitated to open the door and asked warily as he looked Yuri up and down and becoming fearful of being robbed, 'Who are you?'

'I knew their daughter, Nadya. I'm trying to find them.'

They're dead most likely.' He wanted to get inside to safety and quickly opened the door and went to slip in. Yuri planted his boot against the door frame.

'I'm not here to harm anyone. I just want to find her. Please tell me what you know and I will go on my way.'

The man relented. 'Ok. Her father was taken away by the secret police and we never saw him again. The mother and daughter were evicted at the same time but I don't know where they went.'

'How do you know all this. Were you there?'

The man looked uncomfortable and said sadly, 'They were good people. I brought my family to the city hoping to find work and accommodation. I couldn't find either. The authority made us move in here to the Rhiendhart's flat. That's how I know. Now please remove your boot?'

Yuri withdrew his foot and slumped to the ground reeling from what he had heard. Then a thought suddenly struck him. He rememebered the flat where they had spent a lovely evening cuddling. Inber! That was her name. He jumped up and oblivious of the shelling hurried along the street desperately trying to remember where the flat was.

After checking out a number of apartment blocks he turned a corner and there was the building, just as he had remembered it. He ran up the steps and banged on the door. There was no answer. Despondency drained his energy and he sat on the top step staring over a park to the large apartment blocks on the other side, listening to shells whistle overhead. He sat there until his backside became numb and he tiredly got up and walked slowly down the steps out onto the street. He was hungry and headed for the more prosperous area to steal some food.

An hour later with his spoils hidden beneath his thick coats, he wandered back to Inber's flat and spotted a figure exiting the block of flats and walking in the opposite direction away from him.

'Nadya!?' The figure kept on walking. He called again and the figure turned. At first he thought he was wrong but as he drew nearer his heart began to race; he knew it was her. She looked up and stared not believing what she was seeing. Yuri stopped a few paces from her and said, 'Nadya?'

'Yuri?'

He stumbled through the snow to her.

'Yuri!' She flung her arms around him. 'You're safe! You're safe.' She squeezed him and hung on nestling into his neck.

'Nadya, I've thought about you every day. I've searched all over the place.'

'Oh Yuri I feared you were dead.' She hung onto him tightly. Their breath formed thick clouds of moisture around them and she shivered and said, 'I never gave up hope Yuri. Never.' She stood back and appraised him. 'Is it really you?'

He nodded.

'Come to the flat it's freezing out here.'

As they climbed the slippery stairs covered in frozen ice she looked sideways to see if the Supervisor had seen her. She couldn't see him. She opened the door to number seventy three. Their breath hung in the cold air inside the apartment as he tentatively entered surprised at how tidy the few oddments she possessed were arranged. Although everywhere in the city was grimy, tainted by smoke and dust, she had clearly done her best to keep it clean.

He smiled as he looked around. 'Am I dreaming?'

'No. It's real. You are here.' She took a step back to reassure herself. 'A lot has happened.' She looked around the flat. 'It's not much but it's better than the street.'

Yuri shuddered. 'you get used to it.'

Nadya, stroked his stubbled face. 'I thought I'd never see you again.'

'Me too. There were times when it was too painful to think about you; and others when it was all that kept me alive.'

'She nodded and tentavily move closer to him. 'She took his hand and led him to the sofa. 'I haven't seen you for eight years — I thought you were dead. I just want to make sure you're real.' She stroked his hand feeling the calloused knuckles. 'I've grown up now — fear and starvation do that for you, and grief and anger at this stupid war and evil men running our country into the ground.'

Yuri held her hand in both his and kissed her. 'Yes. I've grown up as well for the same reasons. I came to the city to find you and I have. I shan't let you go again. He looked around at the sparse room. 'How do you keep warm?'

She shrugged beneath her thick coat. 'These clothes and sometimes I just lay in bed under the covers. Hunger is the hardest thing to cope with, I think about food all the time.'

Yuri smiled as he took out a loaf of bread and a tin of sardines. He held them out to her.

She gasped. 'How did you get them? The food shop is empty.'

'I've got a system, let's leave it at that.'

She looked at him quizzically. He said, 'Ok. I steal it from rich people.'

'Once upon a time I would have judged you. Not anymore. Even in the Gulag we had some food.'

'Gulag?'

She laughed grimly. 'Oh yes. I've seen a lot in eight years.' She hesitated for a moment and looked at him. 'You are real aren't you? I'm not dreaming?'

He smiled.'Yes I'm real.'

She took out the loaf which she carefully placed on the table and cut off two small pieces. She opened a drawer and took out a small tin which she opened. Any crumbs she collected and carefully placed in the tin. She opened the tin of sardines and smelt the oil then tipped a little onto her piece of bread, smelt it again, savouring the odour then popped it in her mouth sighing with delight as she enjoyed the taste. Yuri was spell bound. She nodded to him to do the same which he did.

'So tell me what happened to you.' He said between mouthfuls.

She sat on the floor between his knees holding his hands, 'The secret police came and took my father away, and threw us out on the street. Mama was terrified; all I could think to do was to go to her sister's. We settled in although Nina, her sister, was worried because the secret police were very active in her village. Mama had been unwell for some time and her health was deteriorating fast. I did what I could for her but Mama had lost the will to fight and died. Nina arranged for a burial which brought us to the attention of agitators in the village who reported her to the secret police. They raided her home and discovered me. Nina said I was just visiting but they checked and discovered I was the daughter of a deported criminal and therefore arrested. I was given seven years in the Gulag. When I was released I came back to Leningrad. I lived with Inber for awhile but she died from illness. I tried writing to you but I got no reply.'

The thunder of shells began outside, the whistle and thud feeling close by. She looked toward the window with tattered curtains partly keeping out the city. 'You can't go out there. You can stay if you like.'

He looked awkward. 'Ok, I can sleep on the floor, no problem.'

She stroked his leg.' So tell me what what happened to you?'

His face darkened as he began — at first haltingly, unable to stop the flow of anger and hurt — to tell her. They talked until late in the night.

She looked at the loaf and said, 'Thank you for the wonderful bread and fish. You're brilliant.' He blushed. 'I'm really tired and it's getting late.' There was an awkward pause. Then she said, 'Yuri I want to make love with you but I feel dirty and...'

'Unclean. I feel the same. We have plenty of time. When it is warmer we will!'

She opened a bedroom door where she stopped and turned to him, 'Goodnight Yuri.'

He stretched. 'Night.' He settled down on the floor and made himself as comfortable as it was possible given the freezing temperatures, enjoying the smells of the apartment and the excitement of being near to her.

He began to drift into the twilight zone that pre—empts sleep, thinking about how suddenly everything had changed. Somewhere in the shadows his father was nodding approval, his mother anxious he would get enough to eat. He drifted into sleep.

The bedroom door opened laying a chink of candle light across his eyes waking him. He sat up to see Nadya framed in the doorway wearing a red dress. He rubbed his eyes to make sure he wasn't seeing things and she said, 'Well? Do you like it?' He mumbled it was perfect. That she was so beautiful. Then he became aware of the oppressive cold air enveloping him in the cold room where he laid huddled in three layers of clothes. He sighed realising it was a dream. He pulled his coat tighter around him trying to ignore the savage cold as it looked for gaps to enter and sap his strength. He remembered the red dress from the house where he stole the food from. Perhaps he would get it for Nadya.

Nadya, wrapped in her extra layers, lay huddled in her cold bed pulling the blankets up tight to keep in her body heat. Her breath hung in the air above her. She tried not to shiver because that sapped vital energy. Her thoughts focused on Yuri lying on the floor a few feet away. If she was this cold, what must it be like for him? Their combined body heat would be more efficient. She smiled to herself and called out to him.

He came into the bedroom and stood beside the bed. 'You ok?'

'Get in here with me. It's too cold out there on the floor.' She moved over to make space for him. He kept his coats on and crept under the thick blanket. She snuggled up to him. She had learnt to live one day at a time and wanted to make love with him but thought ruefully that her cycle had stopped because of the vicious winter and starvation so she probably would not be at risk of getting pregnant, but then their situation was hardly romantic was it? That would have to wait.

She drifted off but the cold woke her up again. Her mother was telling her to keep up her studies at the Academy. A tear formed producing a cold trickle on her cheek. She thought about her father and where he might be. She knew deep inside she would not see him again. She felt anger rise at the world. Would she ever be able to live normally? It hadn't seemed possible she would survive this hell but since Yuri had come into her life things seemed different. He had energy, a vital spark of life that she needed desperately. Maybe she could achieve her dreams. But now was not the time to think of such things. Now it was important to stay alive.

Yuri dozed but his body shivered despite his determination not to do so. He smiled, despite shivering, when he imagined her face as he gave her the red dress. He tried to imagine how she would look in it, swirling her hips and laughing. His urges were subdued, his focus on staying alive. Other things would have to wait.

Vladimir Rostockovitch, forty years old, short fat with greasy hair smoothed over a balding scalp, was the block supervisor to Inber's apartment. He sat hunched over a small stove warming his chubby hands. He sighed as he stared through his grimey window to the beseiged city outside. Still no water in the pipes which meant he had to get the woman from apartment twelve to get it for him from the river. She wouldn't argue; she had seen what happened to those who did. He scratched his fat belly and ate another slice of bread. Unlike many of the inhabitants of Leningrad during that appalling winter, Vladimir Rostockovitch, had eaten well. He had quickly learnt how to spot weaknesses in others and exploit them for his own ends. He wasn't going to starve — or overwork himself.

Vladimir lived on his own. When the seige began, his mother, who had suffered from poor health most of her life, soon succombed to the cold. Vladimir wasn't too bothered about his father; the drunken beatings had made sure of that; as for his mother he would deny she meant much to him because she never stood up for him against his father's rages anyway. To make matters worse her ill health meant he had been her reluctant carer which did not sit comfortably. He remembered how on a drunken occassion his stupid father had spoken out against the system. He thought he was being clever and what did it benefit him? The Gulag thats what. Forced labour and meagre rations.

Vladimir knew he needed to ingratiate himself with the local Commissar which he did by informing him of any behaviour that could be construed as anti Motherland. At first it was a few Jews but he soon realised as circumstances became harsher that people spoke out more openly about their frustrations. He was handsomely rewarded for this information with extra food.

He ran a finger down the list of tenants for his block, noting the crossed through names of the families he had reported. His eye settled on apartment senty three, fourth floor. He knew the previous tenant had died and was pleasantly surprised when he saw the new girl slip into the flat. She kept a low profile but he watched her avidly. It was his plan to spoil her with food and in exchange... He felt a flush of excitement when he pictured her pretty face; he imagined she would undoubtledly be thin beneath all those thick dirty clothes but all the same...

Unlike most of the population whose sexual desires were subdued by the cold and starvation, Vladimir had needs that demanded satisfaction. He knew he was not atractive to women and the derisory comments he had received — on the odd occassion he had taken a risk — served to reinforce his low self esteem.

His sexual frustration was a powerful driver — although he did not possess sufficient self awareness to understand this — and he turned to alcohol and indulgent eating, together with fantasing about the women he watched every day to achieve some level of satisfaction. Such habits required a source of alcohol and food not available to most people. He certainly wouldn't get what he needed queing for hours waiting for meagre handouts. Sleep did not come easily and at night he would wander around the apartment block imagining what the families were doing behind their closed doors. This spying developed into obtaining information he could take to the Secret police.

Yuri woke up early and realised he was in bed with Nadya. She was already awake and studying him with a look of adoration.

He smiled and stretched. 'Morning. You look so beautiful.'

She laughed. 'Hmm and I smell like sweet roses? I haven't even taken these clothes off for days, so God knows what I must...'

He put his hand to stop her and stroked her hair away from her eyes. 'Neither have I. We're lucky to be alive. Our priorities are to stay that way. Other things,' he touched her lips, 'we can look forward to when we are in better shape.'

She kissed him and slipped out of the bed. 'Let's have some bread and sardines!'

Later they hurried out of the apartment and ran through the snow hand in hand.

Vladimir Rostockovitch did a double take as he saw the girl with a man leaving Inber's apartment. It appeared by the way they held hands they were lovers. A shudder of jealousy rattled through him; he would soon put a stop to that.

25. A HELPING HAND

MARCH 1942

In the short space of a month, Yuri and Nadya became inseparable. He said he wanted to be a farmer in the Urals where he would grow vegetables. She wanted to be a famous violinist but would settle for running her own business; she wasn't sure what in. They dreamt they would make it through the siege, having a life together and a family.

On their way foraging for food they passed the botanical gardens, now closed and used as air raid shelters, where Nadya noticed a figure slumped in a doorway. There was a vague familiarity about the shape of the figure that sparked her interest. Usually she would pass quickly by but with Yuri she felt safe and she nudged him in the direction of the figure.

Yuri started to pull her away. 'We can't help. We've hardly enough food for ourselves. Anyway once they get that bad it's too late.'

She pulled him over to the figure. 'I just have a feeling that's all. Come on.' They reached the prone figure and Nadya exclaimed, 'I know him! We were at school together.' She prodded the figure and he stirred but was too weak to speak. She turned to Yuri. 'It's Aleksei Krupin! I went to school with him. We've got to help him. He's a decent person. His father was a clever man, he made all sorts in his workshop.'

Yuri studied the young man huddled in the doorway then looked intently at her, her brown eyes pleading with him. He sighed, 'I'm not sure...'

She held him with those mesmerising eyes he found irresistible, her hand stroking his. He sighed reluctantly, picked the prone figure up and turned toward her apartment.

As he carried him she said, 'You are a good person Yuri. Even though we live in hell we must try and act with honour.'

He laughed. 'You sound just like my father!'

'I wish I could've talked to him.'

He grunted with the effort of carrying the boy, his breath producing large clouds in the cold air. 'He would have loved you.'

Once in the apartment, she heated the oil left from the sardines in a tin into which she grated some cattle cake. 'This might help a little.'

Yuri watched bemused as she tended to the prone figure. As far as he was concerned they already had enough trouble finding food and he wasn't going to feed another too weak to feed themselves. Gradually the man stirred and opened his bloodshot, sunken eyes, his skin a yellow pallor loose over his wasted body. He recognised Nadya but looked warily toward Yuri who watched him dispassionately.

Nadya touched his arm. 'He's Yuri, a friend. You're safe here.' Aleksei sat back and closed his eyes.

Yuri grunted. 'If he's got that bad he's no good at finding food and I'm not going to do it for him.'

She gave him a look that warned him off. He huffed and went back downstairs. She sat down next to Aleksei and held his hand. 'Don't worry Aleksei, he will come round.'

Yuri walked around outside for a few minutes feeling the cold biting into his face as he blew into his hands to keep them warm. He thought of the hardships he had endured over the past few months, a wave of anger flashing over him; partly at the expectation of looking after her friend but more he realised toward those in power who misused it for their own ends. Still, he knew he could not refuse her, so... he took a few deep breaths and went back in.

Aleksei watched as Yuri came back in and sat down with a sullen look on his face. Aleksei felt the effects of the food warming his core as he sat wrapped in a blanket huddled against the cold. He felt awkward. To Nadya he said weakly, 'I can be of use to you both. If you can get me some metal, preferably stove pipe and some other bits and pieces, I will make a stove you could use. It would burn wood or whatever you want.'

Yuri looked up. 'What about the smoke?'

Aleksei looked round to him. 'Leave that to me. I might not be good at finding food but I'm good with my hands, I can make anything with the right tools. Can you get me tools to make the stove?'

Nadya said, 'Yuri?'

Yuri nodded. 'I'll see what I can do. I can get anything on the black market. I just need something to sell in exchange.

Give me a list.' He stood up. 'How did you learn to make things?'

'My father was a gunsmith. I was his apprentice. You get me the materials and I will go to his old workshop and see if anything is left.'

'Ok.'

After a couple of days and more food Aleksei began to look better, some colour returning to his cheeks. He knew he had to prove himself to Yuri and now he felt strong enough to go to his father's workshop. He shuffled through the snow watching his footing on the treacherous pavements holed by the shelling. He looked around, bewildered at the damaged buildings. As he approached the road where he used to live, memories flooded back of hours spent with his father learning his craft.

He reached the workshop and discovered it had been broken into, the broken padlock dangling from the hasp. He tentatively entered to find most of the equipment had been taken. He sighed deeply as he looked around under benches and in cupboards for anything he could use. Eventually he managed to fill a bag with an assortment of files, drill bits, a hammer and oddments of screwdrivers, centre punches, spanners, a tin of gun oil and a worn but useable vice. He stroked the vice affectionately remembering the hours he had spent learning at it. He knew if he left it there it would be stolen so he had to unbolt it from the workbench. He was still very weak from lack of food and it seemed an impossible task to transport the vice. Forever resourceful, he found some lengths of wood and fashioned a rough sled, sufficient to take the vice and bag of tools. Slowly, he dragged them to the apartment block but realised he could not take them up four flights of stairs on his own. He hid them behind a wall and went up to the apartment.

That evening Yuri came in with a big smile on his face. 'I have loads of stuff downstairs! I saw your bits behind the wall and put them there. Why have you brought them here?'

'I thought they would be safer.'

Yuri considered for a moment. 'You can't keep them here. If anyone heard we would be found out and have to leave. Why can't you use your father's workshop?'

'It's been broken into already.'

'I'll get a new lock. We have to take it all back now before it gets stolen.'

Aleksei groaned.

Yuri grabbed his arm. 'Come on.'

As they gathered all the equipment together on their sleds Alkesei asked, 'How did you manage to...'

Yuri put a finger to his nose. 'You just need to know who to ask, especially someone who owes you a favour.'

They arrived at the workshop and took everything inside. Aleksei tried to lift the vice but gave up. Yuri grabbed it and effortlessly placed it in position on the workbench. He looked around. 'Can you manage the rest?' Aleksei nodded as he began sorting through the pile of equipment.

Yuri patted his shoulder. 'I'll get you a sturdy lock and we'll make it safe.' He looked around. 'You're father must have been clever.'

Aleksei stopped and straightened up. 'Yes, he was. He taught me everything he could. We used to talk about all sorts of things as we worked. He read a lot and encouraged me to do the same. He said there were many books in the world but censorship prevented us reading them. The state feared we would want more.'

Yuri leaned on the bench. 'My father was like that. I mean he wasn't clever the same way yours was but he read as much as he could and passed it onto me.'

Aleksie picked up a drill bit and felt its sharp edges, the twists of the metal along its length. 'My father was a gentle man. A thinker. One night they came and took him away. Evidently, he had made a joke about a party official and that was considered "sabotage".' Aleksei picked up a piece of sheet metal and said, 'Let's get to work on this heater.'

'And you're mother?'

'She died of starvation.'

The next day on one of the rare, lulls in the bombardment, Yuri and Aleksei sat by the river Neva. Aleksei idly studied the outlines of the Tauride palace and people hurrying to and fro. 'I wonder how long this is going to go on for.'

Yuri shrugged. 'Got to end sometime.'

'What will you do after?'

'No idea. As long as I'm with Nadya I don't care.'

Aleksei stared into the distance. 'You're very lucky to be with her Yuri.'

'I know.'

'I never really thanked you for saving me.'

Yuri smiled. 'Thank Nadya. I was going to leave you there!'

Aleksei grinned. 'Nadya is very special. You are both very special to me.'

Yuri turned to him. 'And you are to us. We make a good team.'

Aleksei glowed with pride and acceptance. 'And the fire?'

Yuri patted his shoulder, 'A masterpiece!'

Nadya appeared and sat down with them. 'What are you two plotting now?'

Aleksei laughed. 'We couldn't possibly tell you. You could be a spy!' She playfully kicked at him.

He stood. 'Ok, I've got a few things to do before they start shelling again.' He wandered off.

Nadya took hold of Yuri's hand. 'I wish every day could be like this, sunny and warm and no shells or bombers.' She stood. 'Come on. Walk with me.'

He joined her. 'Where are we going?'

'You'll see.'

They walked hand in hand down the Suvorovsky Prospekt listening to radio broadcasts on fixed wire loud speakers wired to poles. Yena Berggolt's poetry cheered them as did the weather.

They paused under a large tree and kissed. She sighed as he put his arms around her aware that this was where she felt safe, what she wanted for the rest of her life. Time seemed to stand still; the madness of the war a distant memory as she nuzzled into his neck smelling him. She sighed and kissed him, stronger waves of passion growing. She could feel him becoming aroused and loved him for being patient and understanding.

She whispered to him. 'Come.'

They hurried back to her apartment. She made him wait outside on the staircase as she went inside. He heard her washing and singing to herself. Yuri looked out over the city at the broken buildings, smoke and dust everywhere, people scurrying for cover as the sirens wailed again, explosions in the distance, and close by, eruptions and screams. Yuri felt he was in a nightmare. Surely this can't go on forever?

The door opened and Nadya poked her head round. 'You can come in now.' He entered and stood spellbound at the vision before him in her red dress complete with white pleats at the waist. 'Well?' she asked demurely.

He stood taking her in. A tiny tear trickled down his cheek as he remebered the dream. He whispered 'Nadya I...' She took his hand and smiled gently steering him toward the bedroom. 'Nadya I...'

She stopped, turned and embraced him whispering in his ear. 'I haven't either. Let's learn together.'

Aleksei had been out looking for firewood and returned with an armful. He hesitated on the stairs when he noticed the tatty bedroom curtains were drawn. He sighed as he sat on the cold concrete steps grasping the firewood. He knew it was inevitable they would consummate their relationship once the winter had passed. He was pleased for them but at the same time sad for himself. He thought of Nadya most of the time even though he tried not to. In fact, the more he tried not to, the more she filled his head. But then he felt as if he was betraying Yuri with his thoughts and chastised himself.

He stood, stretched and decided sitting there feeling sorry for himself would not help. He made his way down the Nevsky Prospect toward the Moscow station hoping to see a friend he had bumped into recently. To find anyone he knew still alive was something he prized. He stopped at the edge of Aleksandrinskaya square. The air raid sirens began their loud plaintive wail. Aleksei spotted two army officers with a policeman checking people's papers. He ducked into an alleyway.

Yuri and Nadya lay entwined. He stroked her hair and kissed her neck.

She smiled up at him studying his face. 'I've wanted to do that since I first met you.'

He sighed. 'Me too.'

They lay in silence enjoying the warmth of each other beneath her tattered blankets.

He sighed again. 'I always want to be with you. I miss you when I go away for a few hours.'

She stroked his face. 'And I miss you. I love your strength and determination.'

He chuckled. 'My father would say stubborness.' He became serious. 'I want us to stay together Nadya.'

She touched his face gently. 'We will.'

They heard the sirens begin to wail. He said, 'Aleksei should have been back by now.'

She sighed into his shoulder. 'It's so nice just lying here.'

He kissed her. 'He's our friend. I don't think he's too good at surviving on his own out there.'

She kissed his mouth gently. 'That's why I love you Yuri.'

He looked into those deep brown eyes and smiled. 'I've loved you from the first second I saw you. You are the most beautiful woman I have ever seen.' He poked her in the ribs. 'Pity you stink!'

She slapped him playfully. 'Pig!'

He quickly dressed and as he left the apartment noticed the bundle of firewood on the steps. So he had been back. So where was he? He hurried onto the chaotic street where people were running to the air raid shelter. Yuri ran against the crowd looking frantically back and forth. He ran desperately trying to think where Aleksei would have gone. On a hunch — because Aleksei had mentioned it previously — he darted toward Aleksandrinskaya square. As he raced out of a side street he ran straight into two army officers and a policeman who grabbed him by the arm and said, 'In a hurry lad?'

Yuri thought quickly and replied, 'Yes I want to get under cover!'

'Plenty of time for that. Show me your ID.'

Yuri made a show of searching his pockets then said apologetically, 'I must have left them at home.'

One of the officers grabbed his other arm and sneered, 'Running away from fighting for his country more like. How old are you?'

Yuri knew he could not bluff his way out.

The second officer said, 'Old enough. You've just been enlisted. You'll come with us.' To the policeman he said, 'We'll take it from here.'

The policeman released his grip and walked away. The two officers handcuffed Yuri to them leaving him no option but to go with them. Yuri asked, 'Can I at least get some belongings from my apartment?'

The first officer sneered, 'You won't be needed them where you're going. We'll provide you with all you need.' The second officer laughed loudly sharing their private joke.

From across the square Aleskei watched with horror as Yuri was taken away. He followed them for a few streets until they stopped at an army lorry. He turned and hurried back to their apartment. Nadya was cleaning some bowls as he rushed in gasping, 'They've taken him!'

She stopped what she was doing and grasped his arms to slow him down. 'Who? Yuri?'

He nodded gasping for breath. 'A policeman and a soldier, an officer I think. They took him in handcuffs to an army lorry.'

She looked bewildered. 'Why?'

'They wander round looking for young men avoiding the army and take them in.'

She slumped on a chair. 'Just took him? How...'

Aleksei put his arm around her shaking shoulders. 'I'm sure he will be in touch as soon as he can.'

Yuri was pushed into the army lorry with three other young men.

They eventually reached the outer perimeter of the city where the Germans were being held back despite the Soviet army's poor resources. Fierce fighting could be heard in the near distance. They were bundled out of the lorry into a makeshift hut where the officers handed them over to a gruff sergeant who asked for their details which he entered into a log and issued them with a number each. A private came in and was ordered to get them kitted out in uniform and issued with a rifle.

Two hours later Yuri sat morosely on his makeshift bunk in a tent holding a rusty rifle which he was attempting to clean. Another soldier came in and sat down beside him.

'So they got you? Ha. Only a matter of time. You see they're running out of bodies to throw at the German machine guns. My names Alek.'

Yuri put his free hand out, 'Yuri.'

Alek looked around to make sure he wasn't overheard and asked quietly, 'Can you shoot?' Yuri nodded. Alek became serious. 'Things are bad here Yuri. Too many officers all thinking they know best. You'll be lucky if you get any training — ammunition is too low — they'll sling you out as machine gun fodder unless you can convince them you are good with a rifle. Tell them you want to be a sniper. You might last a little longer. That's what I did anyway. Try it. Tell you what, I'll speak to the Sergeant, we lost a sniper yesterday so you might be in with a chance.'

Yuri smiled at him. 'That's great thanks.'

The next day Yuri was detailed to go with Alek who took him amongst the ruins of apartment blocks and a factory. Alek beckoned Yuri to stop. 'Now we have to be careful. We'll find a spot say on a third floor overlooking where the bastards are trying to infiltrate through our lines toward the city. Then we wait. We'll soon see if you're any good at it. Patience is the secret to this job.'

After some searching, Alek pointed toward the smashed windows of a block of flats; its walls pockmarked by shells and bullets. They made their way carefully through the building up to the third floor checking for enemies at every turn. Yuri felt sadness, then anger at the tilted pictures on the wall, photos of somebody's loved ones covered in dust on the floor, broken crockery, splintered pieces of furniture; evidence of devoted families who once lived there.

On the third floor Alek pointed toward an open window overlooking a square severely damaged by shelling. Once this had been the meeting place for families in the evening to pass the time of day; now holed and covered in rubble, the ornate facades of the stone buildings scarred by bullets and shelling. Glass that had once fronted shops now lay shattered amongst the bricks and torn stonework of once beautiful buildings. He pointed down toward the square. 'I reckon they'll be coming through there and taking cover in those shell holes. Look for ones with stripes, they're officers. Take out the officers and it breaks the other's morale. Pity we can't take out our own, we might stand more chance of winning.' They settled down behind the cill and set up their rifles. Alek showed him how to set up the sight.

'This job is not easy. If you're spotted they'll fire everything at you. That's the secret. Be cunning. That's why I wrap lagging around the barrel, to stop the light reflecting off it and giving my position away.'

Yuri asked, 'What's the thing on the end of the barrel?'

'Muffler. Stops the sound. Slows the bullet a little over a long distance but close up...'

Yuri examined his own rifle and realised his was the same. They watched and waited listening to the constant thunder of cannons and the rattle of machine guns.

Alek said bitterly, 'Much as I love my country we are a socialist society run by a madman. No way is it true communist. Too much corruption.'

Yuri sighed. 'They took our farm and paid us a pittance for our produce. They murdered my father and brother.'

Alek gave him an appraising look. 'You're pretty tough for a village man.'

Yuri looked down to the square below. 'Give me a German and I'll show you.'

Alek studied the square. 'Patience, Yuri, patience. Revenge is a dish best served cold.' He stiffened. 'There over by the archway. I saw a shadow.'

Yuri looked. 'I can't see— Yes! I saw an arm.'

Alek tightened the grip on his rifle. 'Now then, you watch and learn.'

After a few minutes a soldier appeared and, confident the square was not occupied, made his way stealthily toward the shell hole. A second and then third followed him looking around to make sure their way was clear. Alek whispered, 'When there's more than one, take out the one most likely to escape, in this case the last one over there. If he gets away he'll warn the others.' He aimed for the man, pulled the trigger and before the man had hit the ground he had another shot ready which he put into the second man. The first soldier burrowed down into the shell hole.

Alek said, 'Your turn.'

Yuri lined up the sight on the edge of the shell hole and waited. He could just catch a glimpse of the helmet as the soldier moved around beneath the rim of the crater. Then for a second the top half of the helmet appeared. Yuri squeezed the trigger and there was a dull ting as the bullet ripped into the metal.

Alek smiled at him. 'You're a natural. Stick with me, I'll show you the tricks of the trade.'

They both turned in fear as they heard scuffling behind them as a figure crawled across the floor toward them. Yuri noted with relief that the man was not a German. He was not in uniform and his features were gentle, his skin soft. Certainly not a soldier — or a farmer. Alek beckoned him to join them signing to be quiet and keep his head down. He crept up and tried to see what they were watching.

Alek gestured toward a window. 'There's one of them hiding there. He's taken out two of ours. Fancy a shot Daniel?' The other man gave an imperceptible nod. Yuri watched the window.

Alek whispered, 'Yes...' Daniel fired and a man tumbled forward out of the window thudding onto the road. 'Ha! Good shot!' whispered Alek. 'Yuri meet Daniel.'

The man turned to Yuri and shook his hand. 'Poka.'

Yuri had been studying him noting his coat which was full of bullet holes. He said, 'You're not in uniform.' He considered the accent. 'And not Russian.'

Daniel replied. 'English. Stuck here when the war started. I was an interpreter. Now I kill Germans.'

Yuri was in awe, he'd never met an English man. Alek laughed. 'What a way to meet an English huh?'

Yuri said, 'You fight for us?'

Daniel looked down the road. 'Can't get out of the city, might as well fight with you. Mind you, I'm not too partial to your leader's methods.'

Yuri instinctively looked around before he said, 'He is a monster.'

Daniel cleaned the eye piece of his rifle sight with the tip of his glove. 'I would agree. He's murdered so many of his own people I'm surprised there's anyone left. In England we would never have allowed it. Mind you, we managed to kill quite a few in the last war...'

Yuri was fascinated. 'Do you have a President?'

Daniel smiled. 'No! We have a Parliament and elected Prime Minister.'

Yuri was not sure what he meant. 'But you have a king?'

Daniel nodded.

Yuri checked his rifle was loaded then stopped and asked, 'Do you have serfs?'

Daniel laughed. 'Once, a long time ago!' He became wistful. 'It's a green and pleasant land. Our winters are not as fierce as yours and our summers not as hot. Mind you it rains a lot... We're a tiny island compared to your country. We're a reserved lot but you'd be welcome. You should visit after this is all over.'

Yuri was excited. 'Could I live there?'

'I'm sure we could find room.'

'Do you have secret police, purges?'

Daniel chuckled kindly. 'No. We are free to speak as we feel.'

'What happened to your coat, looks like a lot of bullet holes?'

Daniel laughed. 'The previous owner had no further use for it.'

Alek nudged Daniel and nodded toward another window further down the road. 'There's one just set up in the third window down.'

Daniel whispered to Yuri in English. 'Excuse me old boy, got a bit of business to attend to.' Yuri stared at him fascinated by this strange language but managed to tie it in with his actions. Daniel slowly swung his rifle toward the window and waited. A bullet whined as it ricocheted of their window cill narrowly missing Daniel's head. Then a torrent of machine gun fire blasted through the window throwing splinters of plaster and brick over them.

Alek shouted, 'It's a trap! We've got to get out of here!' He crawled across the floor toward the door beckoning the others to follow. Yuri was close behind him and just through the door opening when it seemed as if the whole window area disappeared in a blinding flash of explosive noise and dust as a tank shell smashed into the room passing over the two bodies now at the top of the stairs and taking out the far wall. Yuri's ears hummed as he wiped dust and debris from his face. He looked over to Alek who was doing the same. They both looked back to the gaping hole where the window had been. Daniel had vanished. Yuri rubbed his eyes looking around desperately. Alek pointed to a heap in the corner and made a slitting gesture across his throat.

Yuri understood. Although he had only known the man a few minutes he realised he represented something he wanted more than anything; freedom. They scrambled down the stairs and onto the street ducking as bullets whined past running as fast as they could until the shooting stopped.

Alek stopped to get his breath. 'Close one.'

Yuri nodded. 'I liked him. His country sounds interesting; a bit different to what I was told at school....'

Alek was gasping for breath. 'If what he says is true...'

Yuri scratched his head. 'Sounded like it to me.

26. DESPERATION

APRIL 1942

As the month progressed the weather began to improve sufficiently to allow the Germans to step up their bombing. It also encouraged people to begin thinking about planting vegetables to eat next winter. The effects of the prolonged cold and deprivation from the seige had suppressed thoughts of romance amongst the populace, and now despite the stirrings of spring they remained buried. Too much had happened and survival remained the driving instinct. They were also under pressure from their own authorities suspicious of any indications of anti Government musings. The NKVD ensured it had spies in the community and encouraged people to spy on each other and report anything that could be construed as anti Government. Propaganda was fervent in pushing the party line and that all would be well. Part of this was achieved through the state radio system brought to the people through the many loudspeakers in the streets.

Vladimir Rostockovitch sat in his office in Nadya's appartment block, listening to the announcement that the front line was being held and the Germans showing signs of weakness against the unstoppable Russian forces.

He scratched the three day stubble on his chin. 'Pig swill,' he muttered then guffawed as he swigged the whiskey given to him for information he had gathered about a Jewish family on the first floor, apartment nine. He had smiled as the police arrived and carted them off. He scratched his fat belly through a stained, once white vest, looking down the list of tenants. His greed pushed him to fawn and do everything he could to please his masters in the NKVD to ensure he continued to receive above his share of rations and odd extras such as the whiskey. So a few Jews spent the rest of their time in a Gulag. So what? He's not their keeper.

His thoughts were as usual with the young woman in number seventy three. He hadn't seen her lover for a while which was interesting. About time to pay her a visit and see how the land lies. The other man who was there didn't look as formidable as her lover. Time to find out. He sat foward as he saw Aleksei leave the building. He grabbed his coat and hurried out.

Aleksie made his way through people shuffling through the slush on the Nevtsky Prospekt toward the station with a pair of shoes under his coat. Vladimir Rostockovitch waddled as fast as he could to keep up with the fleeting figure as it vanished for a few seconds amongst the people. Eventually Aleksei arrived at some railway arches where he disappeared. Vladimir waitied in the shadows of a building not daring to go any further. A few minutes later Aleksei reappeared stuffing a brown parcel under his coat. Vladimir squeezed against the wall as Aleksei hurried past heading deeper into the city. He followed him again along wet, rubble strewn streets dodging in and out of people until Aleksei arrived at a square and joined up with some men. Vladimir had what he wanted.

Nadya was repairing a shoe that was falling to pieces, despite Aleksei insisting he could get her some more, because she wanted to prove she could mend them first. A knock at her door startled her. She did not get callers. Could it be Yuri? Perhaps Yuri had been given some leave? She tentavily opened the door a crack.

Vladimir Rostockovitch peered into the room and said with an official tone, 'I'm Vladimir Rostockovitch, apartment supervisor. I need to check your apartment.' As she began to open the door he pushed his way in. Nadya reeled as his body odour swept after him. He poked around and went into the bedroom. 'I know you slipped in here when the other girl died. But you see I am a kind man and understand how diffcult things are. So, you live alone?' She watched warily. He went on. 'You know it is forbidden to have anyone else here don't you?'

She nodded. He looked around picking up clothes then dropping them on the floor. He bent down and picked up a pair of Yuri's trousers.

'Yours?' She nodded yes. He smiled. 'Yes I suppose in these terrible times even a young woman as pretty as you needs to put warmth before style.' He leered at her. 'And you are very pretty Nadya. It is Nadya isn't it?'

She watched him without speaking, hoping he would go away.

He threw the trousers on the floor and picked up some male underwear. 'These yours too?' She watched him impassivley. He smiled. 'I have to make sure there are no German spies in the block you see. The Germans have spies in the city you know. We can't be too careful if we are to preserve the Motherland. Any wrong doings, anti party actions must be stamped out. Our wonderful President Stalin knows what we need to do. I'm sure you agree with his principles.' She continued watching him. 'Anyway, I hope we can be friends, Nadya...even good friends?' He leered at her as he continued snooping. 'We've all lost

love ones because of this terrible seige. Myself, I am now
alone. Sometimes I would love to have somebody to talk to.
Someone to cuddle even...' He looked in a draw and took out
one of Aleksei's screwdrivers. He turned to her. 'Are you good
with your hands Nadya? I like a woman whose good with her
hands.' He turned to the stove and ran his fingers over it.
'You made this?'

She dropped her eyes. He raised his eyebrows enquiringly.

'A friend did.'

'Ah. Left you some of his tools I see. Careless in these
difficult times. And these are terrible times aren't they? We
must all stick together,' he poked around, 'and be nice to
each other.' She shuddered and wrapped her arms around herself
as he leered at her. 'It must be hard trying to survive on your
own now your family are dead. I assume they are otherwise you
would be with them?' She nodded. 'It's wise Nadya in these
harsh times to accept offers of friendship from those in a
position to make life...bearable. Anyway, I must go, but think
on what I've said. I will be stopping by again soon and
perhaps we can get better aquainted. You will find I could be
very useful to you.' He sauntered to the door inspecting bits
and pieces on the table. He smiled at her, winked and opened
the door then paused. 'Oh by the way? Why do you have a second
mattress and blanket?'

She felt a wave of panic. 'My brother visits sometimes.'

He smiled. 'Ah. I see. Good bye.' He softly closed the door
behind him which seemed more sinister than his actual
presence.

She opened a window to remove the stench and sat hugging
herself rocking to and fro. What a horrible man. Her skin
crawled just thinking about him. So why call now? Obviously he
knows about Yuri and Aleksei. She was frightened of this man
having seen enough of his type from the Gulag. She knew he
would make his move soon; she had to be prepared.

The next day, Aleksei and Nadya sat at the table eating
some fruit he had obtained. She said, 'I miss Yuri so much.
How could they just take him away like that?'

'It's horrible. He must get a chance for leave though. Let's
hope it will be soon.'

She sighed. 'I hope he will be ok.'

Aleksei tried to make light of it. 'It's the Germans you
should fear for!' He became serious. 'He'll be fine Nadya.' He
studied her. 'Are you alright?'

She smiled as she looked up. 'I'm fine.' Then suddenly she rushed to the bathroom. Aleksei could hear her vomiting. She came back pale and shaken.

He put his arm around her. 'You ok?'

'Yes. I'm fine.' She fought hard not to burst into tears.

Later, Vladimir Rostockovitch watched Aleksei leave. He grabbed a bottle of vodka, splashed some cheap perfume on his stubble and left his office. Nadya jumped as her door reverberated to a solid thump and the muffled, foul voice of the Superintendent.

'It is the Superintendent, open at once!'

Nadya reluctantly opened the door and Vladimir bustled in waving the bottle. She retched as his stink enveloped her as he passed.

He put the bottle on the table and said, 'Glasses! We need to celebrate surviving that terrible winter. Look, I bring vodka.'

She hugged her arms tight around herself and pressed her back to the wall. He looked around and found two glasses which he filled from the bottle and offered one to her. She remained motionless, her arms wrapped tightly around her self watching him.

He pushed the glass closer to her face and said menacingly, 'It is not a good idea to make an enemy of me. I can be very useful to you... and your friends.' She looked shocked. He continued. 'Oh yes I know all about your friends and their goings on.' He waggled the glass in her face and said softly. 'Drink.'

She reluctantly took the glass and held it as if it was poison. He nodded for her to drink staring at the rim of the glass then to her lips. She tried to ignore the dribble on his lower lip as he leant in close to her. He emptied his glass in one go and gestured to her to do the same. She threw it in his face. He yowled as the alcohol stung his eyes then lunged at her grabbing her dress at her shoulders trying to pull it down. She tried to push him off but he was too strong, his foul breath on her neck as he tried to kiss it, his hands searching for her breasts. Instinctively she brought up her knee and rammed it between his legs.

He groaned and doubled up in agony on the floor gasping for breath. She backed away from him looking for something heavy to protect herself with. He got to his knees as she grabbed the bottle from the table and held it ready to hit him, the vodka pouring down her arm as she held the bottle aloft.

He got to his feet clutching his crutch and hissed, 'You're going to regret this. I'll make sure you never see your boyfriend again. Or the other one.' He grabbed the door and staggered out shouting over his shoulder. 'You wait and see!'

Nadya collapsed on the floor in tears listening to Vladimir as he staggered down the stairs swearing revenge. She felt a wave of nausea and hurried to the communal bathroom and vomited.

Back in his apartment Vladimir huddled in front of his fire plotting his revenge which was angrily fuelled by the ache in his crutch. First he would get those two men arrested for anti soviet behaviour — easy to invent, his word, a loyal party member against theirs, a couple of drifters — then he would have his way with that bitch before giving her up on falsified evidence. It was obvious she was from the lot who viewed his sort as inferior. Well we'll see who comes out on top shall we? He saw Aleksei enter the building and smiled to himself as he opened a tin of peaches hungrily spooning them into his mouth.

Aleksie entered the apartment and found Nadya curled up on her bed.

'He tentavily poked his head around the door. 'You ok?'

She smiled wanly. 'I'm fine, got a bug or something.'

He sat down. 'I don't know how Yuri does it Nadya. He has made so many contacts and friends who know friends who...well what a reputation he has built! I just hope I don't mess it up.' He looked up to see she was sleeping. He spent a few precious moments watching her beautiful face studying every line commiting it to memory. He sighed and stood then moved to the bed and leant over. He picked a stray length of hair from her eyes and gently put it on the pillow. He listened to her breathing, noted her long black eye lashes and left again.

It was now over a month since Yuri had been taken. Having got up hurriedly, Nadya was throwing up in the bathroom again. The dull crump of a heavy explosion as a shell landed far away caused her to look toward the window. She thought about Yuri, felt his arms around her, his smile reassuring her all was fine.

She sighed and made herself get up from the communal toilet floor. She returned to her apartment feeling weak and alone as she looked around at her few belongings. She instinctively knew she was pregnant.

She was busy cleaning out the stove when Yuri burst in. She turned in surprise fearing it was the monster from down stairs then seeing the figure of Yuri covered in dust and dirt standing there she leapt up and embraced him.

'You're alive!' She hung onto him, 'I've missed you so much. Aleksei saw you being taken.'

He hugged her. 'I wanted to write to you but communications are really bad. Alek, my friend there, said I would be able to get some leave, so I waited.' She hugged him tightly. 'Can I at least put my rifle down?!'

She pulled back a little and took it from him studying his face. She leaned it against the wall. 'You ok?'

He nodded as he stroked her hair. 'Anyway, how are you, you look a little pale.'

She turned and busied herself. 'I'm fine.'

'Where's Aleksei?'

'Out doing what you told him to do. I think he would jump off the roof if you asked him.'

He smiled as he took off his coat which scattered dust onto the floor. 'Ok I won't then.' He sat down. 'After all this is over we go to England.'

She eyed the dust on her newly cleaned floor. 'England? Why? Is it that easy? How do we get out of the country?'

'We'll find a way. We have to Nadya. I met this English man and he told me how beautiful and free it is.'

She decided the dust was not important and hugged him.

'Then that's what we'll do! I'm so glad you're here.' She brushed some grit from his stubbled chin. 'Do you have to go back to the front?'

He sighed, 'Yes. They'll come after me and shoot me as a deserter. But don't worry. I'll be ok. I've managed to avoid the infantry. I'm a sniper.' He kissed her. I'm hungry. Have we any food?'

She playfully punched him. 'Pig!' She opened a cupboard and took out a cardboard box from which she took out a tin of sardines and offered them to him.

He laughed. 'Ha, Aleksei is learning!'

'He does his best but his heart is not in it really. He longs to make things.'

'We should take him to England with us.'

'That would be good.' She put the box back in the cupboard.

She turned and studied him.

He became aware and shuffled around. 'What?'

'Oh nothing.' She smiled to herself.

He nudged her. 'What's so funny huh?'

She leant down kissing him on the cheek. 'You'll see.'

He shrugged. 'See what?'

She kissed his neck pushing herself against him.

'You're a crazy woman.'

She hugged him. 'Perhaps.'

'Is it something I've done?'

She laughed. 'Eat your sardines, have a wash, make love to me then go and do your deals and let me get on with cleaning up this pig sty.'

'Ok. I'll stay for a couple of days and put my face around then I'll have to go back.'

'I know.'

Vladimir Rostockovitch always felt nervous when he entered the police building. He knew full well the awful things that happened to people taken there by the Secret Police, how easily life and death decisions where made and families torn apart. He gingerly knocked on the door of the Commissar and on hearing the terse 'Come' he entered. He waited to be invited to stand before the large imposing desk of Commissar Sidorov who was busy writing. Sidorov stopped, carefully put the cap on his pen and looked up. A thin smile appeared and quickly vanished on his round face. He nodded to a chair opposite his desk. 'Comrade Rostockovitch. What do I owe the pleasure?'

Vladimir swallowed nevously. 'Comrade Sidorov, in these dark times we all struggle to survive. Food is hard to come by as you are well aware, although,' he hastily added, 'I know the party does it's best to look after us.' Commissar Sidorov nodded gravely. Vladimir knew he had to tread carefully. 'You have been most kind in responding to information I have provided you...'

Commissar Sidorov raised an impatient eyebrow. 'Patriotic behaviour deserves a reward. Of course we are all suffering terribly, but if individuals try to undermine the great efforts of our leader comrade Stalin, then they must be flushed out and punished.'

Vladimir nodded sagely. 'In my position as Supervisor of my apartment block I keep a vigilant eye out for such people.'

Commissar Sidorov leant forward. 'You have more names for me?'

'Yes Commissar Sidorov I have been keeping an eye on apartment seventy three. It was occupied by a family but the terrible winter took its toll and left just the daughter; a girl of seventeen. She died and another girl moved in. I've watched them. She has allowed two males to move in with her,' he hastily added, 'without my permission! And she still denies they are there.'

Commissar Sidorov sat back and steepled his fingers on his rotund belly. 'Rest assured if your information is correct you will be amply rewarded.'

'Thank you Commissar.' He leaned forward, ' I'm sure they're in the black market..'

Commissar Sidorov sat foward abruptly. 'There's too much of this type of crime. This is valuable information. I need to stamp it out. Can you get names?'

'Huh! These criminal types are cunning. I can only do my best but they are clever, meet in dark corners and work secretly. They believe themselves to be above the law.'

'Then I suggest you don't alert them that we're onto them. Keep observing and try to get the names of these criminals.'

'Yes of course Commissar. They will lead me to their nest.'

The Commissar picked up his pen, removed the cap and returned to his writing. He said without looking up, 'Anything else?'

Vladimir stood. 'No.Commissar Sidorov, and thank you for...'

The Commissar continued to write. 'You may go.'

'Thank you Commissar.' Vladimire quickly left. When he was outside he let out a deep breath and wiped the sweat from his brow. He hurriedly trudged through the melting snow — avoiding treacherous icicles hanging from disused shop fronts dropping as the temperature rose — back to the apartment block. His food supply was getting low and he needed to gather his evidence as quickly as he could. It was easy to stitch up the two males although her lover did not seem to be about. Nadya was not so easy and would require planted evidence of disident

activities. He smiled to himself as a plan formulated in his
twisted mind.

27. SIDOROV SENDS A MESSAGE

June 1942

Yuri returned to the continuing hit and run of the battle at the fringe of the beleaguered city. He had learnt to differentiate between German footprints in the mud and Russian ones. It was easy most of the time; the Russian prints were less defined because many of the soldiers had no boots and had to wrap cloth around their feet. The German boot prints were crisp. He searched apartment blocks with sections of brick missing where a shell had blasted through from the constant bombardment, empty shops, anywhere he thought looked like a good sniping position.

He failed to find Alek and made his own way — seeking out buildings to conceal himself within and snipe from — in comparative safety. He eventually found a warehouse with good visibility of two roads nearby where he had seen Germans scuttling back and forth. He set up his position.

As he sat and waited his thoughts drifted to Nadya and their last talk. He hadn't thought much about it until now and remembered how mysteriously she was acting and how pale she had looked. He suddenly realised. Would she tell him if she was pregnant? Probably not. He would have to speak to her when he went back in a few days. Yuri thought about England and how it sounded the ideal place to raise a family. After this was over he would take them all there.

He began to doze but was stirred by the sound of movement below. He peeked over the window cill between cobwebs he had left as cover, and saw with horror four tanks parked, their drivers standing around smoking. Around the tanks soldiers leant on them smoking and chatting. Yuri knew he could be in trouble and kept himself hidden, but he was able to peek enough to watch them. He thought when they were relaxed they looked quite human. So how could they carry out the atrocities he had heard about? What caused men to do such evil things? One of them took out a photograph and showed it to another. They studied it and shook hands.

Yuri thought about his family and a tear formed trickling down his dirty face. He looked around him at the area of the warehouse he was in. He noticed pieces of damaged machinery, piles of sacking and broken packing boxes. How Nadya would love to collect all that! He could taste the dust from the floor and smell the damp in the walls. A memory of the farm he had been brought up in flooded him quickly turning to anger.

He looked back outside and saw the drivers getting back into their tanks, the soldiers bustling back and forth getting ready to move. He decided he would let them. He might get a couple of them but it would give away his position.

The tanks were started up belching acrid black smoke from their enormous engines and moved away, the soldiers walking behind them for cover. Reluctantly Yuri remained still until they had gone. Perhaps there would be a few stragglers coming along. He waited. It became dusk and he carefully moved his legs to get the circulation going when he spotted a soldier further away but coming in his direction. He decided to risk a long shot, something he had been successful at a couple of times by practicing the tips Alek had given him about trajectory, weight of the bullet, wind. He sighted on the man and squeezed the trigger. The man fell backwards unaware of what had hit him. Yuri smiled grimly and looked for another target.

Suddenly a bullet whined past thudding into the brick behind him. He tried to see where it had come from then ducked as another bullet ricocheted off the edge of the window. A third then fourth then fifth bullet buzzed close to his head as he crouched down. He was in trouble. The bullets continued for a few seconds then stopped. He waited for a few seconds more then risked a peek over the cill. He felt the thud of a bullet in his shoulder that spun him backwards crashing onto a wooden pallet. He laid stunned, fear creeping over him as for the first time he felt helpless. Another bullet ricocheted into his thigh. He realised his arm felt warm and saw the blood seeping through his coat. He began to feel dizzy and his world went black. His last thought that of green fields and sunshine.

Aleksei and Nadya were eating when a bang on the door jolted them. Nadya opened it to find three police officers and a weasely looking man in a suit who immediately took control as he strutted in, uninvited.

He looked around and studied Aleksei then barked, 'What is your name?'

Aleksei felt his insides melt with fear, his mouth suddenly dry, and his legs shaking, 'Aleksei Krupin sir.'

The man looked him up and down as he held out his hand and said, 'Your identification?'

Aleksei gulped. 'My papers have been stolen Sir.'

The man smiled thinly his eyes flinty and suspicious. 'How unfortunate.'

He turned to Nadya. 'And you?'

She looked defiantly at him, went to a drawer and took out her ration card which she thrust at him. He checked it and handed it back to her. Vladimir appeared at the top of the stairs puffing from the exertion keen to see what was happening.

The weasely man beckoned him in and nodded toward Aleksei. 'This is the one?'

Vladimir smirked. 'One of them yes. Not the leader though. He is bigger, taller. But,' he added, 'I saw this one meeting others in dark alleyways.'

'You would testify to this?'

Vladimir nodded. The weasely man turned to the officers and instructed them to take Aleksei away. Nadya tried to hold onto him but she was pushed away and fell to the floor. The weasely man left. She listened helplessly as Aleksei was dragged down the stairs desperately insisting he had done nothing wrong.

Vladimir stood in the doorway. 'I warned you. You shouldn't make an enemy out of me.' He left shutting the door gently.

She sat on the floor in shock as she looked around at the empty flat in the sudden silence. An air raid siren began its urgent wail but she didn't stir. She rested her hands on her swollen tummy and cried.

Later, Nadya huddled on her bed trying to think what she should do. If Yuri was there she would feel safer but she never knew when he would appear. She knew he had to do what he was doing and was not angry with him but she resented the whole situation that constantly threatened their happiness. She wanted to tell him about the baby but knew it would distract him. It was something she intended to put off for as long as possible hoping their situation would improve but now everything had changed for the worse. She knew it was a matter of time before they would come for her; that pig downstairs would make sure of that.

She tried not to imagine what Yuri was going through. She didn't like to think of the danger he was in aware that he made light of it.

There was a knock at her door. Reluctantly she opened it to Vladimir who smiled smugly and pushed his way in. He sat at her table and watched her as she pushed herself against the wall as if hoping she could melt into it. She eyed him with loathing.

His smile widened. 'So Nadya. Your friend will get the punishment he deserves. It is only a matter of time before we find your other friend.' He stood and studied her. 'You look fatter? Your belly seems bigger.' He stood, poking around bits and pieces on the table then stopped. 'Ah! You have a little one on the way huh? You're going to need all the help you can get. You need to know who your real friends are. People like me can make life good for you. You can't be selfish Nadya. You will have a child to consider soon. I think you must be nice to me huh?'

She gave him a look of disgust and said through clenched teeth, 'Never. I will kill myself before that.'

He laughed. 'I think you mean it! Anyway, we'll see won't we?' He stood and meandered to the door. 'You know where to find me. Don't wait too long though. You may get a knock at your door by the secret police...' He went down the stairs laughing to himself.

Nadya knew she would not see Aleksie again. Her heart felt like breaking at the cruelty of it all. She longed for Yuri to appear and make it all ok. She stared at the door as if to make him come back. Her world felt as if it was collapsing in around her.

It grew dark and the shelling began. She winced at the constant thunder of the guns and the impact of the shells. She had only a little wood left for the stove and virtually no food. Unless she took things into her own hands she would not survive; or their child. She stroked her tummy and spoke softly. 'I'll look after you. Your Daddy will come back soon.' She looked around at the tiny apartment, her few belongings that she took pride in; the fruit bowl her mother had bought one Christmas, a picture of her parents, all of which she knew she had to leave. She desperately wanted to wait for Yuri but the threat from the pig downstairs was too real.

In desperation she tried to think if there was some way she could placate him long enough for Yuri to return, and then they could make a run for it, but she knew what the pig wanted and her flesh crept. If she left a note for Yuri, Vladimir would find it and she didn't know Yuri's contacts to leave a message with them. She could go and search for Yuri and she tried to remember where he said he had been going. There was a village he had mentioned but the name wouldn't come. She paced back and forth thinking as the night descended. She had to dig deep now, it was no time to be scared. She was trapped and had to take control.

Downstairs Vladimir sat deep in thought. It was obvious the girl was too stubborn and no amount of coercion was going to change her mind. The Commissar had made it clear he would not sanction the rewards being released until all three were in custody. He needed to speed matters up but also he needed to be cunning about it. If she was too scared she would run and then he wouldn't get the big fellow, the ring leader. He needed to make her feel safer, until the guy reappeared as he had done recently.

Nadya stood looking out at the surrounding buildings, some on fire and all displaying damage of some sort, wondering how long it would be before they were demolished by the constant barrage. She thought of Yuri, his smile, the way he held her but her reverie was interrupted as her door opened and Vladimir entered. She instinctively backed away, leaning on the table and reaching behind her for a bread knife she had placed there.

He smiled warmly. 'I have been thinking. I may have sounded a little harsh. You've got a week to consider my offer. I am sure by then you will have come to your senses.' He smiled warmly. 'Is there anything I can do for you now?' She gripped the knife tightly, as she shook her head. 'You must trust me Nadya.' He looked at her lasciviously. 'We could be friends, good friends. You have one week. Goodnight.'

She stared at the door. Her mind whirling with fear and loathing. Was it a trick? It must be, Why would he do that? Her stomach turned over; to catch Yuri of course. Her decision was made. Her fear had cleared her mind; she'd remembered the name of the village. She gathered her coat and anything else she could wear to keep warm, looked around once then grabbed any food she could find which she stuffed in her pockets and hurried down the stairs. If Yuri was there, they could take their chances on the Ice Road — she had heard was planned as soon as the weather improved — and get past the seige ring to the "mainland". Better than falling into the hands of the NKVD.

She gritted her teeth against the cold wind as she left the apartment and trudged through the snow towards what she hoped would one day be freedom. As she walked she avoided looking at the decomposing bodies still strewn on the pavement although the early thaw had been short lived, followed by a sharp reminder of the cold winter. Nadya plodded on through the dark and snow following the few remaining road signs toward the village of Murino. She tried not to think of Aleksei or the fate that probably awaited him. She concentrated on Yuri's smile and his voice encouraging her to keep going.

She found she was passing fields now and wondered if she could find any scraps to eat. It was imperative she ate for the sake of her baby and as soon as it was light she would look. As she rounded a bend a solitary cottage came into view picked out by the wane moonlight that shone weakly through a break in the clouds.

With enough light to check for recent footprints in the snow she was satisfied the cottage was not occupied. She tentatively tried the door which she found to her relief was not locked and went in. Apart from the scurry of rats it was empty. She couldn't make out much of the room as she huddled in a corner and pulled her coat tighter around her. She was exhausted and although she could hear the rats re—establishing their territory oblivious of her presence, she was too tired to be frightened and drifted into a fitful sleep. She dreamt of parties and friends calling with cake laughing and giggling, of introducing Yuri to her parents presenting them with their first grandchild.

At first light she awoke and looked around the deserted room. On the walls were family pictures above pieces of furniture now covered with dust. There were curtains at the windows and a rug on the wooden floor. She wondered what family had lived here before this insanity had been foisted on them. She stood and stretched feeling hungry. She left the cottage and noticed her footprints leading toward the front door. Reassuringly there were no others as a thin covering of snow had begun to soften the outline of her foot prints which she now retraced back to the road.

She clambered over a shallow ditch into a field and searched for anything to eat trying to dig over the partially frozen earth with her bare hands. She realized the ground was still too hard and returned to the cottage to find something to dig with. She saw a wooden shed at the rear of the cottage and relieved it was not locked, went inside. She heard rats scurrying into the dark recesses provided by sacks and pieces of wood. She rummaged around and settled for a piece of wood sufficiently thick to dig with.

She returned to the field and began stabbing at the hard surface. At first the wood glanced off the frozen earth but gradually a dent appeared and few fragments of frozen soil broke away. Heartened by this success she kept stabbing away until eventually she broke enough away to reveal a couple of frozen carrots and a potatoe. She stuffed them in her pocket and returned to the cottage. Inside she looked around for anything she could use to cook with and eventually discovered an empty tin. She went outside and put a handful of snow in the tin together with the frozen carrots and potatoes.

From her pocket she took out a piece of flint and a stone which she struck together to light some pieces of dry wood and leaves from the floor. After a number of strikes she managed a spark and carefully blew on the tinder until it flashed alight. Quickly she built a fire with more wood and balanced the tin on a couple of bricks she had found outside. She sat back and watched as the flames blackened the outside of the tin. She kept putting more wood onto the fire until the water began to boil.

As she idly watched the flames she thought of Yuri. Where was he? Was he ok or was he lying wounded or dead somewhere? And Aleksei? What would become of him? What had people done to deserve this? Most surprising of all was how quickly it all seemed to have come upon them. She would never have thought a year ago that she would be doing the things she was now. A wave of anger flooded her at the unfairness of it all as the water boiled and she stirred the carrots with a piece of stick.

She broke up the carrots and potatoes in the tin to make a soup. She ate it slowly savouring every mouthful, not wasting the smallest amount, acutely aware of how hungry she was. A sudden memory of family meals and luxuries such as fresh bread and fruit hit her. How things had changed.

She stood and looked around for anything she could take with her that could be of use. She found a rusty knife and length of string both of which she stuffed in her pockets. In the distance she could hear the rumble of gun fire reminding her of her purpose as she reluctantly left the comparative safety of the cottage and rejoined the road producing footprints in the virgin snow as she continued toward the fighting. A thin smattering of snow began to lie on her coat as she trudged along but she ignored it. She had one purpose now and that was to find Yuri.

She walked for what seemed hours noticing the sound of gunfire grow ever closer as she entered the outskirts of the village she was looking for. From here it would become ever more dangerous and she needed to be wary. The blurred outlines of something appeared from the flurries of snow ahead becoming more solid as it drew nearer taking the form of a group of men; she saw they had guns but couldn't make out if they were German or Russian soldiers. She hid behind a hedge until she made out their Russian uniforms. Quickly she jumped out and shouted to them. The ones at the front kept running but a young man at the back slowed and turned. She ran to him as he turned back to look where his friends were.

He eyed her suspiciously. 'What are you doing? You are mad to be here. Why didn't you go with the others, the Germans are breaking through. If you've got any sense you'll run.' He turned and sprinted after the others.

She began to run after him. 'Wait. Please!' He hesitated half turning as he continued to run. She gasped as she ran after him. 'I'm looking for Yuri, Yuri Kazakof, he's a sniper.'

The soldier threw his arms up in despair. 'Never heard of him. Dead I should think like most of them. Run!'

She slowed and began walking in the direction of the soldiers sobbing with frustration and fear. He couldn't be dead. Not Yuri. He loved her, he would take care. She stopped and looked back toward the village and the increasing sound of gunfire as the Germans approached. She knew it was hopeless to risk going any further into the village and followed the soldiers back the way she had come. Her legs felt weak as she trudged through the snow following the soldier's footprints now superimposed in reverse over her own from earlier.

As she wearily made her way back toward the city she wondered in desperation what she would do now. If she went back to her apartment it was inevitable he would try and have his way with her then turn her in to the authorities. She knew she had little choice but to try and survive on the streets until the Ice Road was passable when she would try and get out of the city before the Germans came.

Her one driving need was to look after their baby; to do that she needed to eat. The wind had picked up again and snow began driving at her face sticking in her eyes. So much for the early thaw! She shivered imagining what it would be like on the streets; the cold, the desperate men looking for any source of food. She was so desperate she began to consider whether she could allow Vladimir near her if it meant she could remain healthy for the baby. She shuddered at the thought. Way off in the distance she could just make out the outline of the city.

Yuri groaned as he became conscious. As he focused he saw Alek crouching beside him.

Alek said, 'Welcome back. Thought you were a gonner. Luckily I managed to stop the bleeding and luckily for you the bullet went right through. Can't promise you won't have an infection in your leg though.'

Yuri tried to sit up but gave up and remained on his back. 'How long...'

Alek was filling a tin with water and said, 'About three days. You were lucky I found you. I couldn't get you back to the unit. We've been pinned down.'

'Thanks Alek.'

Alek smiled. 'You would have done the same for me.'

Yuri nodded then said, 'I have to get back and make sure Nadya is ok.' He made a move to sit up but fell back exhausted.

Alek said, 'We're safe enough here, well behind the lines because we seem to have stopped them getting any closer. The area's not so good for sniping from buildings though so I'm going into the fields where we've got a division pinned down. See if I can pick a few off then I'll come back for you.'

Yuri laid back and nodded that he understood. After Alek had gone he began thinking about Nadya. How they seemed to fit together so well, to see the world the same way and yet in some ways they were very different. When this was all over he would take her to England, this magical place Daniel spoke about. He drifted off beneath a blanket of pain from his shoulder and leg.

Alek crawled into a position he felt comfortable with and set up his rifle. He was lying on his stomach against a grassy bank, partially covered with snow. He could see movement in a wooded area five hundred yards away which gave him a good opportunity to pick a couple off without giving his position away, then he could move further along the bank and do it again. With everything set up he laid and waited. Eventually a shot offered itself and he put a bullet right into the head of a tank driver. Then another of a soldier smoking.

Alek smiled grimly to himself unaware that he was not the only sniper around. A German sniper with many kills to his belt had been watching Alek since he set up his position and now satisfied he had the shot he had been waiting for gently squeezed the trigger and put a bullet straight through Alek's skull. He was dead before he had slumped forward face first into the snow where a large red patch quickly spread outwards.

It became dark and Yuri expected Alek to appear but he didn't. He had no idea where he was other than in a barn as evidenced by bales of straw and machinery. He lay in the straw and fell into another fitful sleep. The next day he was woken by a party of Russian soldiers surprised to find him there. He was taken back to his regiment and the doctor checked him over. He was told he had to rest if he was to keep his leg which was severly infected.

28. RECOVERY

Aleksei lay hunched in the darkness; the only light, that which trickled through gaps around the doors and after a while his eyes grew accustomed to it allowing him to just make out the walls. He tried to stand but the pain in his legs, back and stomach from the guard's beatings made him cry out. He slumped down again. The attempt had been sufficient to indicate the cell was around six feet wide. He assumed it would be a little longer. He nursed his bruised stomach where he had been beaten, tenderly touching the underside of his arms where he had tried to fend off the blows. One guard in particular seemed to enjoy inflicting pain being goaded on by the others.

Aleksei huddled in a corner. He was terrified. He hated physical violence fearing he would not survive many more beatings. He could hear other prisoners groaning in nearby cells; one man crying out for his mother, a plaintive sound that fuelled Aleksei's anxiety. He became aware of the cell floor which felt gritty and when he moved he coughed as fine dust filled his nostrils. His senses, heightened by the darkness, became aware of odd sensations on his ankles and shins. He felt around in the dark and discovered to his horror things crawling on his legs. He frantically brushed at them; temporarily ignoring the pain it caused in his shoulders and arms, and moved to a different part of the floor. He realised it was futile; whatever it was would be all over the floor.

Desperation engulfed him. How much can a person endure before they give in? He was not like Yuri, his skills lay in creating things, poetry, listening to bird song. When did he last hear birds sing? His mind keen to find something to occupy it dwelled on the thought. How could something so beautiful vanish without him noticing? Where had they gone? Was it the shelling drove them away? No. He remembered his neighbours throwing nets over the hedges, which at the time he thought was odd. Now he understood.

His thoughts were interrupted by footsteps outside his cell door. The sound of keys jangling as it was unlocked and swung open on creaking hinges letting in light from the corridor silhouetting the rotund figure of the guard who had administered the beating. Aleksei cowered waiting for the blows hoping he would quickly pass out to avoid the agony.

The man entered and grabbed him by the arm pulling him roughly to his feet uttering in a gravelly voice from excessive smoking and drinking, 'Get up.'

Aleksei struggled against the pain in his body as he was roughly manhandled out into the corridor, he felt like retching as the foul body odour of the guard filled his nostrils. As he was pulled and pushed by the guard he tried to make sense of where he was. He counted five cell doors behind which he sensed lay the poor wretches he had heard earlier.

They reached a door which the guard opened whilst gripping Aleksei's right arm causing pain to shoot through his shoulder from the beatings. He was pulled into another corridor, more brightly lit which assailed his eyes as he tried to hold his free arm up to cover them. They reached a flight of stairs which the guard pushed and dragged him up, each step sending pain through his right leg which could hardly sustain his weight where he had been kicked. They entered another corridor, this one even more brightly lit with windows through which he could tell it was night. They came to an office door and the guard knocked. From inside a muffled voice said 'Come.'

The guard opened the door and his demeanour immediately became subservient as he shoved Aleksei forward toward the desk of Commissar Sidorov. 'Prisoner Krupin Sir,' he said gruffly.

Aleksei's whole body trembled with pain and fear as he waited. He could only see the top of the man's head as he leaned forward writing. Commissar Sidorov stopped writing, carefully picked up the top to his pen and slowly replaced it. Aleksei's fear increased as the cold narrow eyes of Commissar Sidorov met his as he removed a cigarette and tapped it on the cigarette box before closing it. He lit the cigarette and with an exaggerated movement drew on it holding it in his Chupin style.

He said calmly, 'So. You know why you are here?' Aleksei shook his head. The chair creaked as Commissar Sidorov sat back and studied him for a few seconds. 'Then let me enlighten you. In these dark times we must all work together for our Motherland. Our great leader works tirelessly for our well being and despite the evil enemy at our gates he does his best to put in place a system to supply food to us all. Unfortunately there are some who believe they deserve more and step outside the law for their own selfish ends.' He leant forward. 'You have been observed exchanging goods — no doubt stolen from hard working citizens struggling to survive these desperate times — for extra food. Obviously you and your friends consider that you deserve more than the rest of us.'

Aleksei took in the fat belly of the man sitting in judgement over him recalling the bitterness with which his father had described the corrupt bureaucracy that governed them.

The Commissar leaned back and attempted a smile as he continued. 'Give me the name of your associate and provide me with evidence that the woman is as guilty as you and I will consider making your sentence less harsh.' He waited. Aleksei felt weak as his legs wobbled with fatigue and fear.

The Commissar smiled. 'Come now Aleksei. Think of yourself here. Your friends are not here to save you. Do you really think they wouldn't give you up to save themselves? By the looks of you a spell in the Gulag would not be beneficial. Save yourself. Work with me by providing the information I need to maintain law and order in these dark times and you might find life easier.'

Aleksei thought of Yuri and Nadya, their kindness and honesty. He stood upright and said, 'No. I won't.'

Commissar Sidorov picked up his pen, removed the top and went back to his writing. 'Very well. I sentence you to fifteen years at the gulag.' Without looking up he said coldly, 'Take him away.'

Aleksei was dragged back to his cell and thrown in.

The guard laughed as he slammed the door shut. 'Have a nice time ha!'

Despite his pain and discomfort, he felt for the first time in his twenty eight years that he had discovered courage he never believed he possessed and his refusal to give them any information — although probably a death sentence for him — could save the lives of the two people he loved more than anything. He knew his father would have been proud of him; patting his back, his mother kissing his forehead with pride. Whatever happened to him he hoped that his memory would remain with Yuri and Nadya.

As he sat huddled in his coat he thought about his two friends. He recalled the number of mornings that Nadya had been sick recently. He realised how naive he was in not understanding what was happening to her. He could imagine Yuri being a wonderful father and what an example Nadya would set. He felt wistful, thinking how he longed for it to have been his child but... The cold and damp of his cell reminded him of the realities and what was to come.

Nadya arrived back at the city and headed for the Nevsky Prospekt. She wondered whether she would be able to find an apartment left vacant by an unfortunate family. It was dark as she entered an apartment block in the poorer sector of the city where she knew the deaths were higher. She found one on a second floor but to her horror discovered the corpse of an old lady in the bedroom. She shuddered at the macabre sight and hurried out despite bits and pieces lying around that might be useful to her; somehow she just couldn't bring herself to take anything, it seemed too irreverent.

Shelling began again and she took cover in another block of flats. She wondered if her college friend Anna was still there and how wonderful that would be to see a friendly face. She made her way up the five flights of steps to the apartment she remembered visiting in what seemed another life. As she approached the door she saw it was ajar.

Her heart sank as she peeked inside to find it was empty apart from a table and bed. She went in and checked the door would close then sat at the table for a moment to catch her breath. Ok she needed bedding which would hopefully still be at her apartment. She would go there now and get it despite the shelling. With luck she could avoid the pig downstairs and make her escape with her few belongings.

She made her way diving for cover occasionally as a shell whistled overhead until she reached Inber's apartment. She checked under the stairs and found with relief the sledge that Yuri used for moving things. She hurried up the steps and quickly gathered everything together and bundled it all into her sheet which she took downstairs praying he would not poke his head out and catch her. She made it to the sledge and loaded everything onto it quickly pulling it away into the darkness and what she hoped would be comparative safety; at least from that pig.

As she plodded along she felt the presence of the baby inside her. She wanted to feel elated but was too tired and scared as the shells continued to whistle over crashing into buildings causing everything to shudder and shake around her.

She eventually got everything into her new flat and closed the door on the madness outside. She made up her bed and curled up under the thin blanket to get warm thinking sadly of the lovely stove Aleksei had made for them. At least the weather was becoming less cold with brief bouts of weak sun aiding the thaw. As she drifted off she thought about the Ice Road and decided tomorrow she would investigate what was happening. As much as it saddened her, she could see no way of contacting Yuri or leaving a message without putting them both in danger. All she could hope for was that he would find her. She fell into a fitful sleep which provided very little respite from the horrors of her life.

Over the next two months Nadya knew she needed to eat more than the scraps she existed on from the official food shop. She feared being spotted by the supervisor of her previous flat and avoided the area. She was sure he would do all he could to get her arrested and this made her unsure about being in public places where she used to live. However, despite her fears she kept returning to the area, hoping to see Yuri looking for her, keeping to the shadows, venturing out when others took to the air raid shelters.

As she foraged for food she remembered what Yuri had told her about watching the factories and odd shops still open to see where the workers lived. Once, she had gone with him to the railway arches where he met his friends and decided she could leave her address with them to give him when he came back and found Inber's flat empty.

After a few days of following two women connected with a factory and who looked well fed she decided to take her chance and break in to their houses when they were away. Terrified, she looked for unsecured windows and did as Yuri had said and took a little at a time, careful not to be greedy.

Her health began to improve, the sores on her legs going and the ulcers in her mouth reducing. Her baby was kicking which gave her hope. She remained in her friend's flat surviving on whatever meagre rations she could steal and four candles to use as light and a tiny amount of heat; more for psychological comfort than physical.

By speaking to people and listening in to conversations she kept up with the fighting outside the city. The Soviet forces were holding the Germans back but a break in the siege seemed just a distant hope.

She thought of Yuri everyday hoping he would appear, not wanting to imagine him dead.

29. TWO STEPS FORWARD...

June 1942

Yuri's shoulder began to heal but his leg wound remained infected. There was no transport back to the city as the Germans continued to try and break through the Russian defences requiring maximum resistance. Yuri was reluctantly confined to his bunk for two months in a makeshift hospital before he was fit enough to walk; albeit with a limp. He was Yuri granted permission to return to the city.

Yuri rode with other wounded soldiers on a rusty worn out lorry to the city of Leningrad desperate to see Nadya and reassure her he was ok. He climbed the four flights of steps slowing down on the landing when he saw the door was ajar. His stomach sunk as he slowly pushed the door open to find the flat empty. It was obvious she and Aleksei had gone. His mind reeled as he tried to make sense of it. He knew Aleksei had feelings for her but he also knew she only had space in her heart for him; unless she believed he was dead. But she wouldn't give up that easily. He sat on the floor with his head in his hands when he heard footsteps on the stairs.

Vladimir Rostockovitch stuck his head round the door. 'I thought you were gone for good. I suppose you're wondering where your friends have gone?' Yuri stood and towered over him.

Vladimir took a step back. 'I should be careful if I were you, I have friends in powerful places,' slyly he added, 'perhaps I can help you. Your friend Aleksei Krupin was arrested for stealing.' he gave Yuri a knowing look. 'He refused to save himself. He's gone to the Gulag so you can kiss him goodbye. Your girlfriend, well who knows. The authorities are searching for her because a number of anti Soviet propoganda leaflets were found in this very flat. And you, my friend are also wanted.'

Yuri moved close to Vladimir and leant down to him. 'Perhaps I can't save my friend but I'm going to find Nadya and when I know she is safe I am going to come back here and kill you.'

Vladimir tried to bluff. 'No you won't. I have a lot of influencial friends and they'll protect me.' He backed off to the door where he said, 'Anyway, she's most likely dead now

having to live off the streets.' He scuttled away quickly.
Yuri clenched his fists in anger controlling the urge to
follow the nasty little man and kill him there and then.

Yuri was sure the fat little pig would run to the police and
left the apartment immediately to find a spot where he could
sit and think. His heart felt heavy when he thought of Aleksei
who he knew would not be able to survive the harsh regime of a
prsion camp, but he knew it would not help to think of that
now.

Vladimir shut his door and breathed a sigh of relief. That
was a close call. He'd almost forgotten about the girl and her
lover since they had disappeared. His interests were with
Sidorov. The man gave him the creeps — ironic considering his
own evil proclivities — a sure sign all was not as it
appeared. Vladimir and Sidorov were outsiders; unable to
belong to society; doomed to act out their lives in darkness.
And so Vladimir instinctively knew Sidorov must have a secret;
a weakness he would be desperate to hide. It was just a matter
of time before he could discover what it might be. He spied on
him week after week until he struck gold. Commissar Sidovar
had a proclivity for young boys.

Vladimir had no loyalty to the Commissar and was considering
whether it was time to use the information he had on him. He
had to be careful though. The Commissar was not a man to treat
lightly. He was dangerous and rutheless. He needed to think
how to handle it. Vladimir looked at his last bottle of vodka
and sighed. No. It was too dangerous to blackmail the
Commissar. He would have to think of something else and keep
the valuable information he had on the man for such time as he
needed it to protect himself.

In the meantime however, a word with the Commissar about
Yuri would not go amiss. He saw Yuri leave and hurried out
after him taking care to remain hidden, watching Yuri sit
beneath a tree deep in thought. Vladimir picked at his nails
nervously, impatient for him to move on and lead him somewhere
useful with information he could pass onto the Commissar.

Yuri desperately tried to think. So where would she go if
she had to leave the flat suddenly? He had no idea but he knew
she was resourceful; she would give an address to his friends
at the arches! He jumped up and headed across the square
noticing with horror the number of rats scurrying about; the
result of the thaw and dead bodies.

Eventually he reached the arches and waited patiently until
someone he knew appeared.

A tall thin man appeared and embraced Yuri. 'Yuri! We thought you were dead. And Aleksei. We haven't seen him either.'

Yuri smiled sadly. 'He's been sent to the Gulag. I was arrested and sent to the army. I got wounded. Listen, you don't know where Nadya is do you?'

Boris punched him playfully. 'Of course! She left an address in case you bothered to come back.' He nudged him playfully. 'Come, let's have a drink to celebrate you are still alive!' He took out a hip flask and offered it to Yuri who took a swig beore handing it back to him. Boris laughed and took a crumpled piece of paper from his pocket. 'See! Your good friend Boris looks after you huh?'

Yuri took the paper and embraced his friend again. 'Thank you. And you? How has it been here?'

'Shells. Snow. Thaw. No food. Many dead bodies — now stinking in the streets.'

Yuri said, 'I would still rather be here than at the front. We have hardly anything to fight with and the officers are idiots. I must go and find her Boris. I'll see you later. Take care.' He ran off.

He went to the address, climbed the stairs and walked along the concrete landing toward the apartment hoping in his heart that Nadya was there. There was no reply, He tried again then decided he had no choice but to wait.

Vladimir watched from the shadows as he noted the apartment number and hurried to the NKVD building. He was ushered through to the Commissar's office and waited outside for the customery 'come.'

He entered and waited as usual for the Commissar to stop writing. He began to wonder what it was that the man spent so much time writing about. Now that he had the juicy, valuable information on the fat little man behind his grand desk he began to feel less anxious and coughed to get his attention.

The Commissar stopped writing and looked up. 'Yes?'

Vladimir wanted to blurt out what he knew about him and remove that smirk but he replied, 'The blackmarket leader Kazakof is back. He just threatened me. I followed him to an apartment where I think the woman is living.' He held out a piece of paper, 'Here is the address.'

The Commissar motioned for him to sit down and sat back in thought. 'I see. I was beginning to think you had lost interest in supporting the party Vladimir.'

Vladimir leaned forward. 'No, I've been ... busy. If you get your men to that apartment quickly, you should catch him.'

The Commissar called for a guard who appeared immediately.

The Commissar passed on the piece of paper to him saying, 'Get there now and arrest whoever you find.' The guard hurried out.

Vladimir continued. 'This war is a terrible thing Commissar; it makes men do bad things?'He looked down a this hands. 'A friend passed on some gossip...'

The Commissar's eyes narrowed slightly. 'Gossip?'

Vladimir smiled slyly. 'Yes. Of course I do not heed such nonsense but on this occassion I intend to check it out for myself.'

The Commissar studied him. 'Get to the point man.'

Vladimir was enjoying his power. 'Well,' he leaned back and crossed his legs, 'it involves an official, who,' he took on a look of distaste, 'has a nasty habit.'

The Commissar's eyes flashed. 'Habit?'

'yes. A bad habit. One the party would be interested in stopping.'

Sidorov frowned. 'Do you have evidence? A name so that I can catch this evil person?'

Vladimir coughed and said importantly. 'I do. But as I said, it may only be gossip.'

'Of course. We don't want to go making false claims?' The Commissar considered for a moment then stood and paced slowly deep in thought. He paused and asked casually, 'This friend? Is he local?'

Vladimir stood and turned toward him. 'I can't say anymore at the moment...' He eyed the cupboard.

Sidorov smiled. 'Of course. Keep me informed of anything you discover though.' He went to the cupboard. 'I think your efforts with the blackmarket thieves warrants a couple of bottles?'

Vladimir joined him. 'That's very kind of you Sir.'

Sidorov took out two bottles and handed them to him. 'We must work together for the sake of the party.'

Vladimir smiled. 'Yes Commissar.'

Yuri sat at the bottom of the stairs waiting to see if Nadya would appear. He became dopey drifting in and out of sleep. It grew dark and he began to feel he was wasting his time when two men appeared from the shadows coming in his direction. Yuri had been around enough to know they were secret police.

He jumped up as they drew near and knocked one down with a single punch to the head. The second man reached for his gun but Yuri grabbed him before he could get it out and broke his arm. The man cried out in agony and slumped to the ground as Yuri ran off. When he was a safe distance away he stopped and hid behind a tree. He continued to watch as the two men limped away.

An hour passed and then he saw her. Her beautiful face was intent on carrying a box up the stairs. He checked all was clear and ran after her catching her up on the second flight. He shouted to her. She stopped, turned in shock and dropped the box spilling tins and fruit over the stairs.

She ran down the stairs to him and threw herself at him. 'Yuri! Your safe.' She kissed his face and neck as she hugged him until he winced as she grabbed his shoulder. Concerned she said, 'You're hurt? Show me where...'

He tried to pick her up but grimaced at the pain in his shoulder. She took his hand and led him up the stairs to Anna's apartment.

He followed her in and held her close to him whispering, 'I've thought of nothing but you Nadya these past months. I couldn't get back. I was in the field hospital.'

She ran her hands over him in desperation. 'Where are you hurt?'

He took off his coat grunting at the effort it took to get it over his shoulder. 'I was shot here,' He pointed to his shoulder, 'but it went right through. I seem to be ok. And here.' He pointed to his left thigh.

She hugged him close. 'I thought you were dead.'

He smiled grimly. 'So did I. He held her at arms length and studied her. 'Are you ok? You look tired.'

She sat down. 'I tried to look for you. That pig from downstairs had Alekesie arrested and threatened me. I had to leave.'

He looked incredulous. 'You came looking for me? Do you know how dangerous that was?'

Her deep brown eyes flashed defensivly. 'Yes! I do! I needed to find you.'

'I said I would come back.'

'But you didn't!'

He said angrily, 'I was in hospital. Nadya, you could have been killed.'

'I needed to talk to you...'

He said angrily, 'Talk to me?'

She jumped up. 'Yes, talk to you!'

'What is there so important that you have to risk your life to talk to me!

'To tell you I'm pregnant!'

He sat down, rubbing his face with his hands. 'Pregnant..?'

She sat down again and put her arm round his shoulders. 'I didn't want to put pressure on you.'

'You should have told me.'

'I couldn't.'

'You couldn't?'

'They took you away from me, remember?'

He turned and held her. 'I know. It's wonderful news. The timing is...'

She poked him. 'Too late I'm afraid. She's kicking.'

'She?'

'Uhuh.'

He opened her coat surprised by the enormous bump. 'Wow!' He looked worried. 'Are you eating enough is the baby...'

'The baby is fine.'

'A girl? You know?'

She smiled. 'I'm pretty sure. And yes we are eating ok. I've been stealing like you did! I'm not proud of it but these people seem happy to keep it to themselves and I have a baby to think about.'

He hugged her. 'I know. It's been horrible for me too. The Englishman is dead and Alek disappeared.' He became sad. 'He was a good friend to me. He saved my life when I was shot. Just laying in that hospital seemed for ever. I thought of you everyday.'

'Show me where you are hurt.'

He took off his jacket and pulled down his shirt to reveal an ugly scar on his shoulder and on his back below his shoulder blade. He said, 'It's ok now, just hurts sometimes.' He touched his leg. 'The shrapnel in my thigh caused the most problem but it's getting better.'

'I'm sorry about your friends. I would like to hear about them, especially the Englishman.'

'You will. But I'm here to look after you now. Tell me about Aleksei.'

She shuddered. 'That horrible Supervisor at the apartment informed on him and tried to set a trap for you. I had to leave before he got me and I came to look for you but some soldiers who were running away from the village you told me about, said the Germans were breaking through and I should get away when I could. So I came back here.'

He sighed. 'I think we are holding them back Nadya.'

'I hope so.'

'Ok, I will see what provisions I can get us. At least it is getting warmer now. Perhaps we can grow some vegetables. I will have to be careful though because if I'm caught they will send me to the Gulag for sure.'

Nadya held him. 'You won't be leaving me again Yuri Kazakof. Grow a beard and cut your hair.'

He pulled a face. 'There were two secret police followed me here so we will to have to move somewhere else tonight.'

She nodded and began putting belongings together.

He smiled grimly. 'You'll be safe with me.'

She stopped and looked at him. 'I know I will.'

They left the apartment and Yuri loaded up the sledge she had stored behind some shrubs. They made their way toward another block of flats and tried their luck until they found one suitable. It was just as the others and clean having been empty since the winter. The apartment block supervisor was not around and they assumed he had not survived the winter. It was as good as anywhere to prepare for the birth of their baby.

30. TIME OUT

The weather was better now and summer on its way; something the residents of Leningrad could look forward to if it wasn't for the continual bombardment. Good weather meant more air strikes and bombing.

Yuri looked out of the flat window wondering how long the city could withstand such relentless pounding. Then he froze not believing his eyes, 'Nadya! Come here!' She joined him and liked her arm through his. 'Look a tram!' He ran out onto the steps of the flat pulling her after him and pointing down to the road below. 'Sunshine! I'd forgotten what its like.'

Yuri pulled her tight to him as a large slab of snow slid off the roof above them to crash into the court yard below. 'Come on, let's go down to the river.' As they walked hand in hand they passed the food shop expecting to find queues of people but there weren't. Yuri said, 'Have you got your rationcard with you?'

She smiled and dragged him after her into the shop. At first they stood in awe at the food displayed before them. Yuri asked the woman behind the counter, 'Where has all this come from? A few weeks ago you were empty.'

The woman behind the counter was thin and looked tired but smiled back at him. 'They've requisitioned it from the collective farms.'

Yuri shook his head in disbelief. 'And I'm sure it was handed over eagerly to the armed guards.'

The woman shrugged. 'Eat or die. Your choice.' She sat back on a stool to conserve energy.

Nadya bought some bread, a little meat, dried mushrooms, coffee and matches with some coupons she had been issued. They ran out of the shop then walked arm in arm through the city square laughing as they paused at a line of lime trees to reach up and pick the lime buds which only Yuri could reach; the lower ones already stripped for food. They continued on and after a leisurely stroll found their favourite place by the bridge and sat to watch the swirling water. Nadya snuggle up tight to him. 'The thaw at last.'

Yuri shivered. 'I never want to be cold again! Ever! In England it doesn't get as cold as this. We can bring our daughter up there.'

'It sounds wonderful. Are they nice people do you think?'

'The one I met was. Before the Germans blew him to pieces.'

'Promise me you won't go back there Yuri please.' She turned to look at him her eyes pleading. 'Promise me.'

'I think they would shoot me as a deserter if I did.'

'We can't lose this Yuri not after all we've been through. And we have our daughter to care for.'

'How are you so sure it will be a girl?'

'I just do. I suppose you want a boy so you can teach him fighting?'

He laughed. 'I can teach a girl just as well!'

She poked him. 'Our second one will be a boy perhaps.'

'As long as the baby is healthy I don't care. Which is why you must eat more. Come on let's get back and get you fed.'

They made their way slowly back. As they entered the Nevsky Prospekt they stopped to watch four men drag corpes from a basement to put on a lorry as others lifted rotting corpses from the pavement. Further along, teams of women with crowbars were prising blocks of ice up for others to drag to the river on makeshift boards. For the first time in months the bare pavement was exposed hidden by frozen hills of dirt and mounds of frozen sewage.

Yuri sighed, 'Everybody is out on the streets cleaning. I would like to join some of the clear up squads but I'll have to be careful not to be spotted.'

She grabbed his arm, 'No! Not after all we've been through. And your daughter needs you here.'

'She's making demands already?' He tickled her. 'Perhaps you're right. But I should do something. And, you must be really careful because dysentry, typhoid and typhus are going to be everywhere.'

'If only the bathhouse was open. I feel so dirty.'

'There are a few I think. I'll ask around and find out.'

They walked on in silence watching the crowds of people clearing the streets. They stopped at a poster on a lamp post and Yuri read out loud, 'Fifteen hundredths of a hectare will produce 800kg of cabbage, 700kg of beets, 120 kg of cucumbers,

130kg of carrots, 340kg of Swedes, 50kg of tomatoes and 200kg of other vegetables. This is more than enough for an entire family for the whole year. Save ashes from your stove for your vegetable patch.' He turned to her nodding at the poster. 'That's what we should do. Find a piece of ground and do that.'

'Well you *are* a farmer!'

A shadow crossed his face. 'I used to be. Come on let's go.'

They arrived back at their flat and laid the food out on the table. Nadya went down the hall to the communal kitchen and tried the taps. 'I heard there were some flats with water again, but not us. I suppose that means the toilet as well.'

Yuri shouted back to her. 'I tried it this morning.'

'So what are we supposed to do?' She looked out of the window to the courtyard below. 'It didn't seem to matter when it was so cold and everything covered in snow. But now. Oh God it's horrible down there. *Stuff* everywhere.'

Yuri joined her and put his arm around her waist drawing her to him. 'They'll provide piles of sand and a spade for the block. We just have to get on with it.'

Nadya pushed into him, 'Can we grow vegetables like that poster said?'

'We will. Great big ones!'

Later they sat at the table and Yuri reached for hand. 'I can't believe I am here with you. All that time in the Gulag I thought of you every day. I could'nt accept I would never see you again. It was the only thing kept me going.'

She squeezed his hand. 'It was the same for me. I thought about you all the time. We've both lost everyone we loved. I don't think we can ever get over that, but we have each other and,' she stroked her belly, 'our child who will be the most special child in the world.'

'She will. We need to get out of this city as soon as we can and find a way to get to England. I've heard rumours that we are wearing the Germans down and might soon break through. Now that it is mostly women left in the city I am going to stand out. The sooner we get away the better and start a new life.'

'I love you Yuri more than words can say.'

'And I love you Nadya. We will make it work for our parent's sake.'

Through May into September the weather improved and —
strangely — the shelling reduced. Nadya and Yuri found a piece
of land near to their flat and made good use of it. If the
seige was to last another winter, they would be prepared.
Summer arrived with sunshine making the city feel almost
normal; apart from the empty streets and bomb damage. Yuri and
Nadya spent every minute together making up for the years
apart.

She was nearing her term and becoming ungainly. Yuri hovered
around her constantly trying to look after her until she
shouted at him in frustration, 'I'm not an invalid!' They
strolled the short distance to their flat holding hands and
laughing, blissfully unaware of a figure watching them from
behind a tree.

31. BAD TIMING

Vladimir watched from the shelter of a tree unable to believe his luck. He'd found them at last! Well he wouldn't let them slip away again. He followed them to their flat and settled down to wait and see if Yuri still went to his friends. Eventually he saw him leave the flat and men. Vladimir recognised Karl from when he had previously followed Aleksei.

He scurried off to the Commissar's office and waited outside the Commissar's door for the ritual of which he was becoming very tired. He heard 'Come' and opened the door quickly as if to catch the man out.

The Commissar motioned toward the chair. 'Vladimir.'

Vladimir entered the Commissar's office and sat down crossing his legs confidently. 'Your men bungled the last attempt at catching that black market crook and his whore. But I have at last found them. I have another address. Also I have found where one of the gang live. He lives with his elderly mother...' He leaned forward a smug look on his face. 'I hope the information could be useful?'

The Commissar looked thoughtful. 'Name?'

'Karl. I Don't know his full name but I can show your men where he lives.'

'Good. He will do what we want if he wants his mother to survive another winter...' He took out a cigarette. 'Any more news from your "friend"?'

Vladimir shrugged. 'No. But I'm checking it out.'

Sidorov stood and went to the cupboard where he took out two bottles of vodka and handed them over to Vladimir.

'Thank you Commissar.'

Nadya was struggling to get up once she had sat down puffing at the effort and railing at Yuri. 'It's ok for you! You don't have to carry your daughter everywhere. She weighs a ton!'

Yuri continued with the rudimentary stove he had built; a poor effort he was the first to admit after Aleksei's masterpiece. He loaded some wood into it and struck his flint to the dry tinder. It burst into flame. 'See!' he exclaimed. 'I said I could do it.'

She looked at it with pretend scorn. 'Aleksei's was better. It didn't smoke like that for a start.'

He laughed. 'True. Can't have everything.'

She stopped and grabbed at her stomach a look of shock on her face.

He ran to her. 'What is it?'

She grunted and breathed deeply. 'Not long now, I think your daughter is on her way. I just hope she's not a big as you. You big oaf.'

He leant down and kissed her forehead. 'Just tell me what to do.'

She relaxed as the spasm retreated. 'Get plenty of wood for the fire, plenty of cloths and plenty of water. Then we wait.'

He hurriedly put on his coat and dashed out. Nadya settled back and pushed a few more pieces of wood onto the fire. For all her joking it was working well as long as the window was kept slightly open... She thought about a recent conversation she had heard about the Ice Road being opened in February, which meant supplies would hopefully begin to arrive. However, she believed the most important thing was to escape the city and get to Moscow where she could think about making her way to England. Yuri's hopes of seeing England burned bright within her and she was determined their child would see his, and her dream, come true.

Yuri met up with four of his friends and told them about the impending birth. He sensed something was wrong as Karl seemed to shift around restlessly as though he needed to be elsewhere. Yuri stopped mid sentence. 'You ok?'

Karl made light of it. 'Yeah sure Yuri. Got to be somewhere that's all.'

Yuri eyed him with puzzlement then continued. As he spoke Karl suddenly darted off. The other three looked at each other then to Yuri and one of them shouted, 'Run!'

Yuri turned and saw four secret police running toward them. He pushed back into the shadows and held his breath. He heard their footsteps stop and then silence. He let out his breath very slowly. A torch suddenly blinded him as it was shone into his eyes and he tried to make a break for it but was knocked to the ground by a blow to the head. The four men took their time methodically kicking him until he lapsed into unconsciousness.

Nadya grew impatient, nervous and anxious as she began to worry as another contraction struck her. She looked around the apartment realising she needed more wood and the cloths. Should she dare going outside and risk getting caught by her daughter insisting on being born in the street? She knew Yuri would return as quickly as he could. She groaned as another contraction doubled her over.

Yuri was dragged and thrown into a cell in the bowels of the police building. He received another kicking and drifted into unconsciousness as a boot thudded into his head.

He woke after a few minutes and groggily remembered where he was. He assessed the damage. It seemed like a probable broken rib but mostly bruising. He stood groaning and gripping his ribs as he felt around in the dark, sizing up the cell. He could just touch two opposing walls with his outstretched arms although the effort was painful causing him to grunt with the exertion.

He sat down and thought about Nadya, desperate to be there with her when she needed him most. His thoughts were disturbed as he heard footsteps and the cell door opened flooding the cell with the bright light of the corridor. He struggled as his arms were grabbed and tied behind his back then he was pushed and pulled by two guards up a flight of steps into the same corridor Aleksei had been dragged through.

He waited while one of the guards knocked on a door and waited. A muffled 'Come' came from inside. Yuri was shoved into the room toward the desk of Commissar Sidorov who stopped writing, carefully placed the cap on his pen and sat back.

He looked at Yuri appraisingly. 'So, Yuri Kazakof, again! King of the black market huh? Not so clever now are we? I think we have enough to put you away for a long, long time. Could even consider execution. I didn't make the connection at first. The name seemed familiar and then I remembered your father.'

Yuri looked attentively at him with a steady gaze.

Sidorov studied Yuri, 'I know it's no use threatening your sort with physical violence although of course we often have to resort to such crude methods. However, in your case as in your friend Karl's, something more subtle is required. In his case it was his poor frail mother who somehow managed to make it through the terrible winter, presumably from the goods stolen by you and your friends.'

He studied Yuri with a sly smile. 'In your case we need to be even more persuasive.' He stretched his arms lazily. 'Even as we speak your whore is being taken to a cell somewhere in the city where she will give birth to your child.' He laughed. 'What do you think about that eh?'

Yuri shrugged feigning disinterest. Inside he was feverishly thinking.

The Commissar continued. 'So. I have an idea.' He motioned to the guards to leave then nodded to Yuri to sit down. 'There is possibly a way out of this for you Kazakof. Let me explain.'

Nadya was relieved as she heard footsteps on the stairs. She knew he would be there for her. Her relief quickly turned to fear as two policemen barged in, roughly grabbed her and dragged her down the stairs. Outside she was bundled into a lorry used as a makeshift ambulance. Her contractions began to increase but there was nobody to help or comfort her. Eventually she was taken to a hospital where she was put in a ward on her own and closely guarded. A nurse saw her distressed state and objected but was told to be quiet. Nadya was beyond caring as the contractions became more frequent. In the times in between she thought of Yuri and what could have happened to him. What would he do when he returned and she wasn't there? She felt despair as she imagined him searching the streets in panic for her. It seemed that they were destined to be apart.

The nurse gave the guards a disparaging glare as she stood beside Nadya ready to check on her progress. They shuffled out of the door. The nurse looked at Nadya and muttered, 'Pigs.' After the examination she announced it would not be long now. Nadya began crying. She didn't know if she was crying with the pain of the contractions or for the loss of Yuri. Gradually her body took over and her efforts concentrated on the birth of their child.

The Commissar smiled at Yuri. 'I have a problem that requires the services of someone outside the NKVD. At the moment you face life in a prison camp or possible death. The state views your crimes very seriously as undermining the great efforts of our wonderful leader.' He sat back and considered Yuri as he lit a cigarette holding it in his usual manner. 'Now then. You have everything to lose and nothing to gain unless you assist me with my difficulty. It must be heart breaking to not be able to see your child born and grow up. I can imagine the difficulties the child's mother will have when the child is removed from her and placed in a home for "strays".'

32. BETWEEEN A ROCK AND A HARD PLACE

Yuri tried to ignore the pain of not being there for Nadya. He maintained steady eye contact feigning disinterest.

The Commissar continued. 'Here is my proposal. I want you to kill someone. An enemy of the State. You don't need to know why. I give you my promise that if you carry out this task and prove to me the deed is done, I will grant you a full pardon and also that of your female friend.' He sat back drawing on his cigarette, a self satisfied smile on his face.

Yuri studied him in silence. 'You want me to murder a man but not know why?'

The Commissar smiled thinly, 'I prefer to refer to it as an *execution.*'

'Why? You have enough thugs on your payroll. Let them do it.'

The Commissar shrugged. 'It is a complicated matter of which the details do not concern you. It is a matter I would prefer to be kept "unoffical". You would be doing it for your country. What is your answer?'

'Who is it?'

'Sidorov studied the end of his cigarette. The man's name is Vladimir Rostockovitch.'

Yuri grimaced at the pain in his side and said, 'Really?'

Sidorov smiled. 'That should make it easier for you.'

Yuri looked deep into Sidorov's piggish eyes. 'I'm not a murderer.'

Sidorov scrubbed out his cigarette. 'Hmm. Well if you want to see your family again I suggest you change your mind. Think of it as an execution on behalf of your country.'

Yuri stood unsteadily. ' I have no choice if I want to see my family again do I?'

The Commissar stood. 'That's how it is. Let's be honest Kazakof, the world will not be a worse place without that little shit.'

Yuri said, 'How do I know I can trust you?'

'You don't.'

'Then I need some sort of guarantee that we will not be arrested later.'

'Ok. I will put in writing that there is no case for you to answer.'

'And what about the murder?'

'The execution? It is unlikely I would risk bringing up the matter don't you think?'

Yuri thought for a moment 'Ok.'

The Commissar said, 'When it is done report you have seen a body. Be sure not to leave any evidence. What you are doing is for the sake of the Motherland.'

Yuri painfully buttoned his coat. 'If you say so.' He considered for a moment. 'When I do see Nadya?'

'As soon as you've done the deed.'

'No. I must see her now. Where is she?'

The Commissar thought for a moment. 'Very well. She is at a hospital near here. You have twenty four hours to complete the job. If it is not you will never see her or your child again. I will arrange for guards to take you to her. When you have seen her they will remain there waiting for my orders. Have I made myself clear.'

Yuri nodded.

Yuri was escorted by two guards who kept a close watch on him as he was taken to the maternity ward. Nadya was laying back exhaused holding a bundle close to her chest. Yuri rushed to her side as she opened her eyes and smiled at him.

He kissed her forehead and said soflty, 'I'm sorry. They were waiting for me. I tried....'

She shushed him. 'Say hello to your daughter.' She pulled the blanket away to reveal a pink face peacefully sleeping.

He touched the baby's cheek. 'She is so beautiful, like you.'

'She's your's Yuri. You have to look after her now, make sure she is safe.'

'I will.'

Nadya stroked her baby as she said quietly, 'They arrested me and brought me here. I don't know why. I was so worried about you not finding us.' She looked concerned as she saw the two guards standing in the doorway. 'Why are they here?'

He leant in close to her. 'The Commissar has a problem. He wants me to do something before he let's us go.'

She whispered, 'What sort of thing?'

'Don't worry about it. I'll come for you tomorrow. Just trust me ok?'

'I will always trust you. We have to find a way of getting away from here Yuri, there are too many dangers for us.'

He looked grim. 'I know, but it will change. Tomorrow we will be safe.' He kissed Nadya and the baby and left with one of the guards.

Outside the hospital the guard said, 'We stay here.' He turned and went back into the building.

Yuri pulled his coat tight around himself and headed toward the railway arches. He hung around until Andre and Karl appeared as they all did every night to make their plans. Karl looked uncomfortable.

Yuri said, 'I've got a problem. The Commissar is out to get us. He has Nadya in custody and wants me to do something for him.'

Andre asked, 'What sort of thing?'

'Kill a man but I don't know why.'

'Killing Germans is one thing, that's different.'

Yuri agreed. 'I need to get Nadya and our baby away from here.'

Andre said, 'So your leaving us?'

'I don't have a choice. Anyway you can all look after yourselves now. We have a nice little organisation here. If I leave, the Commissar will have no leads to you. Will you help me?' They agreed. He looked to Karl. 'You didn't have any choice. I know he blackmailed you.' He held out his hand.

Karl eagerly took his hand and shook it gratefully. 'I didn't know what to do Yuri.'

'I know. Forget all about it. Just help me out ok?'

Karl looked relieved. 'Anything.'

Yuri went on. 'Ok. The man he wants me to kill is a pig. He has caused us all a lot of problems. As long as he is around he will continue to. So if we're not going to kill him we have to get rid of him.'

Andre asked, 'So what do you suggest?'

'We grab him and take him outside the city and leave him to fend for himself. If he comes back we kill him.'

Karl said, 'Isn't that killing him anyway?'

Yuri shrugged. 'At least he has a choice, more than he's given others.'

Andre was thoughtful. 'Can you trust the Commissar, Yuri?'

'No. We need to find out what it is the little shit has that the Commissar wants him killed for. We need to have a little chat with him.'

Andre smiled. 'Sounds a good idea. Lets go.'

As they headed toward the block of flats Yuri was deep in thought about what he had been asked to do. How was it any different to killing German soldiers? The man was evil like them. He had tried to hurt him and Nadya. He had caused Aleksei to be sent to the Gulag. The man was not fit to live; preying on people for his own ends.

They waited until Vladimir appeared from his apartment and followed him until he entered a dark alleyway. The shelling had begun again and the explosions sounded nearby adding to the chaos as people dashed to the air raid shelters. When Yuri was confident there was nobody around they quickened their pace and caught up with Vladimir who sensed their presence and turned in alarm.

'You! What do you want with me? You've got some cheek.' He tried to back away but saw the other two watching him. He said, 'What do you want? You're just common robbers, well you can't threaten me.' He glared defiantly at Yuri. 'I'll make sure you never see her again like I did your friend. And the baby. You can't...'

Yuri grabbed him by his coat front and lifted him off the ground slamming him against a wall. He put his face close in and growled, 'Why does the Commissar want you dead?'

Vladimir looked stunned. 'Wants me dead?' Yuri lifted him a little higher.

Vladimir stuttered. 'You must have it wrong. How do you know this?'

Yuri squeezed tighter still, causing Vladimir's face to redden. 'I want to kill you because you are an evil little man but I will give you a chance if you tell me what the Commissar is scared about.'

Vladimir realised he had no choice. 'Ok ok, put me down and I'll tell you. But then what will you do? You could still kill me.'

'I could. But unlike you I have integrity. I give you my word I won't kill you.'

Vladimir breathed a sigh of relief as Yuri lowered him to the ground. His confidence began to return. 'Our friend the Commissar likes little boys for his sexual pleasure. He has a link to an orphanage and has a regular supply. I've followed him, taken notes, even,' he smiled smugly, 'got a photograph of him taking one of them into his office.'

Yuri exchanged a look of disgust with his two friends then poked Vladimir in the chest. 'And where is all this evidence?'

'Safe. Hidden in my apartment.'

'Ok. Take us there and hand it all over. Then we will let you go.'

Vladimir looked suspiciously at them all. 'Just like that?'

Yuri nodded. Vladimir straightened his coat and said, 'Lets go then.'

Vladimir gave Yuri a folder full of written notes with dates, addresses and times. The most damning piece of evidence was the black and white photgraph. Yuri took it all and put it carefully in his coat pocket.

They bustled Vladimir back outside and Andre said to Yuri, 'We'll take it from here.'

Vladimir began to look concerned as they grabbed his arms and began walking him away. Over his shoulder he called out to Yuri, 'Where are they taking me? You promised!'

Yuri shouted back. 'We're giving you a choice, more than you've given others.'

The next day he returned to the police building and asked to see the Commissar. After a wait he was shown in to his office. The Commissar sat back and looked Yuri up and down. 'Well?'

Yuri looked at him with disgust, 'It's different now. You won't have to worry about Vladimir anymore. It's me you need to be concerned about.'

The Commissar sat forward attentively. 'You are threatening me? I have your girlfriend and child don't forget.'

Yuri considered for a moment. 'I'm not interested in your sick interests. I just want my woman and child out of the city. You can go to hell for all I care.'

The Commissar looked thoughtful. 'So I presume you now have whatever it was Vladimir had?'

Yuri smiled. 'I have and it is where you would never find it. Let them go and I will tell you where it is.'

The Commissar stood and walked around the desk to stand behind Yuri. He sneered. 'I could squash you like a bug Kazakof. You don't worry me a jot. But all the same you are becoming a nuisance. We seem to have a "stand off". He walked around the office deep in thought. Yuri sat down waiting to see how the game would be played out.

The Commissar stopped and examined a picture on his wall then said, 'I propose an exchange on the Troitsky bridge. You bring the "evidence" and I will bring your family. We meet in the middle. Of course I will have protection as I'm sure will you. When the exchange is completed we go our separate ways. In your case, out of the city.'

Yuri stood and turned to him. 'Ok. When?'

'Tomorrow night? Seven o'clock. The shelling usually starts after then.'

Yuri sat with Karl and told him the plan. Karl looked cynical. 'You trust this pig?'

'No. We need a backup plan which I've sorted. How did it go with Vladimir?'

Karl smiled. 'Oh he's learning what war is about...'

Yuri punched his arm playfully. 'Thanks. He didn't even deserve that.' He was thoughtful. 'That pig Sidorov threatened you about your mother didn't he?'

Karl looked sheepish. 'He said he would make sure she starved and I would go to prison.'

Yuri put his arm round him. 'Don't worry, Sidorov won't bother you again. And, you had no choice.'

Karl looked relieved and said, 'So what do you have in mind?'

33. A DOUBLE CROSS

At seven o'clock the following night Yuri went to the bridge as arranged and waited. His friends waited in the shadows, their faces covered. Two cars pulled up on the far side of the bridge and its headlights flashed in Yuri's direction. He could see guards lined up beside it. The Commissar got out and a figure with a baby was helped out of the other side. Yuri stood and walked to the middle of the bridge and waited watching as they approached him. He gripped the papers in his hand trying to control his nerves. He took deep breaths as they drew closer. When the Commissar and the figure were within ten yards he called out, 'Bring the papers here.'

Yuri moved forward trying to see Nadya to check she was ok. As he reached the Commissar he made to move toward Nadya but a guard stepped in his way. The Commissar held out his hand. Yuri handed the papers over. The Commissar looked at the top sheet and noted close hand writing and a list of dates. He shuffled through them quickly and felt a photograph at the back. He looked up and smiled. 'Ok. I will walk away, and when I am safely in my transport the guard will hand your girl friend and the baby over.' He turned to walk away then stopped and said, 'I don't intend to see you again Kasakof.' He walked quickly back over the bridgetoward a lorry. The lorry reversed at high speed and disappeared.

Yuri sensed something was wrong as he watched the still figure. He ran to Nadya and held her but in horror backed away. He snatched the shawl back from her head to reveal a young girl holding a baby. He shouted, 'you're not Nadya!' The guard raised his rifle and Yuri instinctively kicked at him knocking it away. He turned and ran as gunfire opened up from the far side of the bridge, bullets ricocheting off the ground near his feet.

Yuri's friends fired to give him cover. More guards appeared and began laying down automatic fire at Yuri's friends. He carried on sprinting knowing he could not outrun the bullets and took cover at the side of the bridge. More gun shots came from his friends to try and give him cover but he was pinned down. The guards reached him and dragged him away. Yuri's friends had no chance against the overwhelming gunfire and ran into the dark. After a few minutes they stopped and caught their breath.

Karl checked his pistol and said to Andre, 'You ready?'

Andre nodded and they hurried off toward the hospital.

The Commissar entered his office and locked the door. He opened the file of papers and began looking at them in detail. He soon realised he had been duped. Only the top page was an original, the rest scribbles. The photograph was of a family. He threw the papers down and sat back in thought. He still had the upper hand; he had the girl and Yuri. With some friendly persuasion he was sure Yuri would tell him where the papers were. He needed to bring this tiresome affair to an end.

Yuri was thrown into a cell flinching as the door slammed shut. Hisonly hope now was that Karl would fulfil his promise. Yuri sighed deeply with frustration as he knew Sidorov would have moved her by now. At least the papers were safe with Karl who owing him a debt would ensure they reach the Party Secretary. He lay down on the filthy floor angry with himself for not planning this better.

Commissar Sidorov stood outside Yuri's cell and adjusted his uniform confident in the knowledge he was safe with a guard in front of him. The guard opened the door and Sidorov pushed the guard in following close behind. Yuri shielded his eyes against the light filling the small cell from the corridor outlining the Commissar like an angel of death.

Sidorov smiled as he pushed his shoulders back and straightened, gaining a little height to demonstrate his authority.

'You have something I want. You will give it to me.' He smoothed his uniform picking imaginery objects from his cuffs. 'I understand we must play the inevitable game but after much pain you will eventually tell me where it is. I can save you from that pain if you tell me now. Of course, you have no cards to play, I have the winning hand, but you can save your whore.'

Yuri spat at him. 'Go to hell. I don't believe anything you say.'

Sidorov laughed. 'Oh dear, never mind. Tomorrow we start the interrogation. I have a man I want you to meet. He's very good at what he does.' He stepped out of the cell and the door banged shut. Yuri stared into the darkness that seemed to represent the black abyss that had become his life.

Nadya sat on her hospital bed clutching her baby to her breast counting the seconds before Yuri would return. She felt her life rocked back and forth between good and bad. She looked down at her daughter and smiled. 'Soon your Daddy will be here Anna. Then we can go on an adventure.

A figure appeared in the doorway and she looked up expecting to see Yuri smiling at her. Her heart fell. It was an officious looking woman with cold eyes who asked curtly, 'You are Nadya Rhiendhart?'

Nadya said, 'Yes, what is...'

Two other women entered and one of them held Nadya while the other took the baby from her.

The curt woman said, 'You are a criminal. Criminals can't take their children with them.'

Nadya said shakily. 'Take them where?'

'The Gulag.' To the others she said, Take it away and make sure she is restrained before we move her to a cell.' She turned and was about to leave when Nadya leapt from the bed.

She shrieked, 'Give me back my baby! Why am I a criminal? What have I done wrong?' The two other women grabbed her and struggled as they handcuffed her to the bed.

'That's up to the Commissar. He signs the paper and we do what we're told. That's all we need.' They turned and left. Nadya was in shock as she stared at the empty room; a prisoner locked to her bed, helpless to look after her child. Nadya's mind was spinning in desperation thinking about her daughter. She felt she had betrayed Yuri by letting them take her but what could she have done? She so longed to see his loving face and feel his strong arms around her. But he wasn't there. She knew he never would be now, especially once she arrived at a prison camp.

She was later moved to a police cell and sat in the dark in the silence, beyond crying, feeling drained, desolate and helpless. Memories of her time in the Gulag flooded over her producing an overwhelming tiredness as she knew what she would have to deal with again. It was bad enough before, but this time all she could think about was finding her daughter.

The next day, after a sleepness night, she was shoved and pushed onto a railway carriage with many others for the journey she knew would take days.

She stared at the heavy closed door, wondering how she was going to survive the coming hell. She thought of Yuri and her heart sank knowing she may not see him again. For a while she thought of very little, drifting in and out of a light sleep. Then she woke with a start as the train jolted. She remembered the way prisoners were fed and knew then she had to make an effort; everybody in that carriage was out for themselves. If she continued to remain passive she would die. Fear for her helpless baby drove her to survive.

She knew that all she could do was take one minute at a time.
Perhaps eventually it would be one day at a time. She had
endured this before and she would do it again.

34.YURI MEETS SIDOROV'S FRIEND.

Yuri was woken by the door scraping open and arms grabbing him, lifting him off his feet and dragging him out of the cell into the corridor. He struggled at first but a blow with something hard on his lower back stopped him. He was dragged into a large room with a single light bulb hanging in the middle of the ceiling. Beneath it was a wooden chair on which he was roughly shoved and his hands tied behind his back around the chair.

Sidorov strolled in smoking a cigarette to make sure Yuri knew who was in control here. He stood behind Yuri and whispered in his ear. 'Tell me where they are and we can stop all this unpleasantness.' Yuri didn't respond. He walked around and stood in front of him. 'Very well. I will leave you in the capable hands of Sergei.' He stood aside as a large heavy man, once muscled but now heavy with fat, walked purposefully up to Yuri and punched him in the stomach. Yuri doubled in pain — as much as the ropes would allow — and gasped for breath. He looked up to see Sergei wrapping cloth around his knuckles.

Yuri focused on Nadya and his baby, straining his mind to see their faces. He just had to hang on long enough for Karl to deliver the letter. He assumed Sidorov would not harm Nadya until he had the letters; he needed her as a bargaining tool.

Sergei moved in close again and swung a hard left into Yuri's face followed by a right. He stood back and the Commissar moved up to Yuri and said, 'The papers?'

Yuri spat blood from his mouth followed by a tooth. He spat at the Commissar who stood and nodded to Sergei. 'I prefer not to watch, so I'll leave you to it. You will tell me Yuri, you might as well save yourself the pain. Oh and by the way this is just the warm up. Sergei can do wonders with a knife and pliers.' He wandered out and smiled as he heard the scuffle of feet followed by the grunt and groan as a blow landed.

Karl held the envelope in a shaking hand as he stood outside the NKVD building better known as the Big House. He slowly went up the imposing steps and approached a security man at a desk. 'I have a very important letter that needs to be handed to the Party Secretary. He shifted uneasily. 'I don't know who he is but he will want to see what's in here.'

The guard took it from him. 'Is it a matter of State security?'

Karl nodded enthusiastically. 'Yes it is.'

The guard stood and left his desk. 'I'll take it straight away then.' Karl got out as fast his legs would take him and didn't stop until he was out of breath.

Sergie enjoyed his work. He was surprised that Yuri had not folded by now; his face was a bloody pulp, his shirt front soaked in spittle and blood. He was unconscious as Sidorov came in and walked around Yuri then looked at Sergei who shook his head. The Commissar fetched a bowl of water and threw it in Yuri's face. In a world of unbelievable pain Yuri floated in darkness, chasing the ghostly faces of Nadya and his daughter.

Sidorov prodded Yuri in the chest with his leather gloved hand. Yuri stirred and tried to lift his head. The Commissar held him under the chin with the gloved hand and raised his face. 'You really are a stubborn fellow. Obviously our first method hasn't worked so now we turn to phase two.' He turned to Sergei, 'Show him what to expect.' Sergei took a pair of pliers out of his pocket and went behind Yuri who felt his hands being grabbed. Then an excruciating pain stabbed at his hand as Sergei ripped a nail out. Yuri screamed sending spittle and blood onto the floor.

Sergei came back into view and held a finger nail in the pliers for Yuri to see.

The Commissar tutted. 'Oh dear. Still we have another nine then we move onto the feet. After that I'm afraid it gets quite serious.' He prodded Yuri in the crutch. 'If you get my drift?' He turned to the guards. 'Take him to his cell and leave him for a few hours. I'll be down for him later. Take a break Sergei, I think it might be a long night.'

The security guard knocked tentatively at the door of the Party Secretary, Dmitri Chupin, also the head of Security, and waited. A voice came from inside, 'come in!'

He entered and removed his cap as he held the letter up and said, 'A young chap brought this for your attention Secretary Chupin. He said it was important.'

Chupin sat back at his large desk and lit a cigarette. 'Not another informant telling me somebody's getting too much bread...Give it here.' He opened the envelope and removed a sheaf of papers. A photograph fell onto the desk showing Commissar Sidorov in a compromising position with a young boy who was clearly in distress. He stubbed out his cigarette and waved the security guard away. He shuffled through the papers before throwing them down on the table in disgust. He noticed a scrawled note with the envelope and picked it up to read that Yuri had been arrested again.

Chupin always tried to see the bigger picture but this was too much. He knew Sidorov was nasty; but not like this. He felt disgust and betrayal by the system that had forced him to allow this pervert enough room to exercise his depravity. It had suited his purposes to leave him alone; God knows he didn't have enough to deal with already because of the war without having to wet nurse all his officials as well. Despite its shortcomings — and there were a lot — he believed in the Party and Stalin's vision. He didn't agree with the purges but he had little choice. If Stalin got to hear of this he would...it didn't bear considering. He jumped up, struggled into his thick coat, put on his hat and hurriedly left the office calling for his car. He lit a cigarette as he walked purposefully down the marble stairs.

Yuri laid semi conscious in his cell oblivious of his surroundings. He felt a blanket of pain over the whole of his upper body, especially his face. He tried to open his eyes but they were swollen shut. He moved his mouth and thought his jaw was broken. He ran his tongue around feeling the many gaps which had once held healthy teeth. He tried to sit up and groaned at the pain in his middle and chest which hurt every time he breathed. A throbbing sharp ache came from his left hand which was tied behind his back. He jumped at the familiar jangle of keys in the door and blinding light crashing in from the corridor. Two guards manhandled him to his feet and dragged him to the fateful room he had been in earlier.

The Commissar was waiting for him standing beside Sergei who looked rested and ready for work. In his hand he held the pliers. Yuri was once again tied to the chair but this time his hands were tied in front of him.

The Commissar leant down to him and said, 'Well here we are again Yuri. Where are they?'

Yuri raised his head wearily and tried to open his eyes but they were too swollen. He licked his lips and said, 'Go to hell.'

The Commissar stood back and motioned for Sergei to begin but then stopped him and grabbed a wet cloth from a sink and roughly wiped at Yuri's face forcing him to open his eyes. 'I want you to see what Sergei is doing Yuri. It seems a shame to hide such work behind you. Oh and by the way, I've disposed of your girl friend and her brat. So you might as well tell me what I need to know.'

Yuri strained to look up into Sidorov's eyes as he forced himself to speak against the pain. 'If you have killed her I will hunt you down if it takes the rest of my life.'

Sidorov laughed and addressed Sergie. 'Now that is what I call an idle threat! I mean how on earth do you think you are going to get free from here? Anyway, even if you did it's too late. She's on her way to a Gulag. She'll be dead by next week. The survival rate is very poor, especially if you come from a soft upbringing like hers.' He motioned to Sergei who slowly approached Yuri with a sly smile.

Sergei grinned. 'This is going to hurt. A lot. Cos I'm going to do it very slowly.'

Yuri screamed until he had no breath left and then quietly sobbed. He tried desperately to keep hold of the faces that were so dear to him even though he knew he would not see them again. He had to hold on long enough for the letter to be delivered and bring this monster down.

The Commissar sighed. 'You really are making this hard work you know. We have one hand left then we start on the feet, but I suspect that won't work so perhaps we go straight to the genitals. After all, you've fathered a child now so they aren't really necessary are they.' He stood aside while Sergei grabbed at Yuri's trousers and tugged hard to pull them off. As he struggled the Commissar interrupted him and said to Yuri, 'He's such an eager fellow. We need to undo the belt first don't we!' He undid it and Sergei tugged them free. He grabbed hold of Yuri's underwear and ripped it away. Yuri felt naked and exposed. He didn't know how much more of this he could take. He thought of his father and used the anger to sustain him even though he felt desperately lonely and without hope.

Sergie kicked Yuri's legs apart and drew his knife. The Commissar put his hand up saying, 'I really can't watch. I've tried but it's so....urgh.' He sidled out. Sergei knelt down between Yuri's legs and grinned as he waved the knife. He gave Yuri an enquiring look and satisfied he wasn't going to tell him anything grabbed his knees and forced them apart. One of the guards came round for a closer look.

Loud voices echoed down the corridor which stopped Sergei who looked over his shoulder to see two armed security men enter and roughly pull him away. The Party Secretary Chupin hurried in followed by Sidorov.

Chupin said in a hushed voice, 'What in God's name is going on here?' He moved closer to Yuri and examined his battered face and naked legs. To the guard he said through gritted teeth, 'Cover this man up.'

Commissar Sidorov said, 'It was necessary Party Secretary Chupin. This man is a danger to the Party and people of Leningrad.'

Chupin looked at him coldly with steely eyes. 'The only danger to the party and people of Leningrad is you. You are under arrest.'

Sidorov began to argue but Chupin leant in close to him and whispered, 'I have the papers and photograph.' Yuri gave a choked laugh and spat a tooth out. Chupin looked at Yuri. 'Did you send the papers?' Yuri nodded wearily. Chupin instructed his guards to release Yuri and get him to hospital. He had Sidorov taken to the cell Yuri had been in.

As the cell door closed he said, 'I'll deal with you tomorrow.' The door slammed shut plunging Sidorov into darkness.

Back in his lonely office, Party Secretary Chupin lit a cigarette and considered his options. He was confident he had reacted with such swiftness —which could be verified by the security desk guard who was scrupulous with his recording — that no blame could be attached to him if the matter was to become known to the General. The problem now was what to with him? There had to be a way. Ideally, Sidorov needed to be punished but it wasn't good for such perverted behaviour to be associated with the party, especially when the General was so close to Stalin. Perhaps the best way would be to simply send him to the Gulag.

No. Such a course of action would backfire. What if he were to speak to the General personally? Too risky not knowing the temperament of the man who might become defensive and...No, he needed for Sidorov to disappear in a manner which could not come back on him. An arranged suicide perhaps? Now that was a possibility. God knows Stalin had set enough of them up.

Now that he knew what was happening he would take decisive action, not only for the remaining children of Leningrad but also to cover his own back. He drew on his cigarette as he sat back considering the fellow in the torture room. There was something about him that warranted further interest. After all, why would he put himself through such agony just to hold onto those papers? He must have had another motive. Come to think of it, how did the letter get delivered if he was locked up? There must be others involved. This puts it into another perspective. Are these people dissenters out to cause the

Party trouble? He stubbed out the cigarette and called for his car.

Yuri lay on a hospital bed in agony from so many parts of his body it seemed he was one giant ache. The satisfaction of seeing the Commissar arrested was just dawning on him. He relished the thought of Sidorov going to a Gulag. His thoughts turned to Nadya and their daughter causing a tiny tear to escape his bruised and swollen eyes. He clenched his fists in anger and winced as the damaged fingers screamed out in protest.

His reverie was disturbed by a nudge at his left arm. He turned his head in that direction and tried to open his eyes. His right eyelids parted enough for him to note a man standing by his bed.

The Party Secretary drew up a chair and sat beside him. 'I understand your name is Yuri Kazakof?' Yuri nodded very slightly which was the most he could manage. 'I am The Party Secretary Dmitri Chupin. You received quite a beating to resist giving up those papers. I would like to know more about it all but I understand you are in no state to talk at the moment. I propose to return in a week or so and perhaps you will be a little better. You look a strong fellow and you have youth on your side. If my hunch is right about you I might have something interesting to offer you. For now just rest. I will return in a couple of days.' He patted Yuri's shoulder, stood and replaced the chair then left.

Yuri's mind was racing. Something interesting to offer him? Perhaps Sidorov had been bluffing? Perhaps whatever was on offer would give him the chance to find out what happened to Nadya and the baby. He laid back as despair overwhelmed him again, hate and revenge for Sidorov boiling inside him like a cauldron of pure anger; of course he had not been bluffing, a man as cruel and evil as Sidorov didn't need to. Tears escaped and ran down his bruised and battered face. Overwhelming pain engulfed him. What purpose was there to living anymore? His family gone, his lover and child lost to him. He cried as he had never cried before until he was spent.

The void within him began to fill with images of Sidorov and what he would do to him. Also that pig Sergie. Hatred began to give him a purpose. He would recover and begin the search to find out his family's fate and then go after those responsible. He vowed to himself he would spend however long it would take to track down Sidorov and kill him. Slowly.

Chupin lit a cigarette as he got into his car. His work brought with it a lot of responsibilty and he could do without this Sidorov nonsense. However, he had not risen to his lofty position without a great intelligence which was telling him very clearly that this fellow Kazakof could be useful. If he was right in his hunch — and he usually was — this might be the chance he needed to nail some of these damn German spies in the city. He would keep this to himself for now until he had heard from the fellow, but his instincts told him he was onto something.

Back in his office he shuffled some papers around thinking about filling Sidorov's position quickly before anarchy broke out. He ran through a list of possible names but none leapt out at him; the ones that did were already tied up elsewhere. The other thing that bothered him was how many innocent people were in those cells? Up until now he had not thought about what was happening with Sidorov, trusting all was well but now...

He sighed and stubbed out his cigarette lighting another straight away. One if his strengths was being able to determine priorities. The priority right now was to find a trustworthy successor to Sidorov; everything else would be their responsibility. He placed the cigarette in his ashtray and picked up a file from Moscow stamped URGENT. He sighed and began reading as his cigarette slowly burned away, oblivious that darkness — punctured here and there by fires from the shelling — had descended on the city.

Nadya often thought about Aleksei and Yuri, wondering if she would see either of them again, how he would love to see their baby and enjoy Aleksei being an uncle. However, she had other things to think about now that she was called a Zek, or prisoner of the Gulag.

Time passed slowly as she arrived at her sixth transit camp. She was getting used to it again and learnt a lot of tricks on how to survive. She had discovered before that there was a range of prisoners from violent criminals to political; those who had been convicted of crimes against the state such as making a joke about Stalin or speaking out against the oppressive Socialist system. The whole country was suffering as a result of Stalin's paranoia and determination to dull the populace into submission by edicts, impossible to maintain.

And so Nadya came to see that the lowliest of criminals were acting as guards being able to exercise their pleasure at beating other prisoners up and taking from them anything they had left of any value, usually of sentimental value more than material.

    The conditions in this particular camp were the worst so far. Nadya was herded into a stone cell deep in the bowels of what had once been a palace, but now a transit camp. Rooms originally meant for storage were now cells; this particular cell was ten feet wide by eight feet long and held fifty women, some of whom could not get their feet on the ground. She was in that cell for two weeks and truly believed she had gone to hell, unable to believe she could continue, but she did; she had no choice. The only respite was lining up outside for a roll call every few hours which was of little relief if it was raining and she was forced to stand there for five hours. She began to understand much of this inhuman treatment was because the system had so many to process and transport around the country to work camps that it was forever clogged up.

35. JUSTICE

Nikita Sidorov crouched in the corner of his cell. He had to get out of this place and make a run for it. He could make some excuse to his father and blame others. He called out for Sergie a number of times until he heard the familiar voice outside his cell door.

'Yes?'

'Sergie. It's me the Commissar!'

The gruff voice replied, 'I know. I put you in there myself.'

'You have to get me out of here!'

'You should know I can't, if anyone knows the rules it's you Commissar.'

'As your superior I am ordering you to release me.'

Sergie thought for a moment. 'Why?'

'Because they are going to do something horrible to me. I've done nothing wrong. Simple innocent play with a boy...'

'I saw the picture Commissar. Didn't look very innocent to me.'

Sidorov grew impatient. 'Just get me out of here. I will make it worth your while.'

'How?'

'My father is wealthy. I can make sure you spend this horrible war in safety and comfort.'

'How do I know you will if I release you? Anyway they would know it was me.'

'You can trust me Sergie. Didn't I bring you with me when I was promoted?'

'They would still know it was me.'

Sidorov thought for a moment. 'Not if you were to use one of your fellow officers. Plant some money in his coat. Let me escape and then call the alarm. When they investigate they will find the money and you will be blameless.'

'And where would I get the money?'

Sidorov knew he had no choice but to trust this oaf. 'I have some hidden away. Let me out, handcuff me if you must and I will get it for you.'

'Is it far away?'

'No it's in the building.'

'Then tell me where it is and I'll get it.'

'Forgive me Sergei but how do I know I can trust you?'

Sergie thought for a moment. 'Ok. Wait until the others are asleep and I will let you out. How do I know you will honour our agreement and get me out of here?'

'I give you my word Sergie. Why would I let you down after doing such a favour for me? You're saving my life Sergie. That's not something to forget.'

Sergie's voice came through the door. 'Ok. I'll come back later.'

Yuri was sitting up in his hospital bed feeling more human. Despite many pleas he had not received any news about Nadya and the baby. He was grateful to be alive but the pain of not knowing their fate was worse than any beating. Ok, he still had a lot of bruises, two broken ribs, cracked jaw and a number of missing teeth, but he was alive. He looked down at his bandaged fingers and thought of what he would like to do to that pig Sergei. In fact, he had spent many hours thinking about that; it helped to stop him thinking about Nadya and his daughter.

He looked up as Chupin entered, who pulled up a chair and sat beside the bed. He looked Yuri over. 'Seems you are on the mend? Now then, I want to know what led you to be in that cell, how you obtained the papers and why you held out against the torture. Take your time.'

Yuri sighed and eyed the man for few seconds noting his steady deep blue eyes watching, his expression one of genuine interest. Yuri began.

The Party Secretary Chupin lit a cigarette as Yuri talked. He lit another when he had finished. He sighed. 'Ok my young friend you have had it tough. But it seems you have an inner resilience that has seen you through. Tell me some more about your father.'

Yuri drank some water, wincing at the pain of moving. 'What is there to say? He was an honest man who did his best for his family by trying to make a living from what was left after the state stole everything.'

Chupin smiled. 'He was bitter about this?'

'Of course he was. He believed in our motherland, he was faithful to the Party but it didn't feel right.'

'In what way?'

Yuri looked at him enquiringly, wondering if he could trust this man.

Chupin said, 'You can speak openly to me.'

Yuri hesitated then said, 'He told me that some people where more equal than others.' He looked defiantly at Chupin.

Chupin blew a cloud of smoke as he said, 'Go on.'

'He had been to meetings and met officials who were living well. Far better than anyone my father knew. Our village and the others that we knew survived by making do with what the State left us. He said the principles were good but the men who applied them were corrupt. Since I have been in the city I have seen my own evidence of this.'

'So what do you believe?'

'I am not well educated. I can read and write. I know I can think. I believe this is a great country. We are strong people. My father read as much as he could and passed a lot of what he learnt onto me. But he said he knew there was much we didn't know about the world because of censorship. That made him angry and so he fought to try and get this changed, but he was not stupid; he knew when to keep quiet.' His voice choked. 'Until in the camp it became too bad and he had to do something for his family as he watched them starve in front of him.'

Chupin leaned forward. 'I would like to have met your father. It sounds like he voiced many of my own concerns that I keep to myself. You are aware of the purges we have to endure? It could be anyone.' Yuri closed his eyes feeling exhausted. Chupin said, 'I need someone I can trust who will work for me in keeping this city safe from such corruption. Also we have many German spies here but they are slippery customers. I'm surrounded by incompetent idiots, the tasks my masters in Moscow hand to me are beyond any sane man's ability. I need eyes and ears I can trust so that vermin like Sidorov can be routed out.' He studied Yuri closely. 'Can I trust you?'

Yuri sighed. 'I am an honest man. I have my integrity. As long as you don't want me to bully others or tell lies then yes you can trust me.'

'And if I give you freedom and authority, will you use it for your own ends?'

Yuri opened his eyes. 'Yes. I need to know about Nadya and our daughter. At the moment I don't care much about anything else.'

'And the last time you saw her she was in the hospital?'

Yuri nodded then said, 'Sidorov moved her when he arrested me. My friends went to see.'

Chupin rubbed his eyes. 'I'll see if I can find out where she is,' then said quietly, 'and what if you can't find them?'

Yuri replied quietly. 'Then I will spend my life looking for those who took them away from me.'

General Grigor Sidorov, paced his office deep in thought having just received the news that Commandant Ivakin — in charge of a unit within the Gulag at the Pechora river in the Komi Republic who had been seriously ill — had now died. He had known Ivakin for a number of years and considered him to be one of the better ones. The other news was that his own son Nikita was in custody in the very police station he was Commissar of! He picked up his phone. Chupin answered.

'General Sidorov here. I've just received alarming news that my son Nikita is a prisoner in his own police station!'

Chupin sighed and took a deep breath. 'Yes General that's correct.'

'Damn it Party Secretary Chupin, why?'

'Chupin reached for his cigarettes. 'It is a very delicate matter General.'

'Delicate matter?'

Chupin had to stall for time. 'I would prefer to examine the evidence before making any recommendations.'

There was a long silence at the other end. 'Hmm. I see. Please keep me informed.' The phone went dead. Chupin sat forward and put his head in his hands. He knew he could not deal with the idiot himself and that the General would want to do so. That probably meant it would be covered up as usual. His plan to have the monster removed was the only answer. But it needed a person he could trust to carry it out secretly.

Sergie drank his wine considering his options. He was the first to admit his skills lay in his fists and not intellectual pursuits such as thinking. He didn't trust Sidorov but wasn't sure how he would get by if the new Commissar did not think the same way that Sidorov did, and his *skills* were not needed. He might find himself put straight in the army. No, he had to take the risk that Sidorov was so frightened he would do as he said and get him out of here to a safer place. He glanced over at his colleagues who were both snoring from the excess of wine he had plied them with.

He shuffled down the corridor and stopped outside Sidorov's cell. He paused to make sure he hadn't overlooked anything.

Sidorov stirred as he heard movement outside and pressed himself against the cell door. 'Sergie? Is that you?'

Sergie mumbled it was as he put the keys in the lock and opened the door. He took a step back in case Sidorov tried to attack him, when satisfied he said, 'You can come out now.'

Sidorov scuffled out. 'Sergie. My friend. Thank you.'

Sergie kept his distance and his hand on the gun in his hip holster. 'Ok, let's get the money before they wake up.'

Sidorov nodded and headed down the corridor toward his office. He opened the door and entered. Sergie kept his distance as Sidorov went to a book case and took down a large book which he placed on a shelf nearby ensuring he was between it and Sergie as he opened it. He took out a handful of money which he surreptitiously stuffed into his belt exclaiming, 'There isn't a lot here I'm afraid but you can have what there is.' As he talked he also took out a small pistol and stuffed that into his belt as well. He turned and held out the money to Sergie who tentatively took it.

'Now go and plant it in one of their pockets, let me out and in the morning do your rounds as usual then raise the alarm.'

Sergie looked concerned. 'And how do I know you won't double cross me?'

Sidorov looked hurt. 'I promise Sergie. As soon as I reach my father in Moscow I will have you transferred there with me.'

Sergie struggled with the concept of trusting this man.

Sidorov could see he needed more incentive. He was sure the oaf was illiterate; after all he came from one of the small villages. He went to his desk where he opened a drawer and took out a box containing official forms. He took the top one and held it out to Sergie. 'In here is my fortune. These documents are special bonds handed to me by my father General

Grigor Sidorov. When the country is back on its feet these can be cashed in.' He looked slyly at Sergie. 'See for yourself.' Sergie took it and placed it on the desk where he attempted to read it. He gave up realising it meant nothing to him other than random squiggles. He handed it back to Sidorov and nodded solemnly.

Sidorov put it back in the box and said, 'You look after that and bring it with you when you are summoned to Moscow.'

Sergie looked troubled. 'And if you don't contact me?'

'You have my fortune. So you see, I have every reason to keep my word.'

Sidorov held out the money and nodded toward the room where the other gaolers were sleeping. Sergie took the money and left the room. Sidorov followed a few seconds later as Sergie came out again. Sergie said, 'So what now?'

Sidorov smiled. 'You open the rear door and I disappear. Then you do as we agreed.'

The next morning Sergie roused his colleagues shouting that a prisoner had escaped. They were both confused as Sergie hurried back and forth checking doors and windows. Finally he rang the NKVD building. A message was passed along to Party Secretary Chupin.

Chupin looked up as there was a knock at his door. He checked his watch realising it was at this time each week that Yuri reported to him. He shouted for him to enter.

Yuri walked confidently to the desk and waited to be told he could sit. Chupin indicated the chair opposite him as he knocked ash off his cigarette into the ash tray. With a look of distaste he uttered, 'It appears that Sidorov has escaped. I don't believe for a moment that he is capable of that without the assistance of his hit man, the oaf who damaged you. However, it seems money was found on one of the other guards which suggest they were bribed to let Sidorov free.'

Yuri snorted derisively.

Chupin smiled grimly, 'I agree. Anyway the idiot is free.'

Yuri scowled. 'He can't be allowed to get away with it.'

Chupin sighed, 'No. However, politically it is...delicate.'
Yuri raised his eyebrows in question.

'His father is a general close to Stalin. We have to tread carefully if we want to avoid it coming back on us. The General's already been on the phone to me. I've stalled him...'

Yuri had a thought. 'If an anonymous letter was sent to him with evidence what would he do?'

Chupin looked alarmed. 'Anonymous letter?'

Yuri said, 'I could write one and send copies of the evidence. He couldn't ignore that could he?'

Chupin stood and walked around his desk and put a hand on Yuri's shoulder. 'You walk a thin line my boy.' He picked up his coat and went to the door. 'If you were to get the address of the General and send the letter without my knowing...hmm, he would have to do something then. Not sure what, but he could not ignore it.'

Yuri stood. He put a written report on Chupin's desk. 'These are two individuals I mentioned earlier.'

Chupin paused at the door and turned to Yuri. 'Thank you Yuri. I must go to a meeting now. I hope I never become careless enough to leave my desk drawers unlocked in these troubled times of informers and the like. Especially the second drawer on the right. I suppose if the drawer were damaged it would suggest it had been locked... Good day Yuri, I will action those individuals when I return. Good work.' He left the room. Yuri picked up a letter opener and damaged the draw sufficiently to cover Chupin and took the information he needed.

General Sidorov drew his hands over his thick grey beard as if it would help clear his mind, stopped and picked up the letter which he took over to his window and read. He looked out over Moscow city and sighed. The letter, together with irrefutable evidence, proved his youngest son Nikita guilty of behaviour even he could neither cover up nor ignore. He sat back at his desk and picked up the photograph. He threw it back down in disgust.

Chupin was about to leave for a meeting when his phone rang. He picked it up. 'Hello.'

'General Sidorov. I need to speak to you urgently.'

Chupin sat down and searched for his cigarettes desperately going through his pockets, knowing what was coming. 'Yes General?'

'It is a...delicate matter Party Secretary Chupin concerning my youngest son Nikita. I understand now why you have hesitated in dealing with the matter. I have received an anonymous letter leaving no doubt that Nikita has committed a terrible crime.' Chupin found his cigarettes and smiled grimly to himself thinking *the one we know about*... General Sidorov continued, 'Let us be frank here. That is why you arrested him?'

Chupin shook a cigarette loose and lit it. 'Yes General. The matter has placed me in a difficult position, especially as you requested for him to take up the post of Commissar...However, I hasten to add I did not...'

The General interrupted him. 'Of course not Party Secretary.' He sighed, 'I admit I made a mistake I now deeply regret. I apologise for the trouble it has caused you. I know you had no choice but to arrest him and that it placed you in an impossible position. I have a proposition that might ease your difficulties and solve mine without involving President Stalin.'

Chupin took a deep breath. 'Unfortunately, the situation has changed significantly General.'

'Changed?'

'He's escaped General. He bribed one of the guards.'

There was an intake of breath, 'Escaped?'

'Last night. I've just been informed.'

'I see. Well he won't last long out there. We'll keep a look out for him and when he is back in custody you can leave the matter to me. I can assure you I will deal with it personally and it won't be swept under the carpet.'

'Thank you General.' He placed the phone down gently and blew a smoke ring. He no longer had responsibility in the matter. The Sidorov's could go to hell.

36. EVIL DEEDS

Vasili Gukovsky sat behind his desk and surveyed the office of his new posting as the Commissar to replace Sidorov. He never had liked Sidorov and to now have his job was satisfying although the responsibility that came with it scared him. He was surprised when Party Secretary Chupin approached him; he was sure there were others more qualified but he would do his best. He opened the first of many files and began to read. One of the tasks set by Chupin was for Vasili to discover the depth of corruption that had existed under Sidorov by checking the fate of prisoners who had passed through the police station, and the quality of the evidence against them. There was a knock at his door. 'Come in' he shouted.

Yuri entered and waited until he was invited to sit down. Vasili motioned to a chair opposite his desk. Yuri couldn't help a wry smile as he sat down. Vasili noticed and gave him an enquiring look.

Yuri smiled, 'It's a long story, but the last time I sat here things were a lot different.'

Vasili nodded, 'I see. And you are?'

'Yuri Kazakof. Assistant to Party Secretary Chupin.'

Vasili sat back and lit a cigarette. 'Yes of course, he told me to expect you.'

Yuri eyed the pile of brown manila files. 'Have you read mine yet?' Vasili looked puzzled. Yuri continued, 'Yes there is a file on me in there somewhere.'

Vasili was intrigued. 'And yet you work as the Party Secretary's assistant? A position that I would imagine carries considerable trust and responsibility.'

Yuri smiled, 'Yes that's correct. And when you read it you will see that I was accused of theft. You will also see that the Party Secretary has quashed all the charges made by Sidorov.'

Vasili sat back and studied his cigarette, 'And you are innocent of the charges?'

Yuri shrugged, 'The case is closed as you will see.'

Vasili could see he would get no further in this conversation and said, 'Anyway I haven't come across it yet, but as you can see, I have a lot to read.'

Yuri looked around the room. 'You've made some changes.'

Vasili nodded. 'So, how can I be of assistance?'

Yuri brushed imaginary fluff from his new suit, 'Party Secretary Chupin wants to ensure the many German spies in the city are caught. Can I have your permission to look through the files for some names I have been given?'

'Of course. Help yourself. Anything I can do to help just ask.'

Yuri stood and offered his hand, 'Thank you Commissar.'

After Yuri had left Vasili sat deep in thought. The man's hands were in a terrible state and there were tattoos showing at his wrists which came from the criminal gangs. What the hell was Chupin doing?

Yuri looked through the files for Nadya's. He found nothing. He went back to see Vasili. 'Would you have a list of the orphanages for the district?'

Vasili thought for a moment, 'I'm new to this district but I have staff who would know. Can I ask why?'

'I want to find where my daughter was sent.'

Vasili saw the pain in the man's eyes but something else leaked through into the face; anger. He realised he was discovering there was a more to this man than he had at first thought. 'Leave it with me.'

General Sidorov climbed out of his car and entered a police station in Moscow. He was taken down to his son who was languishing in a cell. The General entered. Nikita stood to hug his father who took a step back and slapped him hard round the face. He spoke through gritted teeth. 'You have brought shame on our family. Your older brother lies in his grave having fought bravely for his country and you, you...' He shuddered. 'Well, I won't bail you out this time.'

'Nikita trembled in front of his father. 'What will you do? I didn't mean to do it. I won't do it again I promise father.'

'Shut up! I'm sending you to Siberia to take the place of Commandant Ivakin who has recently died. You will remain in that God forsaken place until I decide otherwise.' He turned and left.

Nikita Sidorov still smarted from the dressing down he had received from his father as the train rattled over the rails toward his new placement at a Gulag the name of which he was familiar, having sent many people there, but not visited himself. As he watched the countryside pass by, gradually becoming less green as the mountains in the far distance grew closer, pockets of snow still in sheltered areas and fewer trees, he remembered it was a large settlement and the section he would be taking over held approximately forty huts.

That damned Kazakof had caused all this, what a pity he was not at the Gulag... He tried to recall which one the girl had been sent to but it wasn't this one. Pity, that would have been a way of getting revenge for the trouble her boyfriend had caused.

He leant his head against the dirty glass window of the carriage feeling sorry for himself. His father had no idea of his son's complex needs, preferring to judge him harshly for them by sending him to this God forsaken place. Well, sorry father, but there are children born in such places and he would ensure his needs were satisfied. If he was to be condemned to long boring nights he would ensure he had *entertainment.* He drifted into a light sleep.

Nikita Sidorov sat up as the train ground to a halt at a small station, consisting mainly of just a platform and small station master's office. He stood as the train stopped and looked around for someone to take his bags. The carriage was empty and he could not see any porters on the platform. He hurried off the train onto the platform looking around for any sign of life. He was growing impatient. Satisfied the train could not go any further because it was the end of the line he strutted back and forth looking for any sign of life. Even the driver and his mate had vanished. He checked his pocket watch and noted it was seven o'clock in the evening, approximately three hours after it was supposed to arrive. He began to feel angry.

He heard the grinding of a lorry approaching and went through a wooden gate off the platform and down a few steps to a dirt road. In the distance he could hear the lorry getting nearer. He lit a cigarette and waited. After a few minutes a beaten up, dirty lorry drew up alongside him. The driver was a man dressed in a dirty uniform with a cigarette dangling from his lips, unshaven and looking as if he was recovering from a hangover. Sidorov waited as the man switched off the engine and clambered out.

He slammed the door shut and turned to Sidorov. 'Commandant Sidorov?'

Sidorov was expecting a car at least. He looked around and up to the platform where steam from the engine drifted past.

He sneered, 'I don't see anyone else here dressed in police uniform do you?'

The driver sensed he could be in trouble, this one was a lot different to Commandant Ivakin. He straighted and replied, 'No Sir.'

Sidorov held his cigarette in the Chupin fashion which he knew would impress and snapped, 'Get my bags from the carriage. The second from the engine. And hurry up.'

The man scuttled up the steps. Sidorov could judge by the state of the lorry it was going to be a rough camp. He had been told the Settlement Commandant liked an easy life and left the running of each section to their individual Commandants. That suited Sidorov fine and would enable him to make the arrangements he required for the long evenings ahead...

The driver reappeared struggling with two cases and a bag which he had slung over his shoulder. He lost his footing on the steps and tumbled forward landing on one of the cases.

Sidorov bellowed, 'Idiot!'

The man struggled to his feet, Sidorov watching impatiently strutting back and forth as the man struggled to get the bags into the back of the lorry. Sidorov snarled. 'I hope for your sake nothing is broken.'

The driver muttered to himself, 'So do I.'

Sidorov went round to the passenger side and waited impatiently. The driver was midway in opening his own door when he saw Sidorov's head through the window. He muttered, 'fuck' and clambered down hurrying round to the waiting figure. He reached up and opened the door. Sidorov stamped his cigarette out and gave the driver a scathing look of contempt. He pulled himself in and waited for the driver to close the door. He looked around the cab at the driver's detritus scattered everywhere. He brushed a bottle off the seat beside him which clattered on the floor against others by his feet.

The driver got in and closed his door. He was about to start the engine when Sidorov asked, 'Why were you three hours late? I could have been standing there all that time.'

The driver smiled. 'It's always three hours late.'

Sidorov was not surprised. That was how this country ran. He would ensure his part of the camp would be efficient. He looked scathingly at the driver. 'Well? What are you waiting for?'

   The driver started the engine and they lurched forward.
Sidorov heard his cases slide across the floor and bang
against the rear of the lorry. He sighed and lit a cigarette
as he felt empty bottles nudge his feet.

37. THE NET TIGHTENS

Yuri placed his rusted bicycle against a wire fence and looked at the run down building; the tenth out of 130 orphanages he had visited. He entered the grey building and immediately recoiled from an overwhelming atmosphere of the impersonal; as if it was a building devoid of human warmth. He had expected to hear children laughing, running around chasing each other, or sitting in school rooms. Instead there was silence. A heavy thick silence. He looked around at the walls which were peeling paint, their surfaces showing years of neglect, pictures of Stalin and propaganda leaflets dotted here and there. The wooden floors were bare and worn with ill matching boards roughly nailed down where a repair had been needed. He began to wonder if it had been closed.

The childhood he had experienced, although with little material comforts, had been enriching allowing him to become who he was now. He shuddered to think what it would be like growing up here. He wanted to get out as quickly as possible and was about to turn and leave when a tall, thin, balding man with glasses appeared. His grey drab clothes gave the impression of a man tired of his futile existence.

He noticed Yuri and stopped. 'Can I help you?'

Yuri said, 'My daughter was taken from her mother who was then sent to a Gulag. I understand the baby would have been sent here?'

The man considered for a few seconds. 'Possibly. When was this?'

'Six months ago.'

'And what was the child's name?'

Yuri flushed. 'We didn't have time to name her before she was taken.'

The man became wary, his face a blank mask. 'There are many like that sent to the Gulag...'

Yuri stiffened. 'She was not a criminal. She was wrongly accused. We both were.'

'I see. Well, we have had a lot children pass through here. We recently sent some to a safer area now the Ice Road is operational. She could have been amongst them.'

Yuri produced his party card provided by Chupin for just such an occasion. 'Could I please check your records?'

The man nodded. 'Of course. Come with me.' He led Yuri down a corridor, the walls scrawled on with childish drawings and dents at the doors where they had been kicked open. A group of children appeared with a stern looking woman from a room ahead and walked silently past him. He sensed malnutrition. He looked back at them noting their clothes were threadbare, their heads shaved. The man said matter of factly, 'Lice. We shave them to avoid lice.' He opened a door and beckoned Yuri in to a small office. It was untidy with files scattered about on chairs and a desk. There were many pictures of children on the walls with names beneath them.

Yuri studied them. 'Why are some underlined in black?'

The man sat down tiredly at the desk. 'They're the ones who died.'

'And the ones with a red line?'

'They're the ones that have run away. We won't be seeing them again.'

Yuri ran his finger over the pictures silently counting.'

The man said, 'please sit down Comrade..?'

Yuri pulled out a chair. 'Kazakof.'

The man handed him a box file. 'These are all the children we have under one year of age. The females are in the second section.' He stood. 'Good luck. I fear your search will be fruitless. If you need to know anything else I will be back down the corridor we came in by. The second door on the left.'

Yuri opened the file and turned to the second section. All the children listed had names and pictures. Most of them had a parent's name and their fate together with when they entered the orphanage. Nowhere could he find any child that could be his daughter, or any that fitted the dates. He closed the file and looked out of the window to an empty playground. It didn't look as if it had been used for some time.

Yuri returned to the city and sat on the bank of the River Neva angrily twisting a piece of paper containing a list of names of foster parents the man had given him. He didn't know where to start, and worse, the majority were far outside the city. Getting to them with the Germans encircling the city would be tricky — if they were even there now and had not not fled. He watched the water swirl in eddies at the foot of the bridge thinking that was how his life had become; a swirling maelstrom of pain. He had lost his family, Nadya, his daughter and all because of Sidorov. Well...If he couldn't look for his daughter, he would go after Sidorov. He realised he had ripped the piece of paper into small pieces. He stuffed them all in his pocket and headed for Chupin's office.

Party Secretary Chupin hurried up the marble stairs of the NKVD building and reached Yuri waiting patiently outside his office.

'Yuri, sorry to keep you waiting. These interminable meetings....' He opened his office door and bustled through. 'Come in.'

Yuri followed and waited to be invited to sit down at Chupin's desk. Chupin took off his coat and sat down. He lit a cigarette. 'Sit down.'

'I must congratulate you Yuri. Two German spies now in custody, and dangerous ones at that.' He watched Yuri closely as he spoke, noting that he looked fit and strong with an underlying air of confidence.

'Thank you sir. I've also got eyes on the ground.'

Chupin smiled, 'Should I know of these *eyes*?'

Yuri smiled back. 'They're my friends, loyal to me and our country. Now that I have my own apartment and regular food, I make sure they are looked after.'

Chupin laughed, 'They share your apartment?'

Yuri nodded. 'They're my friends. They saved my life by getting the letter to you. I owe them... and you, my life.'

Chupin studied him. 'I made the right decision about you. You interest me, I wish we had the time to speak more freely, but...' he waved a hand over the letters and files waiting for his attention.

'I understand Sir. I want to repay your trust.'

Chupin noted an undercurrent of anger in Yuri's voice.

'Good. And Vasili? Do I need to worry about him?'

'No Sir. He's honest and fair.'

'Hmm. And how are you?'

Yuri looked him at him with an unwavering gaze. 'I have discovered that my daughter was put in an orphanage and has disappeared. I can't trace where she went. I do my job as well as I can but I am looking for the man who destroyed my family, both families.'

Chupin looked concerned as he drew on his cigarette. 'It will do you no good Yuri. I can understand your feelings but they will destroy you. It would be better if you let it be.'

A flash of emotion appeared and vanished on Yuri's face. 'I understand, but I can't. I won't betray you Sir. I will do my work to the best of my ability. But I will continue to look. An idiot like that can't go far.'

Chupin stubbed out his cigarette. 'Ok, I have said what I needed to say. Is there anything else?'

'No Sir.'

Chupin took out a cigarette and offered one to Yuri. 'Good luck.'

38. SECRETS

Ivor Sakrov was stressed trying to organise the transfer of
the children in his care by train deeper into the Russian
countryside away from the German advance. He glanced at the
bulging rows of files on shelves in his office and couldn't
face going through them all to sort out the dead ones; he
would just send them, after all, most would die on the journey
anyway so let somebody else do it. He sat down to catch his
breath and thought about it some more. A creeping fear began
to crawl over him as he realised there was incriminating
evidence buried in those files. He thought for a moment then
snatched the phone and dialled Sidorov's number only to
discover he had been transferred. Eventually he was given a
new number for a Gulag. He rang and Sidorov answered.

Ivor tried to control the shake in his voice as he said,

'We're going to be getting a visitor here from the NKVD.
Thought you should know Sir.'

Sidorov sat forward at his desk and asked quietly, 'Why do
you think this?'

'Because he's been to all the others.'

'Do you have the name of this man?'

'Yuri Kasakof Sir.'

Sidorov froze. How was it possible? 'You're sure of this?'

'Yes Sir, he is very thorough. Asking about a baby.'

'The files?'

Ivor swept a hand over his face anxiously, 'Sir I don't know
what is in them that could...'

'If this fellow arrives then stall him. I will come down
there immediately and deal with it myself. In the meantime
remove any files that relate to ages between nine and twelve.'

'Won't that look suspicious Sir?'

'You said he was looking for a baby. They will be different
files won't they?'

'Yes Sir, but he might check all of them.'

'Then go through the nine to twelve's and tear out any
incriminating...'

'But Sir, he will...'

'Alright Alright. Scribble over anything incriminating, make it look innocent.' He put the phone down. Will he ever be rid of this man who has caused him so much trouble? Well perhaps now is the chance to get rid of him once and for all.

Sidorov watched the landscape flash by as the train headed toward Leningrad. With Kazakof out of the way he could destroy the files — after eliminating Ivor of course as a possible problem in the future — and relax. The train began to slow as the shapes of Leningrad's grand buildings came into view. He smiled to himself thinking once again he had the advantage over Kazakof. He would commandeer a car to make quick progress.

Yuri continued with his list of orphanages crossing each one off in turn. There was one more to check on his list and he made his way toward it down a dirt track. The building was now in a poor state of repair but had once been the home of an aristocrat. It loomed larger as he neared it becoming almost two buildings; one of them a towered wing. He had come to expect the conditions they all shared as another example of Soviet mis— management; bare walls with graffiti, empty playgrounds and children of various ages with shaved heads and sad expressions; what he found most depressing was the distended bellies and skeletal figures that watched him with haunted expressions hoping for food.

He entered the dull lifeless entrance and looked around for someone in charge but found nobody. He spotted a closed door in the corridor which he thought was probably an office and entered. It was empty apart from a desk and two chairs and the usual blackboard with lists of names beside rows of shelves holding files. He took off his coat and after working out the system from the notations on the spines took one down. He flicked through the papers looking for any clues about his daughter, but found none. He took down another file and another without any success, but when he got to the fourth one he stopped and puzzled, looking back at the previous ones and further along to the next in line. He sat down looking back at the shelves. There was an age group missing from nine to twelve.

He sat back in thought and looked up as the door opened and a short fat middle aged man entered, shocked as he saw Yuri and blurted, 'Who are you? You can't just...'

Yuri flashed his ID card and the initials of the NKVD were all that was needed. The man sat down and looked suspiciously at him as Yuri asked, 'You are in charge?'

The man shifted nervously. 'Yes.'

Yuri stood and examined the shelves of files. 'There seem to be some files missing. The man began to redden.

Yuri asked in his official tone, 'Your name?'

'Ivor Sakrov. I've done nothing wrong.'

Yuri stood and wandered around the small room. 'Good. So why are some files missing?'

Ivor sat down and looked at the shelves. 'Oh those. Yes we are preparing to transfer the children to somewhere safer. They're probably packed away as the rest will be.'

'I see. I'm searching for a baby about twelve months old.' He watched the man carefully as he added, 'her mother was arrested and sent to the Gulag by Commissar Sidorov.' The man shifted uncomfortably. Yuri asked, 'Do you know Commissar Sidorov Ivor?' The man nodded that he didn't. Yuri studied him closely, 'Sure?' The man nodded again vigorously. 'How many children do you have here?'

'The maximum is fifty but...we lose a lot unfortunately.'

'Lose?'

'Many are weak when they arrive and die, others run away.' He glanced up at the board.

Yuri studied him closely. 'It's very quiet here. Where are the children?'

'They're in their rooms. We are getting things ready for them to be transferred away from here because of the Germans.'

'Where to?'

Ivor looked uncomfortable as he said, 'I don't know they haven't told us, we just have to get them ready for the train in two days time.'

Yuri looked around again and walked to the door. 'I will need to see those missing files Ivor. I will return soon.' Outside he looked back at the dour building and shuddered knowing Ivor was hiding something.

Yuri returned to the orphanage a couple of days later. He browsed through the files stopping at one in particular of a twelve year old boy where Sidorov was mentioned in a scribbled note poorly covered up at the side of an entry. He had to study the note for some time before he could make out what it said. He looked up at the list on the board and saw the

child's name listed as having run away. He read it again.
Definitely Sidorov's name and his telephone number together
with *will collect on Wednesday*; somebody had been very
careless. He continued going through the files focusing on
those of children under a year old. He found two but after
delving deeper discarded them. He sat deep in thought.
Obviously this was how Sidorov got the children for himself
and then either killed them himself, or more likely, got his
oaf Sergie to do it for him. Rage tried to break through but
he kept the lid tightly down. If he was to get Sidorov he had
to play cunning. The chances were Ivor had tipped Sidorov off
and he was on his way to cover his tracks and probably try to
kill him as well.

   He shouted for Ivor who scurried in. 'There's nothing of
interest in those for my investigation, you can pack them away
again.' He noted that Ivor almost gasped with relief.

39. DEPARTURE

November 1942

Nadya had learnt the art of patience and watching, observing, noting guards shifts, which ones were open to bribery or other favours in exchange for information and odd items. One in particular called Boris was a reasonable man but with strong sexual needs which she exploited. She had long ago given up feeling dirty or wrong; this was about survival in order to find her daughter. She longed to believe she could find Yuri but time in the Gulag had taught her not to have too much hope.

After a few weeks at the camp she had her escape planned. She had told nobody — other than mis-information to send search parties in the wrong direction — where she came from and her plans. Every night beneath her blanket she completed a rucksack made up of bits and pieces of material she had collected. For a needle she used a nail and for cotton, unravelled threads. She estimated from bits and pieces of information to be approximately two hundred miles across a mixture of terrain. She didn't care or allow her fear to get in the way of her plans to find her daughter; she was determined to succeed or die in the process.

She waited for a moonless night and slipped out of the hut. The guard she had used was waiting for her in the pitch dark behind her hut. She made out his shadow and approached him making out his smile in the darkness. He put aside his rifle and opened his flies. She knelt down before him, shut her eyes and focused on her daughter, how she would look now, the colour of her hair. She felt him tense and finished him then quickly stood and whilst he was recovering smacked him hard over the head with a piece of pipe. He slumped to the ground. She grabbed her rucksack and dashed on hands and knees to the wire which she managed to slip under and drag the rucksack after her, furiously spitting in disgust as she did so. She ran in the darkness toward the forest making her way North in the opposite direction she intended to travel until she got to the railway tracks and changed direction doubling back on herself heading south toward Leningrad. Her pulse raced as she jogged silently along the track her focus on her daughter.

Nadya was making slow progress as she struggled over tufted grass hillocks on a swamped area which she had stumbled upon. Now she had to fight to get through it using valuable energy. She was surviving on virtually no food and was constantly searching for anything she could find or steal from farm houses. Much of the journey was through forests which afforded her cover and meagre food such as berries and roots. Water was a constant problem and she had to go out of her way at times to find a fresh stream as she pushed herself to move forward avoiding populated areas and roads in case they were looking for her. She slept in barns and took milk from solitary cows when she could.

Every night she pictured her daughter and Yuri believing she would see them again but at times her spirits dropped and she cried as she plodded on through fields and swamps. At night she would find cover and hide as best she could from predators such as bears. Her clothing was in tatters and she had been forced to steal a piece of tarpaulin from a barn to wrap around her to keep out the rain. At night she used it as a shelter. As she plodded along for mile after mile — at times delirious with hunger and tiredness — she thought about her parents and the awful way their lives had ended. She thought of Yuri and his love for her and their daughter and the cruelty of their separation.

It seemed to Nadya as she at last saw Leningrad in the distance that she had been walking forever. She had long ago stopped worrying about blisters and cuts or whether they might be infected, nothing mattered now but to reach the city and find her daughter. She reckoned she had one more day's travel and would have to risk the road to speed her journey. It was getting dark and the heavy snow clouds brought it sooner than she expected. She kept to the forest and built her shelter, building a small fire from twigs and small branches on which she carefully constructed a stand to put a tin of water on to boil. She took out a couple of potatoes she had found and dropped them in. She looked around at what totalled her life and thought in wonder how she arrived here, living like a tramp and smelling like one as well no doubt; how her mother would have disapproved! She savagely poked the fire.

The next day she completed her journey and crossed the river Neva by Bank pedestrian bridge into the city. In the distance she could hear the rumble of artillery guns and the scream of shells over head. She made her way to the centre of the city looking out for any familiar faces but saw none. She looked in horror at the number of frozen dead bodies on the pavements.

She thought about Yuri and where he might be but now had to accept she wouldn't see him again. She went to Inber's apartment and knocked on the door of a neighbour she had been friendly with. The door opened and a young woman looked out suspiciously until after close examination exclaimed 'Nadya?'

Nadya collapsed and sank to her knees in the snow. 'Can you help me Ingrid?'

Ingrid helped her up and inside her apartment. 'Come here you poor thing, let's get those horrible rags off you.' Nadya was barely able to walk now that she had reached her destination and sobbed with exhaustion. Ingrid said, 'I don't have much to offer you I'm afraid the siege has made sure of that but whatever I can do...I don't have any water because the pipes are frozen but I collected some from the river this morning and you could wash with that?'

Nadya leant against the wall and smiled thinly. 'That would be wonderful. Thank you.'

Later after she had washed weeks of filth from her body she put on some old clothes that Ingrid gave her and sat in the tiny bedroom recalling what had happened and her plans to find her daughter.

Ingrid listened intently then said, 'I've heard they are planning to ship a lot of orphans from a home near to the front line by train to a safer area in the next couple of days.'

Nadya thought for a moment, 'Then I'd better start with that one. Do you know what it's called?'

Ingrid touched her shoulder, 'No but I can soon find out. Get some rest because you can't keep going like you have been. I'm sorry I have so little food to offer you.'

Nadya smiled, 'Oh you would be surprised what I've been eating...Please I won't eat your food. You need it. Don't worry about me.' She was falling asleep as she spoke and Ingrid watched her for a moment then fetched a plate and left a crust of bread and half an apple beside her. She quietly closed the door and went out into the snow.

Nadya awoke twelve hours later her stomach griping and demanding food. She looked around for her friend and heard her in the communal kitchen down the corridor. Nadya saw the plate beside her and smiled. She stood on shaky legs and carefully caried the plate following the sounds into the kitchen to find Ingrid cooking a tin of beans over a wood fire in the sink; the smoke filling the room even though a window was open. Nadya hardly noticed the incongruity as she smelt the beans.

Ingrid looked round and laughed, 'No I didn't think I would ever be doing this either. How did you sleep?'

Nadya sat down weakly, 'Better than I can remember for a long time.'

Ingrid took the tin off the fire and tipped the contents into two bowls giving Nadya a spoon. Nadya held it with amazement as she said, 'It's the first time in months since I last did this!' She tentatively took a mouthful and a tear trickled down her cheek. 'Thank you for your kindness Ingrid.'

'We have to try and remain civilised for as long as we can. There are terrible things happening in this city; so many people starving. I have some good friends and we try and share whatever we find.'

Nadya finished the meagre ration in seconds then pushed the plate left out for her earlier in front of Ingrid. 'Did you manage to find out anything?'

Ingrid looked pleased with herself as she said, 'You must be meant to find her because by chance as I was asking around, a man stopped and said he used to work there. He gave me this.' She handed over a piece of paper with written directions on it.'

Nadya studied it for a few minutes then said, 'I know where it is! I must go there now.'

Ingrid asked, 'How will you get there?'

Nadya thought for a moment, 'I'll find a bicycle. There must be one somewhere.'

Ingrid took her hand and went to the rear of the apartment and pulled a rusty bicycle from a shed. 'There. Is that ok?'

Nadya hugged her. 'Perfect. I will return it.'

Ingrid said, 'Don't bother the owner died ages ago, I was keeping it to sell for food.'

Nadya hugged her. 'I promise I will bring it back.'

Nadya wobbled on the bike through the snow toward her destination determined to find her daughter, and if she wasn't at this one she would go to all the others until she found her, and if she had been fostered or adopted she would search until she knew she was safe at least.

Eventually she saw the large old building in the distance and as she grew nearer she could see it had a towered wing attached to the main building. She noticed a lot of activity at the entrance to the wing where lorries were waiting. She knew the station was nearby and assumed they were using the lorries to transport boxes etc. She pedalled harder and could now make out small children standing in lines being supervised by older ones. Nurses were carrying babies and putting them in prams. Nadya was upon them now and dropped the bicycle as she ran toward the lines of nurses and babies. She frantically looked at each one not giving the startled nurses time to question her. She reached the end of the line and stood desperately looking around.

A woman came up to her. 'Are you looking for someone?'

Nadya spun round. 'Yes! I'm looking for my daughter.'

The woman looked kind and said, 'Why do you think she is here?'

Nadya put her arms up in frustration, 'I don't. I just need to make sure before the train leaves.'

'What's her name?'

Nadya looked crestfallen. 'I didn't have time to name her before they took her away from me.'

The woman looked around at the chaotic scene and said, 'You are not the first one. Those babies we named ourselves and tried to find them foster homes. The siege has made it difficult and we have a lot still here. There are more upstairs, come with me.'

She led her up what was once a grand staircase and along a wood panelled corridor to a large bedroom. Two nurses were wrapping three babies to take down stairs. Nadya hurried to the nearest nurse and peered at the baby. Her heart sunk. She hurried to the second nurse and froze, motionless. She swiped the tears of frustration from her eyes and saw it was her daughter. She grabbed her from the nurse and sobbed with joy as she held her to her breast. The nurse was taken by surprise and alarmed but the woman smiled and said, 'This is the mother can't you tell?' The nurse looked at the babies deep brown eyes and black hair. The shape of her face was that of Nadya. Yet when Nadya was to look at her later she could see so much of Yuri. Nadya held her daughter tightly and made it clear she would not give her up without a fight. The woman smiled and said, 'We'll go to the office and I will give you papers to say she is your baby and we have gladly released her to her mother.'

Nadya was overwhelmed as she followed her down the stairs fearing someone to come along and take her daughter away from her.

40. THE TOCSIN RINGS

Sidorov left the station and hurried toward the orphanage. He had to wait for the right opportunity but he felt sure Yuri would appear. As he neared the bustling crowd of nurses and children at the entrance to the orphanage he skirted around them and slipped inside. Warily he made his way to the office where Ivor was packing the last few boxes of files and office equipment. He almost bumped into Nadya as she came down the grand staircase carrying a baby. She was so absorbed she didn't notice him. What luck! Ivor looked up in fear as Sidorov entered the office and shut the door. 'Is he here?'

'No Sir.'

'Ok. I will wait in the cellar. When he arrives he will come in here. Drop something heavy on the floor as a signal and I will get him.'

'Something heavy?'

'Use your brain Ivor. Do you want to spend the rest of your life in the Gulag?'

'No Sir.'

Sidorov slipped out and down to the cellar. He checked his gun was loaded and waited sure in the knowledge Yuri would come back.

Yuri returned having decided to try and speak to some of the older children. As he reached the orphanage he noticed the transfer was underway. He looked for Ivor but couldn't see him, assuming he was in the office. He saw babies being put into prams and felt despair at not finding his daughter. Well if couldn't find her he would search for Sidorov; the architect of all their heartache. He entered the building and went to the office to find Ivor packing boxes. 'Where's Sidorov?' He snapped.

Ivor avoided his eyes, 'Who?'

'Don't play games with me I'm not in the mood. I know what has been going on here.' Ivor remained passive avoiding eye contact. Yuri suddenly realised. 'He's here isn't here?' Ivor remained silent. Yuri grabbed him by his collar and dragged him up. He transferred his grip to the front of Ivor's jacket and lifted him off the floor. 'Tell me or I'll break your neck.' He shook him so violently that Ivor dropped a large book he was holding.

In the cellar Sidorov heard a dull thud and hurried up the stairs, gun at the ready. From the office he heard a crash and yelp from Ivor. Sidorov took a deep breath and rushed the door. Yuri was bending over Ivor slowly strangling him. Sidorov shut the door behind him as Yuri dropped Ivor and stood to look at who had entered. 'Don't look so surprised Kazakof. We both know you came to find me. Well here I am.'

Yuri stared at him with deep loathing. For so long he had dreamed of finding Sidorov and once again had been thwarted. It would end here anyway he decided tiredly. 'Now what?'

'It's simple. I kill you and take the woman.'

Yuri felt a flush of excitement. Was Nadya here? How could she be? But Sidorov had no need to lie. Immediately Yuri felt energised. 'I know she is dead. Our daughter probably and all because of you.'

'Oh dear, how sad for you to be so close to them both after so long and not be able to see them. Oh yes. Believe me, they're here.'

Yuri had been watching Sidorov's eyes waiting for the sign he needed to jump him. For a second Sidorov was lost in his cruelty and need to torture; just enough of a lapse for Yuri to spring forward and grab the gun. Sidorov was caught off guard and the gun fired sending a bullet into the ceiling. Ivor screamed and grabbed at the door, keeping well out of the way as the two men tussled. Sidorov knew he would not be a match for Yuri's immense strength and desperately sought to shoot him. They toppled onto a pile of boxes and Yuri lost his grip. Sidorov smashed him viciously over the head with the gun and aimed at the semi conscious body. He spun round as he heard running footsteps in the corridor to see Nadya holding her baby close to her with one arm and in the other an iron bar which she swung at him. It caught his shoulder and he turned to tussle it away from her dropping the gun in the process. He heard Yuri groan and Sidorov desperately tried to grab the gun as he pushed Nadya away. She saw Yuri on the floor but had no time to feel anything other than to protect him. She took another swing at Sidorov but hampered by holding the baby she lost her balance.

Sidorov pointed the gun at her and waved her down the corridor. He couldn't risk being caught between them both; he needed to get some space where he could shoot them both in safety. Groggily, Yuri knelt, hanging onto the side of a box shaking his head to clear it. A thumping ache swamped his

brain and he felt blood trickle down his forehead. As his
senses returned, he remembered seeing Nadya in the doorway. He
forced himself up and stumbled along the corridor to see
Sidorov waving a gun at Nadya. Yuri shook his head again and
ran toward the man he had hated for so many years. With a
grunt he launched himself into Sidorov and they tumbled to the
ground. Sidorov swung the gun wildly and managed to hit Yuri
on the head again. Yuri hung onto to Sidorov and shouted,
'Nadya! Take the baby and get on the train. I'll find you.'

She watched in horror as Sidorov, realising Yuri was
stunned, began to get the upper hand. 'No!'

'Go now! For the sake of our child!'

Nadya looked back to train as the station master blew his
whistle. Sidorov hit Yuri again in the face with his pistol
but lost the gun as Yuri swung his arm to defend himself.
Nadya knew she could not help and ran toward the train just
managing to scramble into the last carriage as it began to
roll. Holding her baby with fierce determination and tears
streaming down her face she watched as Sidorov scrambled to
his feet and ran away toward the road. Yuri struggled to his
feet wiping blood from his face looking for Sidorov. He looked
back to the train and saw Nadya at the rear carriage window.

Nadya could see Sidorov disappearing toward the road and
with horror realised Yuri was going to go after him. She
screamed, 'Leave him Yuri! He's not worth losing us for.' Yuri
looked from her back to the fleeing Sidorov. Torn between love
and hatred so deep it now totally consumed him. 'Yuri! Even if
you kill him he will haunt you forever. Choose life!' Yuri
looked back toward Sidorov who, now sufficiently far away, had
stopped and was watching to see what Yuri would do next. Like
a flash of light Yuri seemed to awake from his world of
vengeance and turned toward Nadya.

'You can make it Yuri. Run!'

He made his choice and ran with all his strength toward the
platform focused purely on the two people most important to
him. Nadya desperately leaned out of the carriage window
beckoning Yuri to catch the train as it began to pick up
speed. Sidorov realised his secret was with Yuri and he knew
he would use it against him. He spotted a soldier at the end
of the platform and ran to him snatching his rifle, 'Give me
that you oaf. Can't you see a criminal is escaping!'

Yuri ran as he had never run before focused on the rear of the
train as it slowly pulled away from him but it seemed however
hard he pounded his feet into the ground he couldn't catch up
with it. People on the platform turned in alarm as Yuri dashed
through them.

In desperation he swung his arms harder to get better momentum but he knew it was no good. She was being taken away from him and he could do nothing to stop it. To come so far and still lose her was unbearable. With every sinew of his body he tried to catch up with the train as it inexorably drew away into the mist outside of the station. Now the ground was becoming rough and partly covered with snow as Yuri ran for everything he held dear disappearing from him. He focused on Nadya's face as she hung out of the carriage window encouraging him to keep going. Then her face seemed to change into horror as in the distance she saw Sidorov aiming a rifle at Yuri. 'No!' She screamed as she saw the puff of smoke from the barrel. She watched in horror as Yuri stumbled and fell forward into the snow. She snatched the emergency chord and the wheels screeched to grip the track. As the train ground to a stop, she leapt out desperately holding the baby to her chest as she ran to the prone figure. Even from a distance she could see a red patch spreading into the snow beneath Yuri's prone body. She fell to her knees and pulled him into a sitting position, holding him close to her. Blood was seeping through his coat and his face was deathly white. She looked around in desperation as people from the platform and the train ran to her as she screamed, 'Please help me!'

Sidorov smiled as he turned to make his escape and handed the rifle back to the soldier.

A woman knelt beside Nadya and opened Yuri's coat. 'I'm a nurse, let me see.' Nadya let go and with her baby close to her chest she looked around for Sidorov. She saw him heading toward a car. The nurse was working fast stemming the flow of blood helped by two other nurses who had joined them. As if in a dream as she watched Sidorov, Nadya asked, 'Will he live?'

The nurse looked up at her. 'He might, if we can stop the blood flow. The bullet went straight through.' Nadya handed her baby to one of the nurses and said, 'Please look after her. He is her father.' She walked quickly toward Sidorov who had reached the car. She had no idea what she intended to do other than stop this monster before he hurt anyone else. Amongst the crowd forming a circle around the nurses and the prone body of Yuri, was the soldier from whom Sidorov had snatched the rifle. 'Did she say he is the father of the baby?'

One of the nurses looked up at him. 'Yes. She had just been reunited with her daughter less than an hour ago.'

He scratched his head as he turned to see Nadya walking purposefully toward a car. 'Why is she walking away?' He turned and ran after Nadya. 'What's happening?' He realised the figure getting into the car was the man who had snatched his rifle. 'Who is he?'

Nadya sneered, 'A monster who has killed too many people and ruined too many lives. He has to die.' The soldier felt a chill run down his spine. He grabbed her arm. 'Talk to me. He said the man he shot was a criminal.'

Nadya stopped and turned to him. 'Yuri was no criminal. He is the father of our child who he,' she nodded toward Sidorov, 'took our child, put me in the Gulag and murdered my parents. He is an evil man who must be stopped.'

The soldier asked, 'Who is he?'

'Nadya spat the name. Nikita Sidorov.' She walked quikly on.

The soldier unshouldered his rifle and said in a chilling tone, 'A name not easy to forget, especially when he was the one who had my family deported. First time I've seen what he looks like.' He knelt and brought the rifle into a firing position as Sidorov started the car engine. He took careful aim and fired. A red spray covered the inside of the car window and the figure slumped forward. Nadya stopped in shock and turned to him. The soldier smiled grimly. 'He deserved worse than a quick death.' He turned and walked away. Nadya looked back at him then back at the car. She slumped to the ground exhausted.

41. THE FINAL JOURNEY

It was early 1943 as Yuri and his family stood at the railings of the British Merchant Navy ship, Ocean Gypsy, in the port of Archangel.

Yuri put his arm round Nadya's shoulders and sighed. 'I know we're not safe yet but we will be.'

She huddled close to him to keep out the cold wind of approaching winter. 'If we stayed we would be killed so there isn't much choice. We've come too far and been through so much Yuri. We deserve some luck.'

He squeezed her, 'And we will.' He gently pushed his finger into the bundle Nadya held close to her breast. 'Won't we Yena, Maya, Kazakof?'

THE END

Printed in Poland
by Amazon Fulfillment
Poland Sp. z o.o., Wrocław

54109004R00169